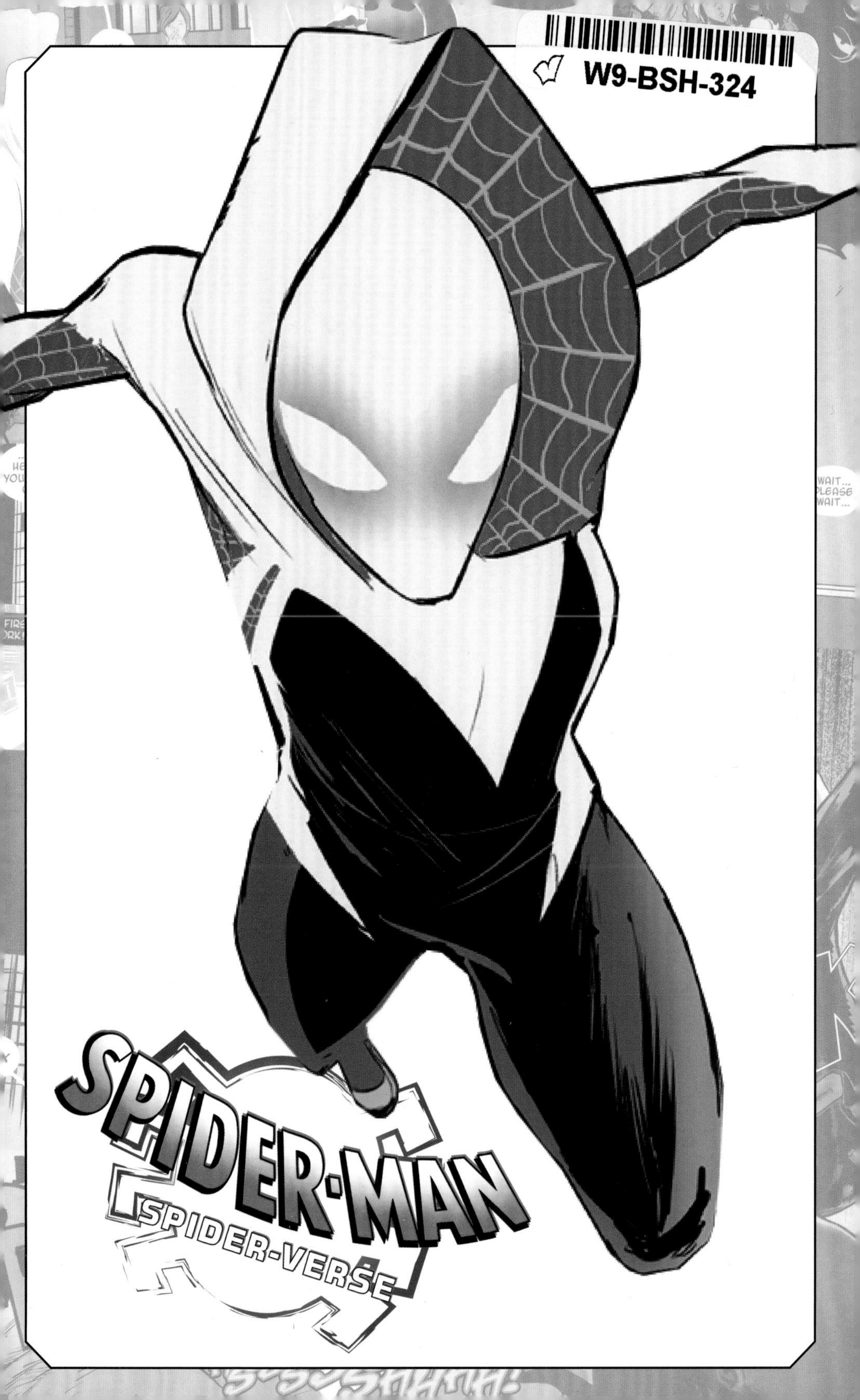
WAIT...
PLEASE
WAIT...
SPIDER-MAN
SPIDER-VERSE

SPIDER-MAN CREATED BY STAN LEE & STEVE DITKO

COLLECTION EDITOR: **JENNIFER GRÜNWALD** ASSISTANT EDITOR: **CAITLIN O'CONNELL**
ASSOCIATE MANAGING EDITOR: **KATERI WOODY** EDITOR, SPECIAL PROJECTS: **MARK D. BEAZLEY**
VP PRODUCTION & SPECIAL PROJECTS: **JEFF YOUNGQUIST** SVP PRINT, SALES & MARKETING: **DAVID GABRIEL**
BOOK DESIGNERS: **JAY BOWEN** WITH **ADAM DEL RE**

EDITOR IN CHIEF: **C.B. CEBULSKI** CHIEF CREATIVE OFFICER: **JOE QUESADA**
PRESIDENT: **DAN BUCKLEY** EXECUTIVE PRODUCER: **ALAN FINE**

SPIDER-MAN: SPIDER-VERSE — SPIDER-GWEN. Contains material originally published in magazine form as EDGE OF SPIDER-VERSE #2, SPIDER-GWEN (2015A) #5, and SPIDER-GWEN (2015B) #1-2 and #13. First printing 2018. ISBN 978-1-302-91417-2. Published by MARVEL WORLDWIDE, INC., a subsidiary of MARVEL ENTERTAINMENT, LLC. OFFICE OF PUBLICATION: 135 West 50th Street, New York, NY 10020. Copyright © 2018 MARVEL No similarity between any of the names, characters, persons, and/ or institutions in this magazine with those of any living or dead person or institution is intended, and any such similarity which may exist is purely coincidental. **Printed in Canada.** DAN BUCKLEY, President, Marvel Entertainment; JOHN NEE, Publisher; JOE QUESADA, Chief Creative Officer; TOM BREVOORT, SVP of Publishing; DAVID BOGART, SVP of Business Affairs & Operations, Publishing & Partnership; DAVID GABRIEL, SVP of Sales & Marketing, Publishing; JEFF YOUNGQUIST, VP of Production & Special Projects; DAN CARR, Executive Director of Publishing Technology; ALEX MORALES, Director of Publishing Operations; DAN EDINGTON, Managing Editor; SUSAN CRESPI, Production Manager; STAN LEE, Chairman Emeritus. For information regarding advertising in Marvel Comics or on Marvel.com, please contact Vit DeBellis, Custom Solutions & Integrated Advertising Manager, at vdebellis@marvel.com. For Marvel subscription inquiries, please call 888-511-5480. **Manufactured between 9/7/2018 and 10/9/2018 by SOLISCO PRINTERS, SCOTT, QC, CANADA.**

10 9 8 7 6 5 4 3 2 1

SPIDER-MAN
SPIDER-VERSE
SPIDER-GWEN

EDGE OF SPIDER-VERSE #2

WRITER: **JASON LATOUR**
ARTIST: **ROBBI RODRIGUEZ**
COLOR ARTIST: **RICO RENZI**
LETTERER: **VC'S CLAYTON COWLES**
COVER ART: **ROBBI RODRIGUEZ**
ASSISTANT EDITOR: **ELLIE PYLE**
EDITOR: **NICK LOWE**

SPIDER-GWEN (2015A) #5

WRITER: **JASON LATOUR**
ARTIST: **ROBBI RODRIGUEZ**
COLOR ARTIST: **RICO RENZI**
LETTERER: **VC'S CLAYTON COWLES**
COVER ART: **ROBBI RODRIGUEZ**
ASSISTANT EDITOR: **DEVIN LEWIS**
EDITOR: **NICK LOWE**

SPIDER-GWEN (2015B) #1-2 & #13

WRITER: **JASON LATOUR**
ARTIST: **ROBBI RODRIGUEZ**
COLOR ARTIST: **RICO RENZI**
LETTERER: **VC'S CLAYTON COWLES**
COVER ART: **ROBBI RODRIGUEZ**
ASSISTANT EDITOR: **ALLISON STOCK**
ASSOCIATE EDITOR: **DEVIN LEWIS**
EDITOR: **NICK LOWE**

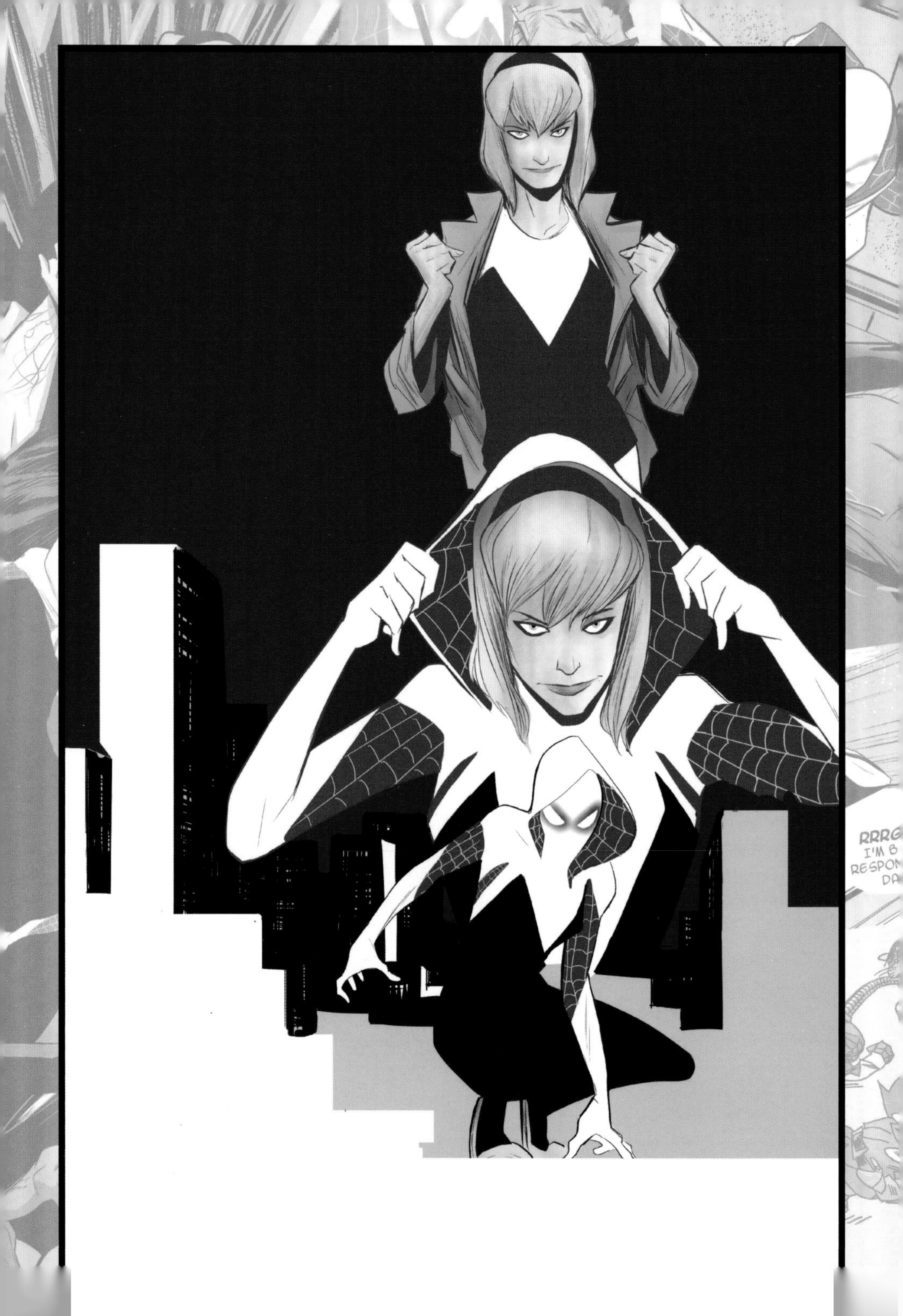

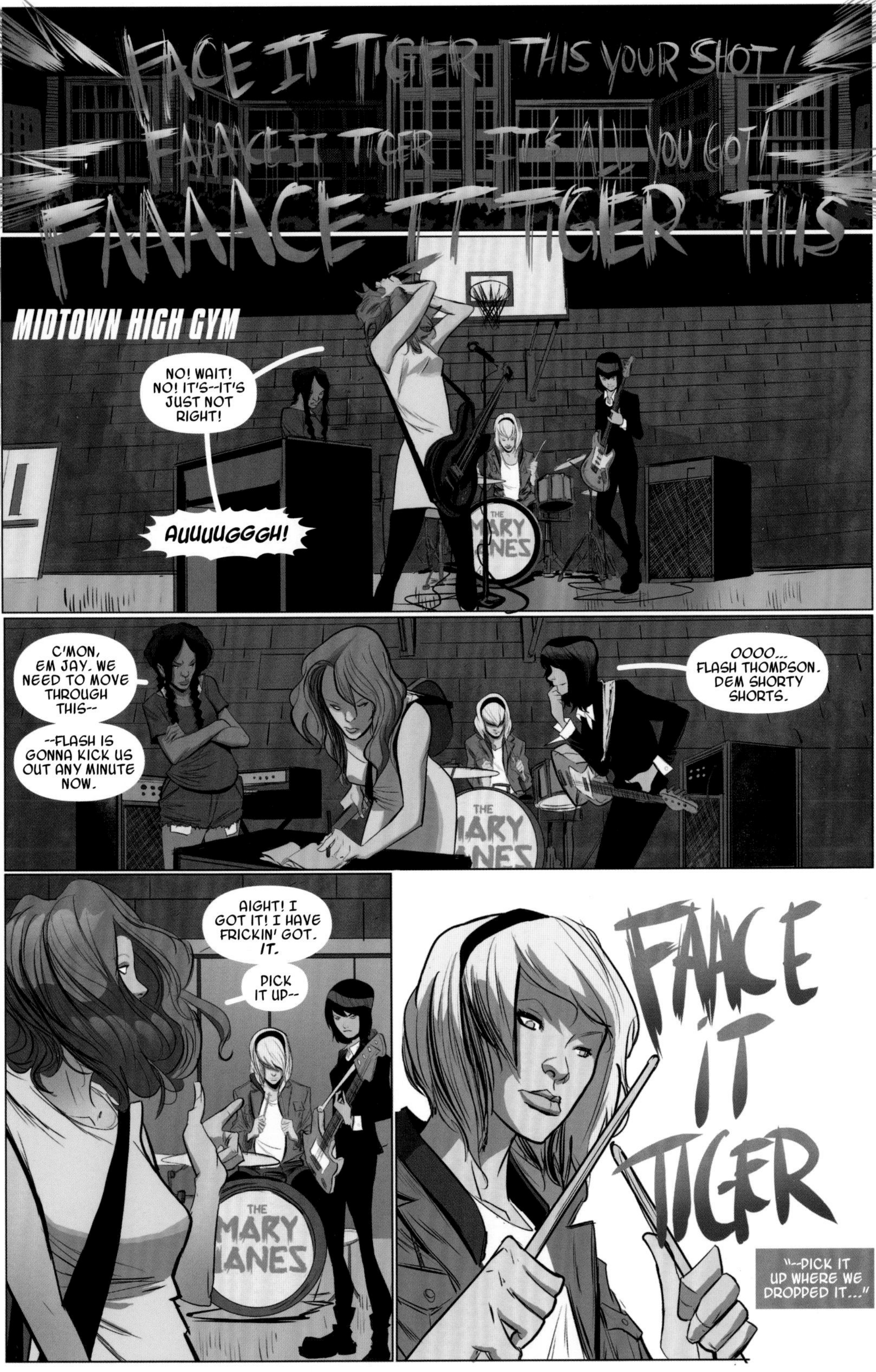

FACE IT TIGER THIS YOUR SHOT!
FAAACE IT TIGER IT'S ALL YOU GOT!
FAAACE IT TIGER THIS
MIDTOWN HIGH GYM
NO! WAIT! NO! IT'S--IT'S JUST NOT RIGHT!
AUUUUGGGH!
THE MARY JANES
C'MON, EM JAY. WE NEED TO MOVE THROUGH THIS--
--FLASH IS GONNA KICK US OUT ANY MINUTE NOW.
OOOO... FLASH THOMPSON. DEM SHORTY SHORTS.
AIGHT! I GOT IT! I HAVE FRICKIN' GOT. IT.
PICK IT UP--
FAACE IT TIGER
"--PICK IT UP WHERE WE DROPPED IT..."

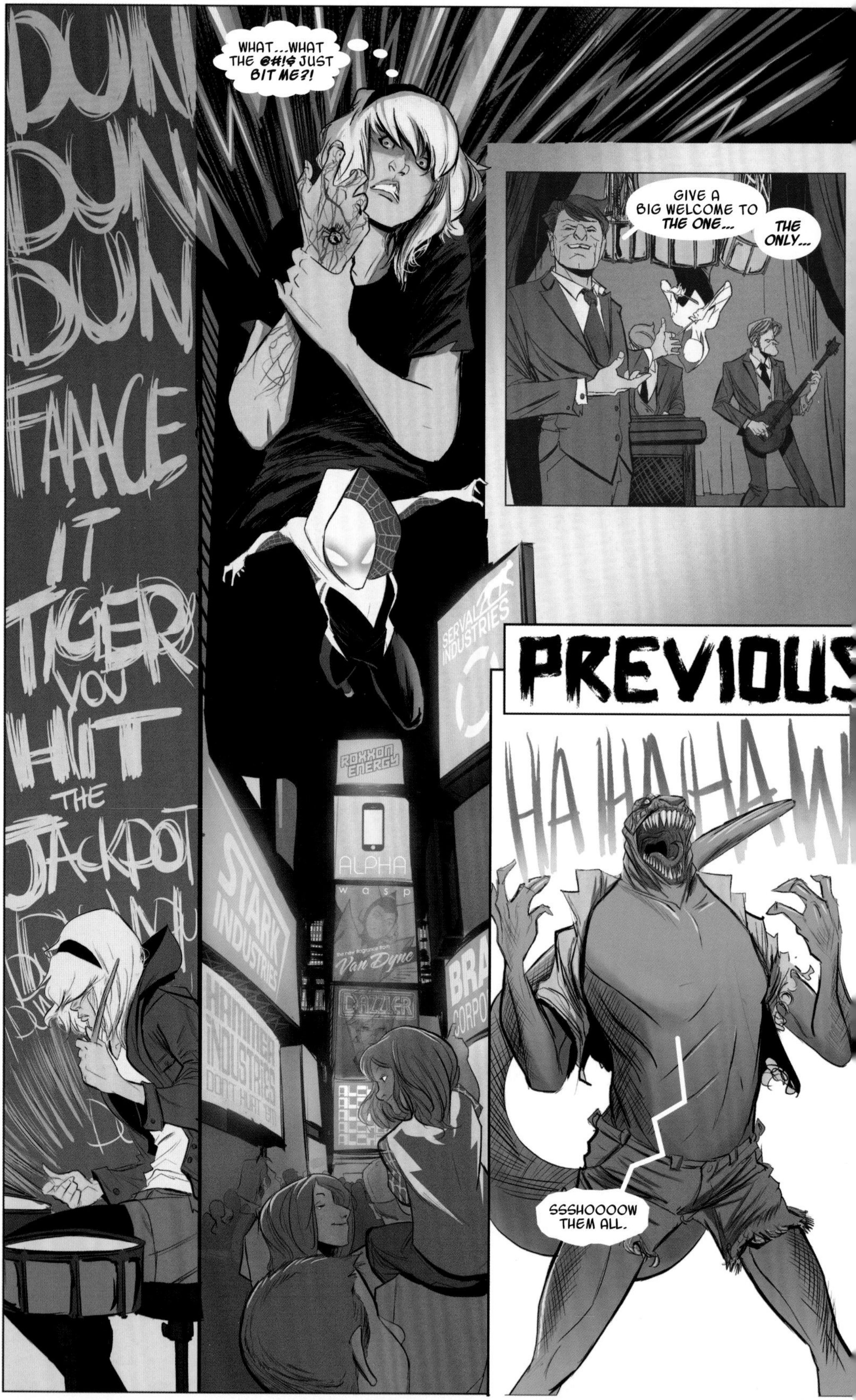
DUN DUN DUN
FAAACE IT TIGER YOU HIT THE JACKPOT
WHAT...WHAT THE @#!$ JUST BIT ME?!
SERVAL INDUSTRIES
ROXXON ENERGY
ALPHA
wasp
The new fragrance from Van Dyne
DAZZLER
STARK INDUSTRIES
HAMMER INDUSTRIES DON'T HURT 'EM
GIVE A BIG WELCOME TO THE ONE...
THE ONLY...
PREVIOUS
HA HA HA HA
SSSHOOOOW THEM ALL.

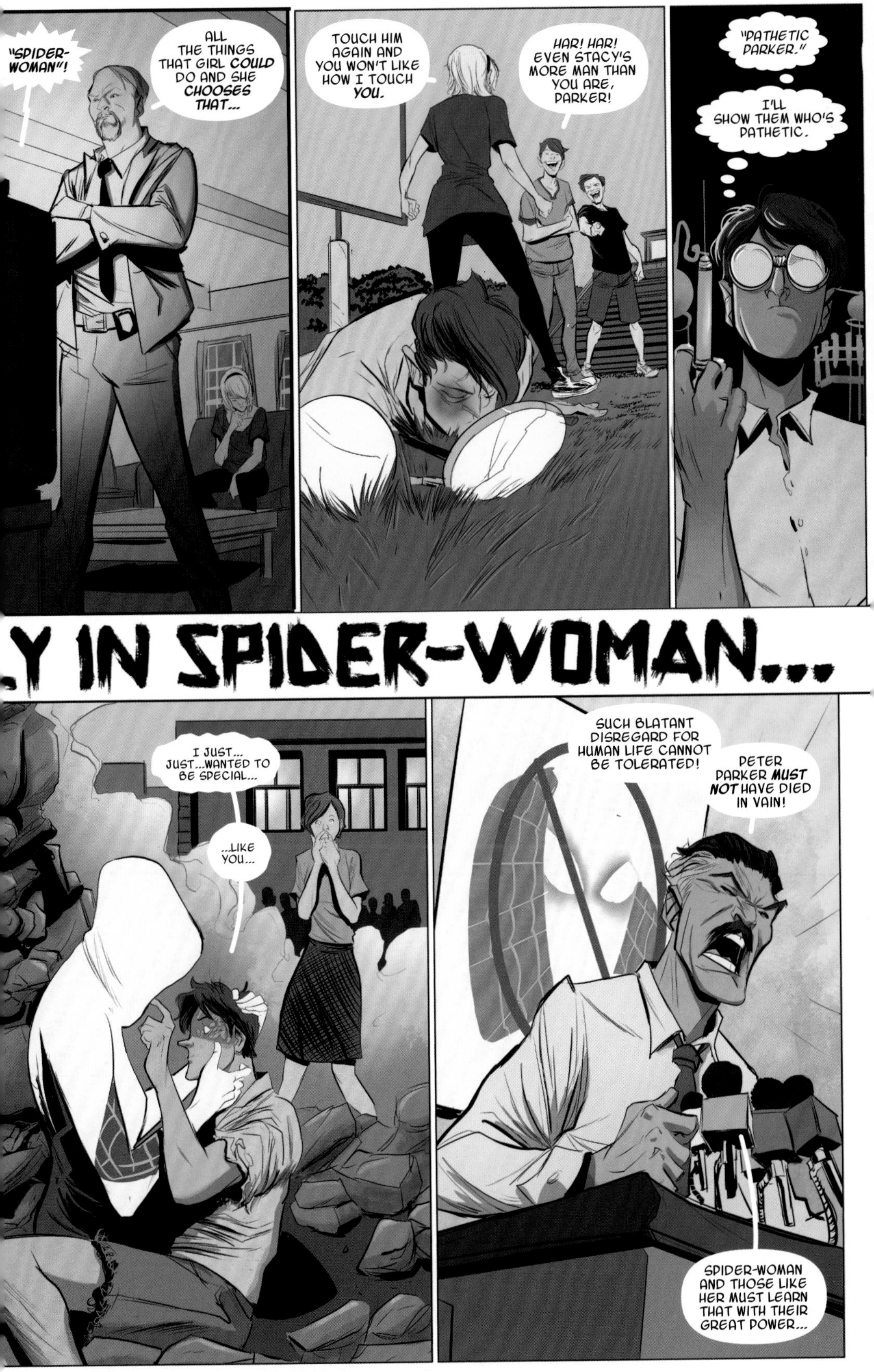
"SPIDER-WOMAN"!
ALL THE THINGS THAT GIRL COULD DO AND SHE CHOOSES THAT...
TOUCH HIM AGAIN AND YOU WON'T LIKE HOW I TOUCH YOU.
HAR! HAR! EVEN STACY'S MORE MAN THAN YOU ARE, PARKER!
"PATHETIC PARKER."
I'LL SHOW THEM WHO'S PATHETIC.
.Y IN SPIDER-WOMAN...
I JUST... JUST...WANTED TO BE SPECIAL...
...LIKE YOU...
SUCH BLATANT DISREGARD FOR HUMAN LIFE CANNOT BE TOLERATED!
PETER PARKER MUST NOT HAVE DIED IN VAIN!
SPIDER-WOMAN AND THOSE LIKE HER MUST LEARN THAT WITH THEIR GREAT POWER...

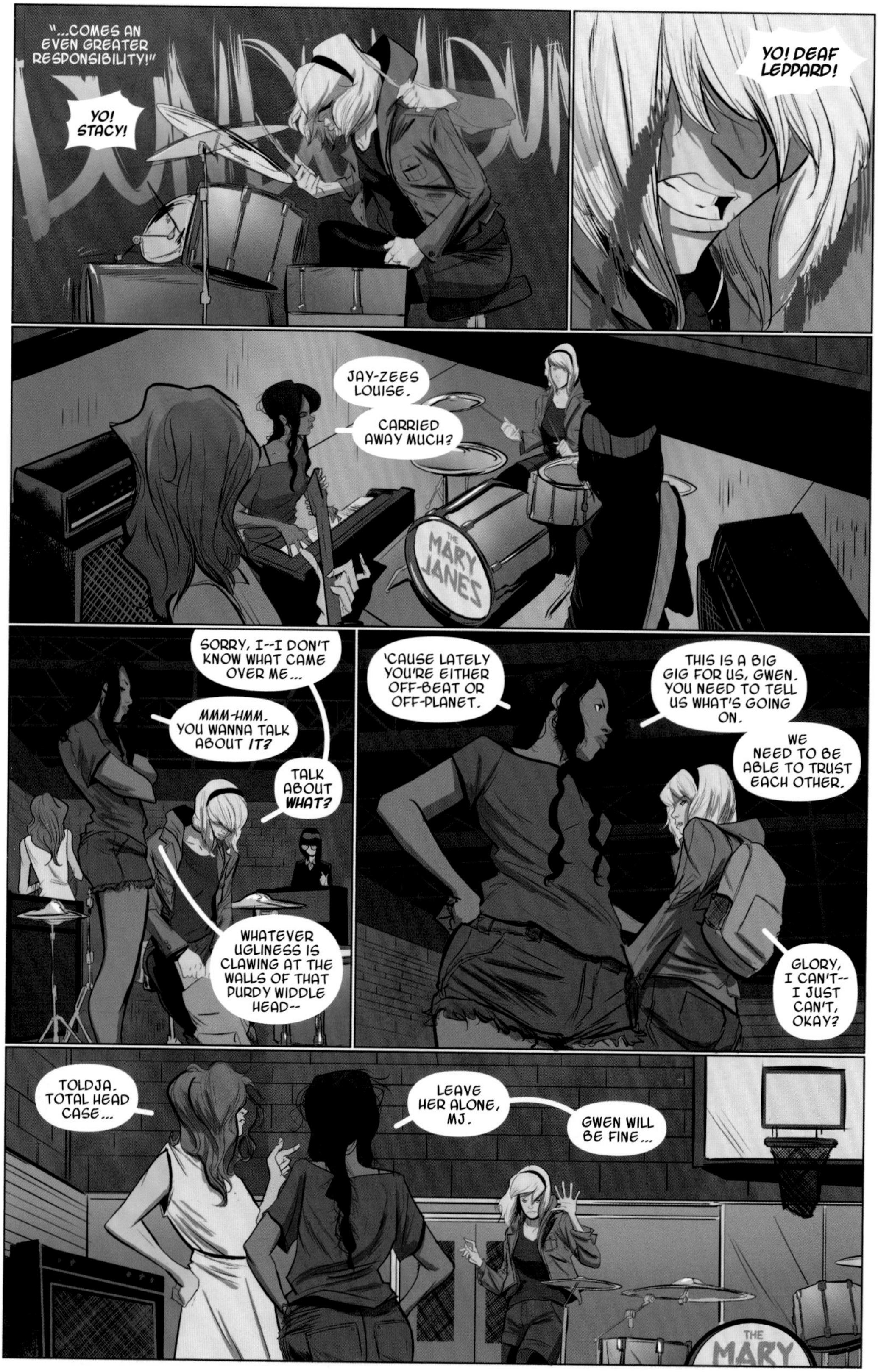
"...COMES AN EVEN GREATER RESPONSIBILITY!"
YO! STACY!
YO! DEAF LEPPARD!
JAY-ZEES LOUISE.
CARRIED AWAY MUCH?
THE MARY JANES
SORRY, I--I DON'T KNOW WHAT CAME OVER ME...
MMM-HMM. YOU WANNA TALK ABOUT IT?
TALK ABOUT WHAT?
WHATEVER UGLINESS IS CLAWING AT THE WALLS OF THAT PURDY WIDDLE HEAD--
'CAUSE LATELY YOU'RE EITHER OFF-BEAT OR OFF-PLANET.
THIS IS A BIG GIG FOR US, GWEN. YOU NEED TO TELL US WHAT'S GOING ON.
WE NEED TO BE ABLE TO TRUST EACH OTHER.
GLORY, I CAN'T-- I JUST CAN'T, OKAY?
TOLDJA. TOTAL HEAD CASE...
LEAVE HER ALONE, MJ.
GWEN WILL BE FINE...
THE MARY

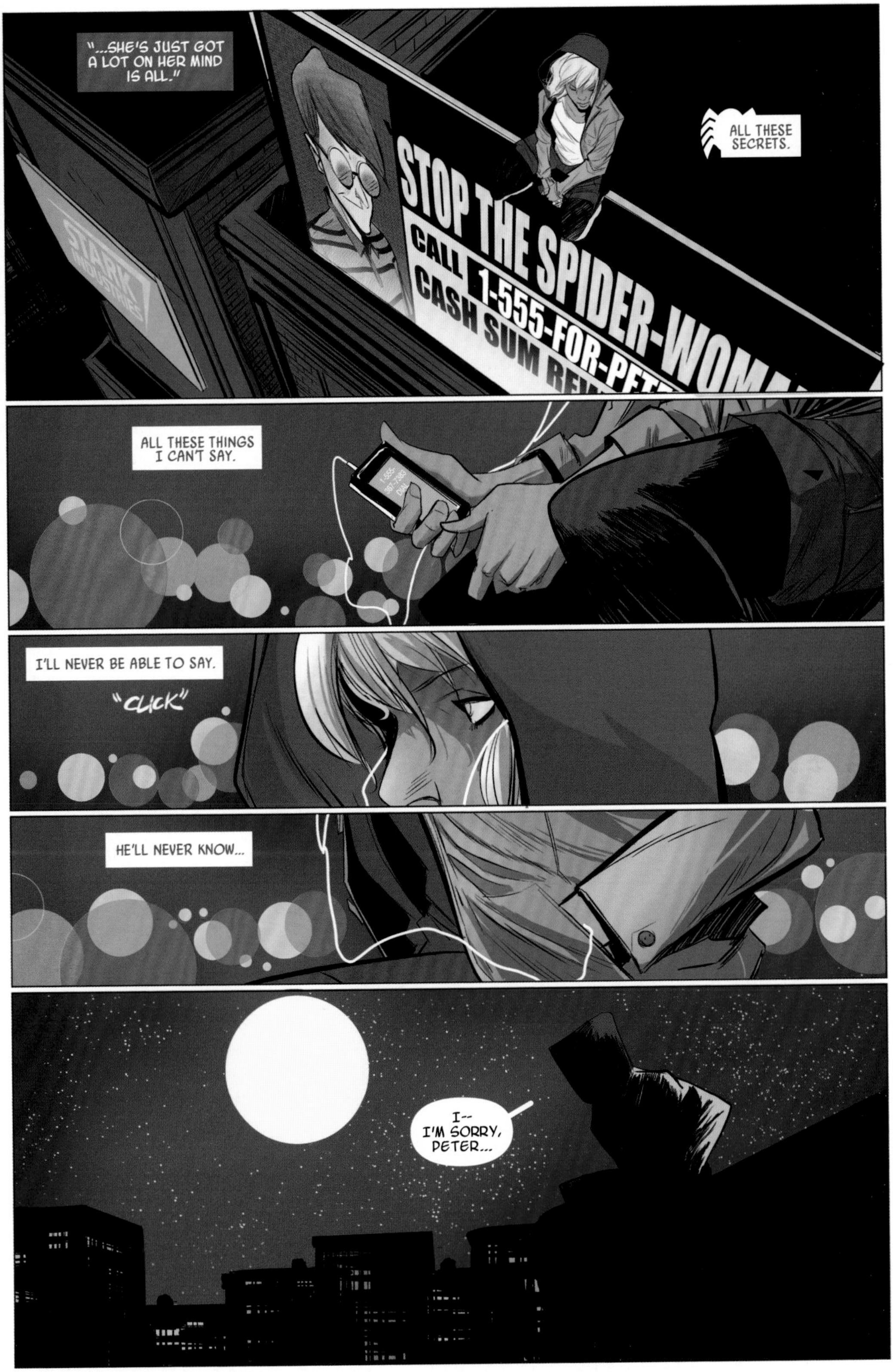
"...SHE'S JUST GOT A LOT ON HER MIND IS ALL."
STARK INDUSTRIES
STOP THE SPIDER-WOMA
CALL 1-555-FOR-PETE
CASH SUM REW
ALL THESE SECRETS.
ALL THESE THINGS I CAN'T SAY.
I'LL NEVER BE ABLE TO SAY.
"CLICK"
HE'LL NEVER KNOW...
I-- I'M SORRY, PETER...

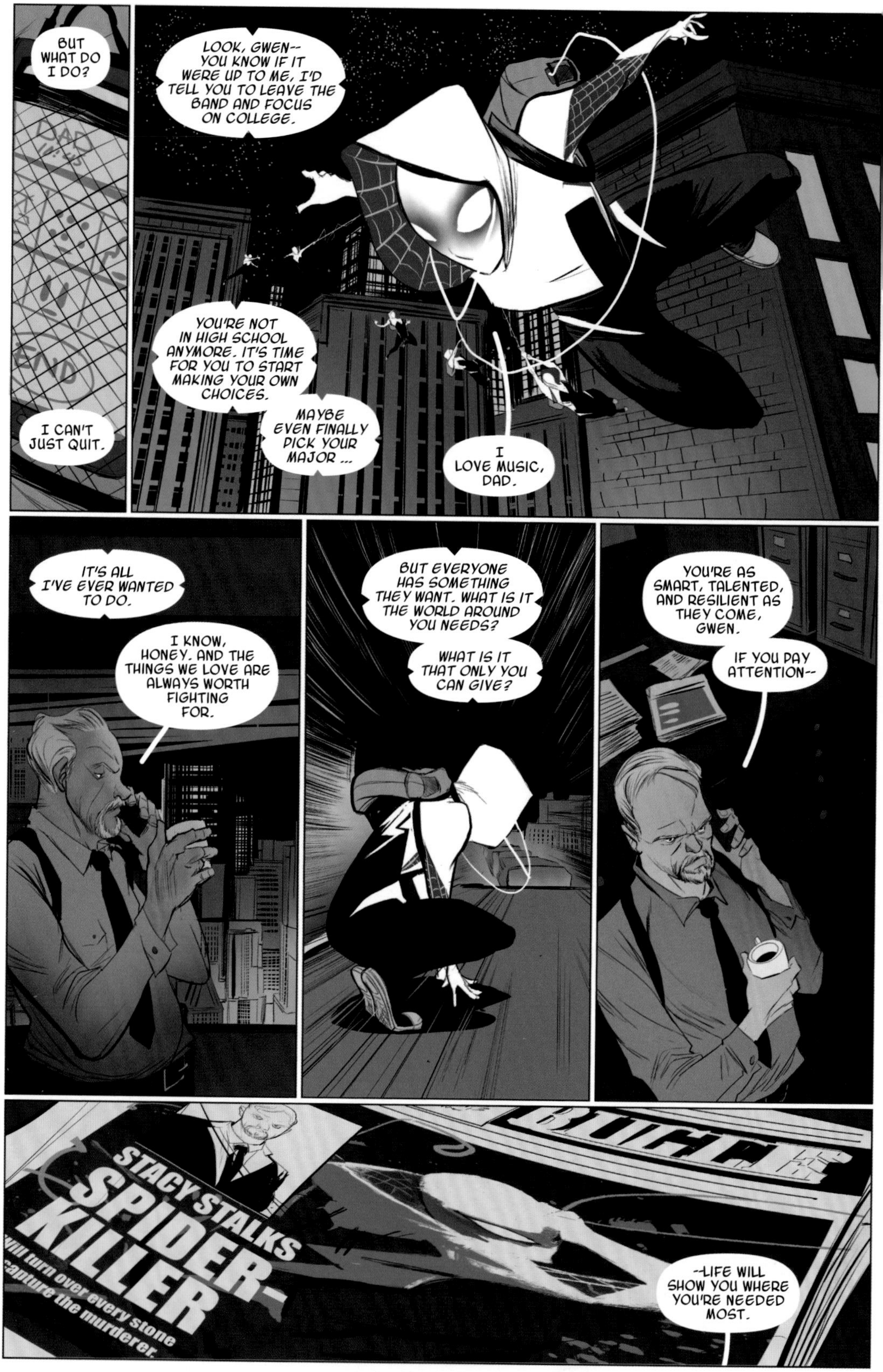
BUT WHAT DO I DO?
LOOK, GWEN-- YOU KNOW IF IT WERE UP TO ME, I'D TELL YOU TO LEAVE THE BAND AND FOCUS ON COLLEGE.
YOU'RE NOT IN HIGH SCHOOL ANYMORE. IT'S TIME FOR YOU TO START MAKING YOUR OWN CHOICES.
MAYBE EVEN FINALLY PICK YOUR MAJOR ...
I CAN'T JUST QUIT.
I LOVE MUSIC, DAD.
IT'S ALL I'VE EVER WANTED TO DO.
I KNOW, HONEY. AND THE THINGS WE LOVE ARE ALWAYS WORTH FIGHTING FOR.
BUT EVERYONE HAS SOMETHING THEY WANT. WHAT IS IT THE WORLD AROUND YOU NEEDS?
WHAT IS IT THAT ONLY YOU CAN GIVE?
YOU'RE AS SMART, TALENTED, AND RESILIENT AS THEY COME, GWEN.
IF YOU PAY ATTENTION--
STACY STALKS SPIDER-KILLER
--LIFE WILL SHOW YOU WHERE YOU'RE NEEDED MOST.

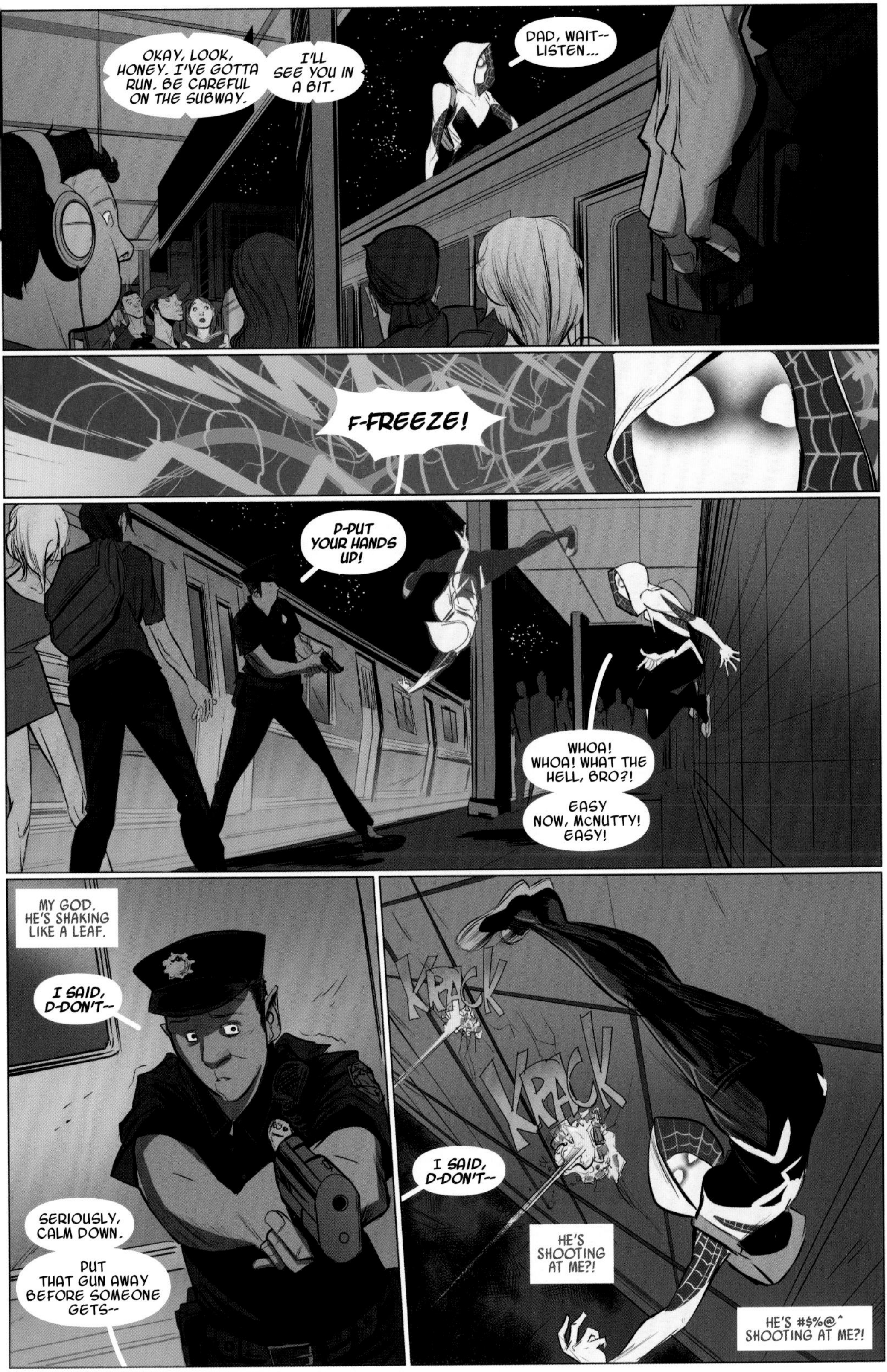
OKAY, LOOK, HONEY. I'VE GOTTA RUN. BE CAREFUL ON THE SUBWAY.
I'LL SEE YOU IN A BIT.
DAD, WAIT-- LISTEN...
F-FREEZE!
D-PUT YOUR HANDS UP!
WHOA! WHOA! WHAT THE HELL, BRO?!
EASY NOW, McNUTTY! EASY!
MY GOD. HE'S SHAKING LIKE A LEAF.
I SAID, D-DON'T--
SERIOUSLY, CALM DOWN.
PUT THAT GUN AWAY BEFORE SOMEONE GETS--
KRACK
KRACK
I SAID, D-DON'T--
HE'S SHOOTING AT ME?!
HE'S #$%@^ SHOOTING AT ME?!

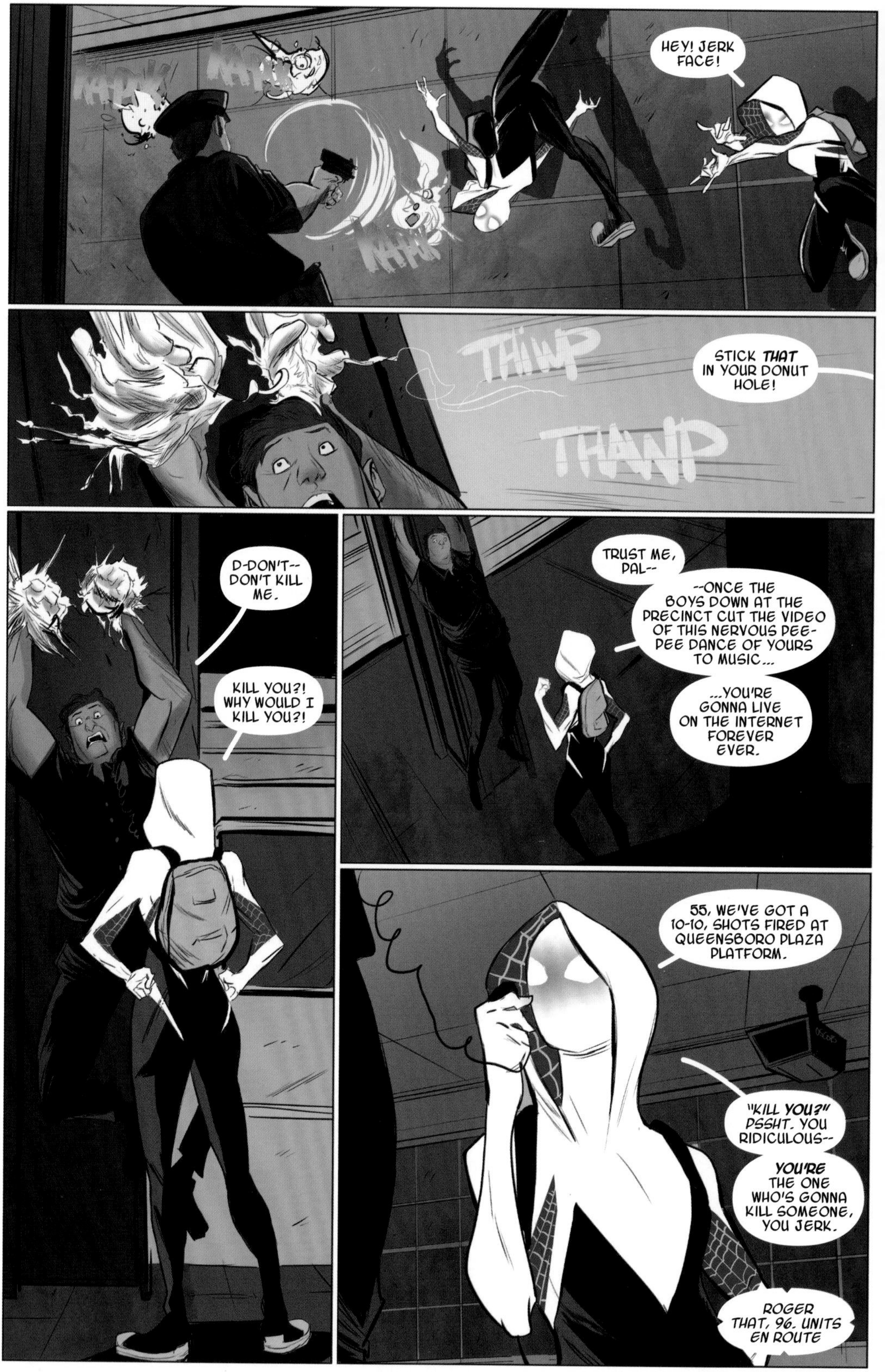
KA-BLAM
HEY! JERK FACE!
THWP
THWP
STICK THAT IN YOUR DONUT HOLE!
D-DON'T-- DON'T KILL ME.
KILL YOU?! WHY WOULD I KILL YOU?!
TRUST ME, PAL--
--ONCE THE BOYS DOWN AT THE PRECINCT CUT THE VIDEO OF THIS NERVOUS PEE-PEE DANCE OF YOURS TO MUSIC...
...YOU'RE GONNA LIVE ON THE INTERNET FOREVER EVER.
55, WE'VE GOT A 10-10, SHOTS FIRED AT QUEENSBORO PLAZA PLATFORM.
"KILL YOU?" PSSHT. YOU RIDICULOUS--
YOU'RE THE ONE WHO'S GONNA KILL SOMEONE, YOU JERK.
ROGER THAT, 96. UNITS EN ROUTE

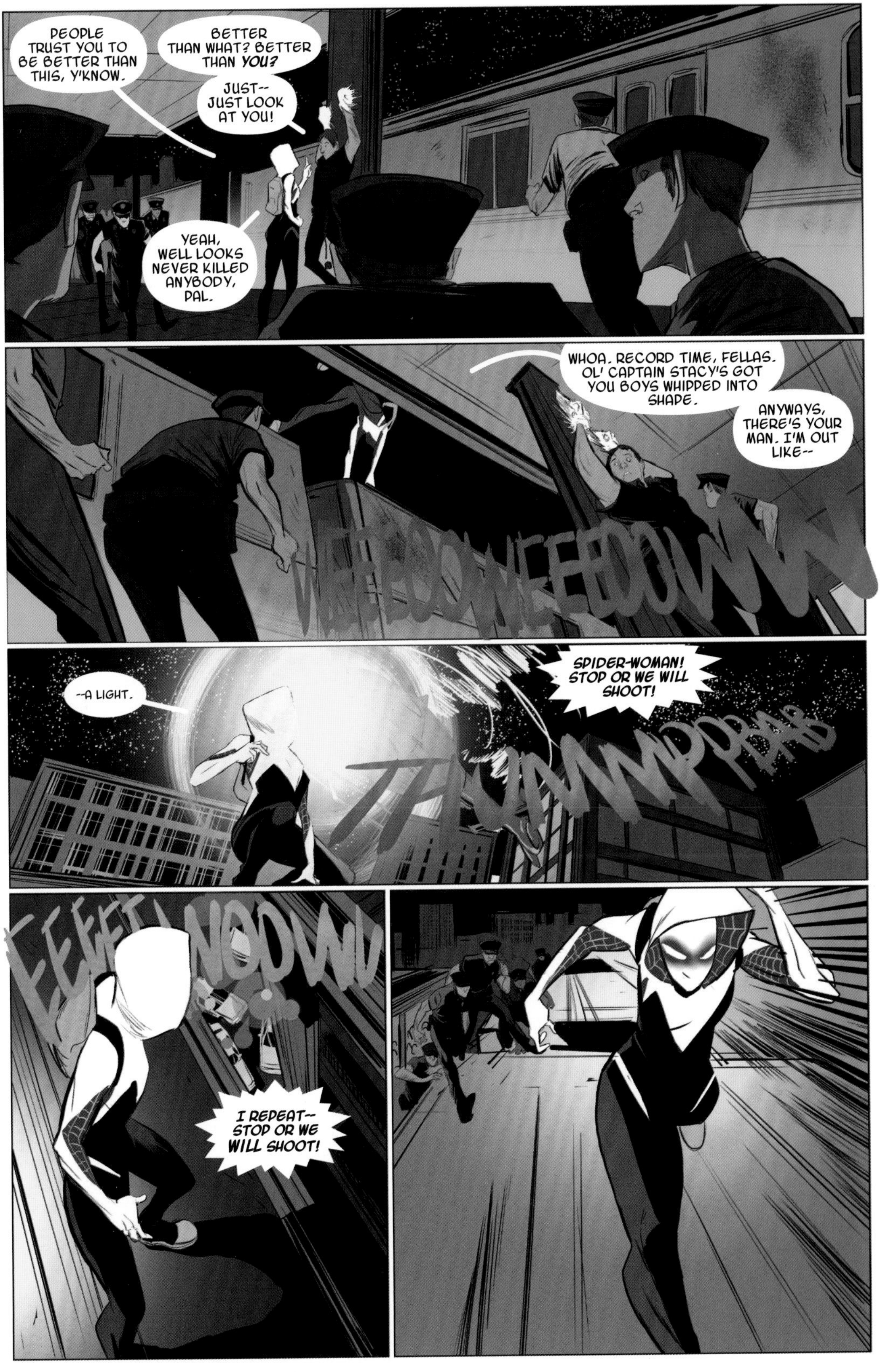
PEOPLE TRUST YOU TO BE BETTER THAN THIS, Y'KNOW.
BETTER THAN WHAT? BETTER THAN *YOU?*
JUST-- JUST LOOK AT YOU!
YEAH, WELL LOOKS NEVER KILLED ANYBODY, PAL.
WHOA. RECORD TIME, FELLAS. OL' CAPTAIN STACY'S GOT YOU BOYS WHIPPED INTO SHAPE.
ANYWAYS, THERE'S YOUR MAN. I'M OUT LIKE--
--A LIGHT.
SPIDER-WOMAN! STOP OR WE WILL SHOOT!
I REPEAT-- STOP OR WE **WILL** SHOOT!

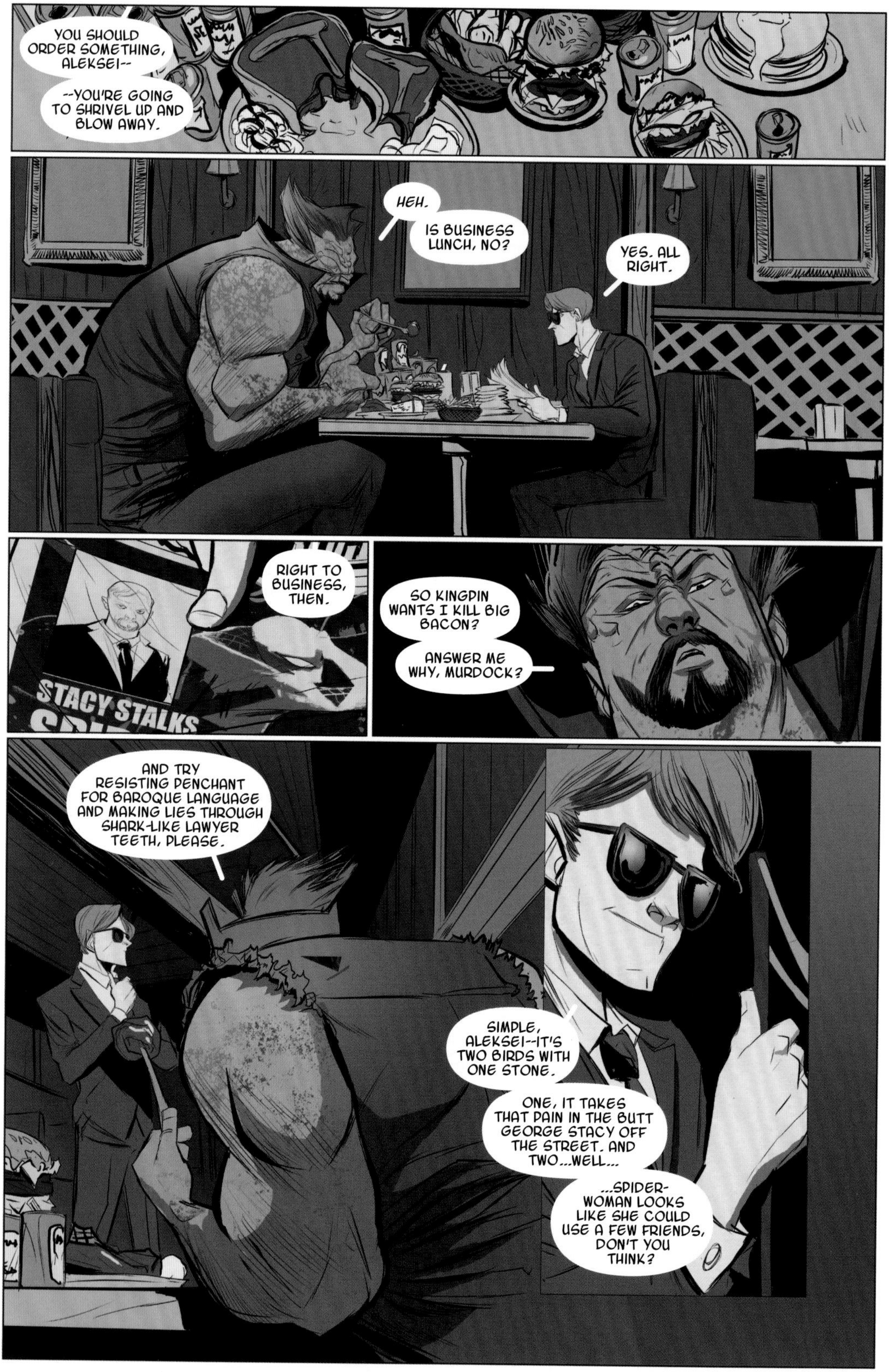
YOU SHOULD ORDER SOMETHING, ALEKSEI--
--YOU'RE GOING TO SHRIVEL UP AND BLOW AWAY.
HEH.
IS BUSINESS LUNCH, NO?
YES. ALL RIGHT.
RIGHT TO BUSINESS, THEN.
STACY STALKS
SO KINGPIN WANTS I KILL BIG BACON?
ANSWER ME WHY, MURDOCK?
AND TRY RESISTING PENCHANT FOR BAROQUE LANGUAGE AND MAKING LIES THROUGH SHARK-LIKE LAWYER TEETH, PLEASE.
SIMPLE, ALEKSEI--IT'S TWO BIRDS WITH ONE STONE.
ONE, IT TAKES THAT PAIN IN THE BUTT GEORGE STACY OFF THE STREET. AND TWO...WELL...
...SPIDER-WOMAN LOOKS LIKE SHE COULD USE A FEW FRIENDS, DON'T YOU THINK?

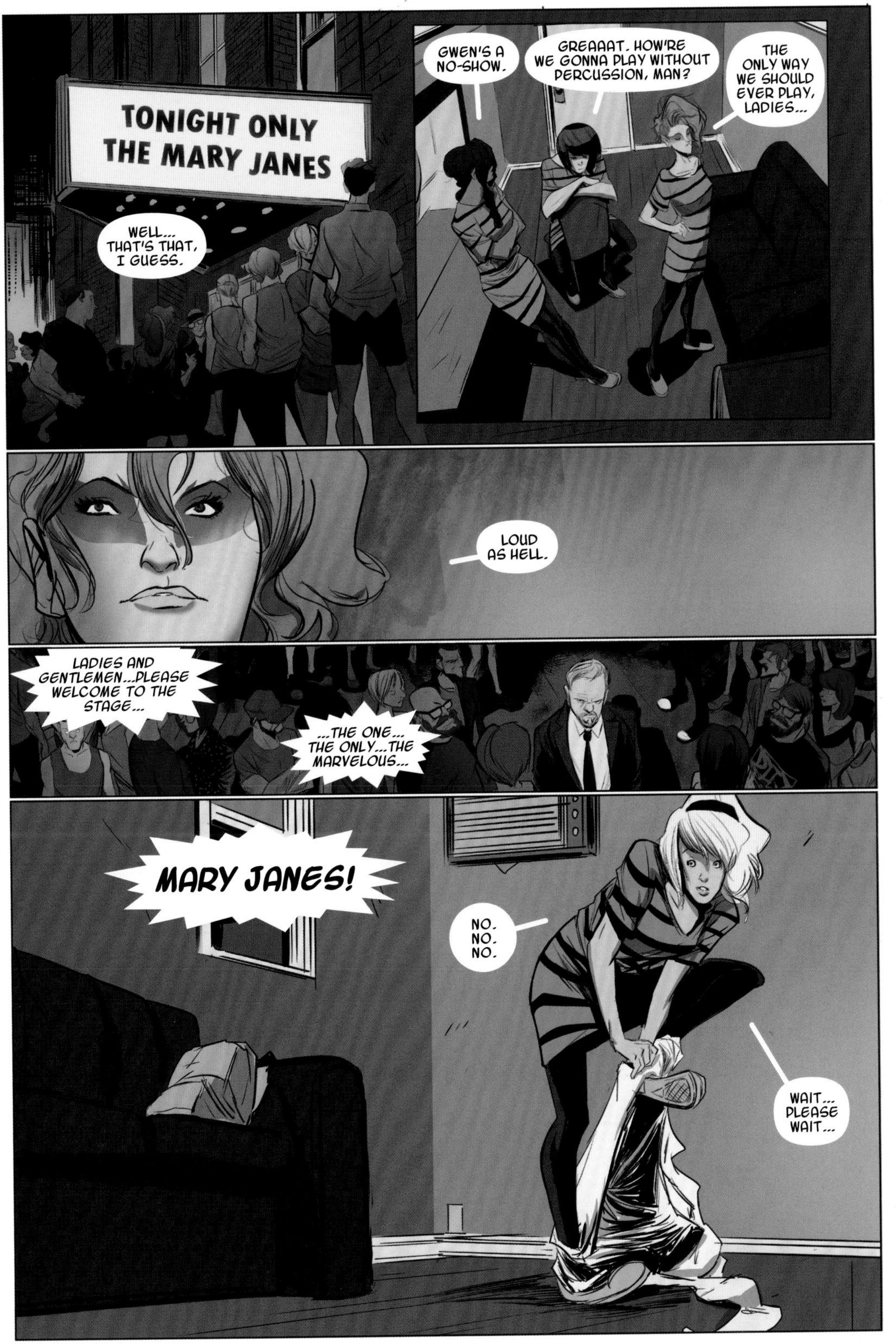
TONIGHT ONLY
THE MARY JANES
WELL... THAT'S THAT, I GUESS.
GWEN'S A NO-SHOW.
GREAAAT. HOW'RE WE GONNA PLAY WITHOUT PERCUSSION, MAN?
THE ONLY WAY WE SHOULD EVER PLAY, LADIES...
LOUD AS HELL.
LADIES AND GENTLEMEN...PLEASE WELCOME TO THE STAGE...
...THE ONE... THE ONLY...THE MARVELOUS...
MARY JANES!
NO. NO. NO.
WAIT... PLEASE WAIT...

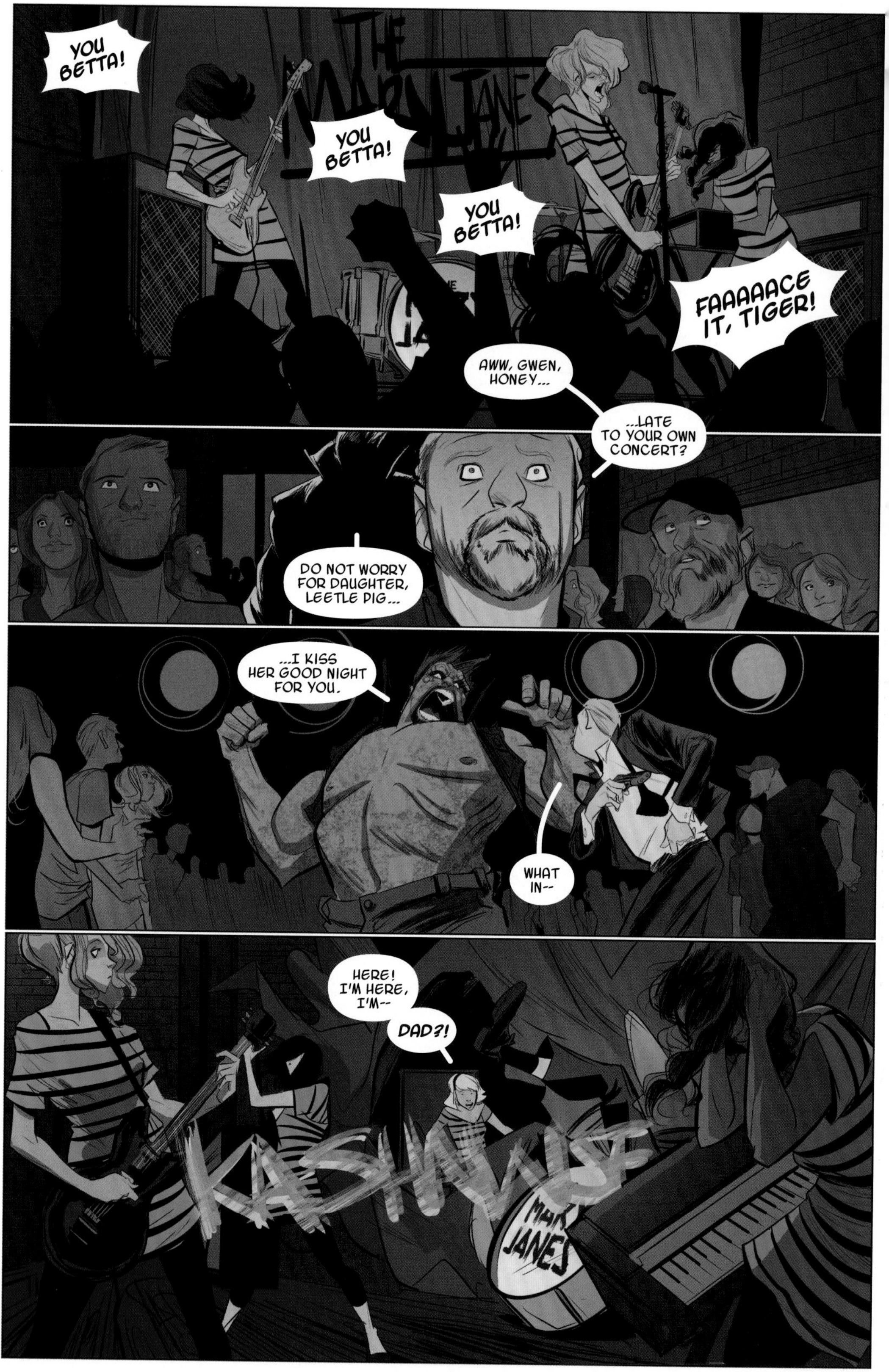
YOU BETTA!
YOU BETTA!
YOU BETTA!
FAAAAACE IT, TIGER!
AWW, GWEN, HONEY...
...LATE TO YOUR OWN CONCERT?
DO NOT WORRY FOR DAUGHTER, LEETLE PIG...
...I KISS HER GOOD NIGHT FOR YOU.
WHAT IN--
HERE! I'M HERE, I'M--
DAD?!
KASHWASH

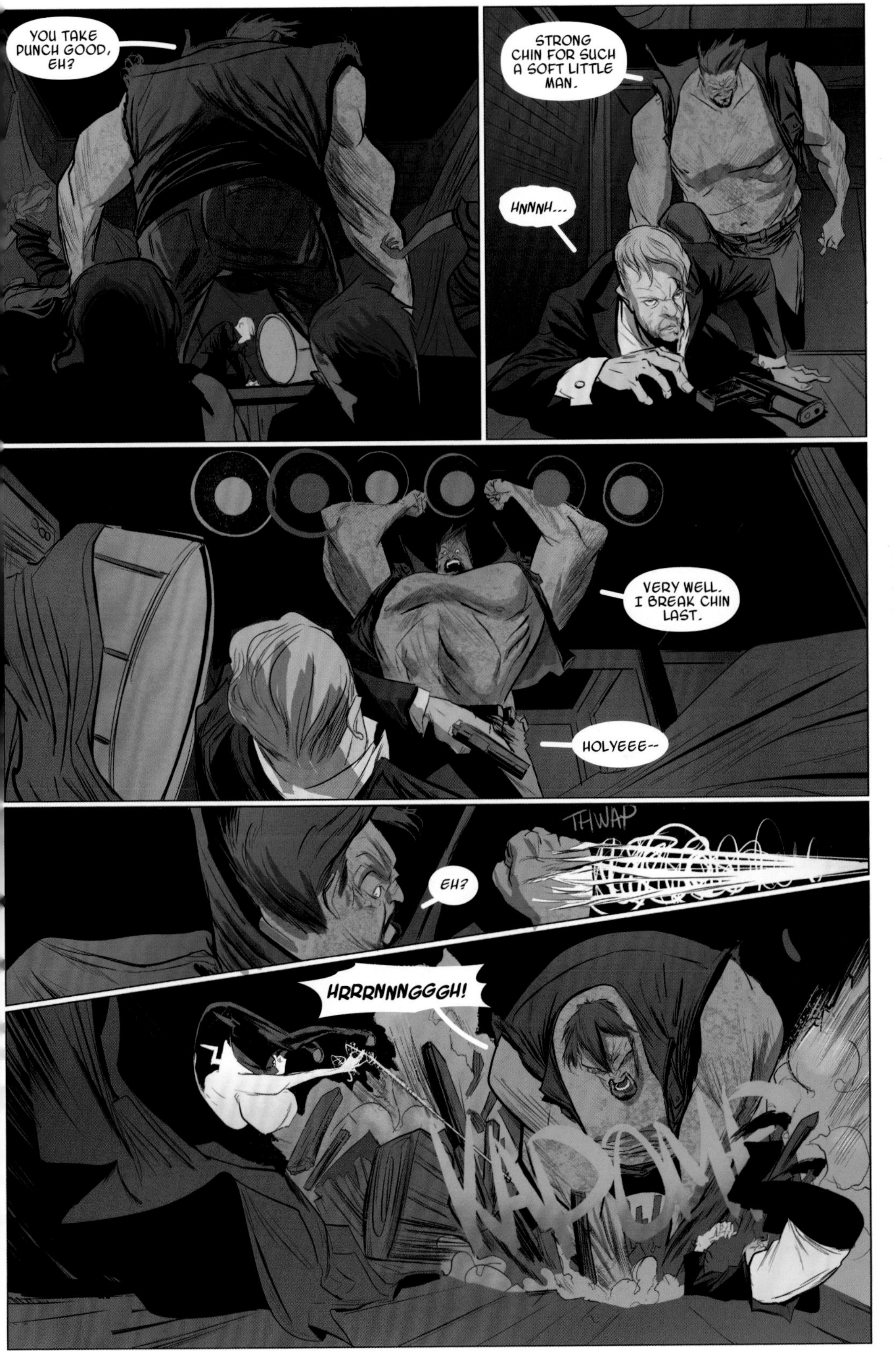
YOU TAKE PUNCH GOOD, EH?
STRONG CHIN FOR SUCH A SOFT LITTLE MAN.
HNNNH...
VERY WELL. I BREAK CHIN LAST.
HOLYEEE--
THWAP
EH?
HRRRNNNGGGH!

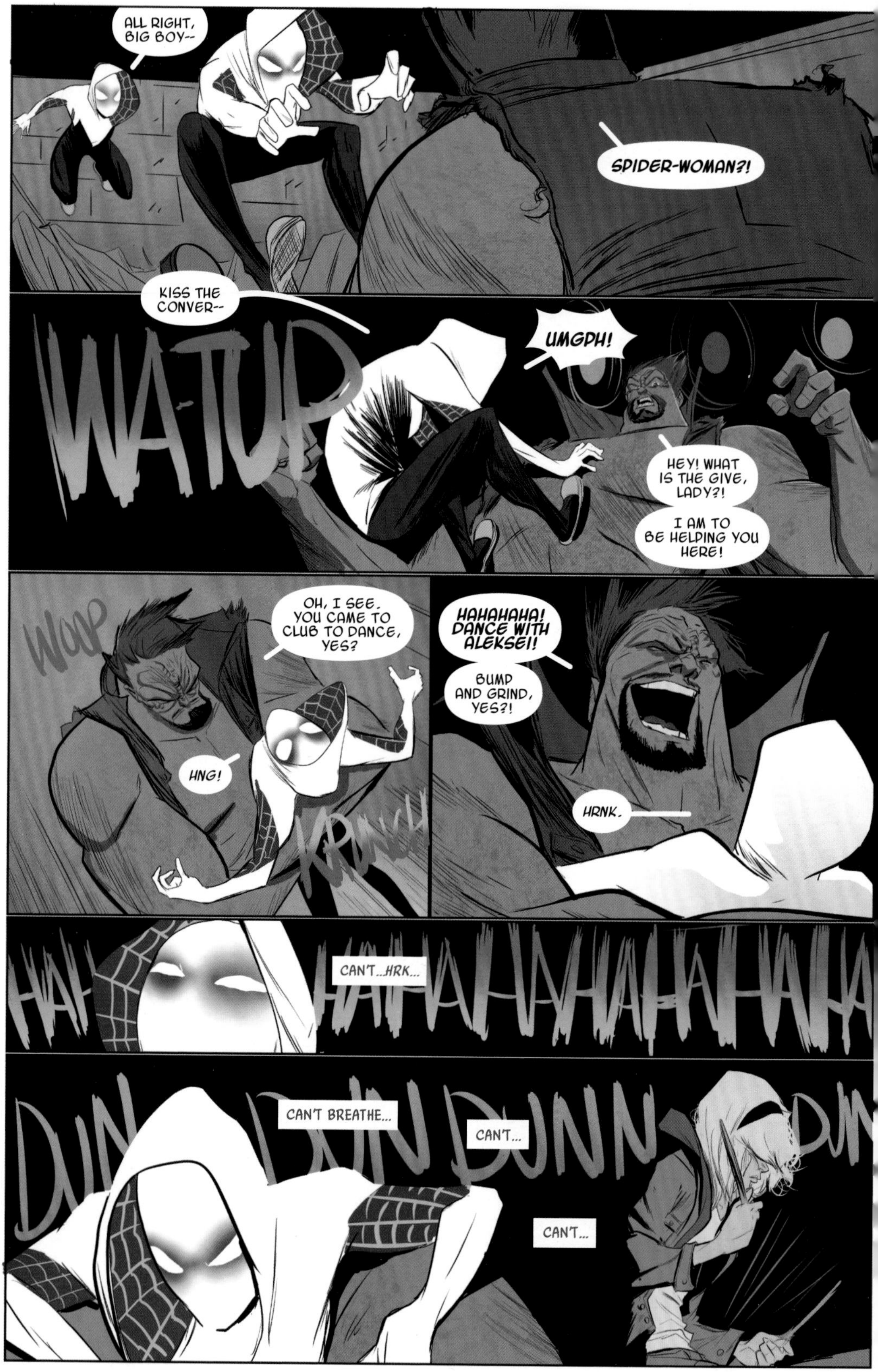
ALL RIGHT, BIG BOY--
SPIDER-WOMAN?!
KISS THE CONVER--
WATUP
UMGPH!
HEY! WHAT IS THE GIVE, LADY?!
I AM TO BE HELPING YOU HERE!
WOOP
OH, I SEE. YOU CAME TO CLUB TO DANCE, YES?
HNG!
KRUNCH
HAHAHAHA! DANCE WITH ALEKSEI!
BUMP AND GRIND, YES?!
HRNK.
CAN'T...HRK...
CAN'T BREATHE...
CAN'T...
CAN'T...

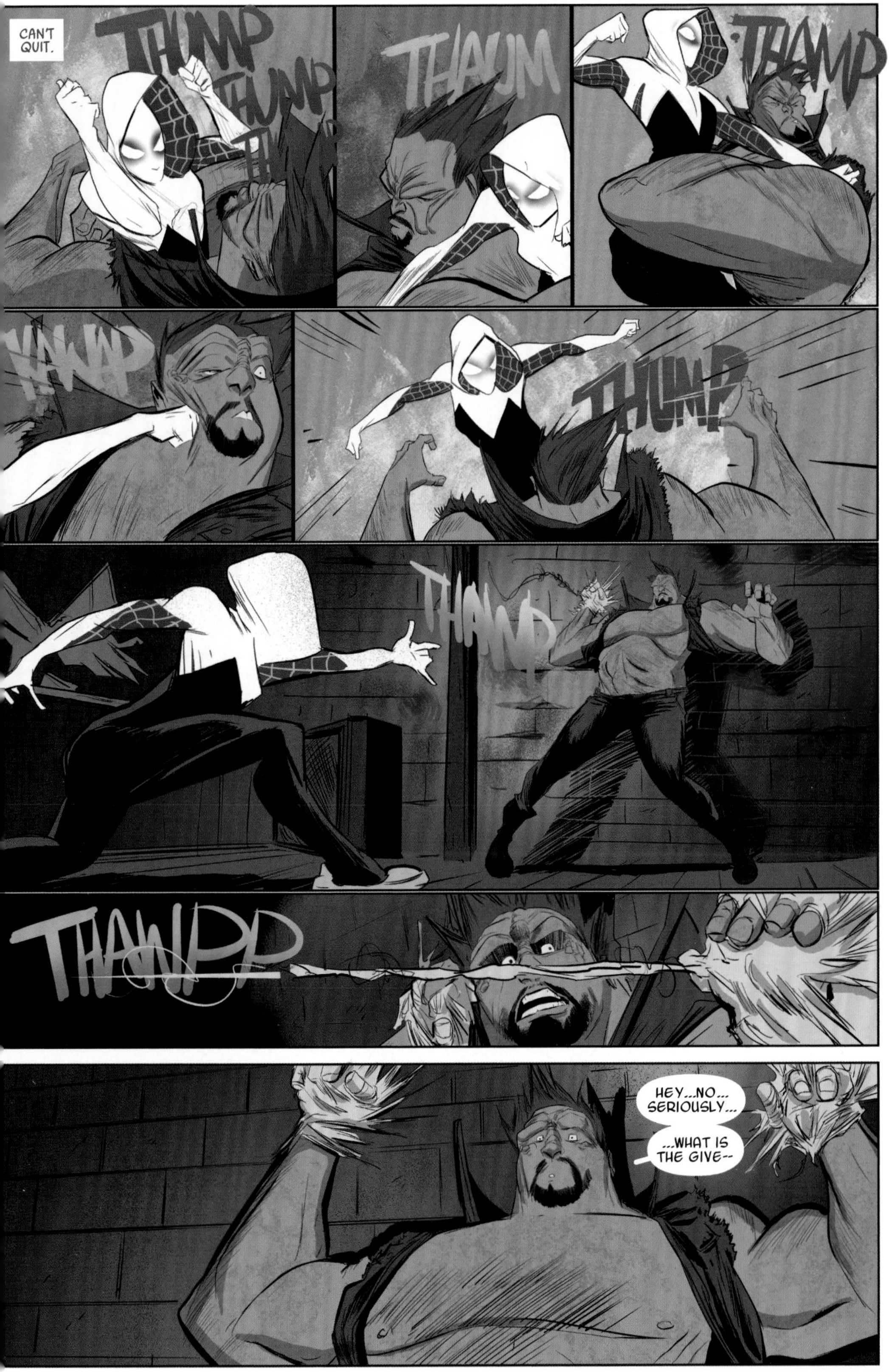
CAN'T QUIT.
THUMP
THUMP
THUMP
THAUM
THAMP
YAWP
THUMP
THAMP
THAWPP
HEY...NO... SERIOUSLY...
...WHAT IS THE GIVE--

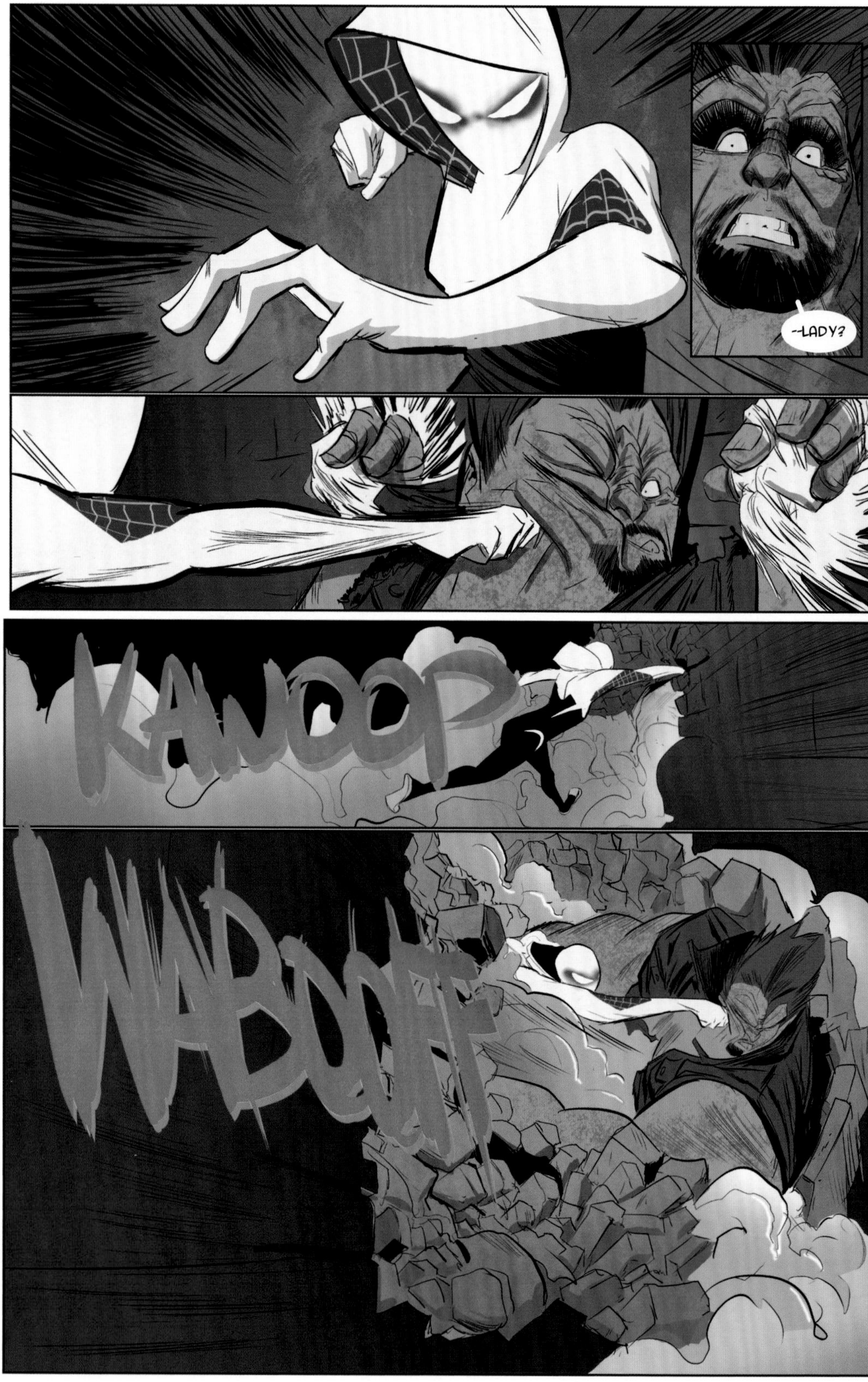

--LADY?
KAWOOP
WABOOFF

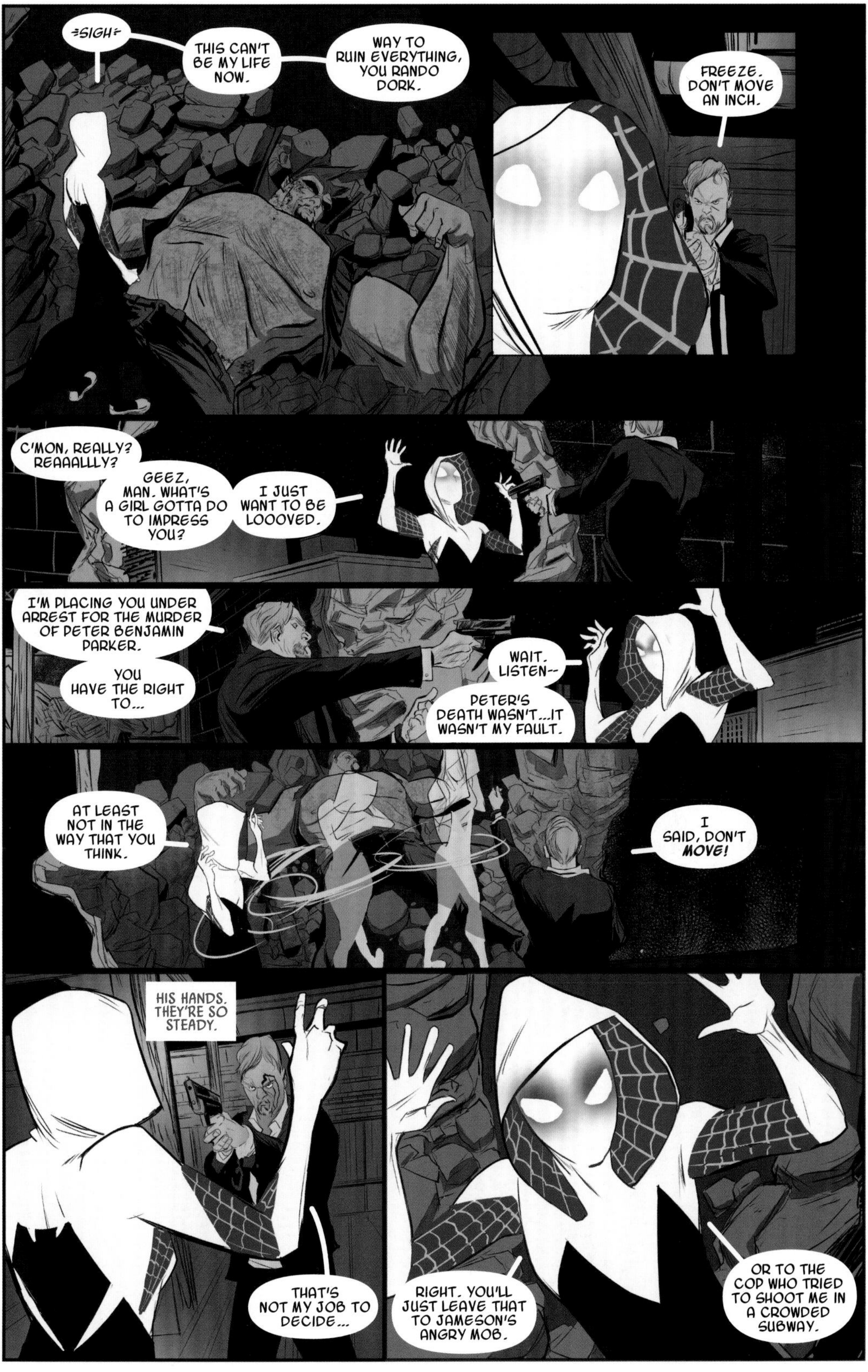
≈SIGH≈
THIS CAN'T BE MY LIFE NOW.
WAY TO RUIN EVERYTHING, YOU RANDO DORK.
FREEZE. DON'T MOVE AN INCH.
C'MON, REALLY? REAAALLLY?
GEEZ, MAN. WHAT'S A GIRL GOTTA DO TO IMPRESS YOU?
I JUST WANT TO BE LOOOVED.
I'M PLACING YOU UNDER ARREST FOR THE MURDER OF PETER BENJAMIN PARKER.
YOU HAVE THE RIGHT TO...
WAIT. LISTEN--
PETER'S DEATH WASN'T...IT WASN'T MY FAULT.
AT LEAST NOT IN THE WAY THAT YOU THINK.
I SAID, DON'T *MOVE!*
HIS HANDS. THEY'RE SO STEADY.
THAT'S NOT MY JOB TO DECIDE...
RIGHT. YOU'LL JUST LEAVE THAT TO JAMESON'S ANGRY MOB.
OR TO THE COP WHO TRIED TO SHOOT ME IN A CROWDED SUBWAY.

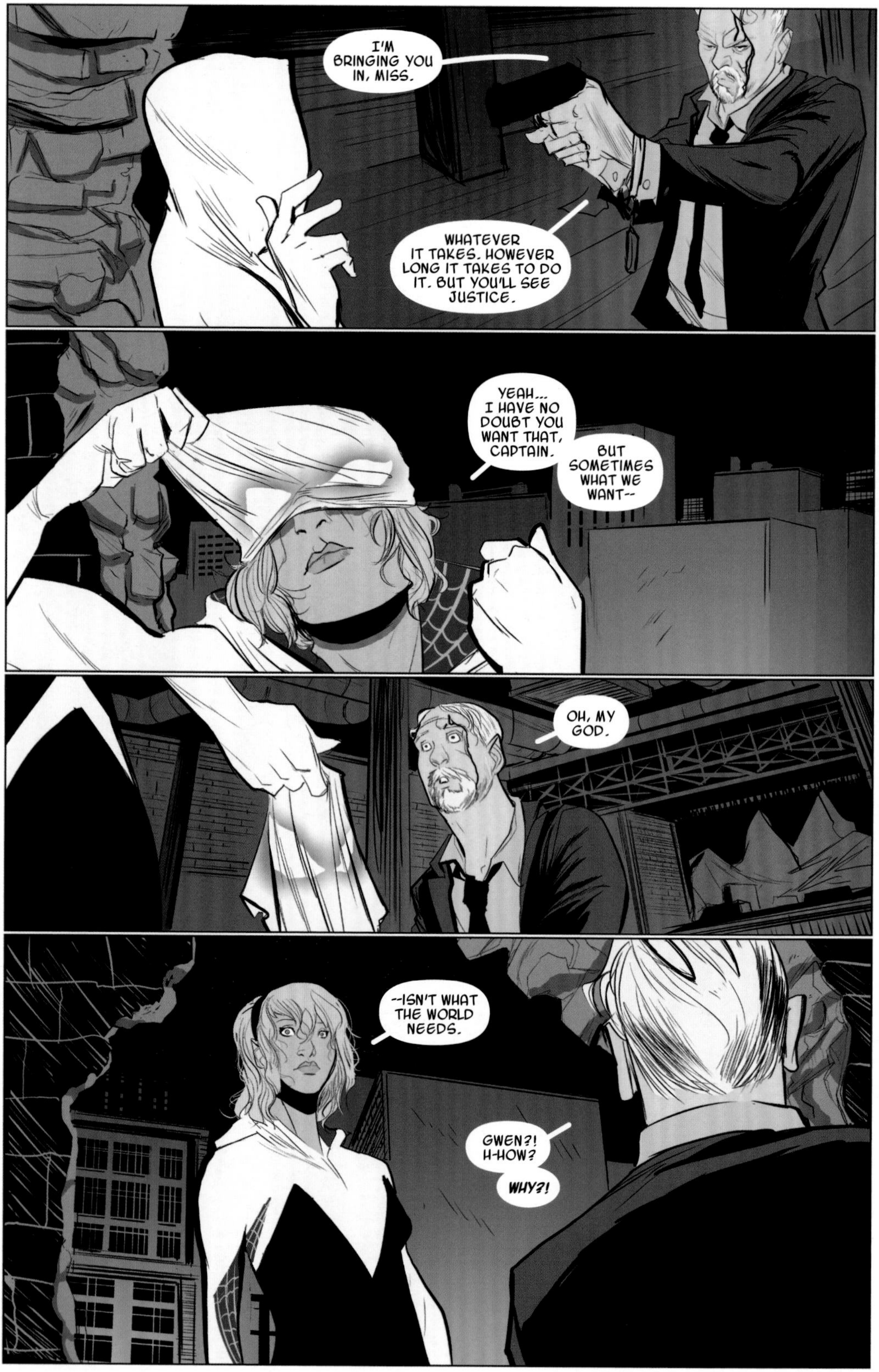
I'M BRINGING YOU IN, MISS.
WHATEVER IT TAKES. HOWEVER LONG IT TAKES TO DO IT. BUT YOU'LL SEE JUSTICE.
YEAH... I HAVE NO DOUBT YOU WANT THAT, CAPTAIN.
BUT SOMETIMES WHAT WE WANT--
OH, MY GOD.
--ISN'T WHAT THE WORLD NEEDS.
GWEN?! H-HOW?
WHY?!

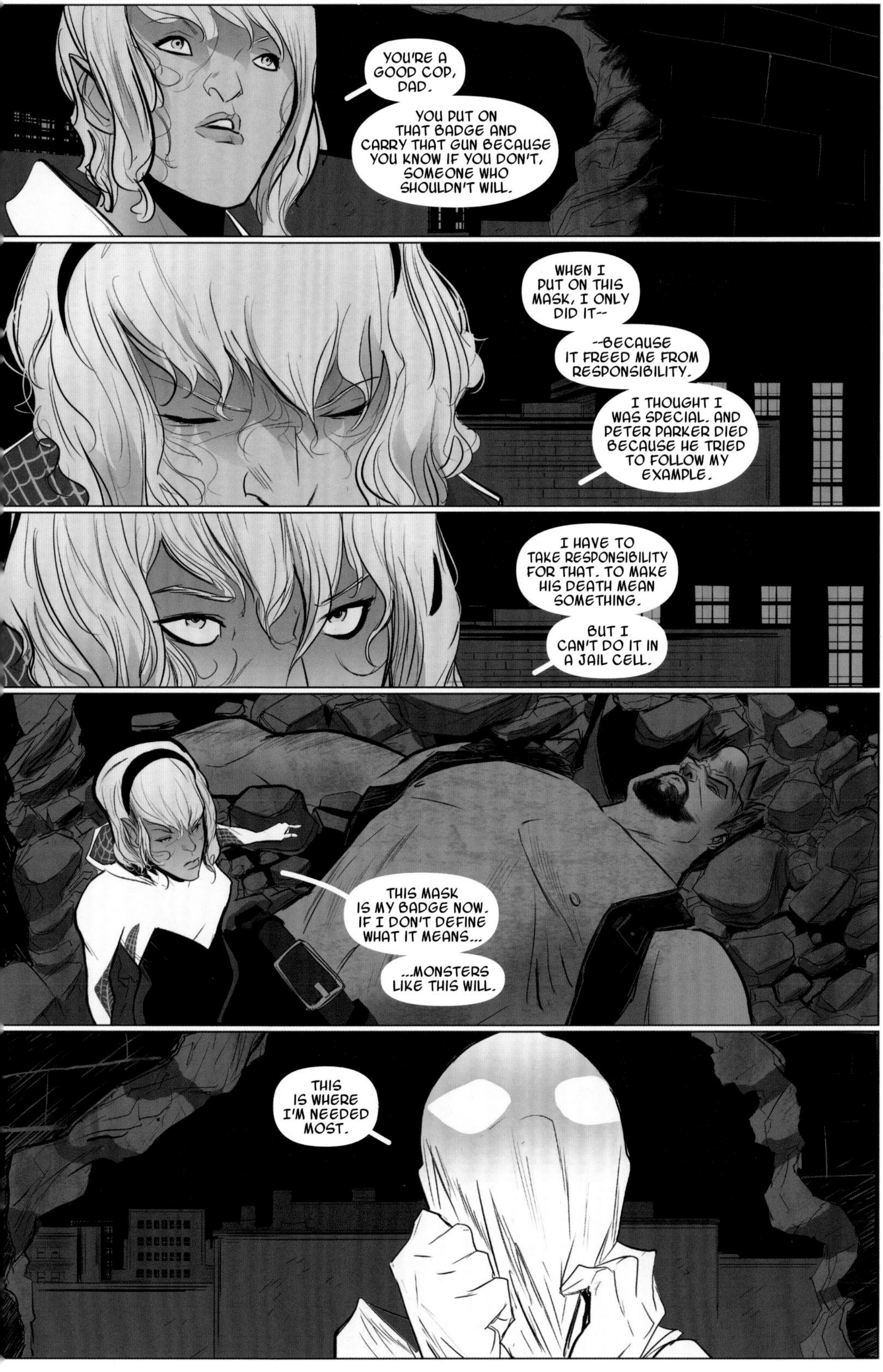
YOU'RE A GOOD COP, DAD.
YOU PUT ON THAT BADGE AND CARRY THAT GUN BECAUSE YOU KNOW IF YOU DON'T, SOMEONE WHO SHOULDN'T WILL.
WHEN I PUT ON THIS MASK, I ONLY DID IT--
--BECAUSE IT FREED ME FROM RESPONSIBILITY.
I THOUGHT I WAS SPECIAL. AND PETER PARKER DIED BECAUSE HE TRIED TO FOLLOW MY EXAMPLE.
I HAVE TO TAKE RESPONSIBILITY FOR THAT. TO MAKE HIS DEATH MEAN SOMETHING.
BUT I CAN'T DO IT IN A JAIL CELL.
THIS MASK IS MY BADGE NOW. IF I DON'T DEFINE WHAT IT MEANS...
...MONSTERS LIKE THIS WILL.
THIS IS WHERE I'M NEEDED MOST.

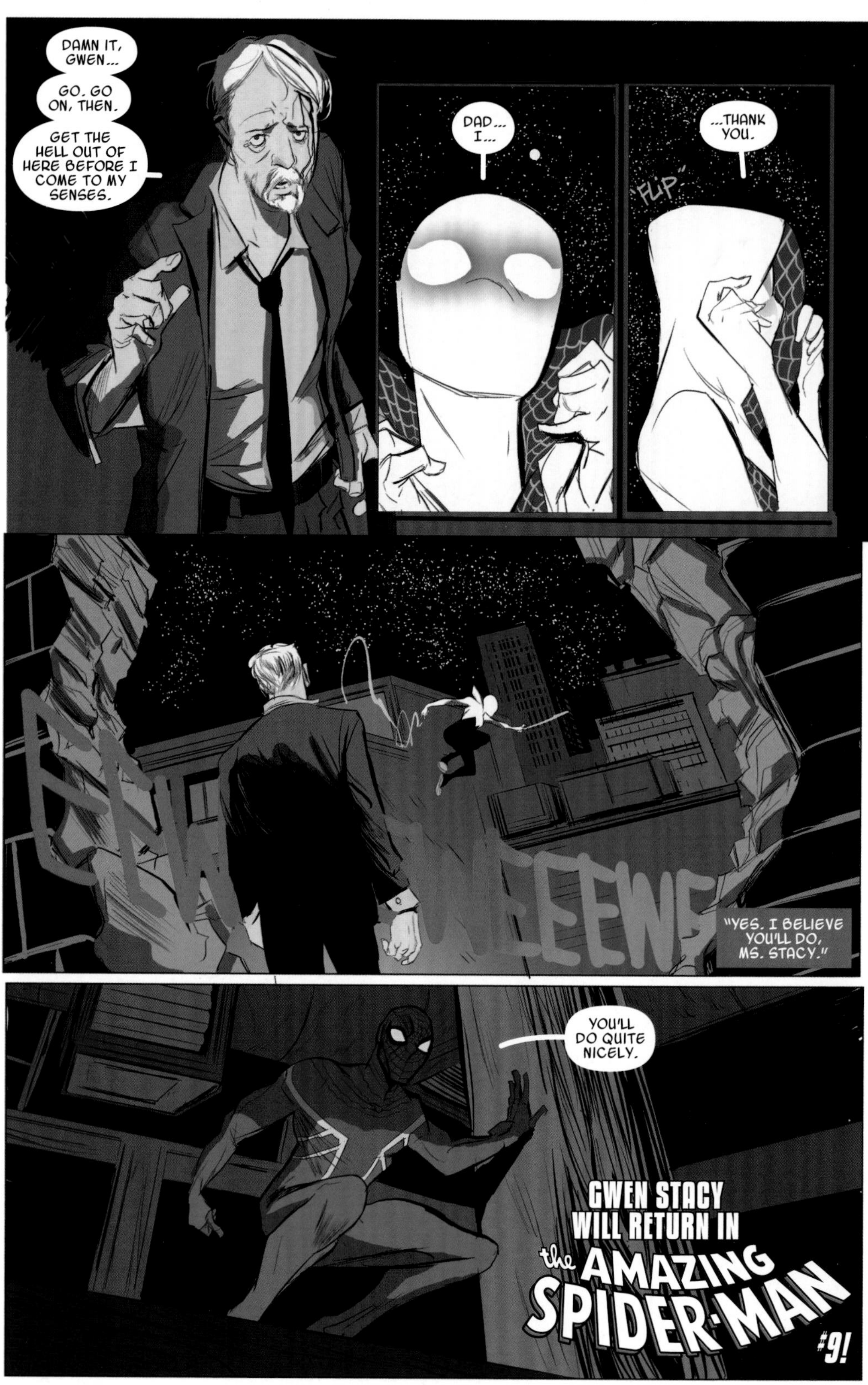
DAMN IT, GWEN...
GO. GO ON, THEN.
GET THE HELL OUT OF HERE BEFORE I COME TO MY SENSES.
DAD... I...
...THANK YOU.
FLIP
"YES. I BELIEVE YOU'LL DO, MS. STACY."
YOU'LL DO QUITE NICELY.
GWEN STACY WILL RETURN IN
the AMAZING SPIDER-MAN
#9!

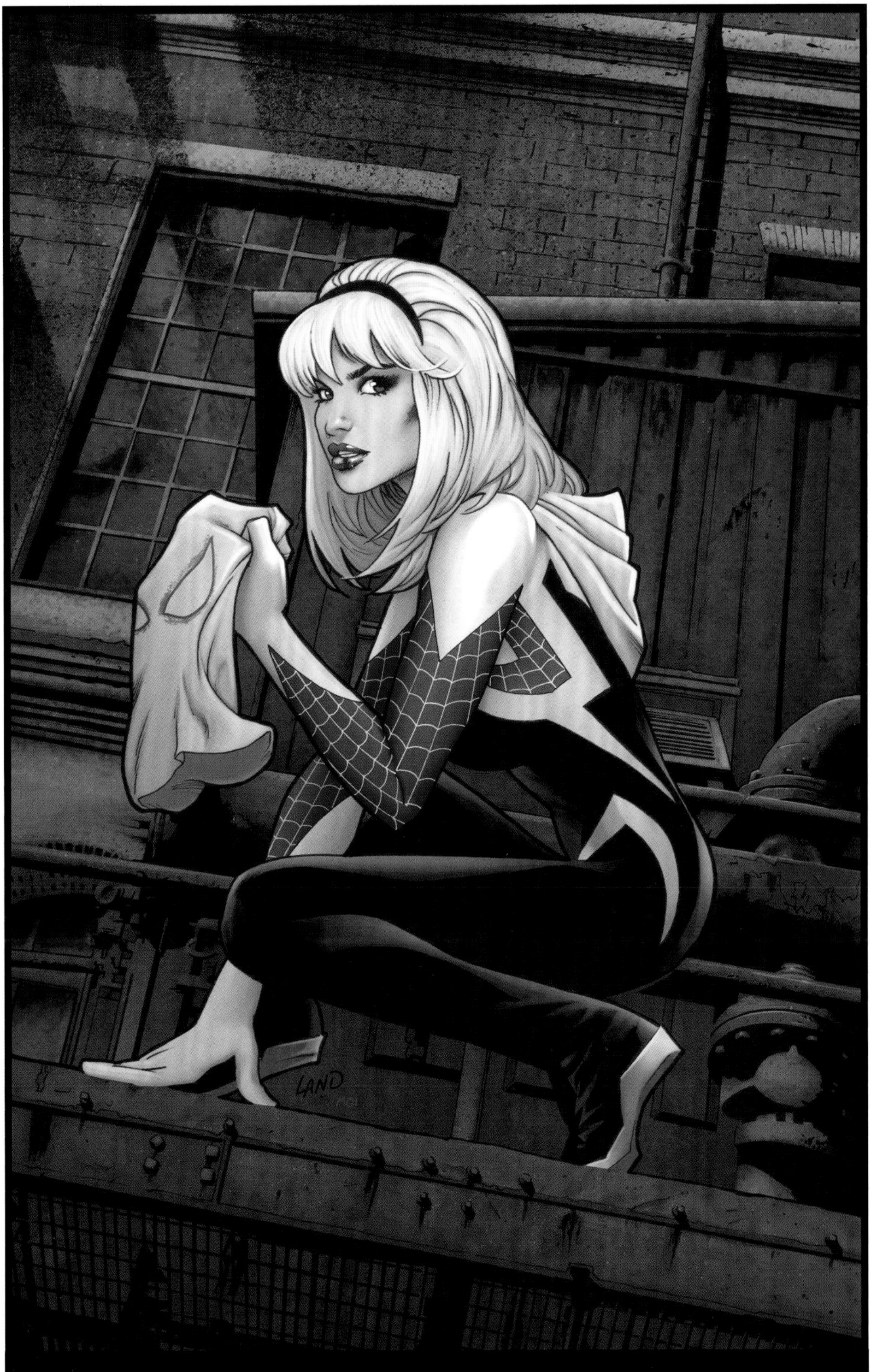
LAND

EDGE OF SPIDER-VERSE #2 VARIANT

BY GREG LAND & MORRY HOLLOWELL

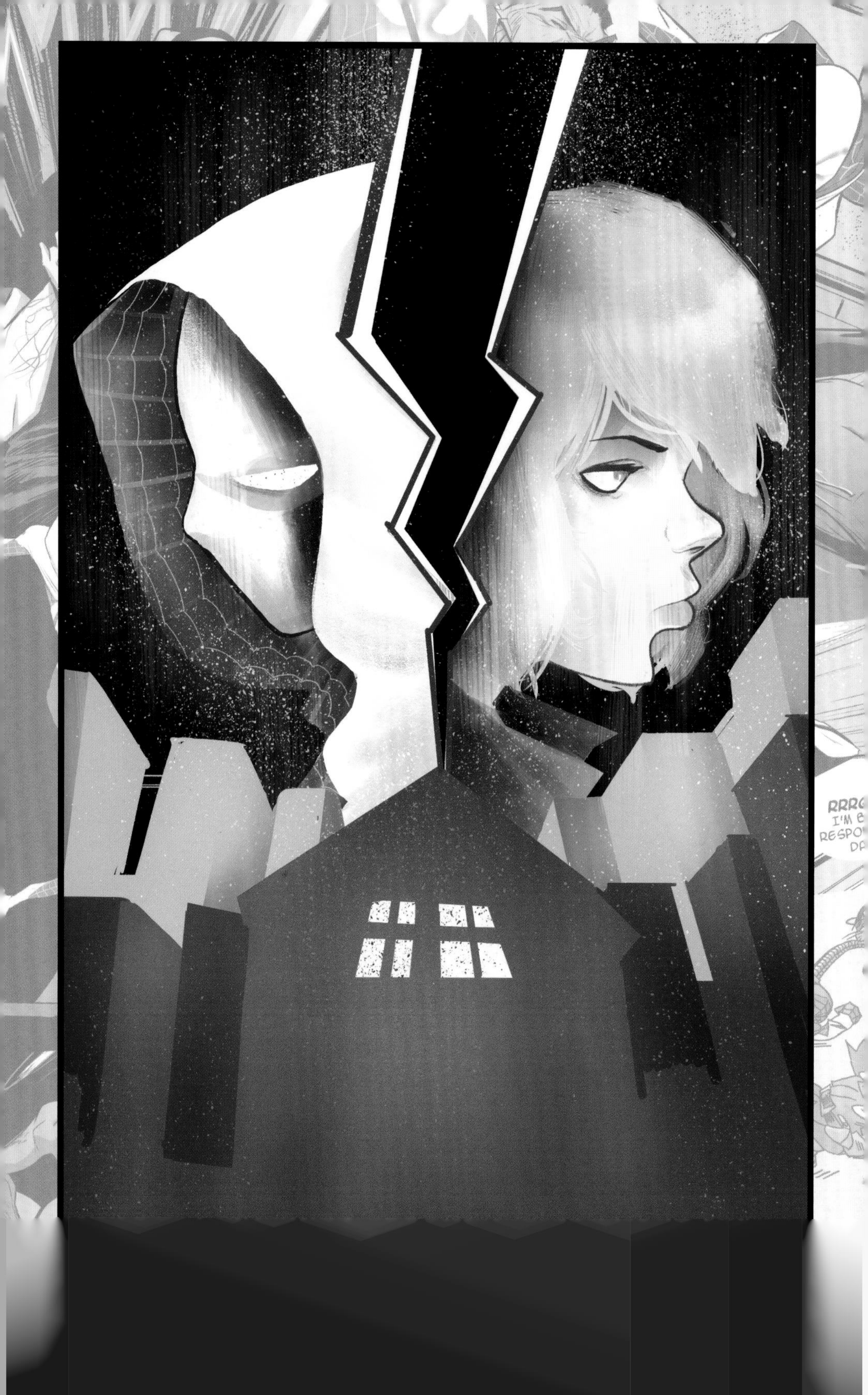

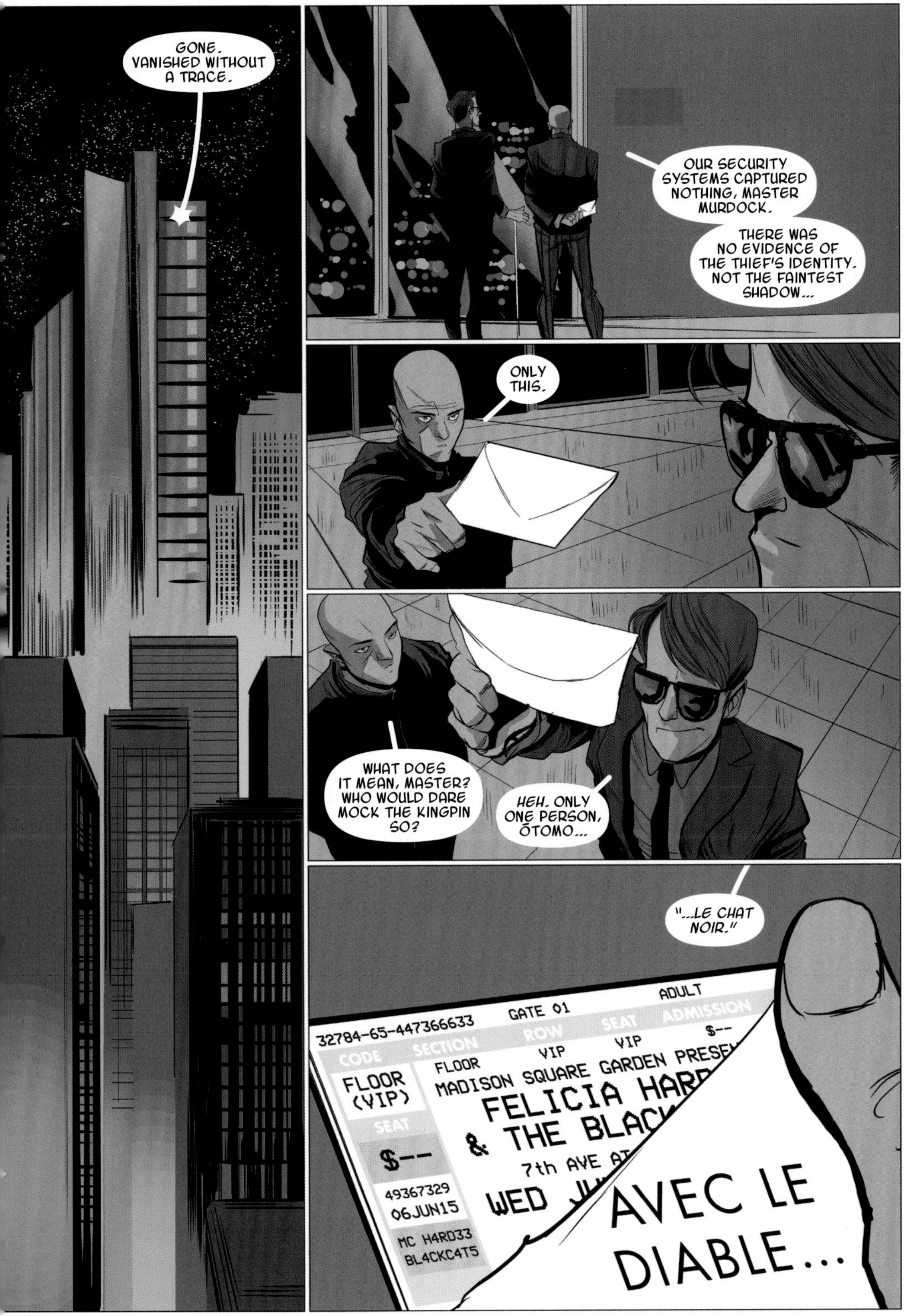
GONE. VANISHED WITHOUT A TRACE.
OUR SECURITY SYSTEMS CAPTURED NOTHING, MASTER MURDOCK.
THERE WAS NO EVIDENCE OF THE THIEF'S IDENTITY. NOT THE FAINTEST SHADOW...
ONLY THIS.
WHAT DOES IT MEAN, MASTER? WHO WOULD DARE MOCK THE KINGPIN SO?
HEH. ONLY ONE PERSON, ŌTOMO...
"...LE CHAT NOIR."
ADULT
GATE 01
32784-65-447366633
ADMISSION
SEAT
ROW
SECTION
CODE
$--
VIP
VIP
FLOOR
FLOOR (VIP)
MADISON SQUARE GARDEN PRESE
FELICIA HAR
& THE BLAC
7th AVE A
WED J
SEAT
$--
49367329
06JUN15
MC H4RD33
BL4CKC4T5
AVEC LE DIABLE...

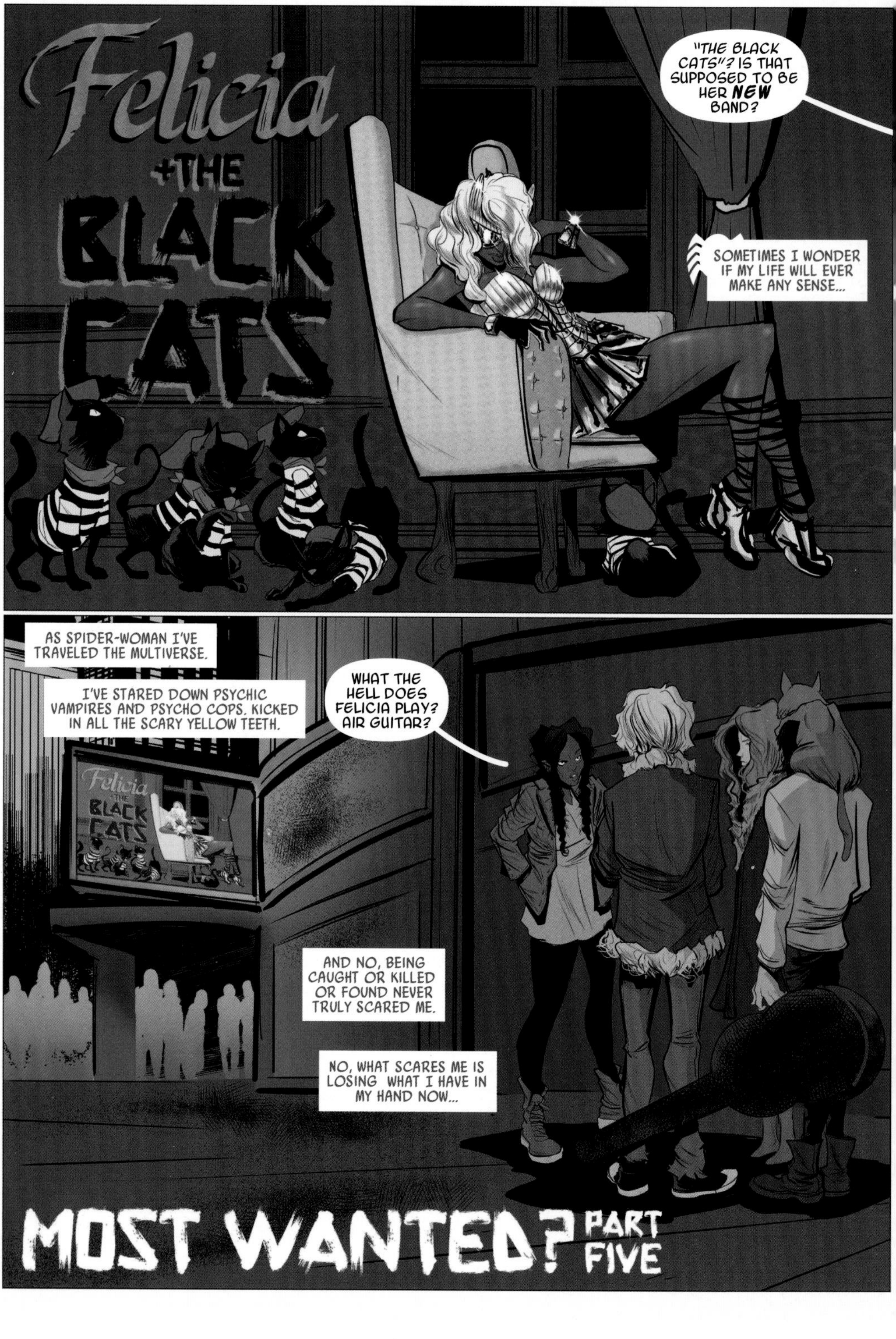
Felicia + THE BLACK CATS
"THE BLACK CATS"? IS THAT SUPPOSED TO BE HER NEW BAND?
SOMETIMES I WONDER IF MY LIFE WILL EVER MAKE ANY SENSE...
AS SPIDER-WOMAN I'VE TRAVELED THE MULTIVERSE.
I'VE STARED DOWN PSYCHIC VAMPIRES AND PSYCHO COPS. KICKED IN ALL THE SCARY YELLOW TEETH.
WHAT THE HELL DOES FELICIA PLAY? AIR GUITAR?
Felicia + THE BLACK CATS
AND NO, BEING CAUGHT OR KILLED OR FOUND NEVER TRULY SCARED ME.
NO, WHAT SCARES ME IS LOSING WHAT I HAVE IN MY HAND NOW...
MOST WANTED? PART FIVE

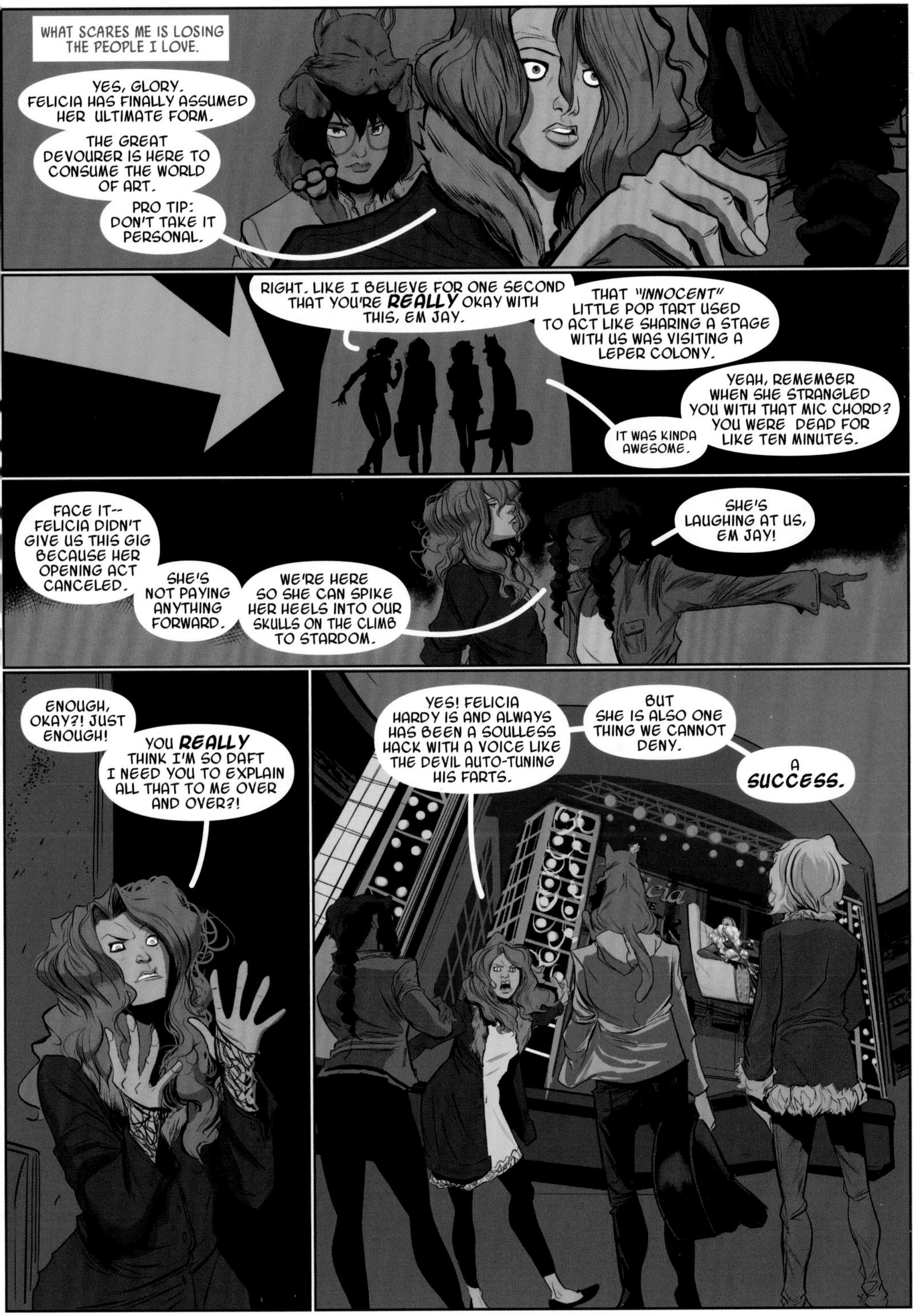
WHAT SCARES ME IS LOSING THE PEOPLE I LOVE.
YES, GLORY. FELICIA HAS FINALLY ASSUMED HER ULTIMATE FORM.
THE GREAT DEVOURER IS HERE TO CONSUME THE WORLD OF ART.
PRO TIP: DON'T TAKE IT PERSONAL.
RIGHT. LIKE I BELIEVE FOR ONE SECOND THAT YOU'RE **REALLY** OKAY WITH THIS, EM JAY.
THAT *"INNOCENT"* LITTLE POP TART USED TO ACT LIKE SHARING A STAGE WITH US WAS VISITING A LEPER COLONY.
YEAH, REMEMBER WHEN SHE STRANGLED YOU WITH THAT MIC CHORD? YOU WERE DEAD FOR LIKE TEN MINUTES.
IT WAS KINDA AWESOME.
FACE IT-- FELICIA DIDN'T GIVE US THIS GIG BECAUSE HER OPENING ACT CANCELED.
SHE'S NOT PAYING ANYTHING FORWARD.
WE'RE HERE SO SHE CAN SPIKE HER HEELS INTO OUR SKULLS ON THE CLIMB TO STARDOM.
SHE'S LAUGHING AT US, EM JAY!
ENOUGH, OKAY?! JUST ENOUGH!
YOU **REALLY** THINK I'M SO DAFT I NEED YOU TO EXPLAIN ALL THAT TO ME OVER AND OVER?!
YES! FELICIA HARDY IS AND ALWAYS HAS BEEN A SOULLESS HACK WITH A VOICE LIKE THE DEVIL AUTO-TUNING HIS FARTS.
BUT SHE IS ALSO ONE THING WE CANNOT DENY.
A **SUCCESS.**

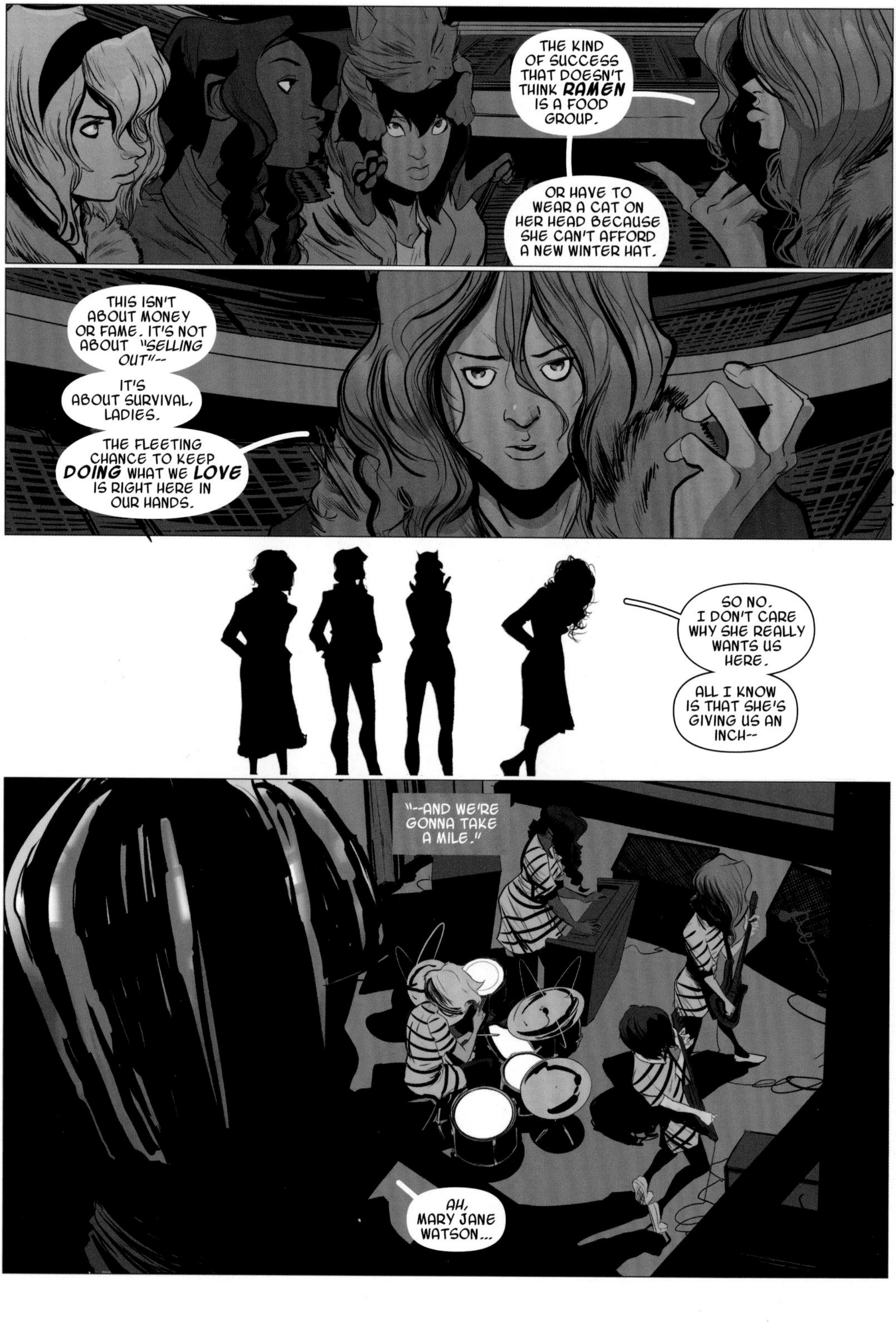
THE KIND OF SUCCESS THAT DOESN'T THINK RAMEN IS A FOOD GROUP.
OR HAVE TO WEAR A CAT ON HER HEAD BECAUSE SHE CAN'T AFFORD A NEW WINTER HAT.
THIS ISN'T ABOUT MONEY OR FAME. IT'S NOT ABOUT "SELLING OUT"--
IT'S ABOUT SURVIVAL, LADIES.
THE FLEETING CHANCE TO KEEP DOING WHAT WE LOVE IS RIGHT HERE IN OUR HANDS.
SO NO. I DON'T CARE WHY SHE REALLY WANTS US HERE.
ALL I KNOW IS THAT SHE'S GIVING US AN INCH--
"--AND WE'RE GONNA TAKE A MILE."
AH, MARY JANE WATSON...

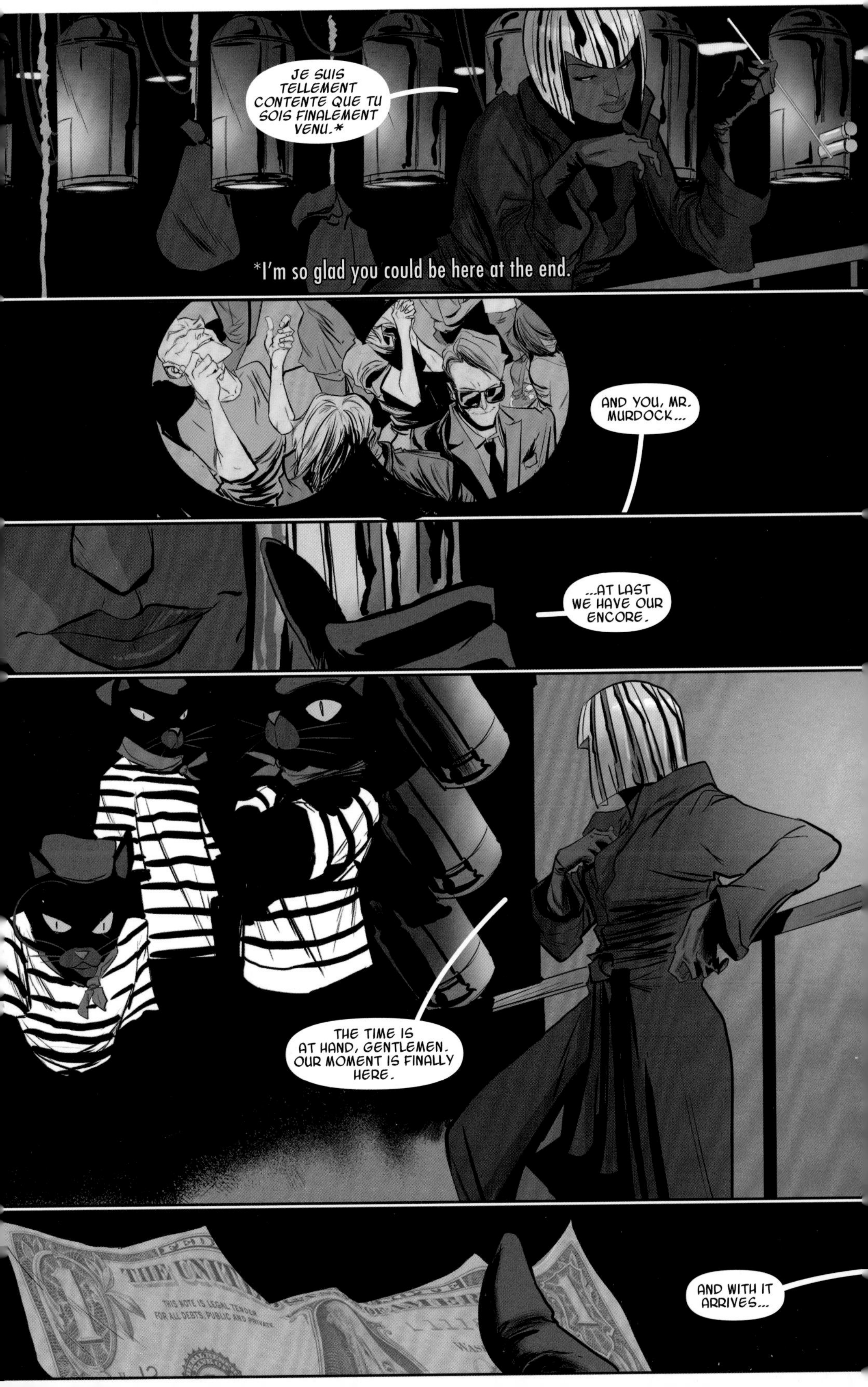
JE SUIS TELLEMENT CONTENTE QUE TU SOIS FINALEMENT VENU.*
*I'm so glad you could be here at the end.
AND YOU, MR. MURDOCK...
...AT LAST WE HAVE OUR ENCORE.
THE TIME IS AT HAND, GENTLEMEN. OUR MOMENT IS FINALLY HERE.
AND WITH IT ARRIVES...

"LA VENGEANCE DU CHAT NOIR!"

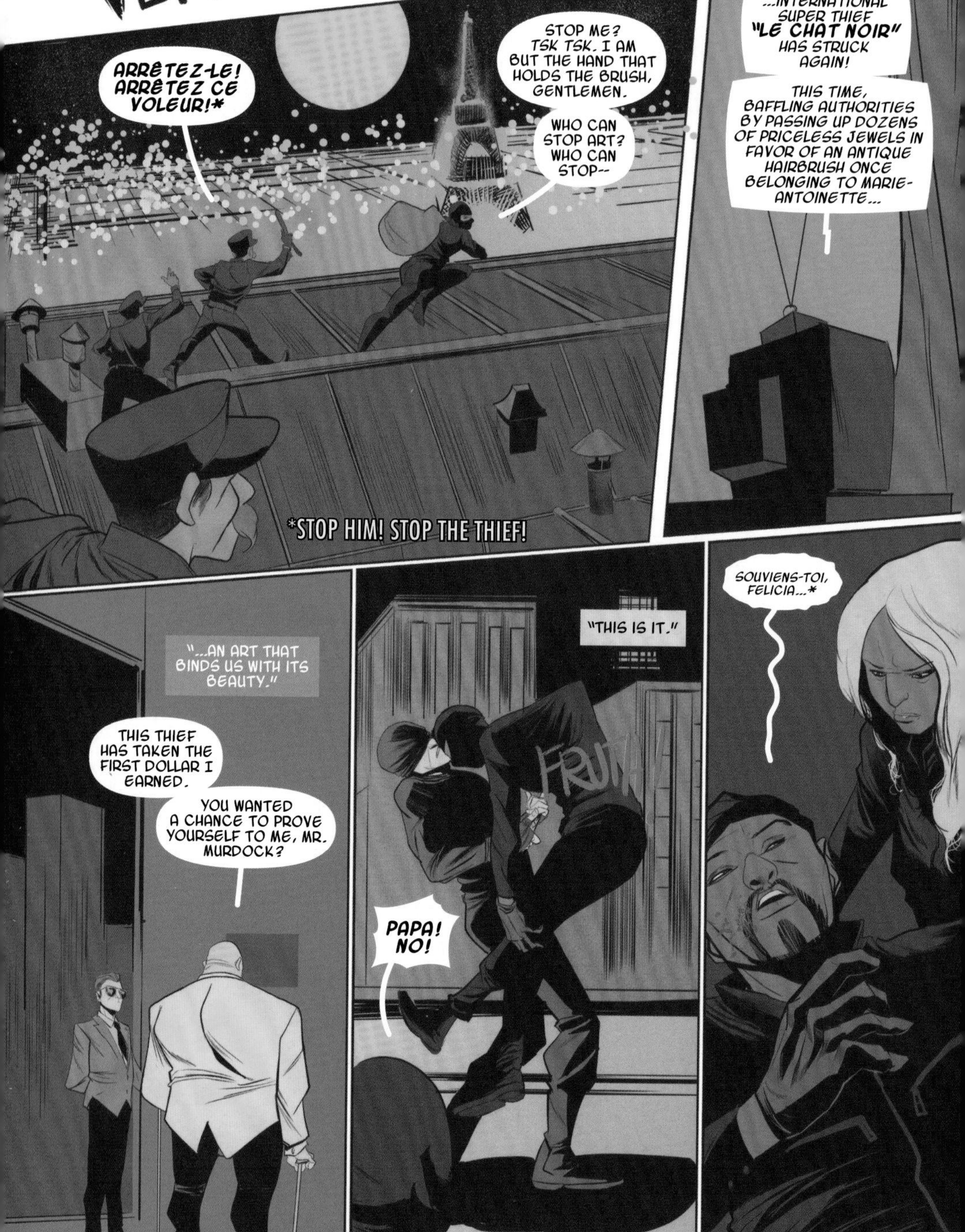

ARRÊTEZ-LE! ARRÊTEZ CE VOLEUR!*
STOP ME? TSK TSK. I AM BUT THE HAND THAT HOLDS THE BRUSH, GENTLEMEN.
WHO CAN STOP ART? WHO CAN STOP--
*STOP HIM! STOP THE THIEF!
...INTERNATIONAL SUPER THIEF "LE CHAT NOIR" HAS STRUCK AGAIN!
THIS TIME, BAFFLING AUTHORITIES BY PASSING UP DOZENS OF PRICELESS JEWELS IN FAVOR OF AN ANTIQUE HAIRBRUSH ONCE BELONGING TO MARIE-ANTOINETTE...
"...AN ART THAT BINDS US WITH ITS BEAUTY."
THIS THIEF HAS TAKEN THE FIRST DOLLAR I EARNED.
YOU WANTED A CHANCE TO PROVE YOURSELF TO ME, MR. MURDOCK?
"THIS IS IT."
PAPA! NO!
SOUVIENS-TOI, FELICIA...*
*Remember, Felicia...

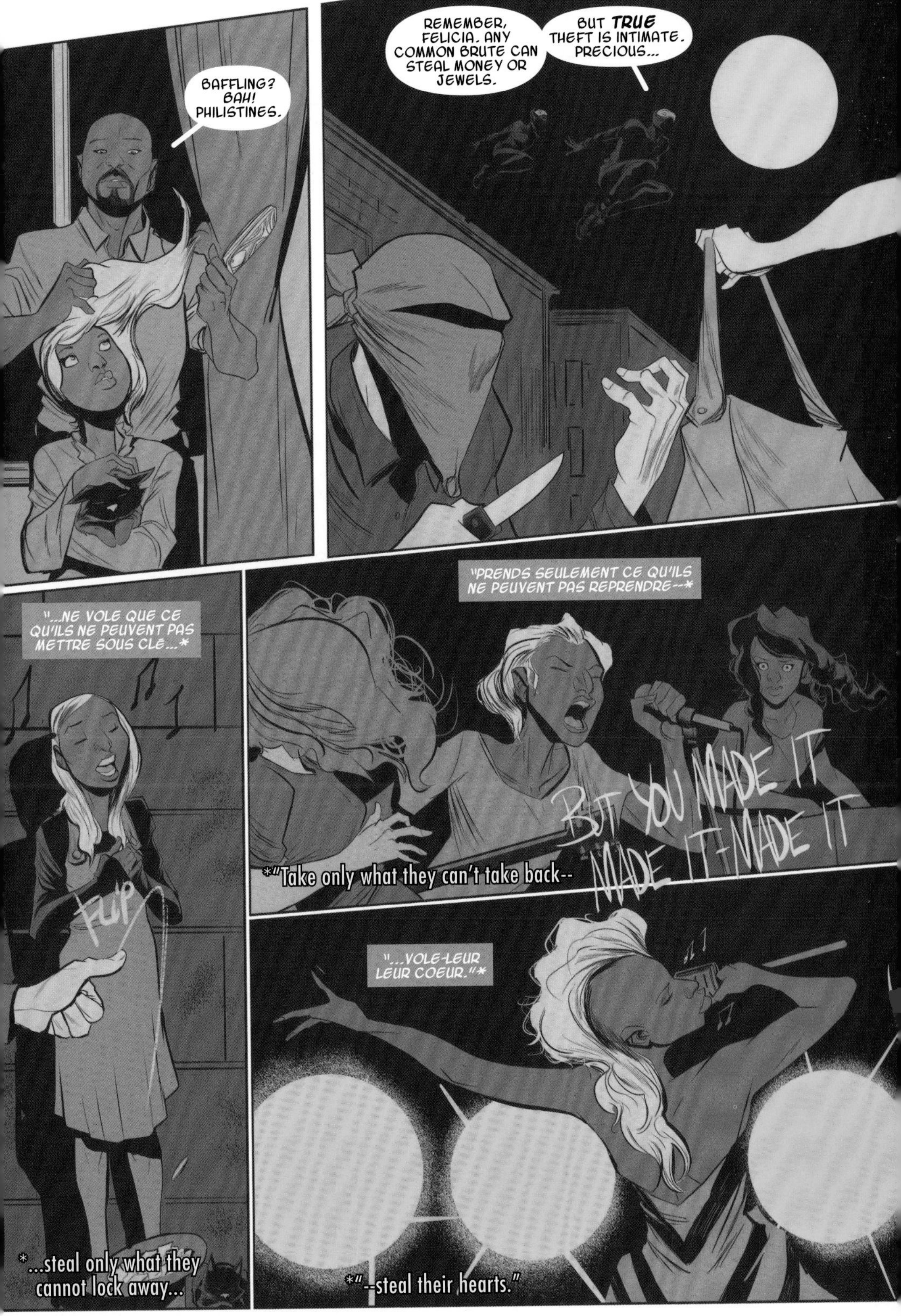
BAFFLING? BAH! PHILISTINES.
REMEMBER, FELICIA. ANY COMMON BRUTE CAN STEAL MONEY OR JEWELS.
BUT **TRUE** THEFT IS INTIMATE. PRECIOUS...
"...NE VOLE QUE CE QU'ILS NE PEUVENT PAS METTRE SOUS CLE...*
FLIP
*...steal only what they cannot lock away...
"PRENDS SEULEMENT CE QU'ILS NE PEUVENT PAS REPRENDRE--*
BUT YOU MADE IT
MADE IT-MADE IT
*"Take only what they can't take back--
"...VOLE-LEUR LEUR COEUR."*
*"--steal their hearts."

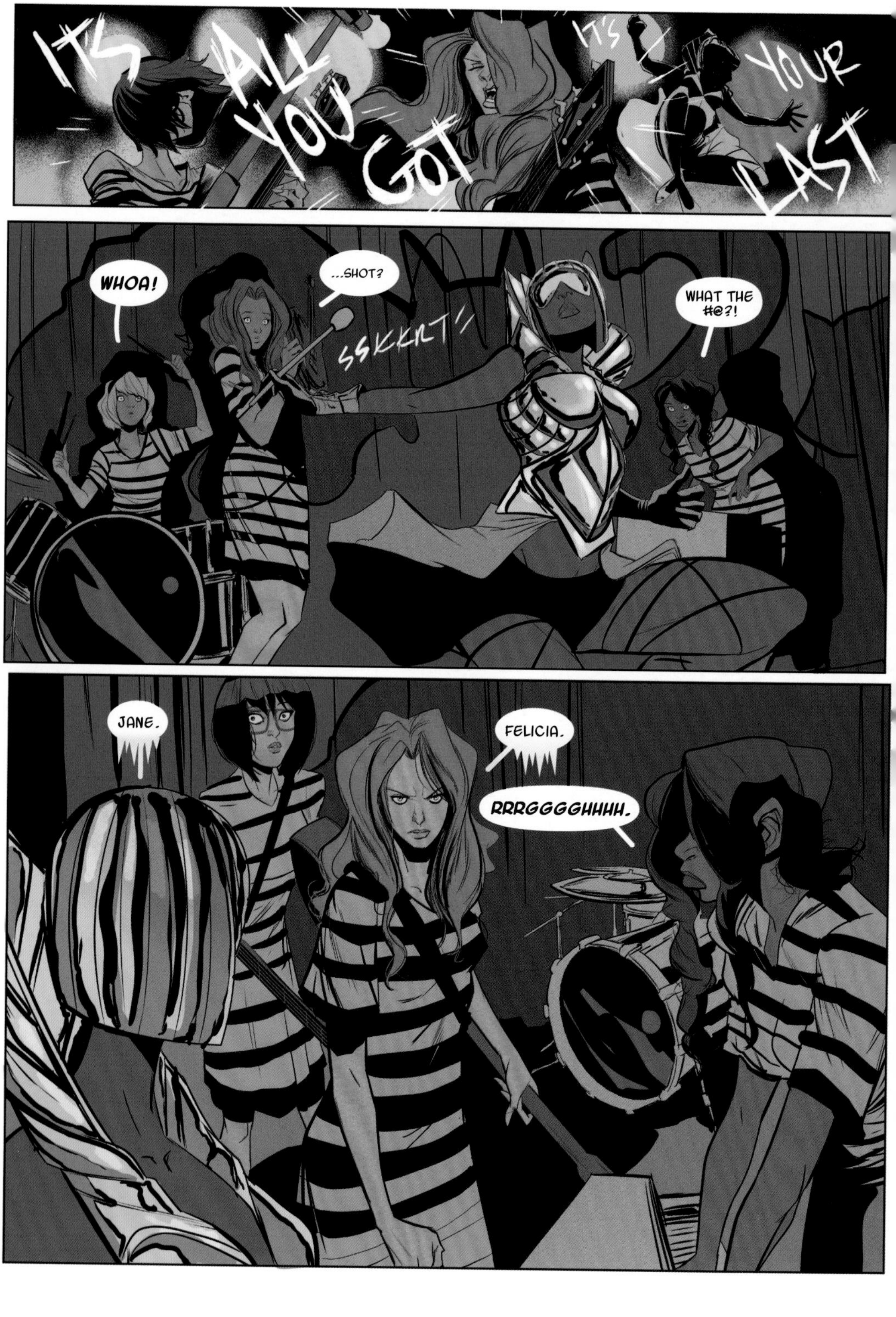
IT'S ALL YOU GOT
IT'S YOUR LAST
WHOA!
...SHOT?
SSKKRT
WHAT THE #@?!
JANE.
FELICIA.
RRRGGGGHHHH.

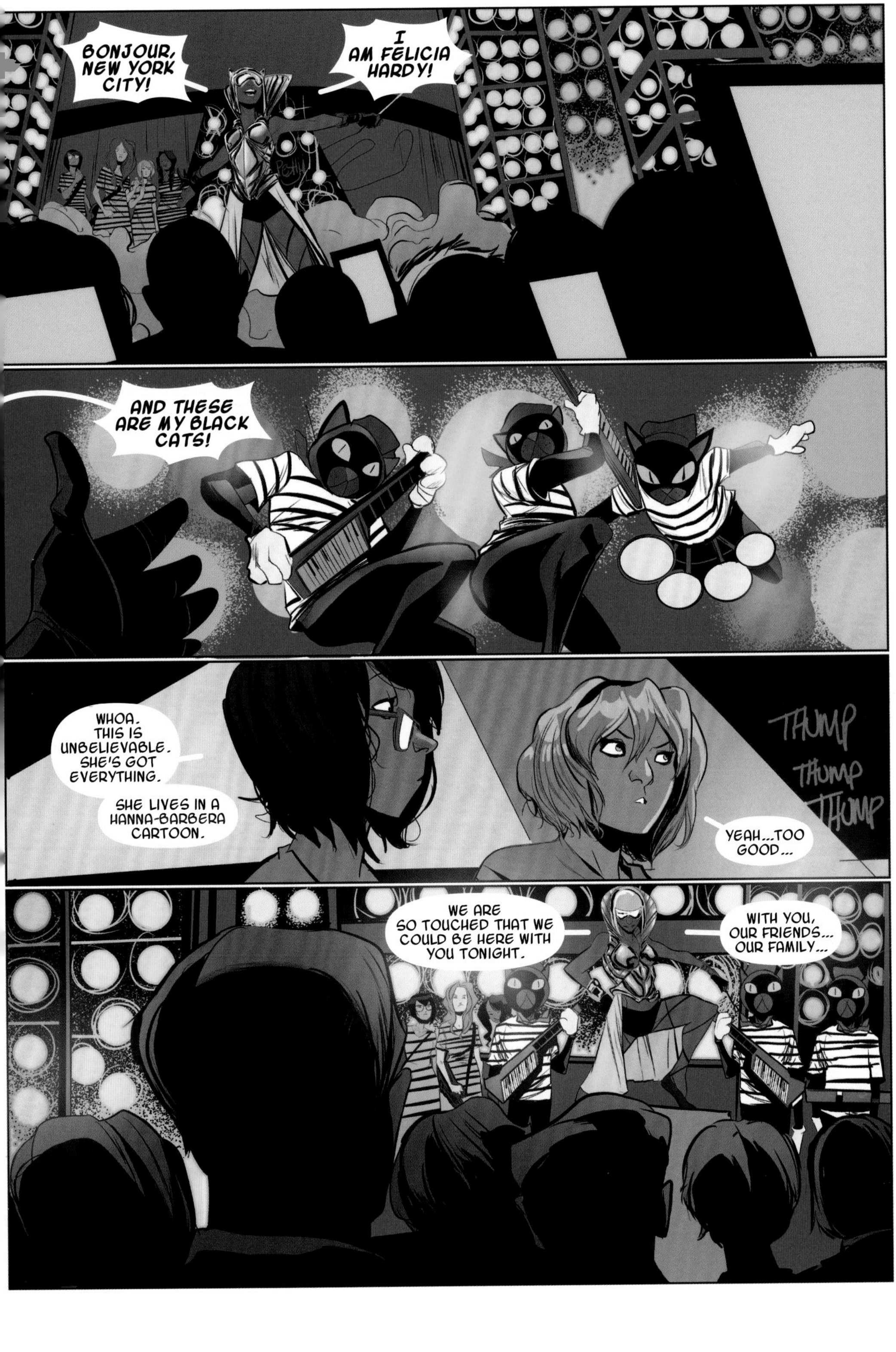
BONJOUR, NEW YORK CITY!
I AM FELICIA HARDY!
AND THESE ARE MY BLACK CATS!
WHOA. THIS IS UNBELIEVABLE. SHE'S GOT EVERYTHING.
SHE LIVES IN A HANNA-BARBERA CARTOON.
THUMP THUMP THUMP
YEAH...TOO GOOD...
WE ARE SO TOUCHED THAT WE COULD BE HERE WITH YOU TONIGHT.
WITH YOU, OUR FRIENDS... OUR FAMILY...

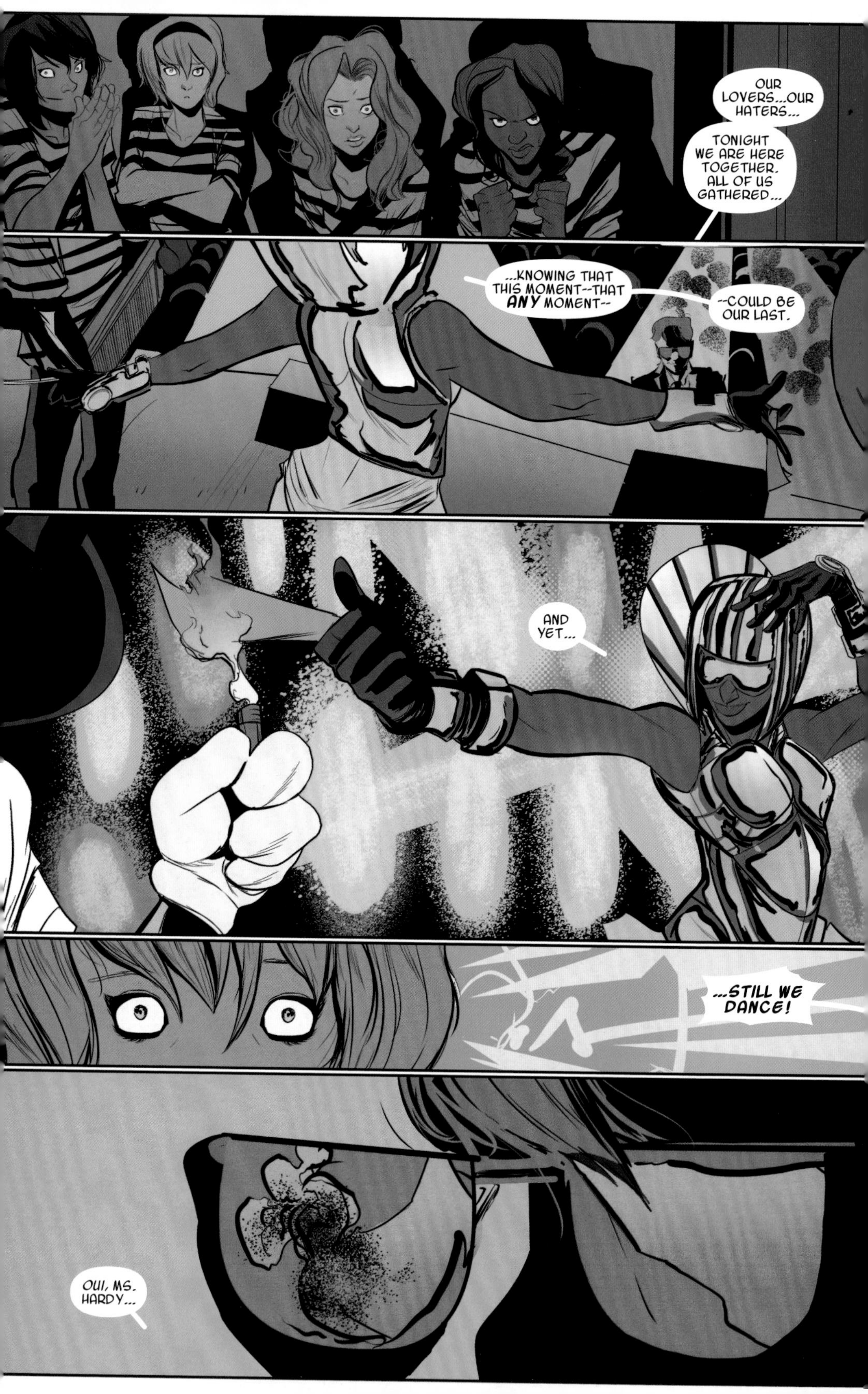
OUR LOVERS...OUR HATERS...
TONIGHT WE ARE HERE TOGETHER. ALL OF US GATHERED...
...KNOWING THAT THIS MOMENT--THAT ANY MOMENT--
--COULD BE OUR LAST.
AND YET...
...STILL WE DANCE!
OUI, MS. HARDY...

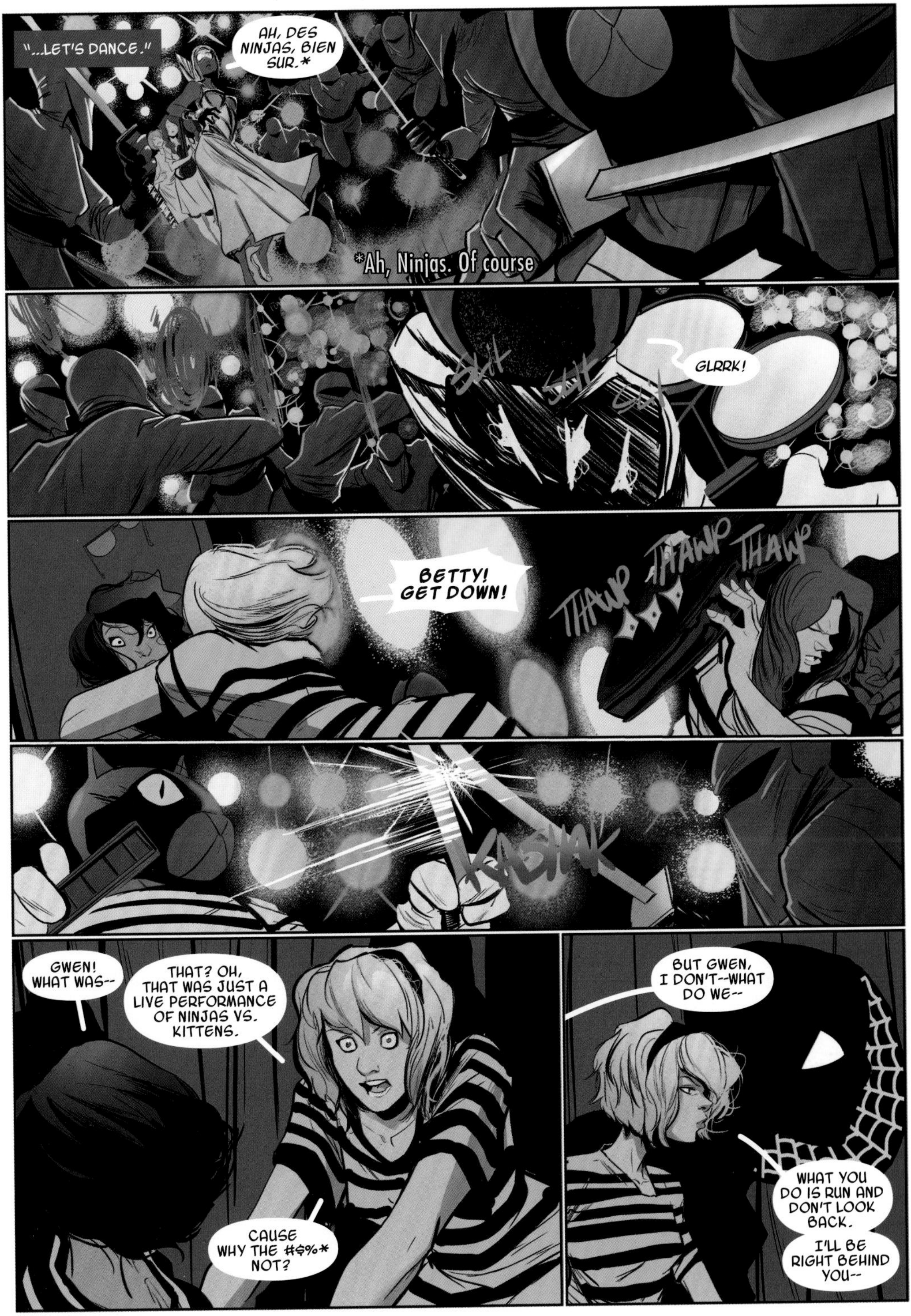
"...LET'S DANCE."
AH, DES NINJAS, BIEN SUR.*
*Ah, Ninjas. Of course
GLRRK!
BETTY! GET DOWN!
THAWP THAWP THAWP
KASHAK
GWEN! WHAT WAS--
THAT? OH, THAT WAS JUST A LIVE PERFORMANCE OF NINJAS VS. KITTENS.
CAUSE WHY THE #$%* NOT?
BUT GWEN, I DON'T--WHAT DO WE--
WHAT YOU DO IS RUN AND DON'T LOOK BACK.
I'LL BE RIGHT BEHIND YOU--

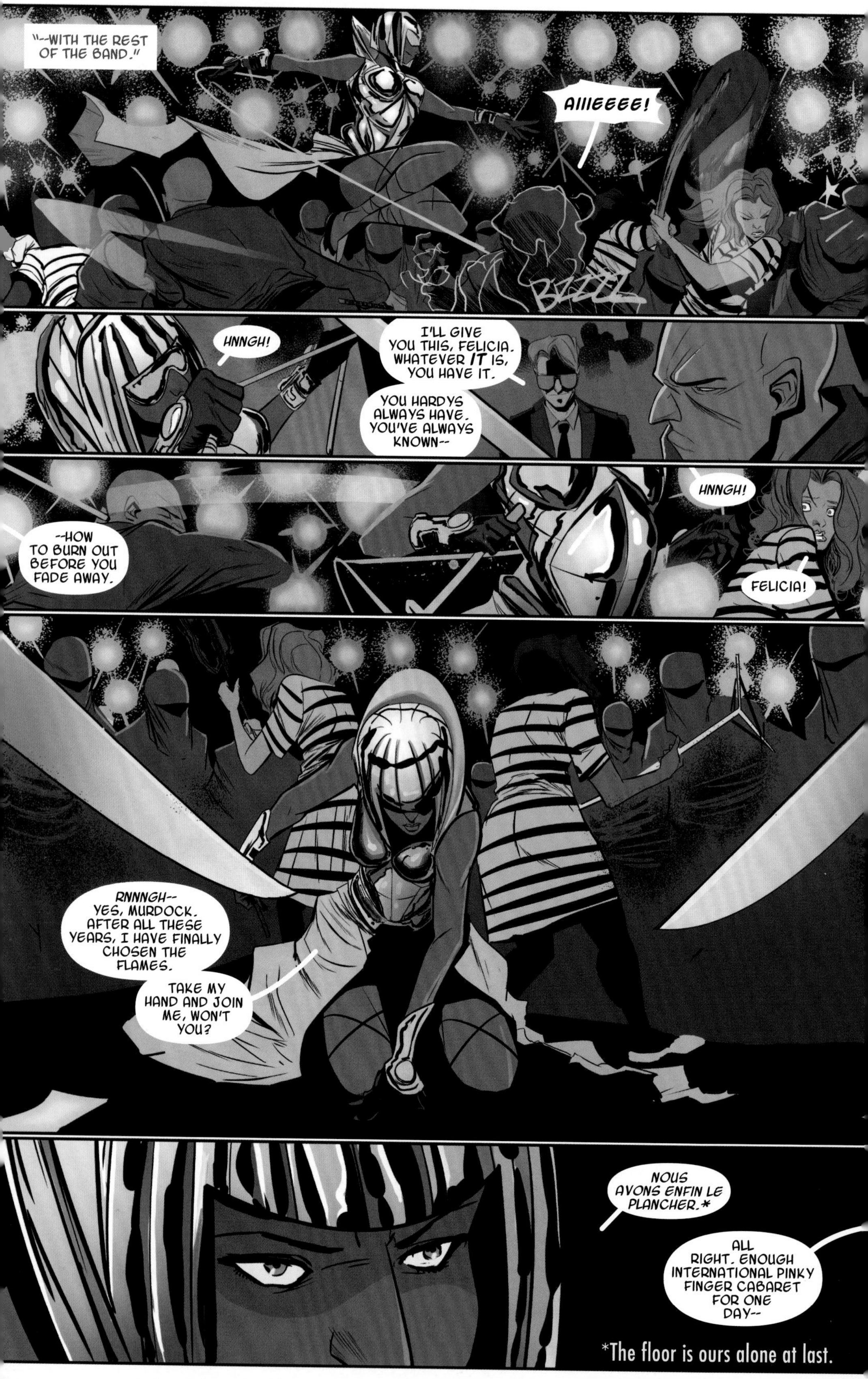
"--WITH THE REST OF THE BAND."
AIIIEEEE!
BZZZZ
HNNGH!
I'LL GIVE YOU THIS, FELICIA. WHATEVER IT IS, YOU HAVE IT.
YOU HARDYS ALWAYS HAVE. YOU'VE ALWAYS KNOWN--
--HOW TO BURN OUT BEFORE YOU FADE AWAY.
HNNGH!
FELICIA!
RNNNGH-- YES, MURDOCK. AFTER ALL THESE YEARS, I HAVE FINALLY CHOSEN THE FLAMES.
TAKE MY HAND AND JOIN ME, WON'T YOU?
NOUS AVONS ENFIN LE PLANCHER.*
ALL RIGHT. ENOUGH INTERNATIONAL PINKY FINGER CABARET FOR ONE DAY--
*The floor is ours alone at last.

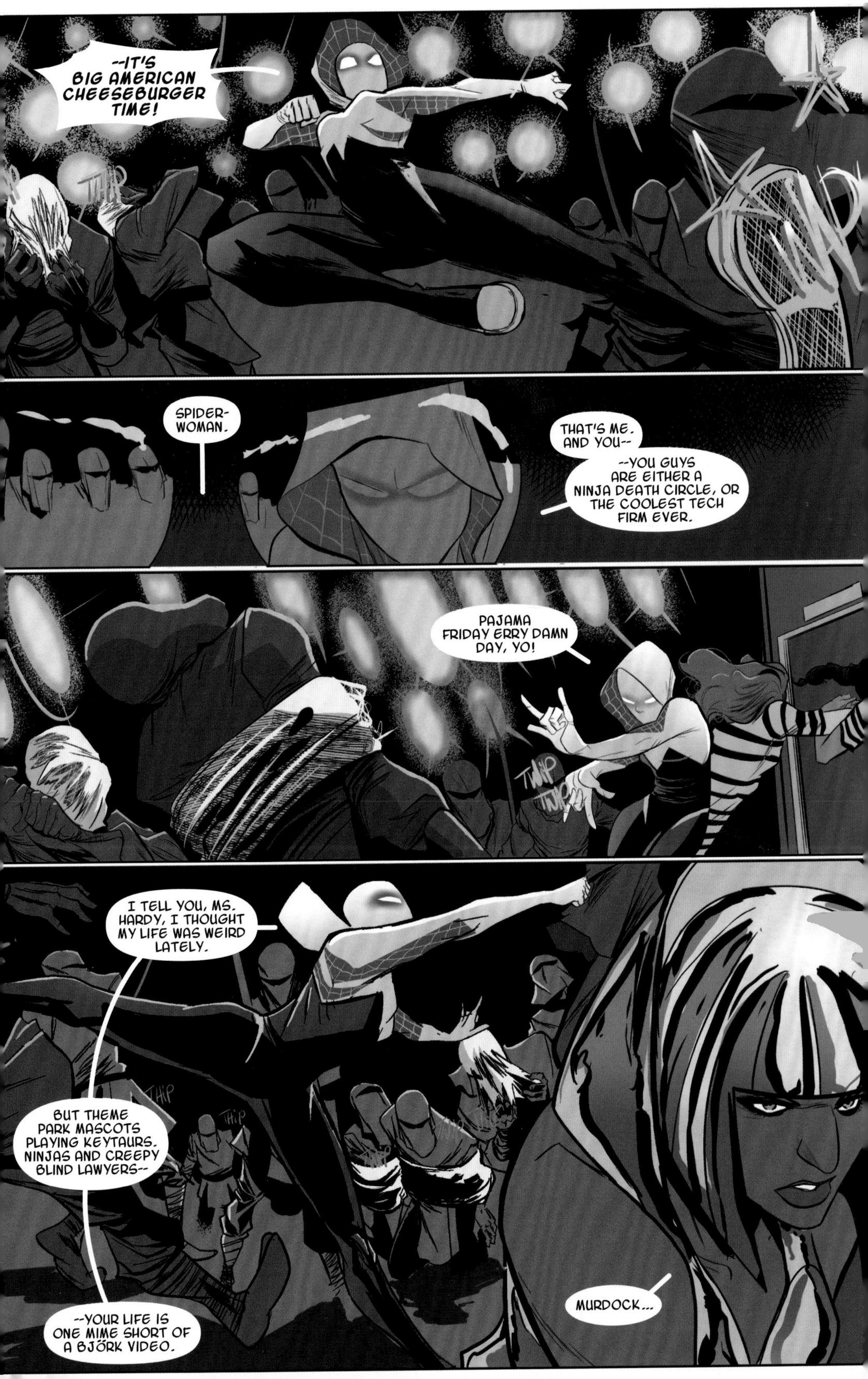
--IT'S BIG AMERICAN CHEESEBURGER TIME!
THIP
THWAP
SPIDER-WOMAN.
THAT'S ME. AND YOU--
--YOU GUYS ARE EITHER A NINJA DEATH CIRCLE, OR THE COOLEST TECH FIRM EVER.
PAJAMA FRIDAY ERRY DAMN DAY, YO!
TWIP
THWIP
I TELL YOU, MS. HARDY, I THOUGHT MY LIFE WAS WEIRD LATELY.
BUT THEME PARK MASCOTS PLAYING KEYTAURS. NINJAS AND CREEPY BLIND LAWYERS--
--YOUR LIFE IS ONE MIME SHORT OF A BJÖRK VIDEO.
THIP
THIP
MURDOCK...

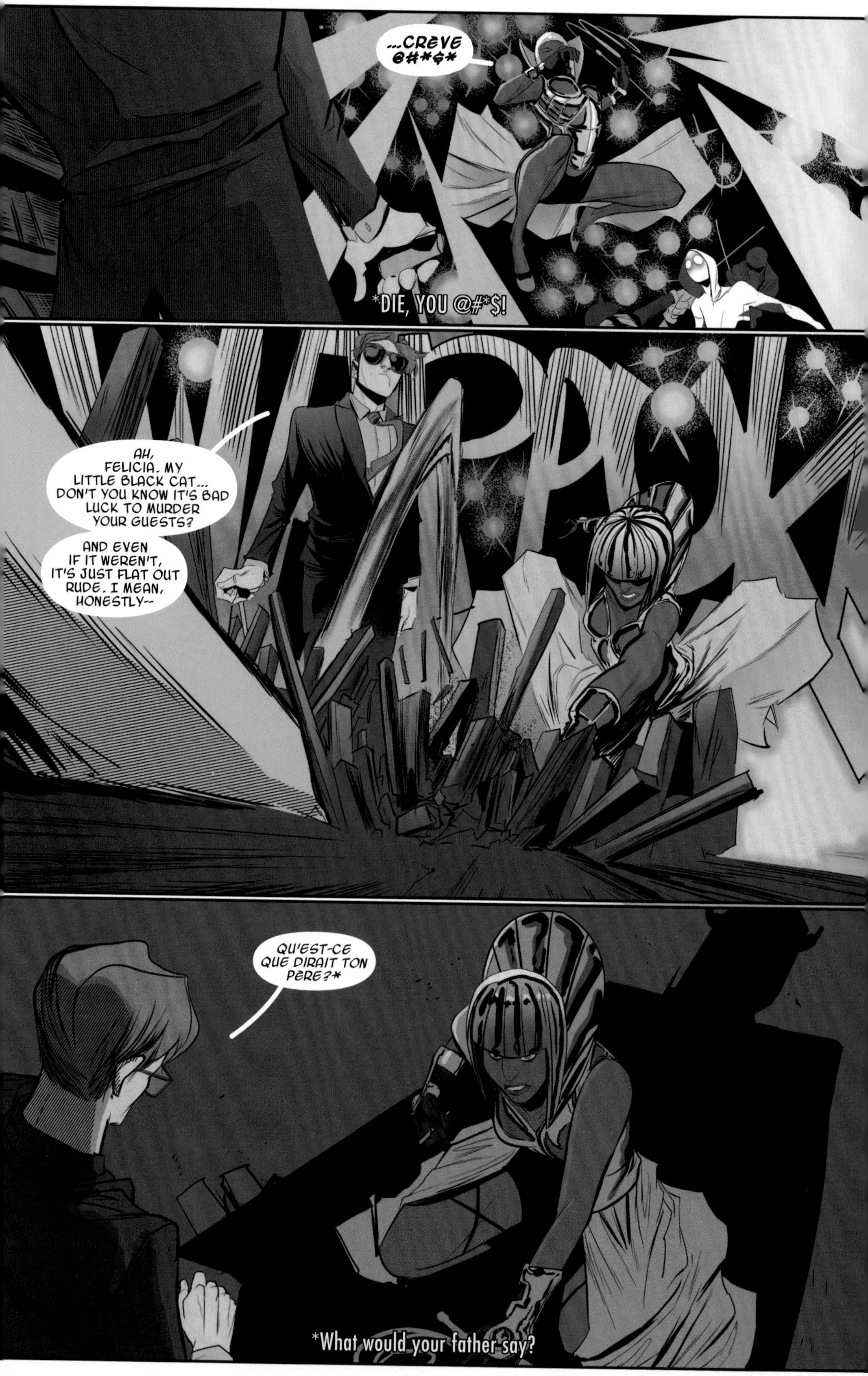
...CREVE @#*$*
DIE, YOU @#$!
AH, FELICIA. MY LITTLE BLACK CAT... DON'T YOU KNOW IT'S BAD LUCK TO MURDER YOUR GUESTS?
AND EVEN IF IT WEREN'T, IT'S JUST FLAT OUT RUDE. I MEAN, HONESTLY--
QU'EST-CE QUE DIRAIT TON PÈRE?*
*What would your father say?

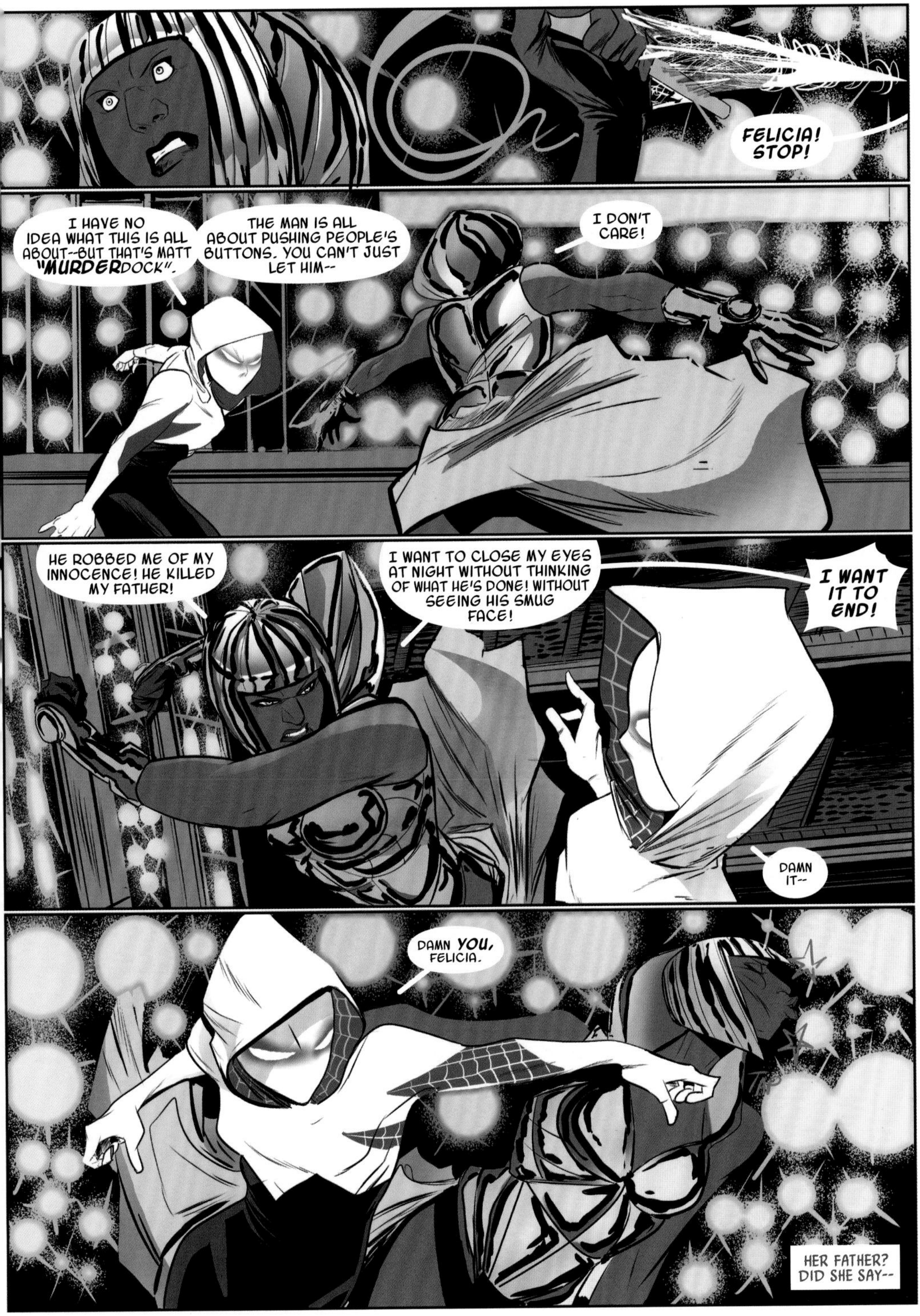
FELICIA! STOP!
I HAVE NO IDEA WHAT THIS IS ALL ABOUT--BUT THAT'S MATT "MURDERDOCK".
THE MAN IS ALL ABOUT PUSHING PEOPLE'S BUTTONS. YOU CAN'T JUST LET HIM--
I DON'T CARE!
HE ROBBED ME OF MY INNOCENCE! HE KILLED MY FATHER!
I WANT TO CLOSE MY EYES AT NIGHT WITHOUT THINKING OF WHAT HE'S DONE! WITHOUT SEEING HIS SMUG FACE!
I WANT IT TO END!
DAMN IT--
DAMN YOU, FELICIA.
HER FATHER? DID SHE SAY--

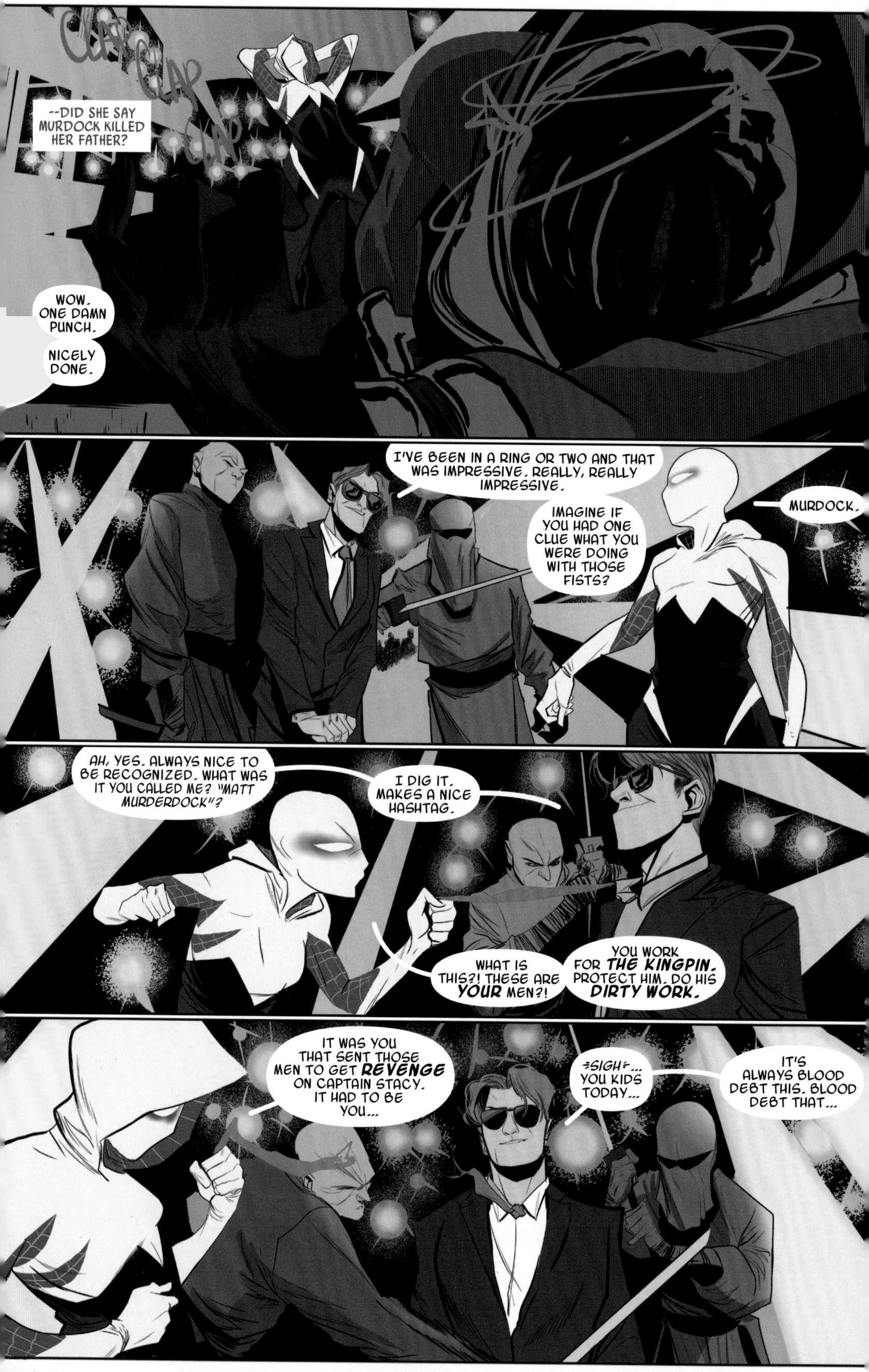
CLAP CLAP CLAP
--DID SHE SAY MURDOCK KILLED HER FATHER?
WOW. ONE DAMN PUNCH.
NICELY DONE.
I'VE BEEN IN A RING OR TWO AND THAT WAS IMPRESSIVE. REALLY, REALLY IMPRESSIVE.
IMAGINE IF YOU HAD ONE CLUE WHAT YOU WERE DOING WITH THOSE FISTS?
MURDOCK.
AH, YES. ALWAYS NICE TO BE RECOGNIZED. WHAT WAS IT YOU CALLED ME? "MATT MURDERDOCK"?
I DIG IT. MAKES A NICE HASHTAG.
YOU WORK FOR THE KINGPIN. PROTECT HIM. DO HIS DIRTY WORK.
WHAT IS THIS?! THESE ARE YOUR MEN?!
IT WAS YOU THAT SENT THOSE MEN TO GET REVENGE ON CAPTAIN STACY. IT HAD TO BE YOU...
≈SIGH≈... YOU KIDS TODAY...
IT'S ALWAYS BLOOD DEBT THIS. BLOOD DEBT THAT...

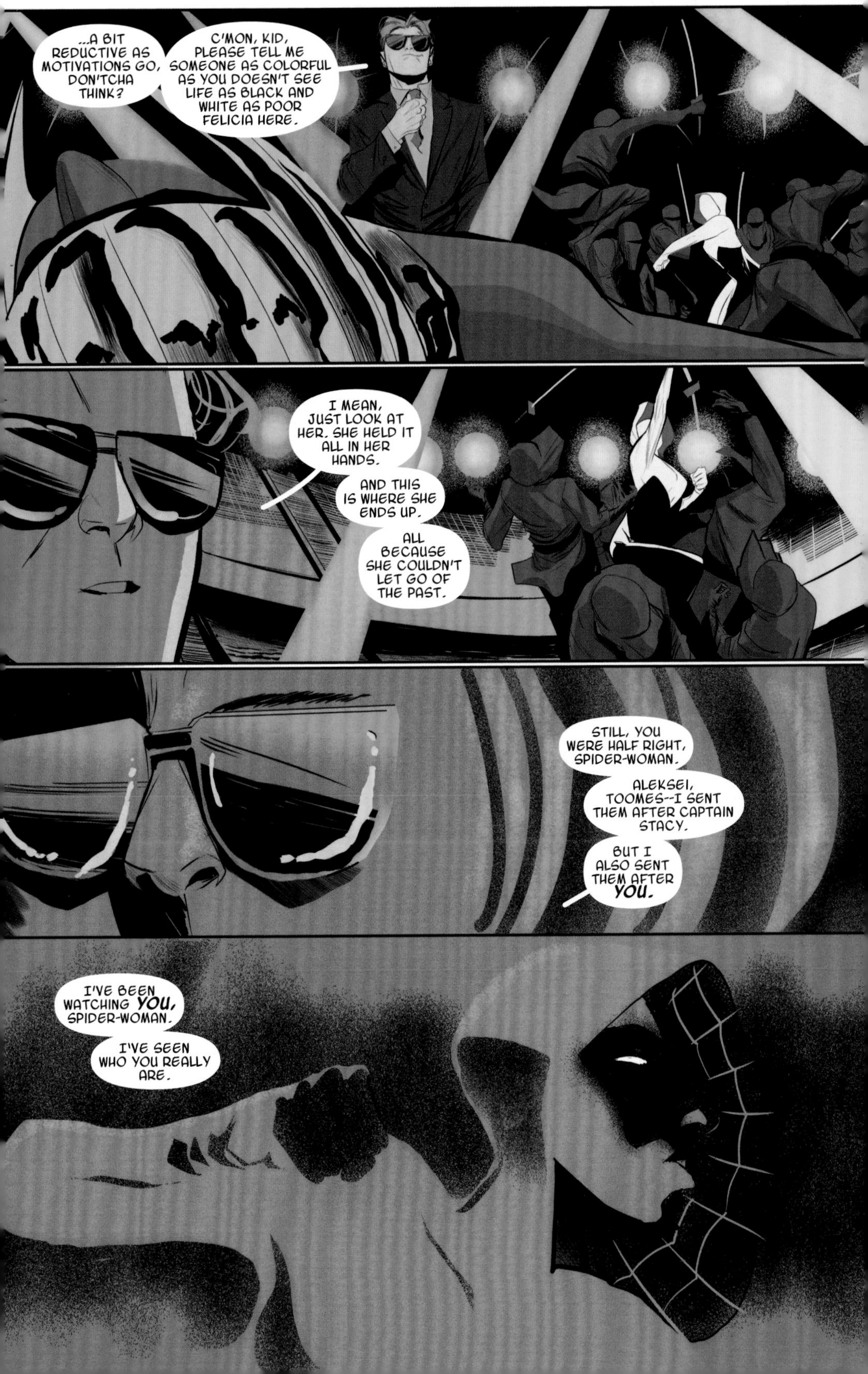
...A BIT REDUCTIVE AS MOTIVATIONS GO, DON'TCHA THINK?
C'MON, KID, PLEASE TELL ME SOMEONE AS COLORFUL AS YOU DOESN'T SEE LIFE AS BLACK AND WHITE AS POOR FELICIA HERE.
I MEAN, JUST LOOK AT HER. SHE HELD IT ALL IN HER HANDS.
AND THIS IS WHERE SHE ENDS UP.
ALL BECAUSE SHE COULDN'T LET GO OF THE PAST.
STILL, YOU WERE HALF RIGHT, SPIDER-WOMAN.
ALEKSEI, TOOMES--I SENT THEM AFTER CAPTAIN STACY.
BUT I ALSO SENT THEM AFTER YOU.
I'VE BEEN WATCHING YOU, SPIDER-WOMAN.
I'VE SEEN WHO YOU REALLY ARE.

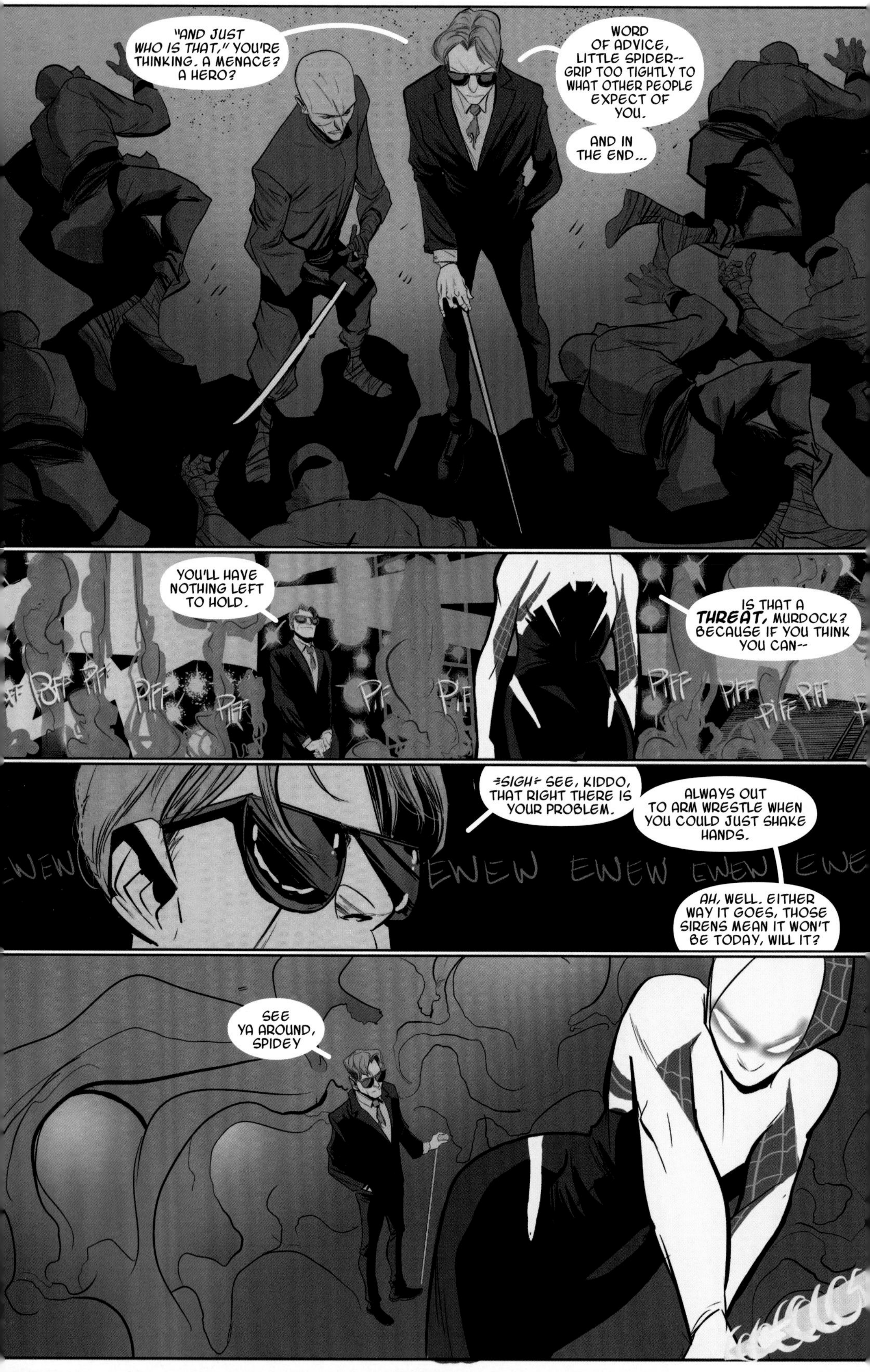
"AND JUST WHO IS THAT," YOU'RE THINKING. A MENACE? A HERO?
WORD OF ADVICE, LITTLE SPIDER-- GRIP TOO TIGHTLY TO WHAT OTHER PEOPLE EXPECT OF YOU.
AND IN THE END...
YOU'LL HAVE NOTHING LEFT TO HOLD.
IS THAT A THREAT, MURDOCK? BECAUSE IF YOU THINK YOU CAN--
PFF PIFF PIFF PIFF PIFF PIFF
≠SIGH≠ SEE, KIDDO, THAT RIGHT THERE IS YOUR PROBLEM.
ALWAYS OUT TO ARM WRESTLE WHEN YOU COULD JUST SHAKE HANDS.
EWEW EWEW EWEW EWEW
AH, WELL. EITHER WAY IT GOES, THOSE SIRENS MEAN IT WON'T BE TODAY, WILL IT?
SEE YA AROUND, SPIDEY

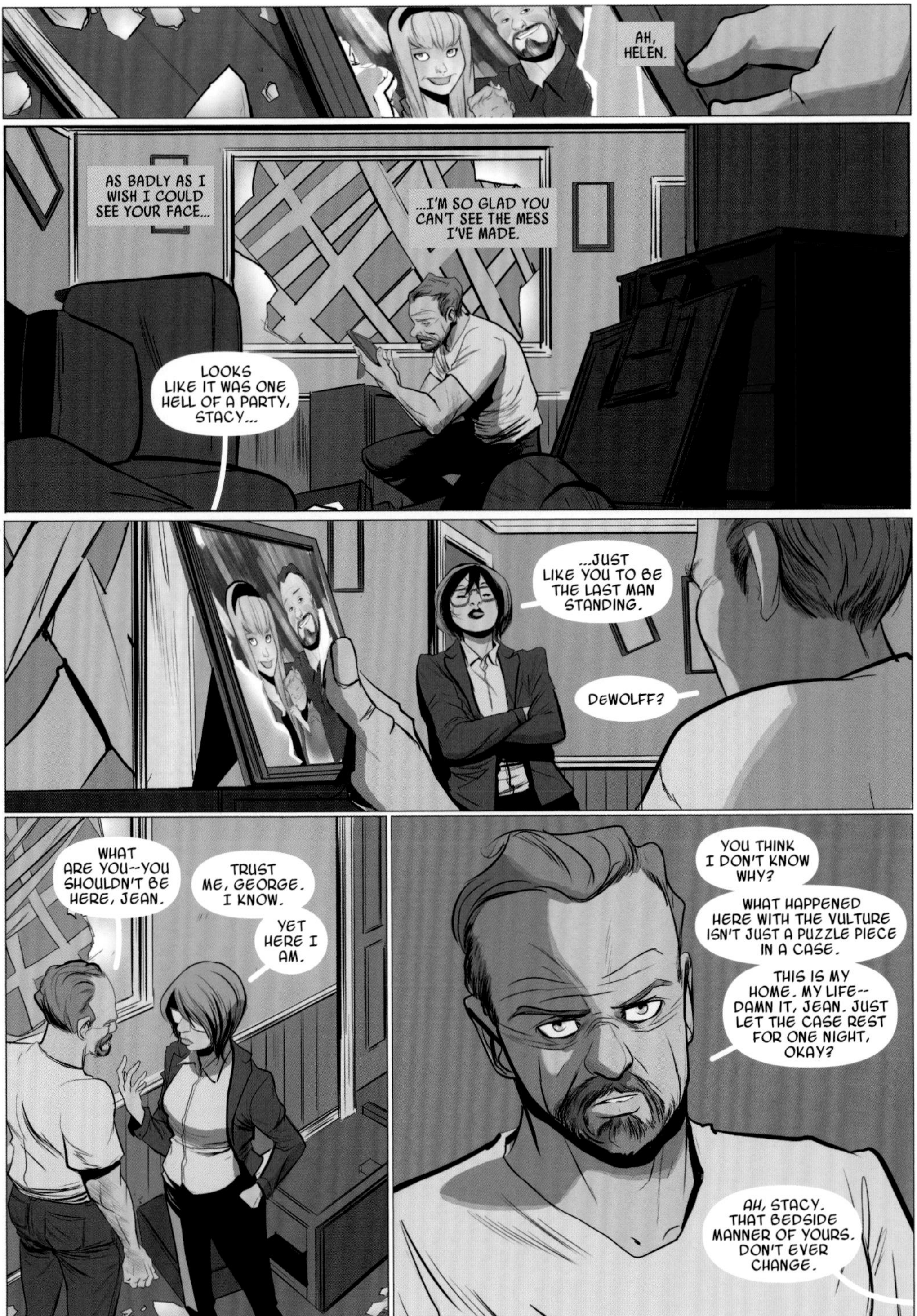
AH, HELEN.
AS BADLY AS I WISH I COULD SEE YOUR FACE...
...I'M SO GLAD YOU CAN'T SEE THE MESS I'VE MADE.
LOOKS LIKE IT WAS ONE HELL OF A PARTY, STACY...
...JUST LIKE YOU TO BE THE LAST MAN STANDING.
DEWOLFF?
WHAT ARE YOU--YOU SHOULDN'T BE HERE, JEAN.
TRUST ME, GEORGE. I KNOW.
YET HERE I AM.
YOU THINK I DON'T KNOW WHY?
WHAT HAPPENED HERE WITH THE VULTURE ISN'T JUST A PUZZLE PIECE IN A CASE.
THIS IS MY HOME. MY LIFE-- DAMN IT, JEAN. JUST LET THE CASE REST FOR ONE NIGHT, OKAY?
AH, STACY. THAT BEDSIDE MANNER OF YOURS. DON'T EVER CHANGE.

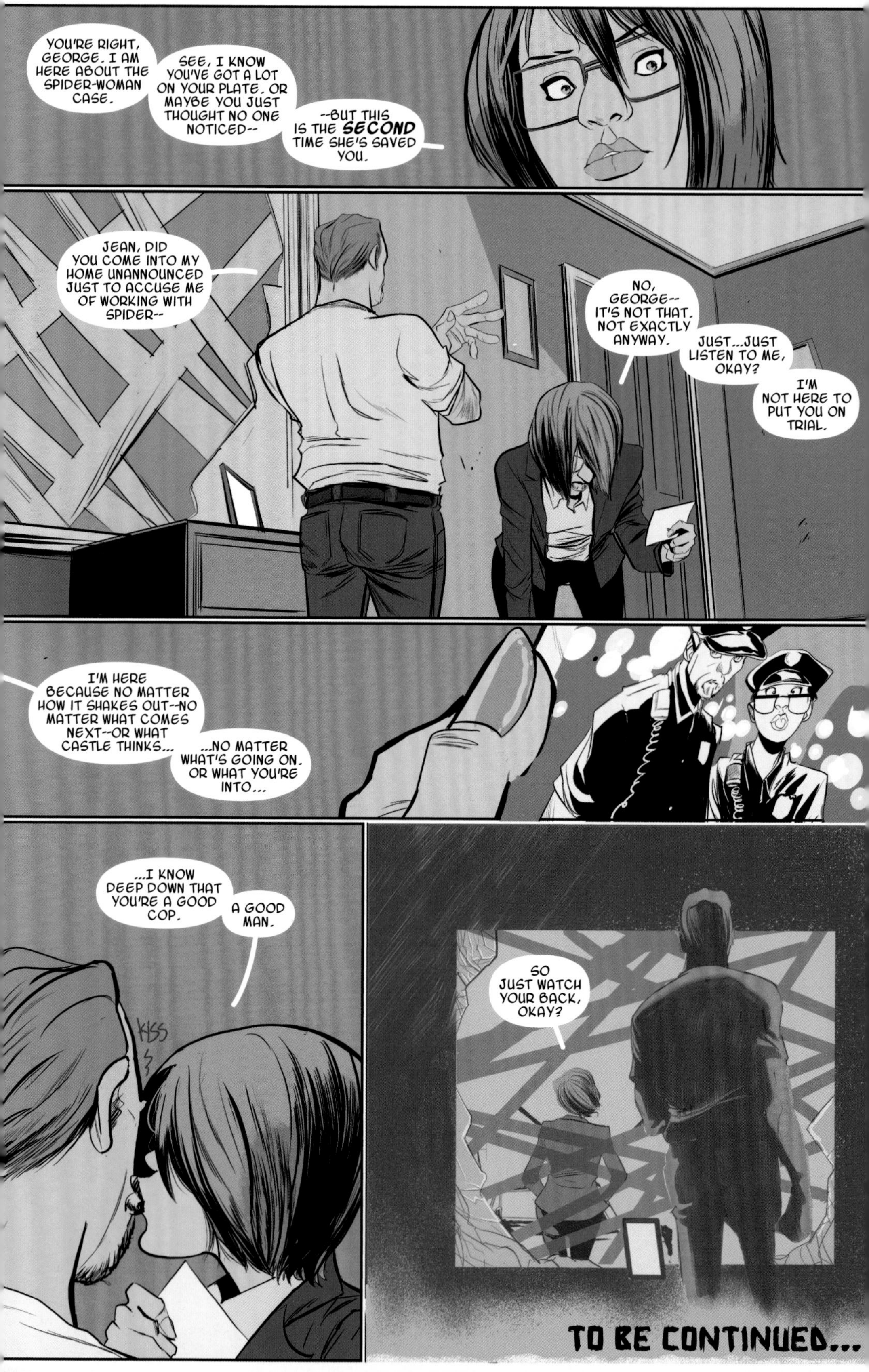
YOU'RE RIGHT, GEORGE. I AM HERE ABOUT THE SPIDER-WOMAN CASE.
SEE, I KNOW YOU'VE GOT A LOT ON YOUR PLATE. OR MAYBE YOU JUST THOUGHT NO ONE NOTICED--
--BUT THIS IS THE SECOND TIME SHE'S SAVED YOU.
JEAN, DID YOU COME INTO MY HOME UNANNOUNCED JUST TO ACCUSE ME OF WORKING WITH SPIDER--
NO, GEORGE-- IT'S NOT THAT. NOT EXACTLY ANYWAY.
JUST...JUST LISTEN TO ME, OKAY?
I'M NOT HERE TO PUT YOU ON TRIAL.
I'M HERE BECAUSE NO MATTER HOW IT SHAKES OUT--NO MATTER WHAT COMES NEXT--OR WHAT CASTLE THINKS...
...NO MATTER WHAT'S GOING ON. OR WHAT YOU'RE INTO...
...I KNOW DEEP DOWN THAT YOU'RE A GOOD COP.
A GOOD MAN.
KISS
SO JUST WATCH YOUR BACK, OKAY?
TO BE CONTINUED...

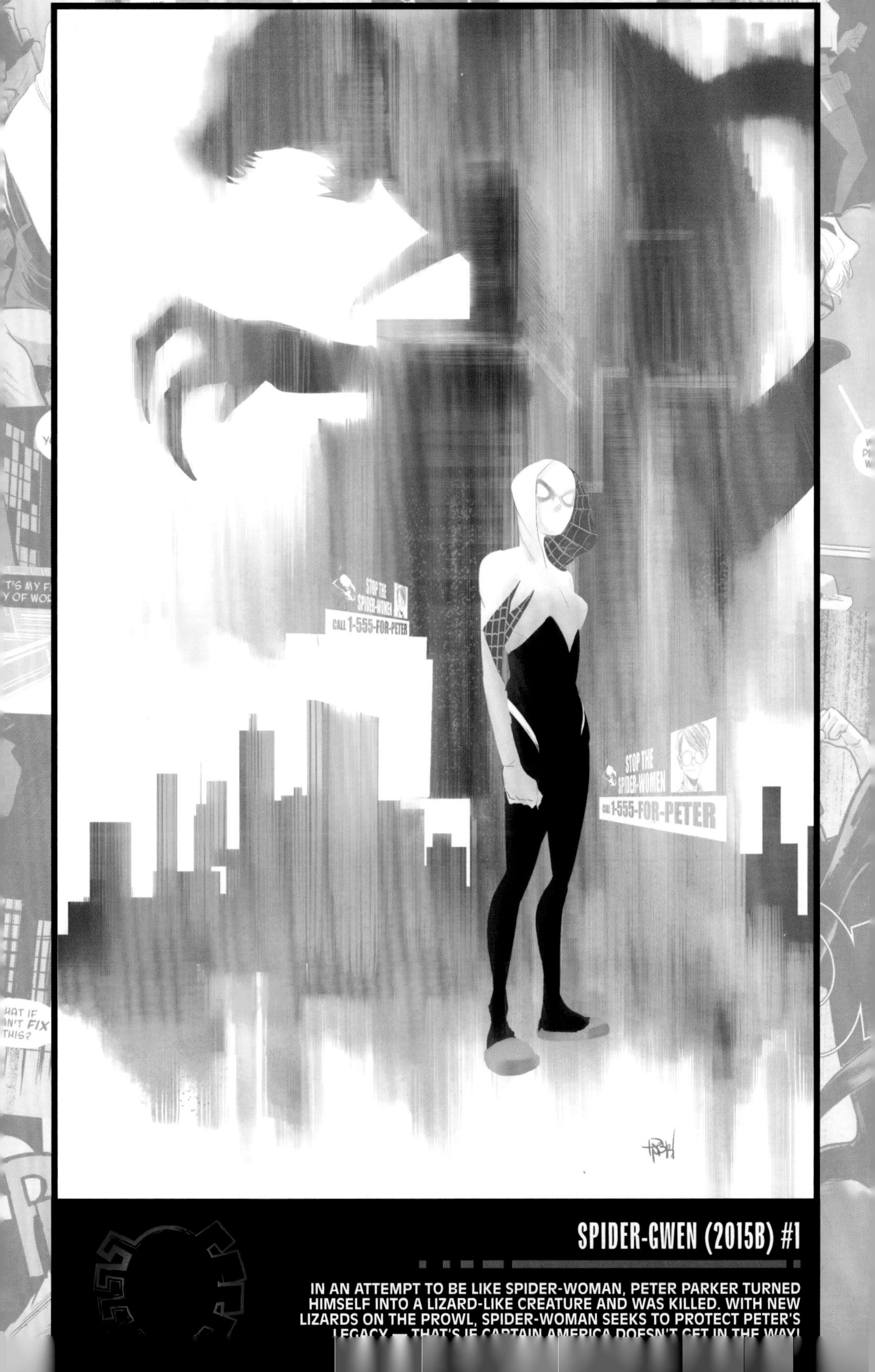
STOP THE SPIDER-WOMEN
CALL 1-555-FOR-PETER
STOP THE SPIDER-WOMEN
CALL 1-555-FOR-PETER

SPIDER-GWEN (2015B) #1

IN AN ATTEMPT TO BE LIKE SPIDER-WOMAN, PETER PARKER TURNED HIMSELF INTO A LIZARD-LIKE CREATURE AND WAS KILLED. WITH NEW LIZARDS ON THE PROWL, SPIDER-WOMAN SEEKS TO PROTECT PETER'S LEGACY — THAT'S IF CAPTAIN AMERICA DOESN'T GET IN THE WAY!

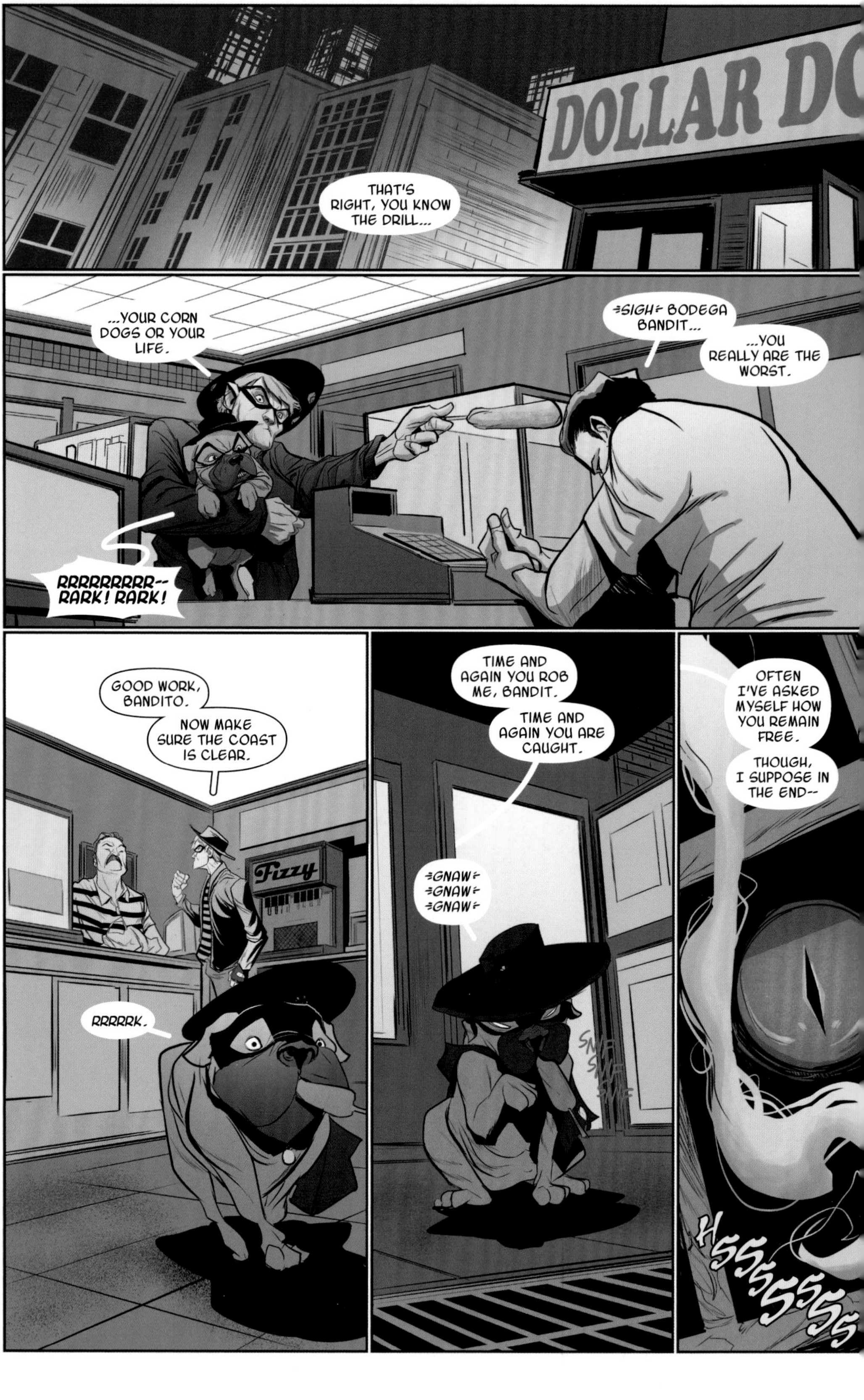
DOLLAR DO
THAT'S RIGHT, YOU KNOW THE DRILL...
...YOUR CORN DOGS OR YOUR LIFE.
=SIGH= BODEGA BANDIT...
...YOU REALLY ARE THE WORST.
RRRRRRRRR-- RARK! RARK!
GOOD WORK, BANDITO.
NOW MAKE SURE THE COAST IS CLEAR.
Fizzy
RRRRRK.
TIME AND AGAIN YOU ROB ME, BANDIT.
TIME AND AGAIN YOU ARE CAUGHT.
=GNAW= =GNAW= =GNAW=
SNIF SNIF SNIF
OFTEN I'VE ASKED MYSELF HOW YOU REMAIN FREE.
THOUGH, I SUPPOSE IN THE END--
HSSSSSSS

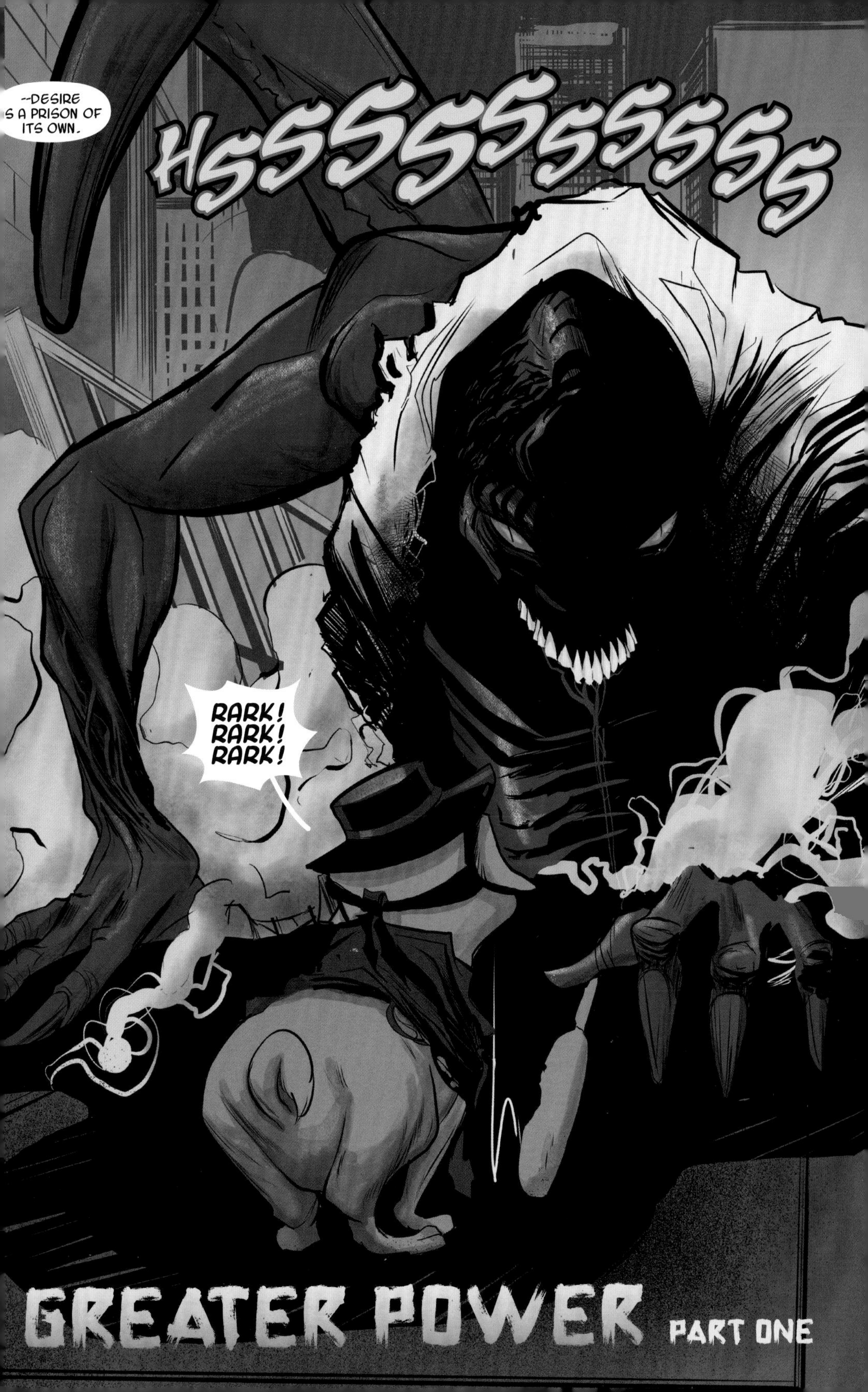
--DESIRE S A PRISON OF ITS OWN.
HSSSSSSSSSS
RARK! RARK! RARK!
GREATER POWER PART ONE

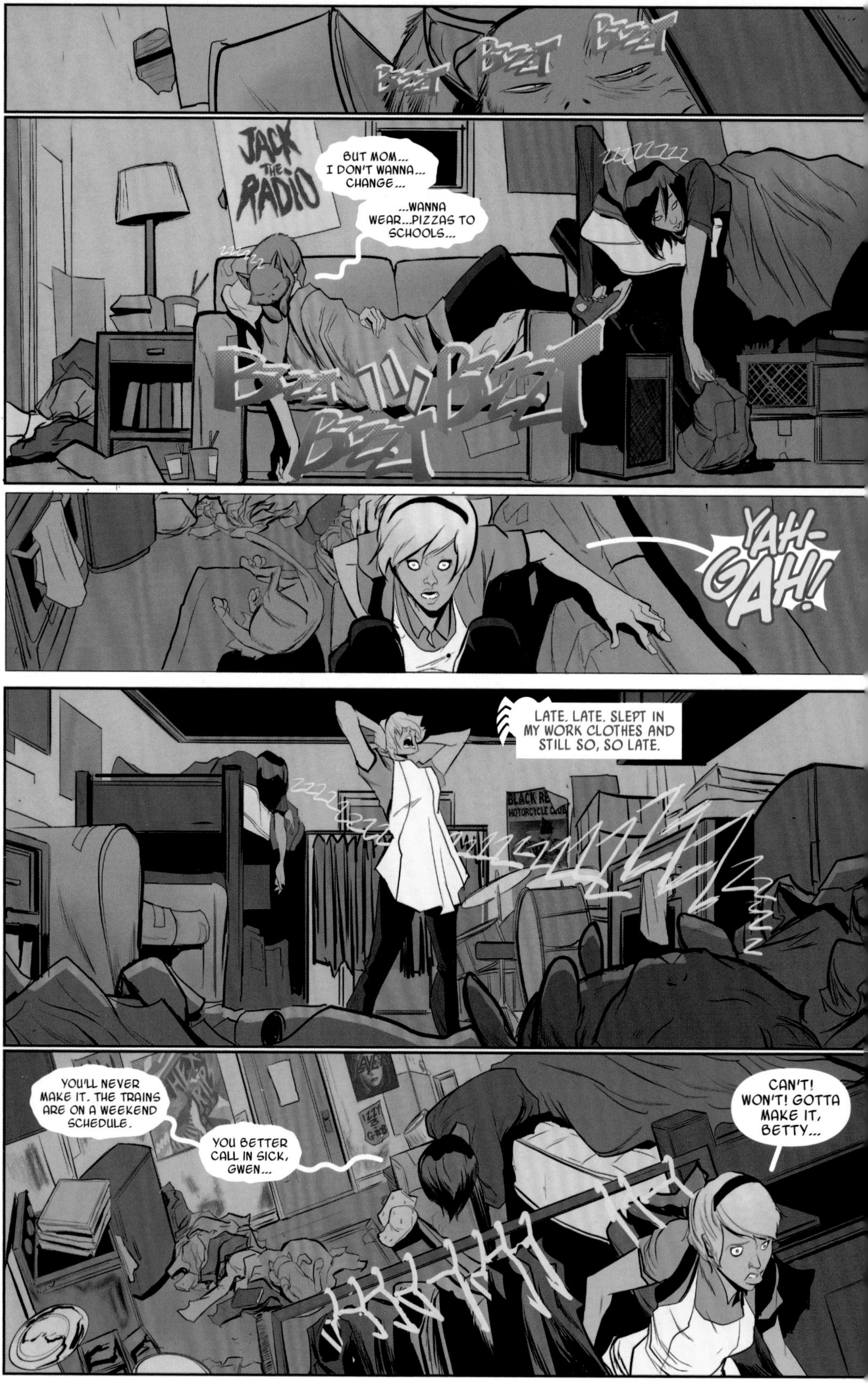
BEEP BEEP BEEP
JACK the RADIO
BUT MOM... I DON'T WANNA... CHANGE...
...WANNA WEAR...PIZZAS TO SCHOOLS...
BEEP BEEP BEEP
YAH-GAH!
LATE. LATE. SLEPT IN MY WORK CLOTHES AND STILL SO, SO LATE.
BLACK RE MOTORCYCLE CLUB
YOU'LL NEVER MAKE IT. THE TRAINS ARE ON A WEEKEND SCHEDULE.
YOU BETTER CALL IN SICK, GWEN...
CAN'T! WON'T! GOTTA MAKE IT, BETTY...

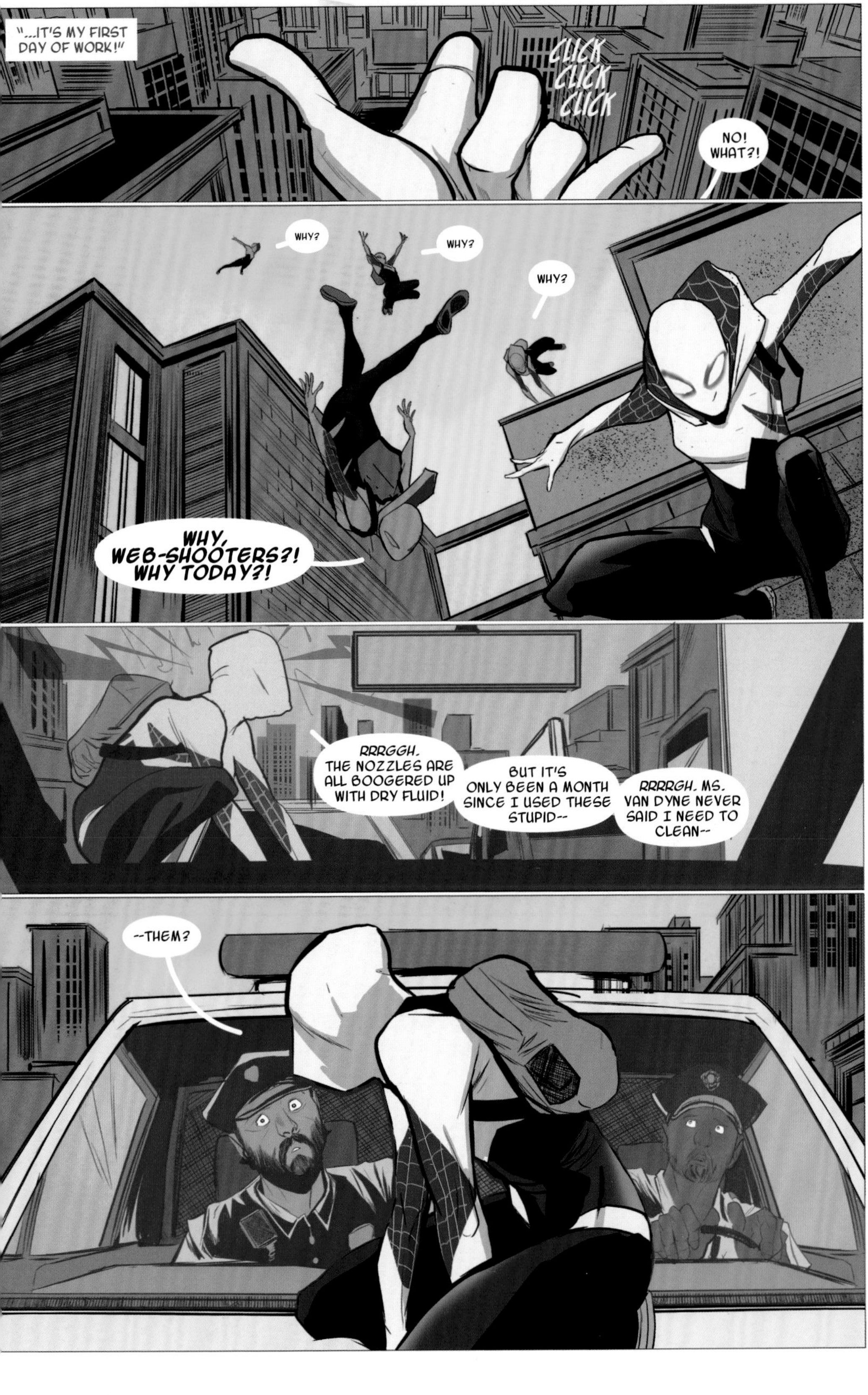
"...IT'S MY FIRST DAY OF WORK!"
CLICK CLICK CLICK
NO! WHAT?!
WHY?
WHY?
WHY?
WHY, WEB-SHOOTERS?! WHY TODAY?!
RRRGGH. THE NOZZLES ARE ALL BOOGERED UP WITH DRY FLUID!
BUT IT'S ONLY BEEN A MONTH SINCE I USED THESE STUPID--
RRRRGH. MS. VAN DYNE NEVER SAID I NEED TO CLEAN--
--THEM?

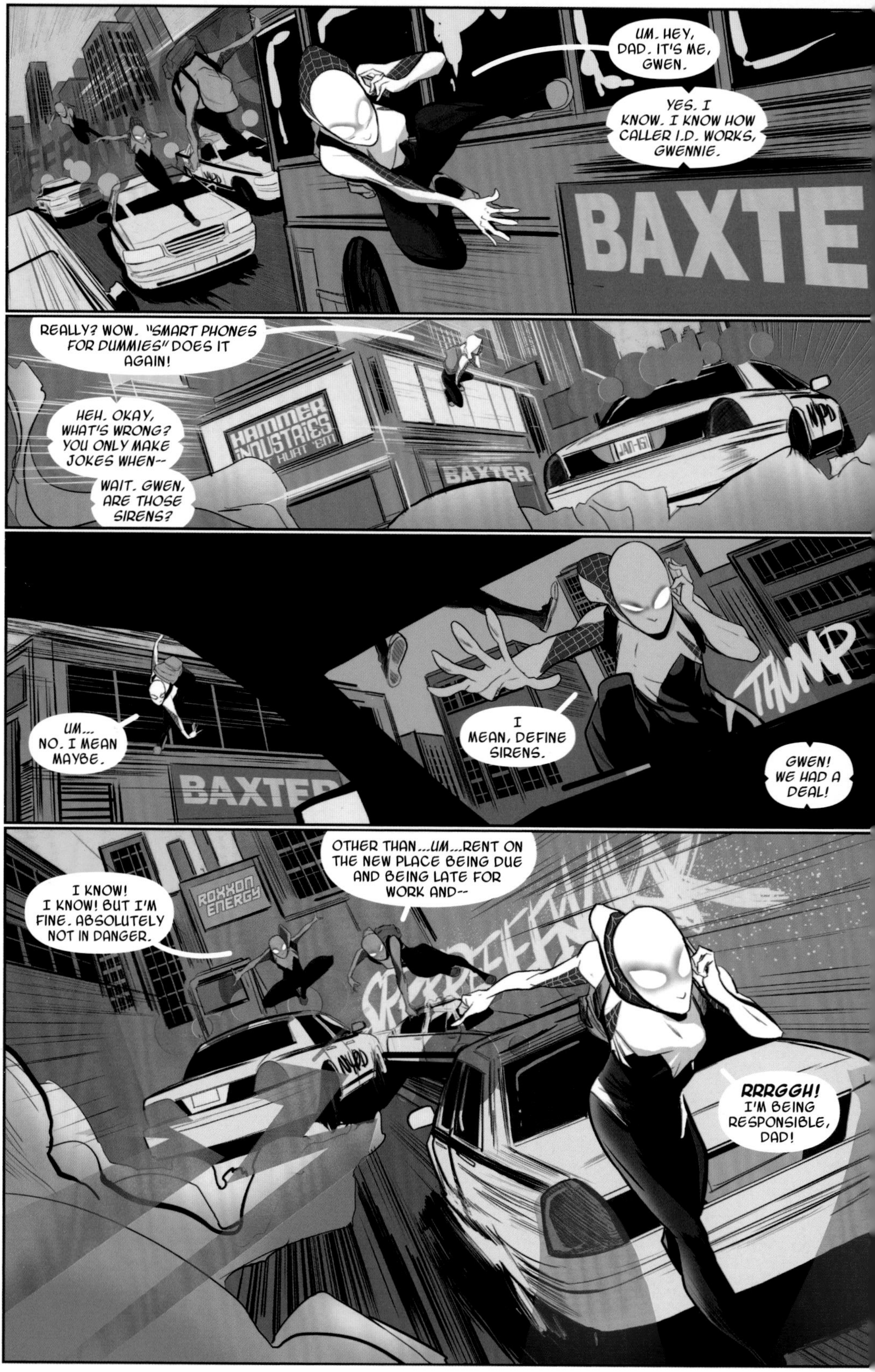
UM. HEY, DAD. IT'S ME, GWEN.
YES. I KNOW. I KNOW HOW CALLER I.D. WORKS, GWENNIE.
BAXTE
REALLY? WOW. "SMART PHONES FOR DUMMIES" DOES IT AGAIN!
HEH. OKAY, WHAT'S WRONG? YOU ONLY MAKE JOKES WHEN--
WAIT. GWEN, ARE THOSE SIRENS?
HAMMER INDUSTRIES
BAXTER
NYPD
UM... NO. I MEAN MAYBE.
I MEAN, DEFINE SIRENS.
THUMP
GWEN! WE HAD A DEAL!
BAXTER
I KNOW! I KNOW! BUT I'M FINE. ABSOLUTELY NOT IN DANGER.
OTHER THAN...UM...RENT ON THE NEW PLACE BEING DUE AND BEING LATE FOR WORK AND--
ROXXON ENERGY
NYPD
RRRGGH! I'M BEING RESPONSIBLE, DAD!

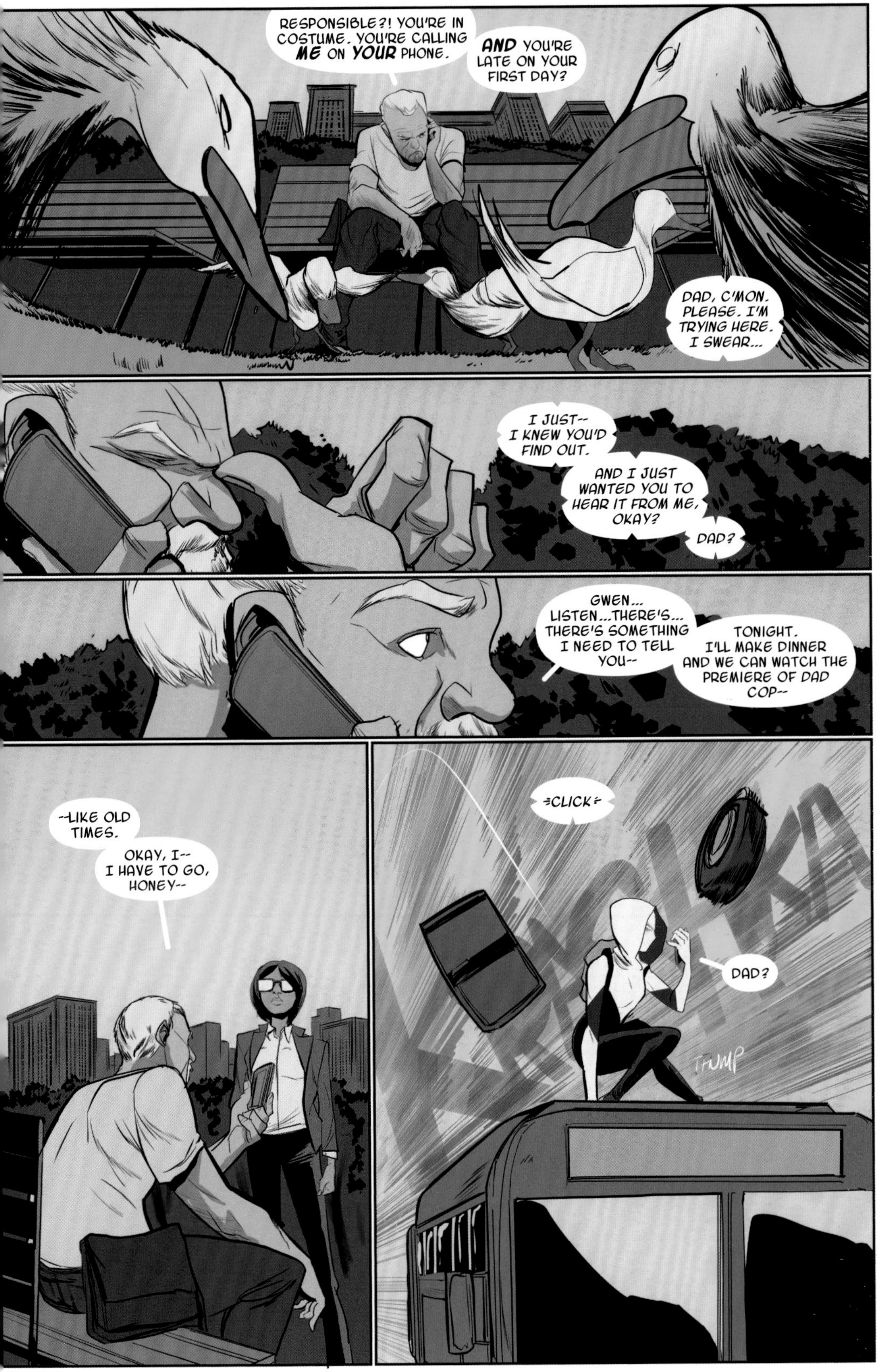
RESPONSIBLE?! YOU'RE IN COSTUME. YOU'RE CALLING ME ON YOUR PHONE.
AND YOU'RE LATE ON YOUR FIRST DAY?
DAD, C'MON. PLEASE. I'M TRYING HERE. I SWEAR...
I JUST-- I KNEW YOU'D FIND OUT.
AND I JUST WANTED YOU TO HEAR IT FROM ME, OKAY?
DAD?
GWEN... LISTEN...THERE'S... THERE'S SOMETHING I NEED TO TELL YOU--
TONIGHT. I'LL MAKE DINNER AND WE CAN WATCH THE PREMIERE OF DAD COP--
--LIKE OLD TIMES.
OKAY, I-- I HAVE TO GO, HONEY--
=CLICK=
DAD?
THUMP

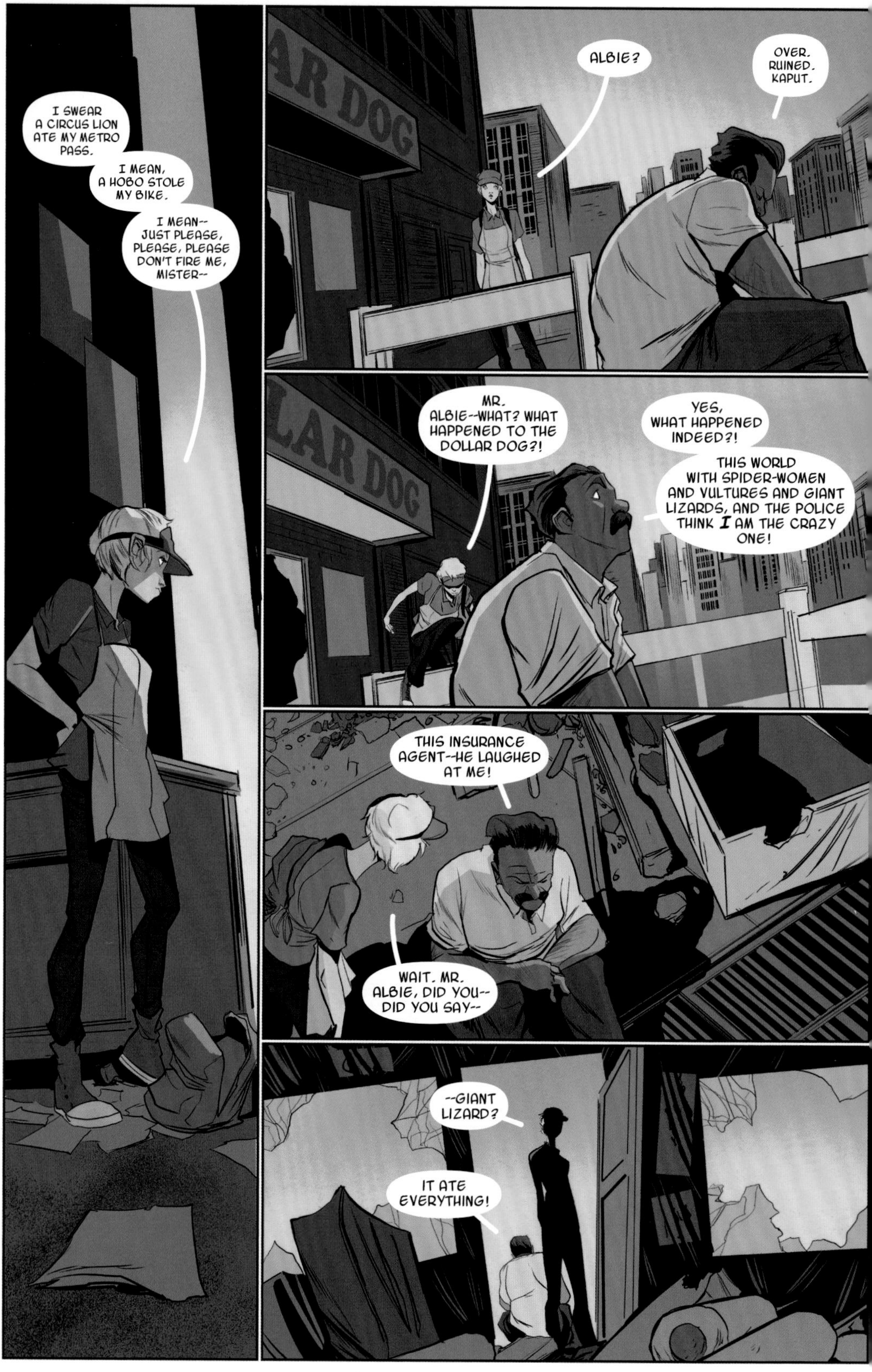

I SWEAR A CIRCUS LION ATE MY METRO PASS.
I MEAN, A HOBO STOLE MY BIKE.
I MEAN-- JUST PLEASE, PLEASE, PLEASE DON'T FIRE ME, MISTER--
AR DOG
ALBIE?
OVER. RUINED. KAPUT.
LAR DOG
MR. ALBIE--WHAT? WHAT HAPPENED TO THE DOLLAR DOG?!
YES, WHAT HAPPENED INDEED?!
THIS WORLD WITH SPIDER-WOMEN AND VULTURES AND GIANT LIZARDS, AND THE POLICE THINK *I* AM THE CRAZY ONE!
THIS INSURANCE AGENT--HE LAUGHED AT ME!
WAIT. MR. ALBIE, DID YOU-- DID YOU SAY--
--GIANT LIZARD?
IT ATE EVERYTHING!

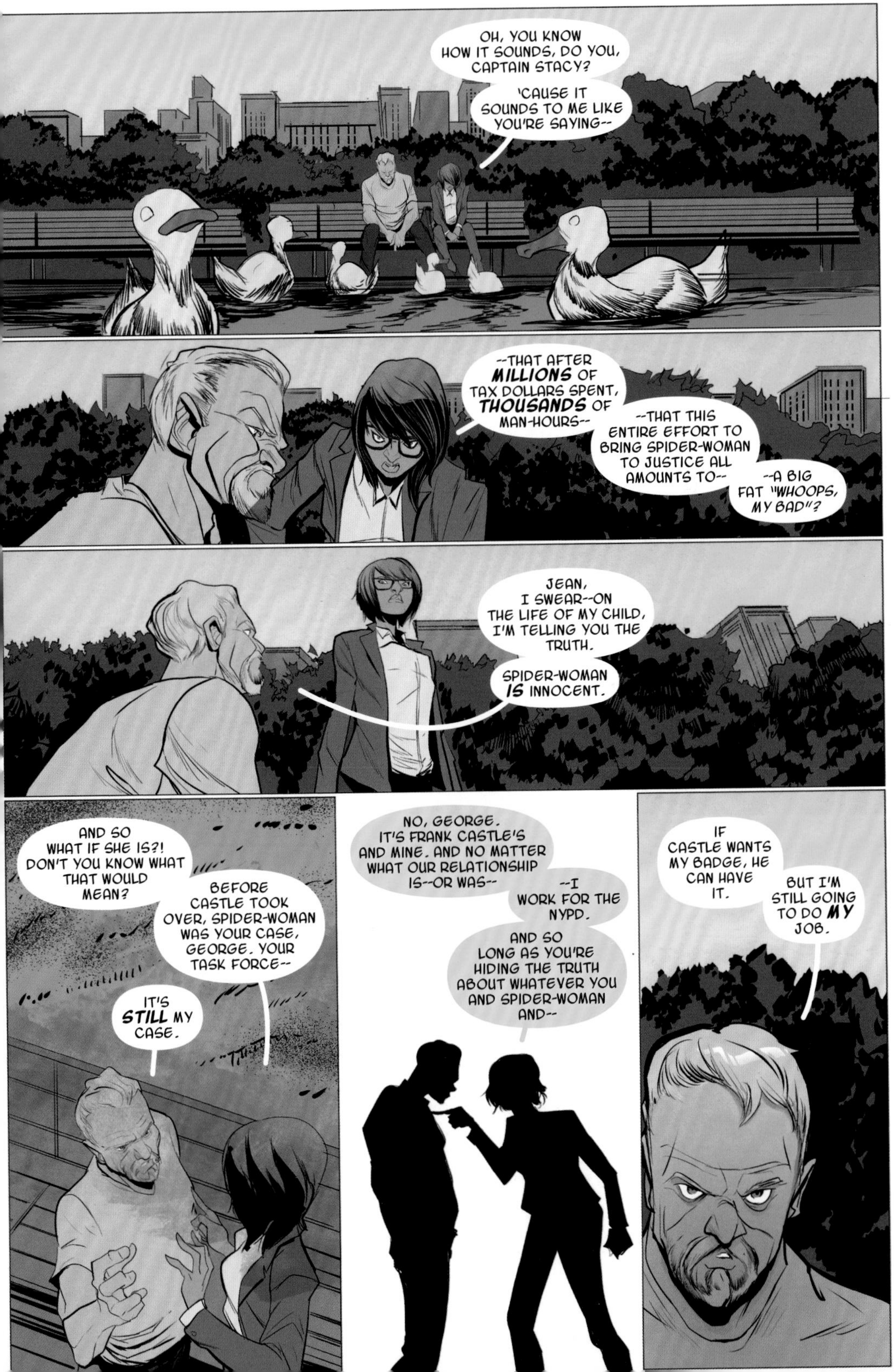
OH, YOU KNOW HOW IT SOUNDS, DO YOU, CAPTAIN STACY?
'CAUSE IT SOUNDS TO ME LIKE YOU'RE SAYING--
--THAT AFTER **MILLIONS** OF TAX DOLLARS SPENT, **THOUSANDS** OF MAN-HOURS--
--THAT THIS ENTIRE EFFORT TO BRING SPIDER-WOMAN TO JUSTICE ALL AMOUNTS TO--
--A BIG FAT "WHOOPS, MY BAD"?
JEAN, I SWEAR--ON THE LIFE OF MY CHILD, I'M TELLING YOU THE TRUTH.
SPIDER-WOMAN **IS** INNOCENT.
AND SO WHAT IF SHE IS?! DON'T YOU KNOW WHAT THAT WOULD MEAN?
BEFORE CASTLE TOOK OVER, SPIDER-WOMAN WAS YOUR CASE, GEORGE. YOUR TASK FORCE--
IT'S **STILL** MY CASE.
NO, GEORGE. IT'S FRANK CASTLE'S AND MINE. AND NO MATTER WHAT OUR RELATIONSHIP IS--OR WAS--
--I WORK FOR THE NYPD.
AND SO LONG AS YOU'RE HIDING THE TRUTH ABOUT WHATEVER YOU AND SPIDER-WOMAN AND--
IF CASTLE WANTS MY BADGE, HE CAN HAVE IT.
BUT I'M STILL GOING TO DO **MY** JOB.

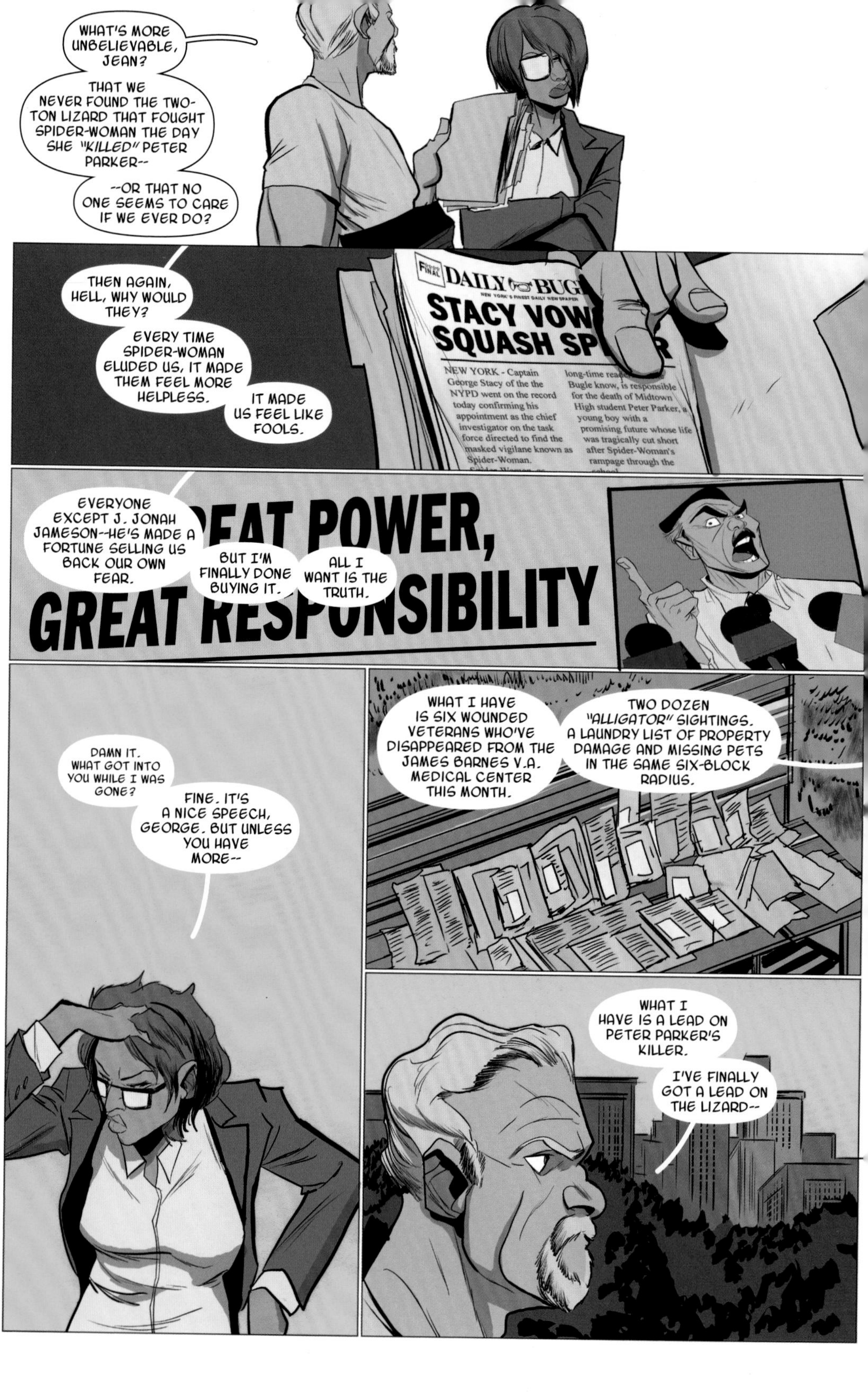
WHAT'S MORE UNBELIEVABLE, JEAN?
THAT WE NEVER FOUND THE TWO-TON LIZARD THAT FOUGHT SPIDER-WOMAN THE DAY SHE "KILLED" PETER PARKER--
--OR THAT NO ONE SEEMS TO CARE IF WE EVER DO?
THEN AGAIN, HELL, WHY WOULD THEY?
EVERY TIME SPIDER-WOMAN ELUDED US, IT MADE THEM FEEL MORE HELPLESS.
IT MADE US FEEL LIKE FOOLS.
FINAL
DAILY BUG
NEW YORK'S FINEST DAILY NEWSPAPER
STACY VOW
SQUASH SP
NEW YORK - Captain George Stacy of the the NYPD went on the record today confirming his appointment as the chief investigator on the task force directed to find the masked vigilane known as Spider-Woman.
long-time rea Bugle know, is responsible for the death of Midtown High student Peter Parker, a young boy with a promising future whose life was tragically cut short after Spider-Woman's rampage through the
EVERYONE EXCEPT J. JONAH JAMESON--HE'S MADE A FORTUNE SELLING US BACK OUR OWN FEAR.
BUT I'M FINALLY DONE BUYING IT.
ALL I WANT IS THE TRUTH.
EAT POWER,
GREAT RESPONSIBILITY
DAMN IT. WHAT GOT INTO YOU WHILE I WAS GONE?
FINE. IT'S A NICE SPEECH, GEORGE. BUT UNLESS YOU HAVE MORE--
WHAT I HAVE IS SIX WOUNDED VETERANS WHO'VE DISAPPEARED FROM THE JAMES BARNES V.A. MEDICAL CENTER THIS MONTH.
TWO DOZEN "ALLIGATOR" SIGHTINGS. A LAUNDRY LIST OF PROPERTY DAMAGE AND MISSING PETS IN THE SAME SIX-BLOCK RADIUS.
WHAT I HAVE IS A LEAD ON PETER PARKER'S KILLER.
I'VE FINALLY GOT A LEAD ON THE LIZARD--

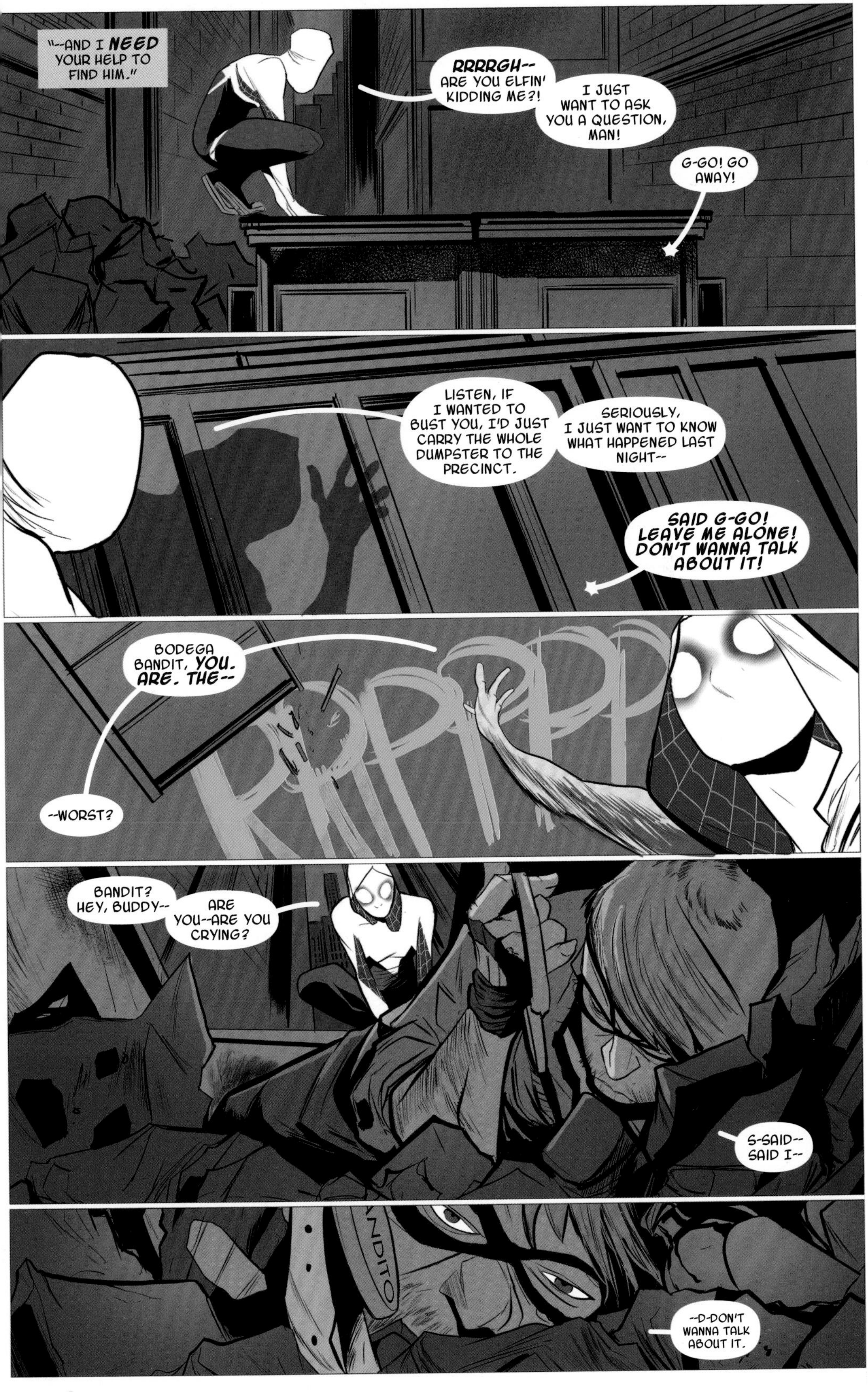
"--AND I NEED YOUR HELP TO FIND HIM."
RRRRGH-- ARE YOU ELFIN' KIDDING ME?!
I JUST WANT TO ASK YOU A QUESTION, MAN!
G-GO! GO AWAY!
LISTEN, IF I WANTED TO BUST YOU, I'D JUST CARRY THE WHOLE DUMPSTER TO THE PRECINCT.
SERIOUSLY, I JUST WANT TO KNOW WHAT HAPPENED LAST NIGHT--
SAID G-GO! LEAVE ME ALONE! DON'T WANNA TALK ABOUT IT!
BODEGA BANDIT, YOU. ARE. THE--
RRIPPPP
--WORST?
BANDIT? HEY, BUDDY--
ARE YOU--ARE YOU CRYING?
S-SAID-- SAID I--
--D-DON'T WANNA TALK ABOUT IT.

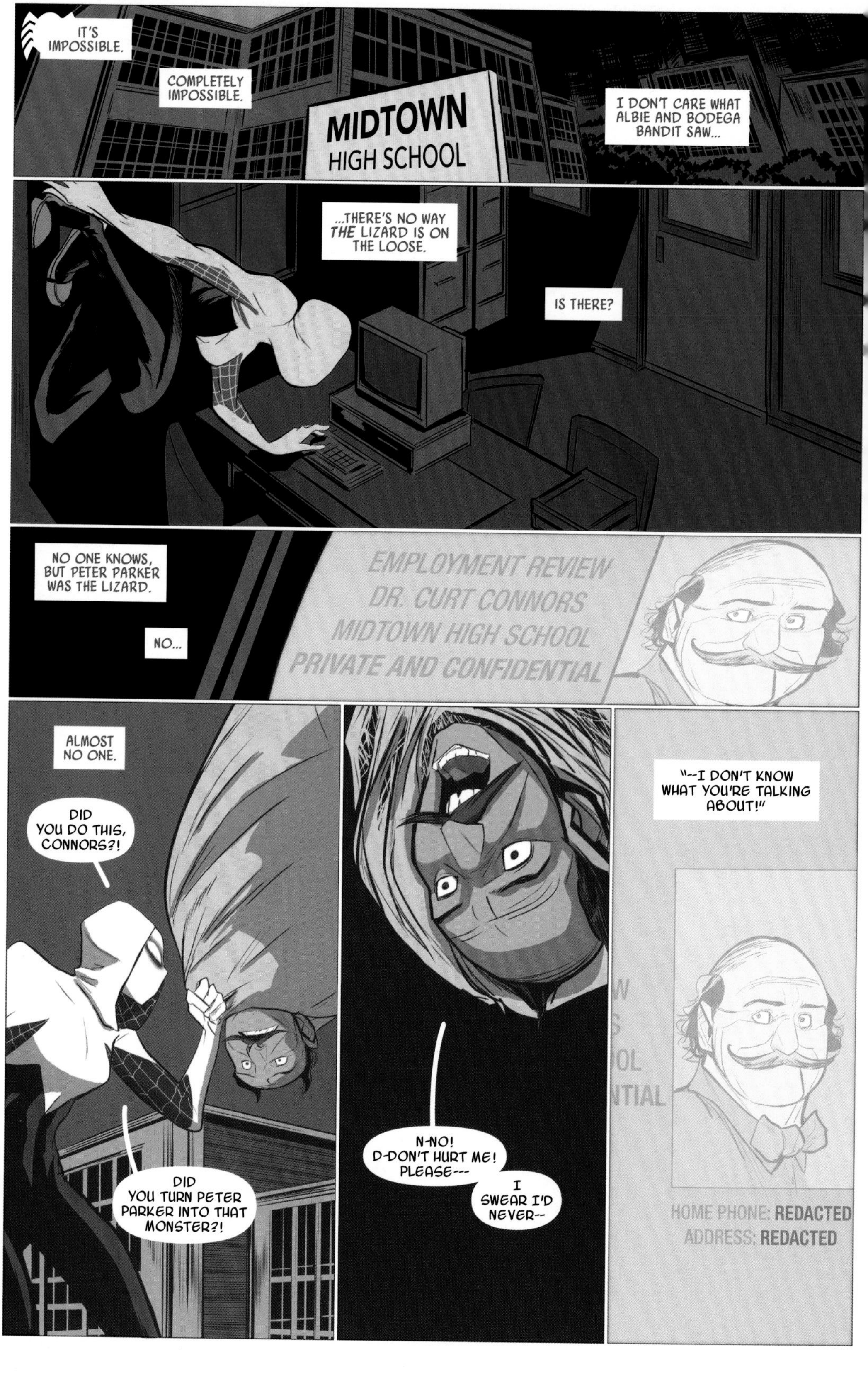
IT'S IMPOSSIBLE.
COMPLETELY IMPOSSIBLE.
MIDTOWN HIGH SCHOOL
I DON'T CARE WHAT ALBIE AND BODEGA BANDIT SAW...
...THERE'S NO WAY *THE* LIZARD IS ON THE LOOSE.
IS THERE?
NO ONE KNOWS, BUT PETER PARKER WAS THE LIZARD.
NO...
EMPLOYMENT REVIEW
DR. CURT CONNORS
MIDTOWN HIGH SCHOOL
PRIVATE AND CONFIDENTIAL
ALMOST NO ONE.
DID YOU DO THIS, CONNORS?!
DID YOU TURN PETER PARKER INTO THAT MONSTER?!
N-NO! D-DON'T HURT ME! PLEASE---
I SWEAR I'D NEVER--
"--I DON'T KNOW WHAT YOU'RE TALKING ABOUT!"
HOME PHONE: REDACTED
ADDRESS: REDACTED

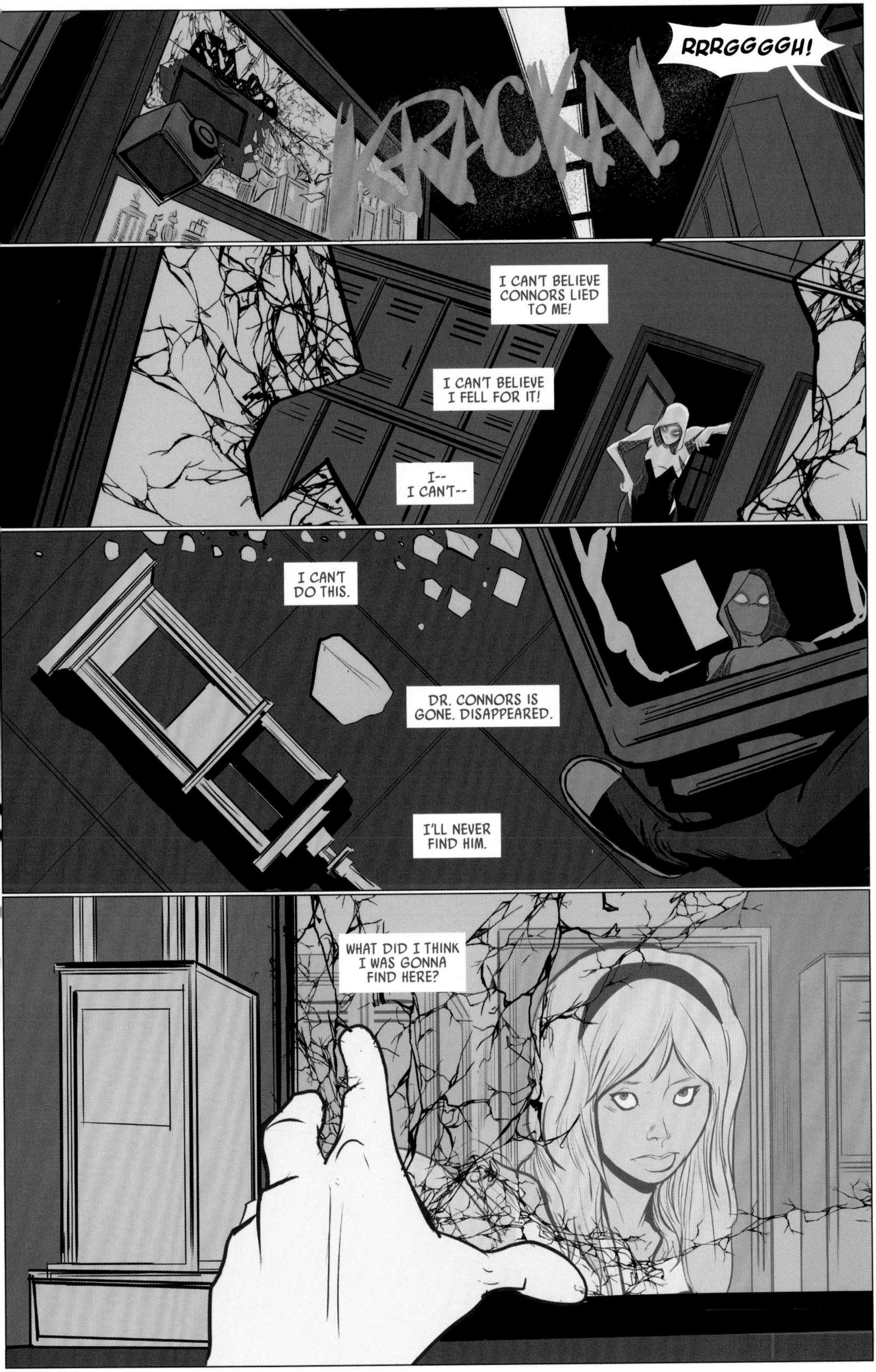
KRACKA!
RRRGGGGH!
I CAN'T BELIEVE CONNORS LIED TO ME!
I CAN'T BELIEVE I FELL FOR IT!
I-- I CAN'T--
I CAN'T DO THIS.
DR. CONNORS IS GONE. DISAPPEARED.
I'LL NEVER FIND HIM.
WHAT DID I THINK I WAS GONNA FIND HERE?

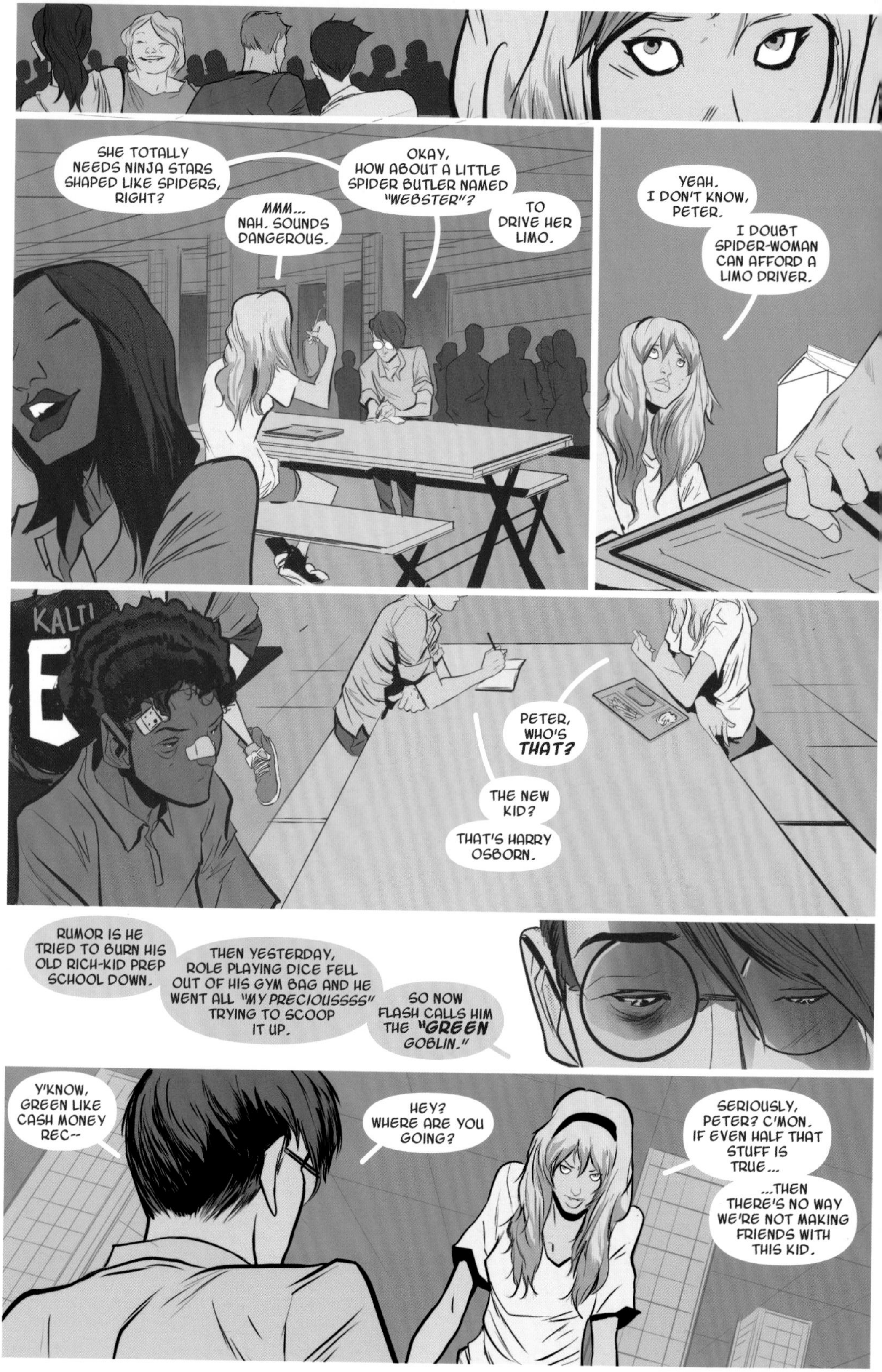
SHE TOTALLY NEEDS NINJA STARS SHAPED LIKE SPIDERS, RIGHT?
OKAY, HOW ABOUT A LITTLE SPIDER BUTLER NAMED "WEBSTER"?
MMM... NAH. SOUNDS DANGEROUS.
TO DRIVE HER LIMO.
YEAH. I DON'T KNOW, PETER.
I DOUBT SPIDER-WOMAN CAN AFFORD A LIMO DRIVER.
KALT
PETER, WHO'S THAT?
THE NEW KID?
THAT'S HARRY OSBORN.
RUMOR IS HE TRIED TO BURN HIS OLD RICH-KID PREP SCHOOL DOWN.
THEN YESTERDAY, ROLE PLAYING DICE FELL OUT OF HIS GYM BAG AND HE WENT ALL "MY PRECIOUSSSS" TRYING TO SCOOP IT UP.
SO NOW FLASH CALLS HIM THE "GREEN GOBLIN."
Y'KNOW, GREEN LIKE CASH MONEY REC--
HEY? WHERE ARE YOU GOING?
SERIOUSLY, PETER? C'MON. IF EVEN HALF THAT STUFF IS TRUE...
...THEN THERE'S NO WAY WE'RE NOT MAKING FRIENDS WITH THIS KID.

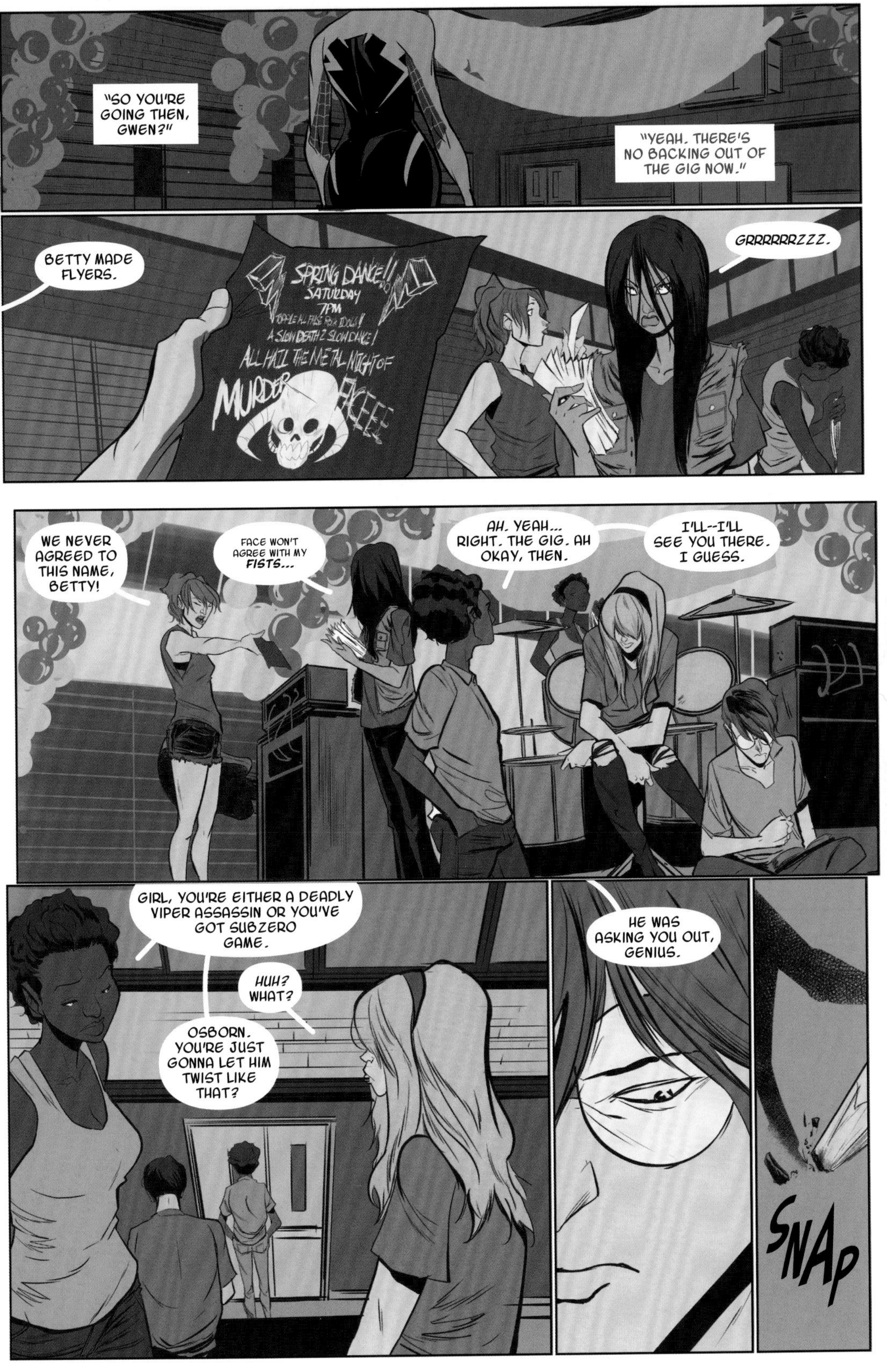
"SO YOU'RE GOING THEN, GWEN?"
"YEAH. THERE'S NO BACKING OUT OF THE GIG NOW."
BETTY MADE FLYERS.
SPRING DANCE!!
SATURDAY
7PM
TOPPLE ALL FALSE ROCK IDOLS!
A SLOW DEATH 2 SLOW DANCE!
ALL HAIL THE METAL NIGHT OF
MURDER FACEEE
GRRRRRRRZZZ.
WE NEVER AGREED TO THIS NAME, BETTY!
FACE WON'T AGREE WITH MY **FISTS...**
AH. YEAH... RIGHT. THE GIG. AH OKAY, THEN.
I'LL--I'LL SEE YOU THERE. I GUESS.
GIRL, YOU'RE EITHER A DEADLY VIPER ASSASSIN OR YOU'VE GOT SUBZERO GAME.
HUH? WHAT?
OSBORN. YOU'RE JUST GONNA LET HIM TWIST LIKE THAT?
HE WAS ASKING YOU OUT, GENIUS.
SNAP

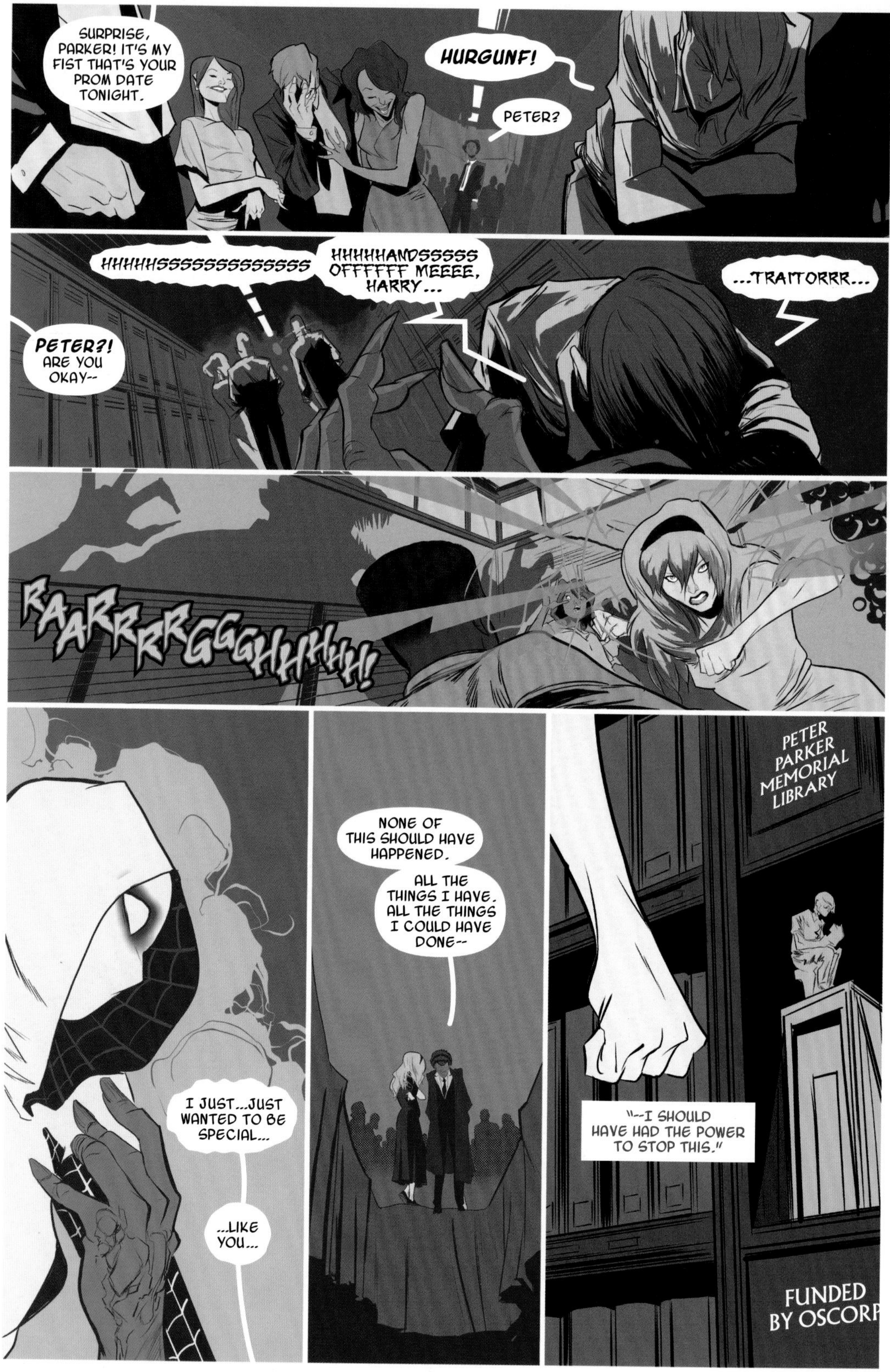
SURPRISE, PARKER! IT'S MY FIST THAT'S YOUR PROM DATE TONIGHT.
HURGUNF!
PETER?
HHHHHSSSSSSSSSSSSSS
HHHHHANDSSSSS OFFFFFF MEEEE, HARRY...
...TRAITORRR...
PETER?! ARE YOU OKAY--
RAARRRRGGGHHHHH!
I JUST...JUST WANTED TO BE SPECIAL...
...LIKE YOU...
NONE OF THIS SHOULD HAVE HAPPENED.
ALL THE THINGS I HAVE. ALL THE THINGS I COULD HAVE DONE--
PETER PARKER MEMORIAL LIBRARY
"--I SHOULD HAVE HAD THE POWER TO STOP THIS."
FUNDED BY OSCORP

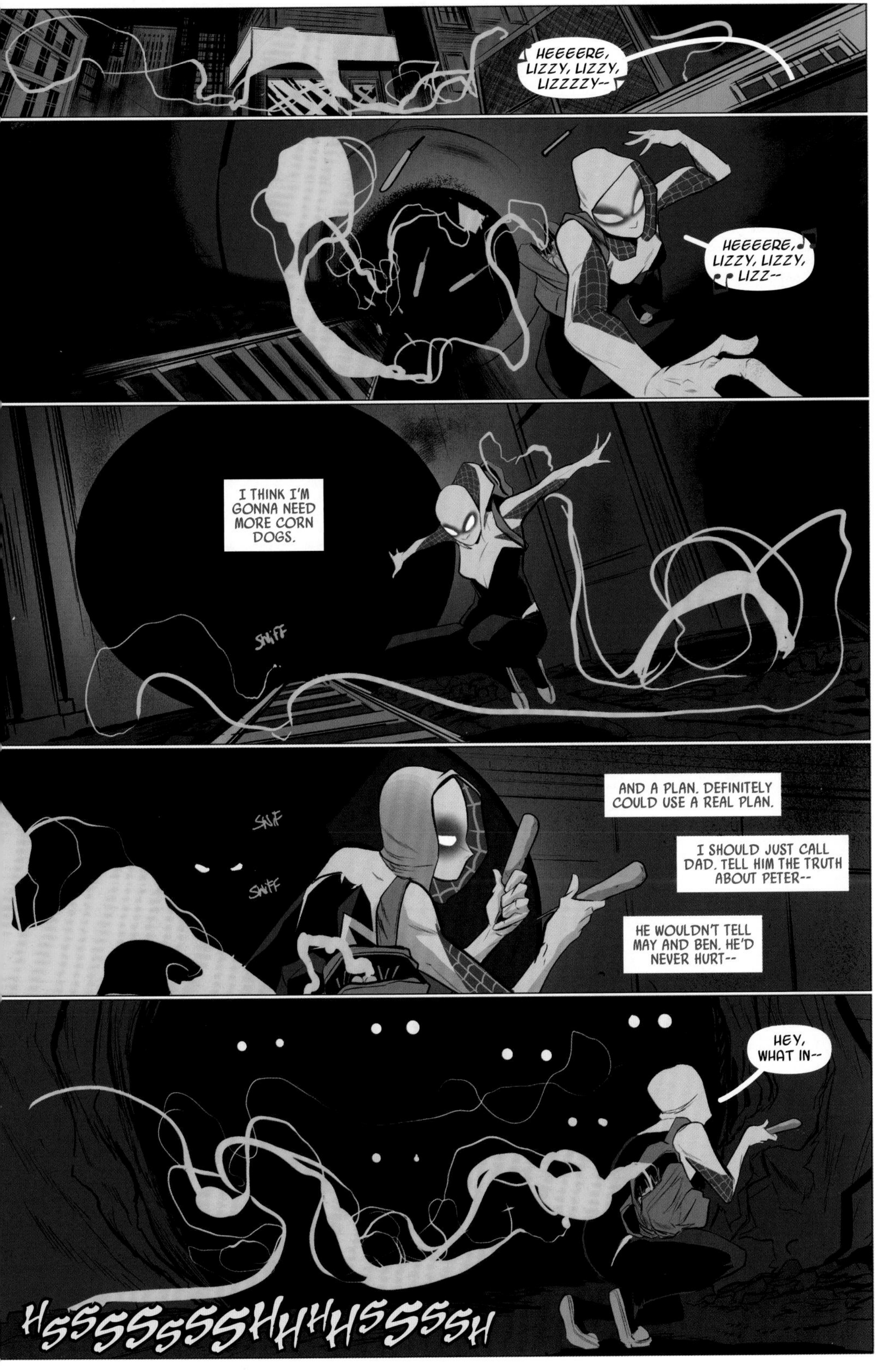
HEEEERE, LIZZY, LIZZY, LIZZZZY--
HEEEERE, LIZZY, LIZZY, LIZZ--
I THINK I'M GONNA NEED MORE CORN DOGS.
SNIFF
AND A PLAN. DEFINITELY COULD USE A REAL PLAN.
SNIFF
SNIFF
I SHOULD JUST CALL DAD. TELL HIM THE TRUTH ABOUT PETER--
HE WOULDN'T TELL MAY AND BEN. HE'D NEVER HURT--
HEY, WHAT IN--
HSSSSSSSSHHHHSSSSH

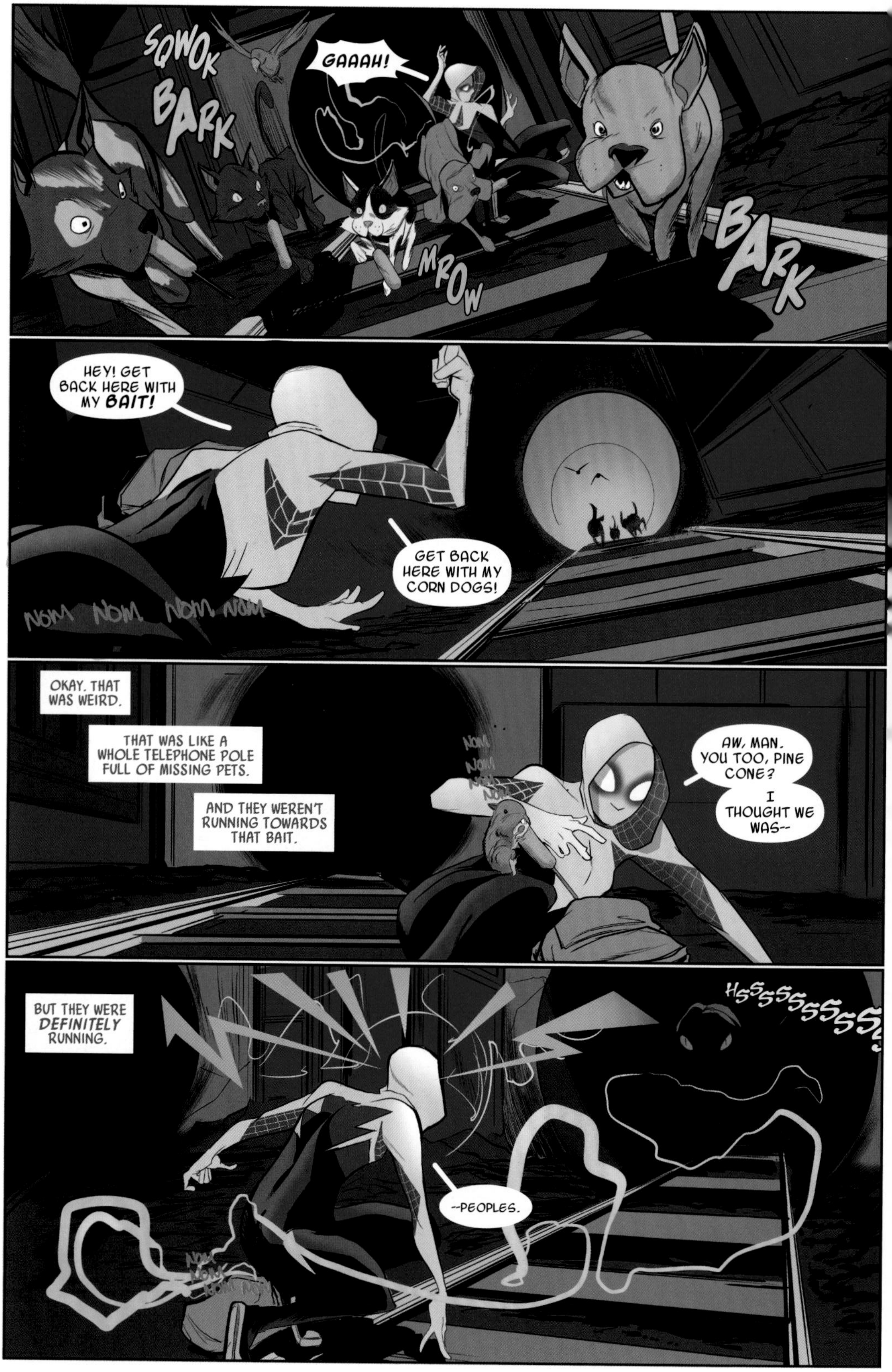
SQWOK
BARK
GAAAH!
MROW
BARK
HEY! GET BACK HERE WITH MY BAIT!
GET BACK HERE WITH MY CORN DOGS!
NOM NOM NOM NOM
OKAY. THAT WAS WEIRD.
THAT WAS LIKE A WHOLE TELEPHONE POLE FULL OF MISSING PETS.
AND THEY WEREN'T RUNNING TOWARDS THAT BAIT.
AW, MAN. YOU TOO, PINE CONE?
I THOUGHT WE WAS--
BUT THEY WERE DEFINITELY RUNNING.
HSSSSSSSSSS
--PEOPLES.

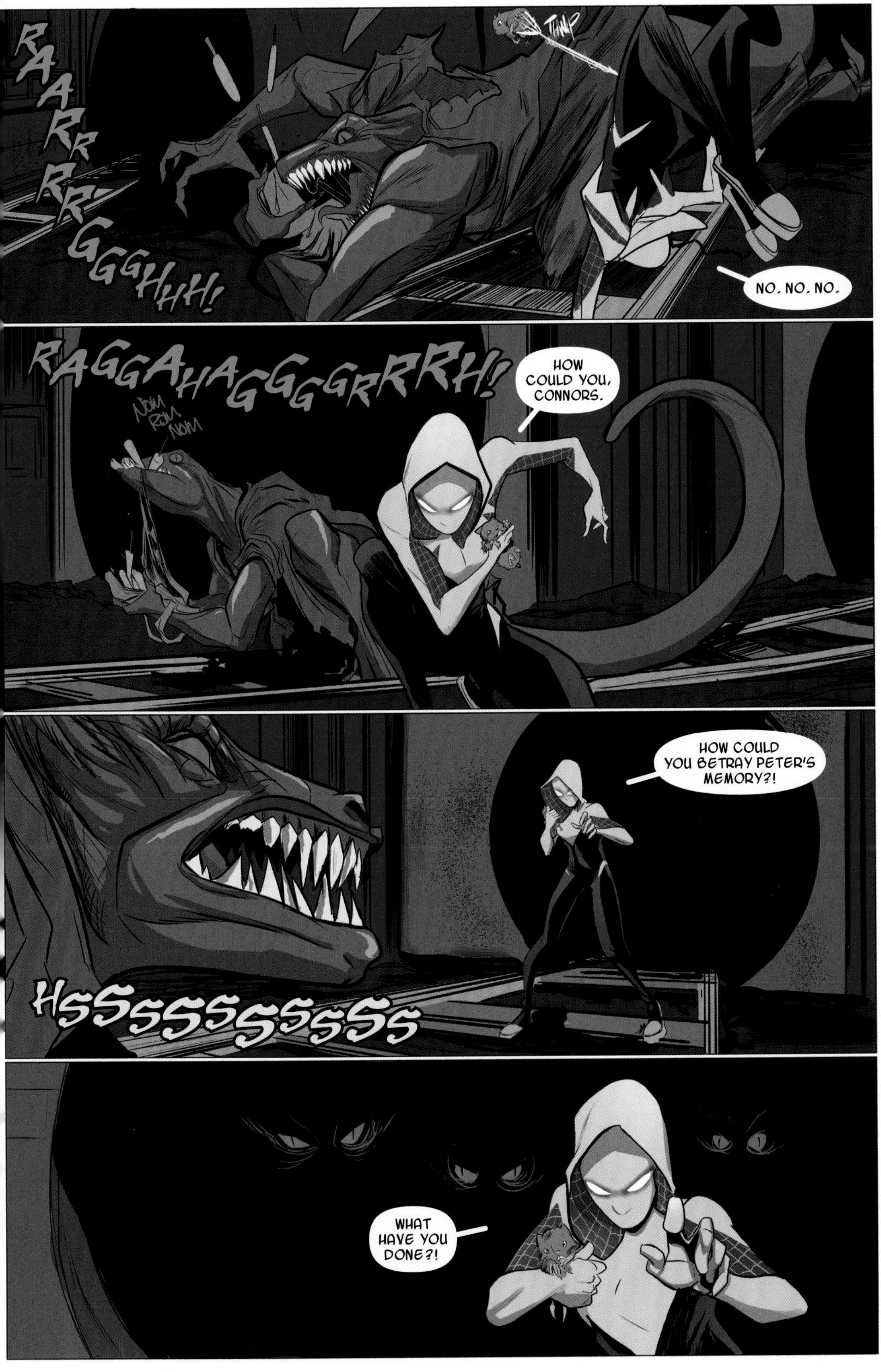
RAARRRRGGGHHH!
THWP
NO. NO. NO.
RAGGAHAGGGGRRRH!
HOW COULD YOU, CONNORS.
NOM NOM NOM
HOW COULD YOU BETRAY PETER'S MEMORY?!
HSSSSSSSSSSS
WHAT HAVE YOU DONE?!

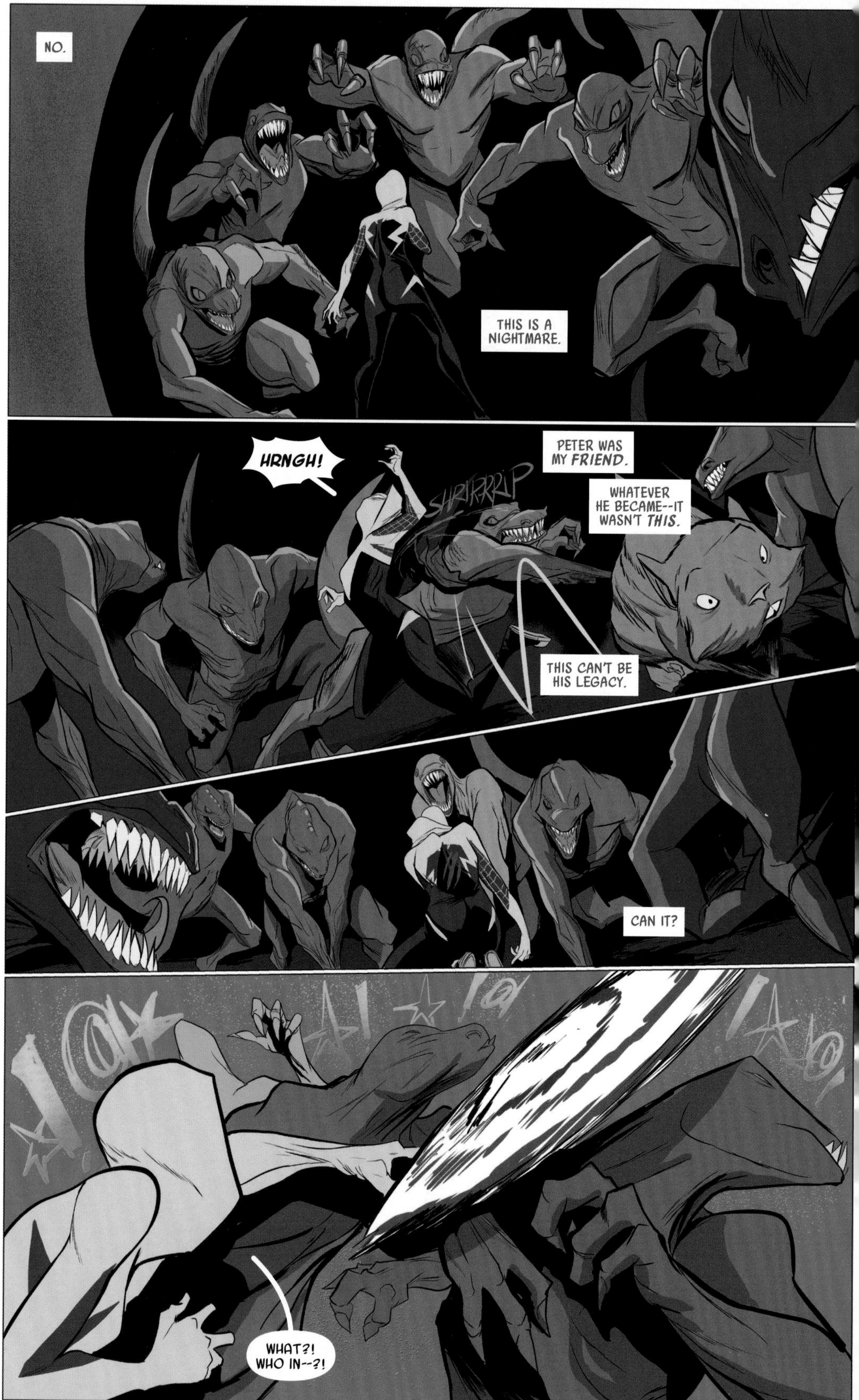
NO.
THIS IS A NIGHTMARE.
HRNGH!
PETER WAS MY FRIEND.
WHATEVER HE BECAME--IT WASN'T THIS.
SHRRRRRIP
THIS CAN'T BE HIS LEGACY.
CAN IT?
WHAT?! WHO IN--?!

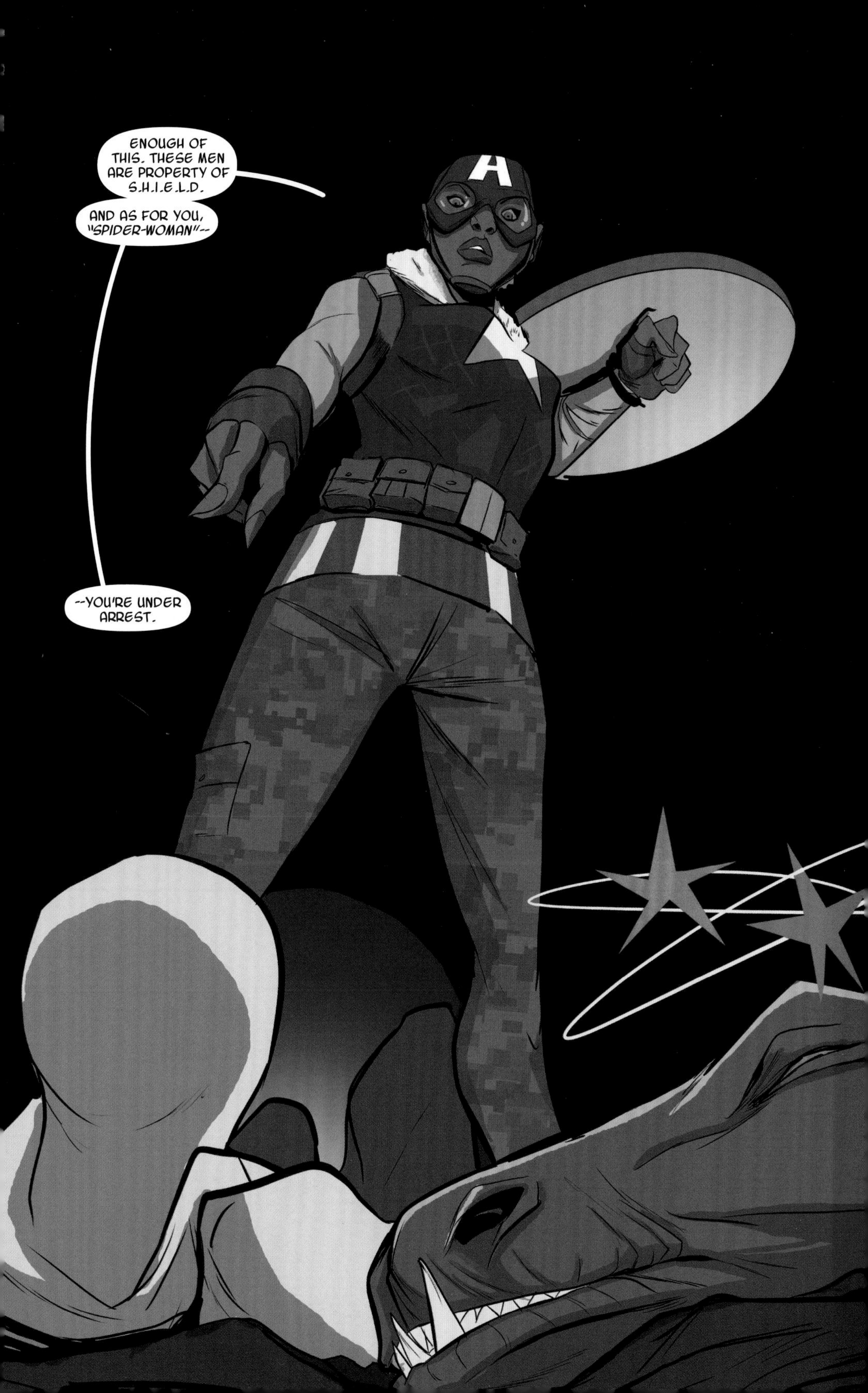
ENOUGH OF THIS. THESE MEN ARE PROPERTY OF S.H.I.E.L.D.
AND AS FOR YOU, "SPIDER-WOMAN"--
--YOU'RE UNDER ARREST.

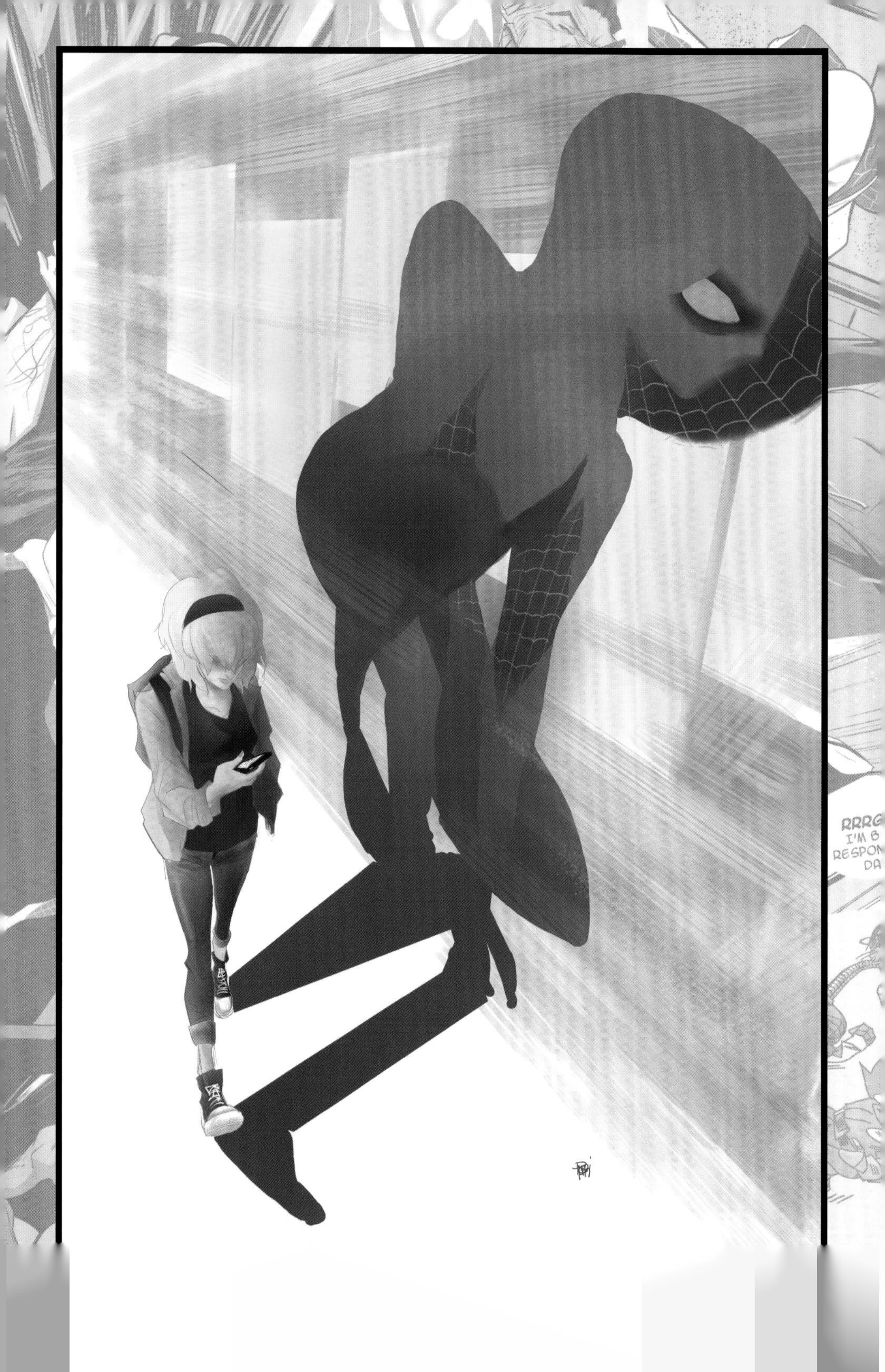
RRRG
I'M B
RESPON
DA

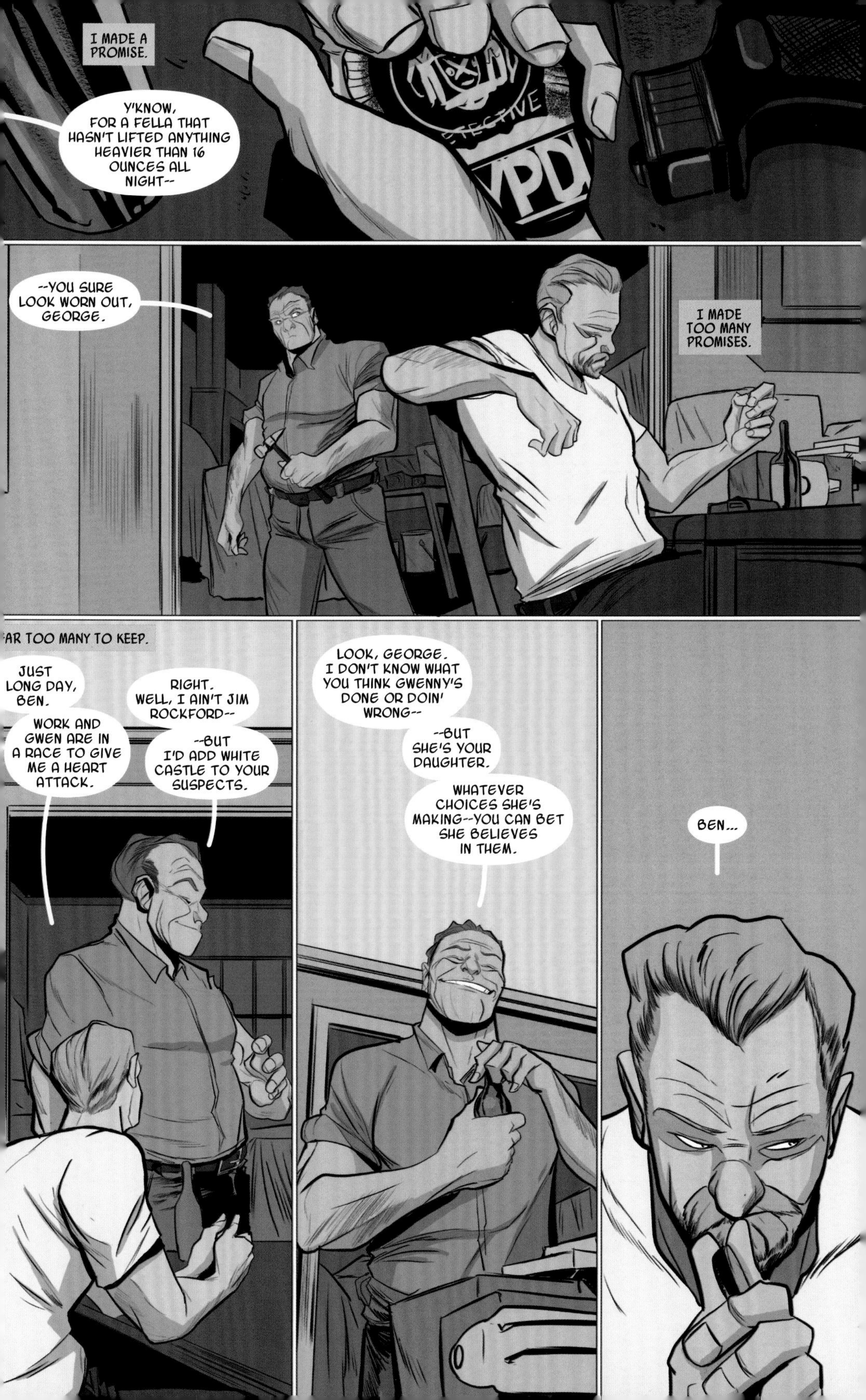
I MADE A PROMISE.
Y'KNOW, FOR A FELLA THAT HASN'T LIFTED ANYTHING HEAVIER THAN 16 OUNCES ALL NIGHT--
--YOU SURE LOOK WORN OUT, GEORGE.
I MADE TOO MANY PROMISES.
FAR TOO MANY TO KEEP.
JUST LONG DAY, BEN.
WORK AND GWEN ARE IN A RACE TO GIVE ME A HEART ATTACK.
RIGHT. WELL, I AIN'T JIM ROCKFORD--
--BUT I'D ADD WHITE CASTLE TO YOUR SUSPECTS.
LOOK, GEORGE. I DON'T KNOW WHAT YOU THINK GWENNY'S DONE OR DOIN' WRONG--
--BUT SHE'S YOUR DAUGHTER.
WHATEVER CHOICES SHE'S MAKING--YOU CAN BET SHE BELIEVES IN THEM.
BEN...

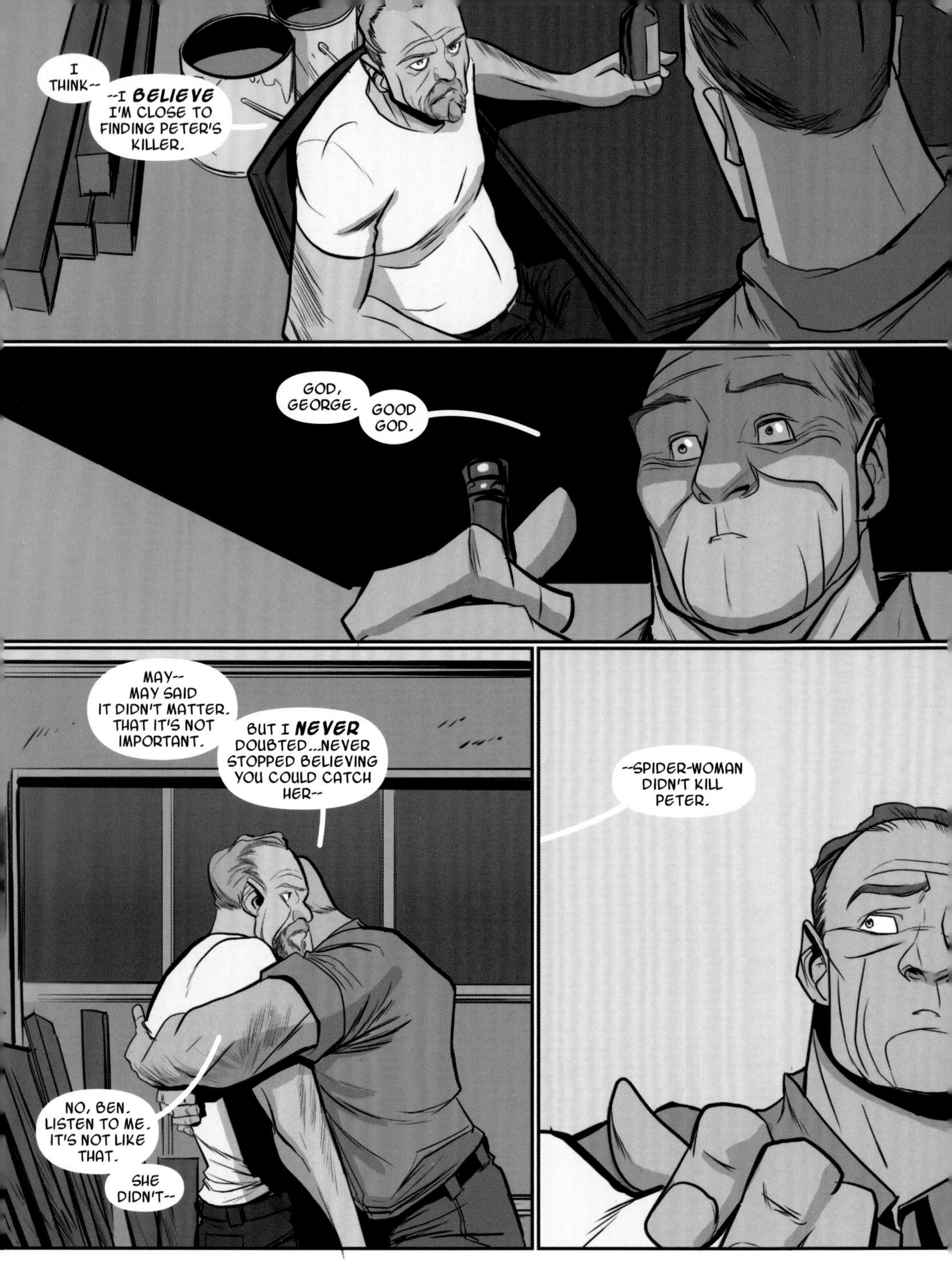
I THINK--
--I BELIEVE I'M CLOSE TO FINDING PETER'S KILLER.
GOD, GEORGE.
GOOD GOD.
MAY-- MAY SAID IT DIDN'T MATTER. THAT IT'S NOT IMPORTANT.
BUT I NEVER DOUBTED...NEVER STOPPED BELIEVING YOU COULD CATCH HER--
NO, BEN. LISTEN TO ME. IT'S NOT LIKE THAT.
SHE DIDN'T--
--SPIDER-WOMAN DIDN'T KILL PETER.

GREATER POWER

PART TWO

LATOUR RODRIGUEZ RENZI COWLES

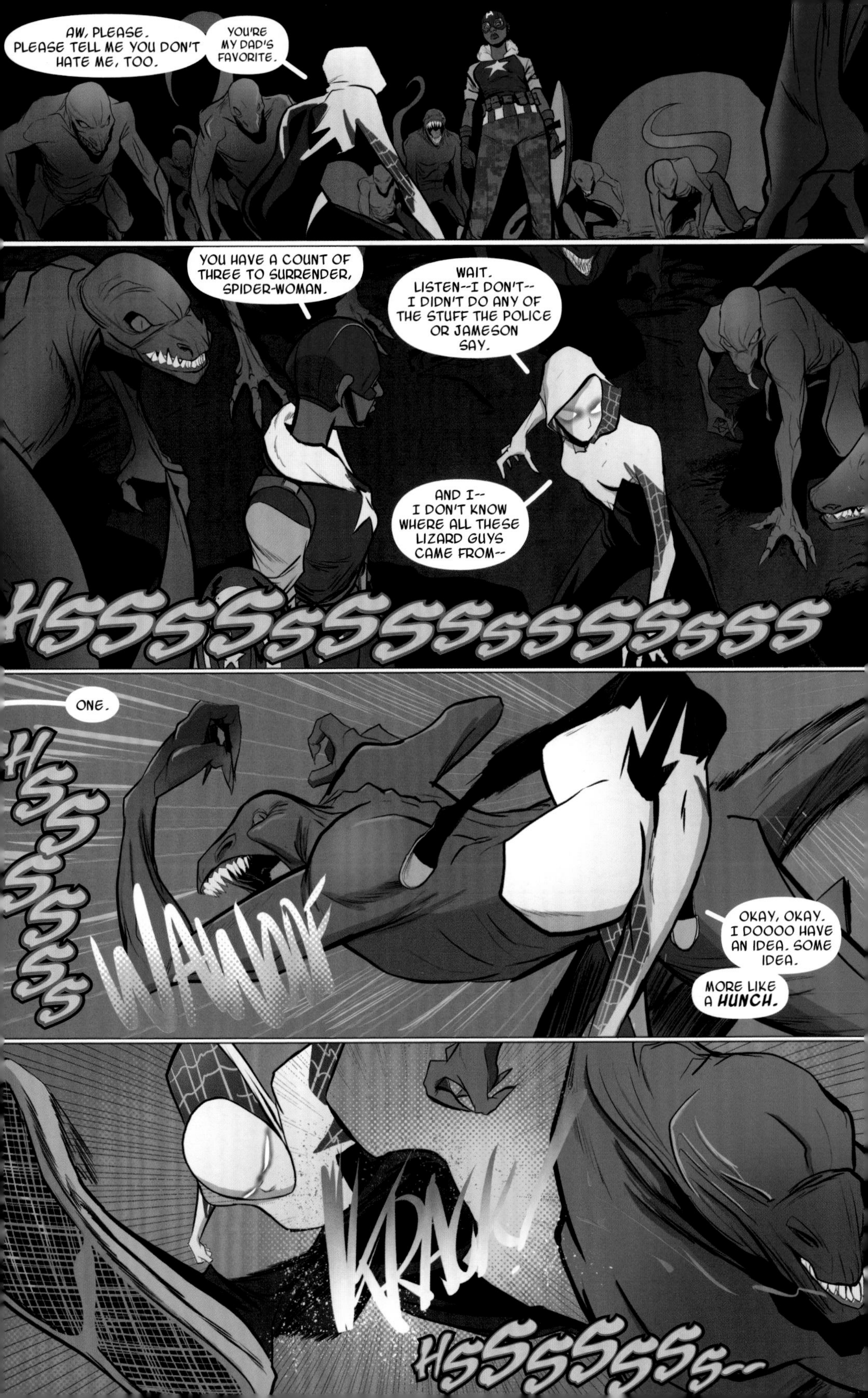
AW, PLEASE. PLEASE TELL ME YOU DON'T HATE ME, TOO.
YOU'RE MY DAD'S FAVORITE.
YOU HAVE A COUNT OF THREE TO SURRENDER, SPIDER-WOMAN.
WAIT. LISTEN--I DON'T-- I DIDN'T DO ANY OF THE STUFF THE POLICE OR JAMESON SAY.
AND I-- I DON'T KNOW WHERE ALL THESE LIZARD GUYS CAME FROM--
HSSSSSSSSSSSSSSSSS
ONE.
HSSSSSSS
WAAAK
OKAY, OKAY. I DOOOO HAVE AN IDEA. SOME IDEA.
MORE LIKE A HUNCH.
KRACK
HSSSSSSSS--

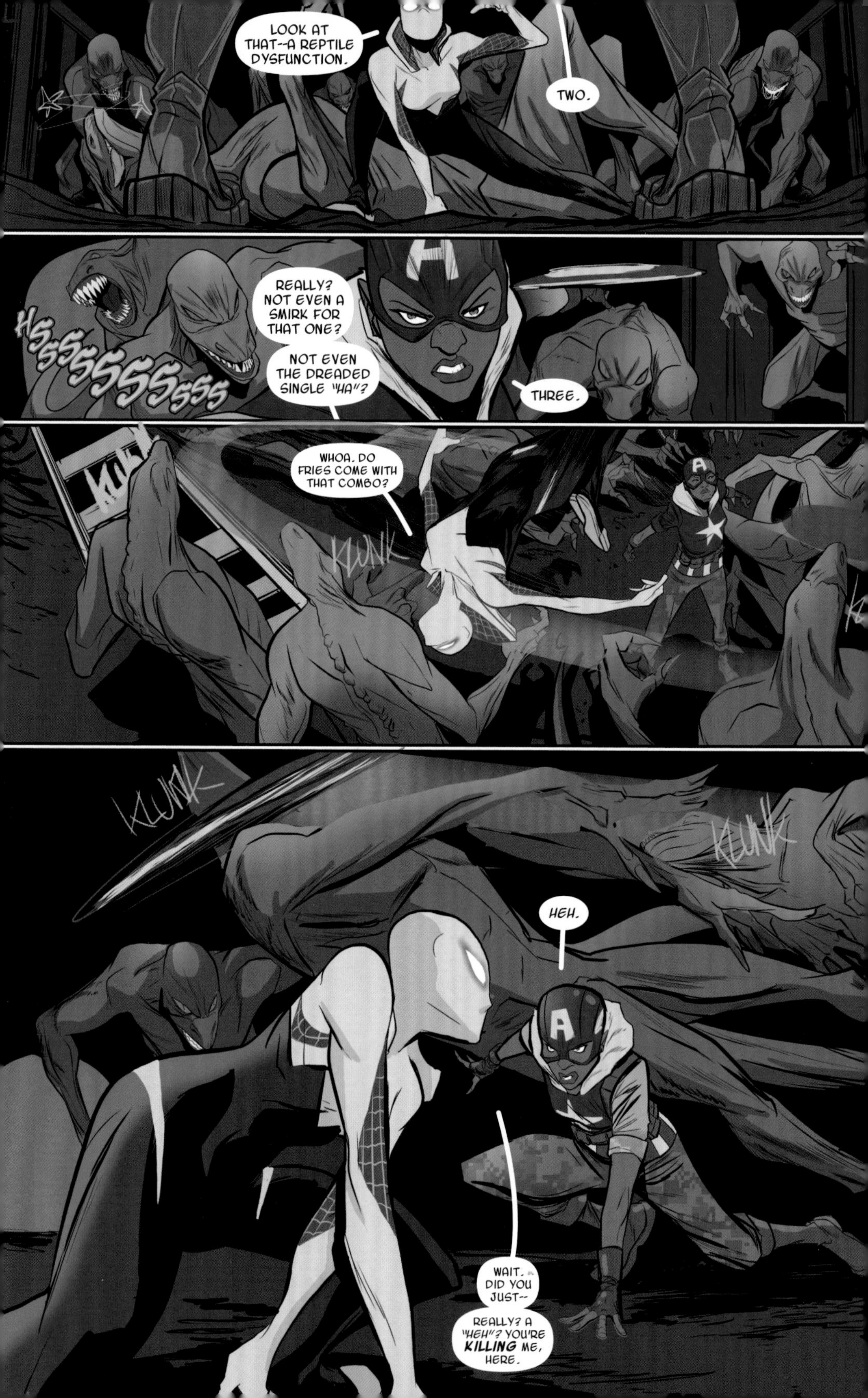
LOOK AT THAT--A REPTILE DYSFUNCTION.
TWO.
REALLY? NOT EVEN A SMIRK FOR THAT ONE?
NOT EVEN THE DREADED SINGLE "HA"?
HSSSSSSSSSSSS
THREE.
WHOA. DO FRIES COME WITH THAT COMBO?
KLUNK
KLUNK
KLUNK
HEH.
WAIT. DID YOU JUST--
REALLY? A "HEH"? YOU'RE **KILLING** ME, HERE.

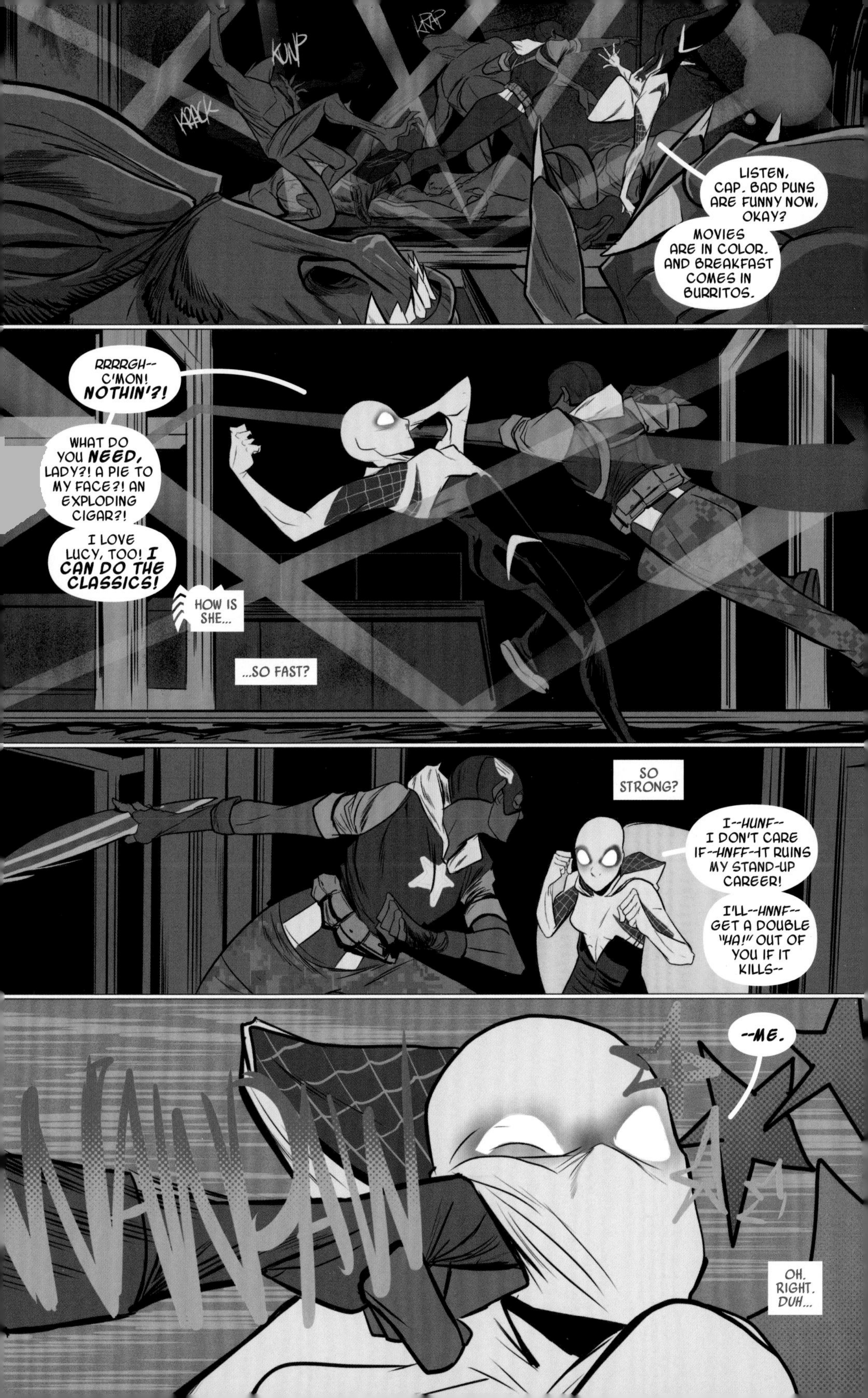
KRACK
KUNP
KRAP
LISTEN, CAP. BAD PUNS ARE FUNNY NOW, OKAY?
MOVIES ARE IN COLOR. AND BREAKFAST COMES IN BURRITOS.
RRRRGH-- C'MON! NOTHIN'?!
WHAT DO YOU NEED, LADY?! A PIE TO MY FACE?! AN EXPLODING CIGAR?!
I LOVE LUCY, TOO! I CAN DO THE CLASSICS!
HOW IS SHE...
...SO FAST?
SO STRONG?
I--HUNF-- I DON'T CARE IF--HNFF--IT RUINS MY STAND-UP CAREER!
I'LL--HNNF-- GET A DOUBLE "HA!" OUT OF YOU IF IT KILLS--
--ME.
OH. RIGHT. DUH...

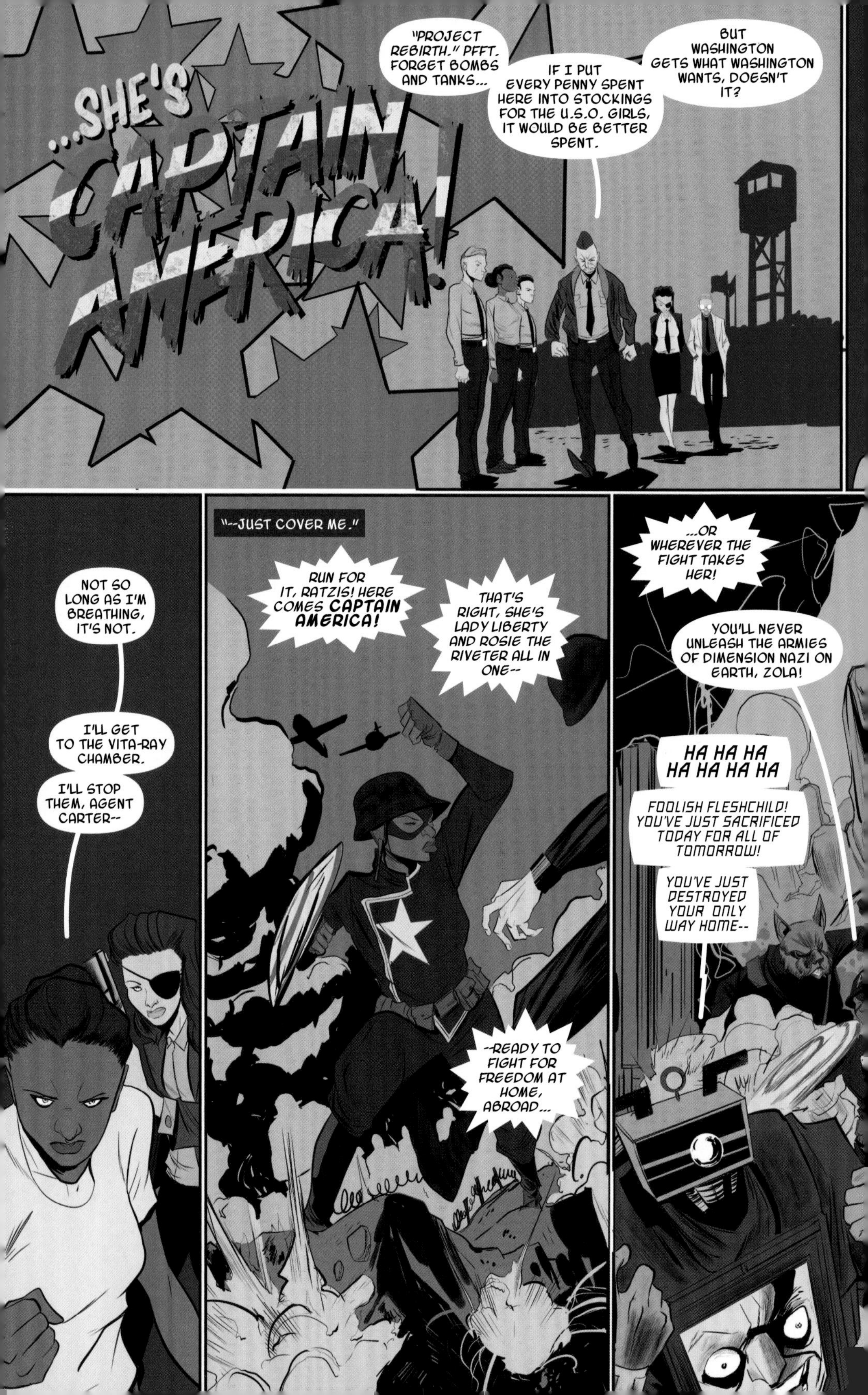
...SHE'S CAPTAIN AMERICA!
"PROJECT REBIRTH." PFFT. FORGET BOMBS AND TANKS...
IF I PUT EVERY PENNY SPENT HERE INTO STOCKINGS FOR THE U.S.O. GIRLS, IT WOULD BE BETTER SPENT.
BUT WASHINGTON GETS WHAT WASHINGTON WANTS, DOESN'T IT?
NOT SO LONG AS I'M BREATHING, IT'S NOT.
I'LL GET TO THE VITA-RAY CHAMBER.
I'LL STOP THEM, AGENT CARTER--
"--JUST COVER ME."
RUN FOR IT, RATZIS! HERE COMES CAPTAIN AMERICA!
THAT'S RIGHT, SHE'S LADY LIBERTY AND ROSIE THE RIVETER ALL IN ONE--
--READY TO FIGHT FOR FREEDOM AT HOME, ABROAD...
...OR WHEREVER THE FIGHT TAKES HER!
YOU'LL NEVER UNLEASH THE ARMIES OF DIMENSION NAZI ON EARTH, ZOLA!
HA HA HA HA HA HA HA
FOOLISH FLESHCHILD! YOU'VE JUST SACRIFICED TODAY FOR ALL OF TOMORROW!
YOU'VE JUST DESTROYED YOUR ONLY WAY HOME--

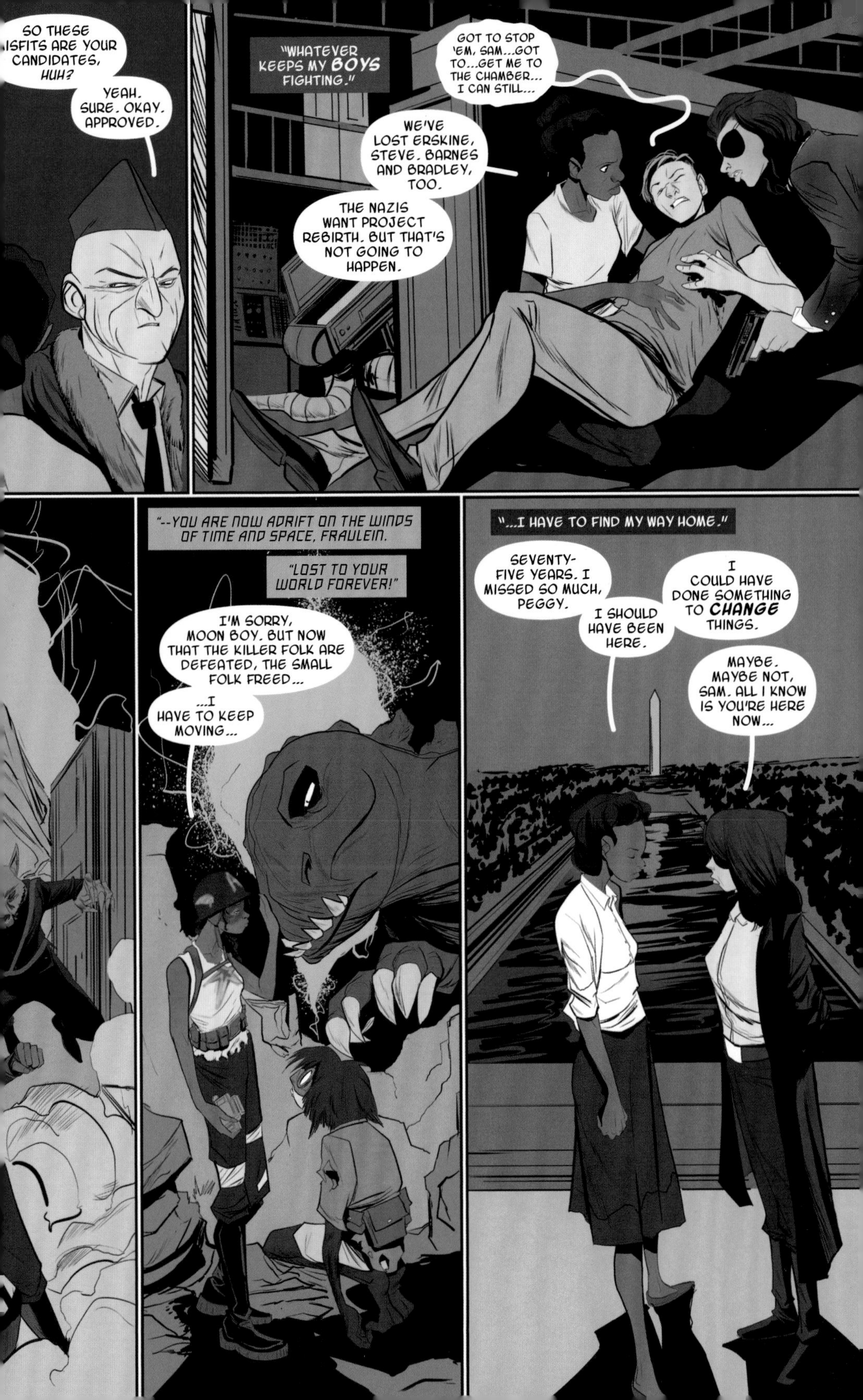
SO THESE
ISFITS ARE YOUR CANDIDATES, HUH?
YEAH. SURE. OKAY. APPROVED.
"WHATEVER KEEPS MY BOYS FIGHTING."
GOT TO STOP 'EM, SAM...GOT TO...GET ME TO THE CHAMBER... I CAN STILL...
WE'VE LOST ERSKINE, STEVE. BARNES AND BRADLEY, TOO.
THE NAZIS WANT PROJECT REBIRTH. BUT THAT'S NOT GOING TO HAPPEN.
"--YOU ARE NOW ADRIFT ON THE WINDS OF TIME AND SPACE, FRAULEIN.
"LOST TO YOUR WORLD FOREVER!"
I'M SORRY, MOON BOY. BUT NOW THAT THE KILLER FOLK ARE DEFEATED, THE SMALL FOLK FREED...
...I HAVE TO KEEP MOVING...
"...I HAVE TO FIND MY WAY HOME."
SEVENTY-FIVE YEARS. I MISSED SO MUCH, PEGGY.
I SHOULD HAVE BEEN HERE.
I COULD HAVE DONE SOMETHING TO CHANGE THINGS.
MAYBE. MAYBE NOT, SAM. ALL I KNOW IS YOU'RE HERE NOW...

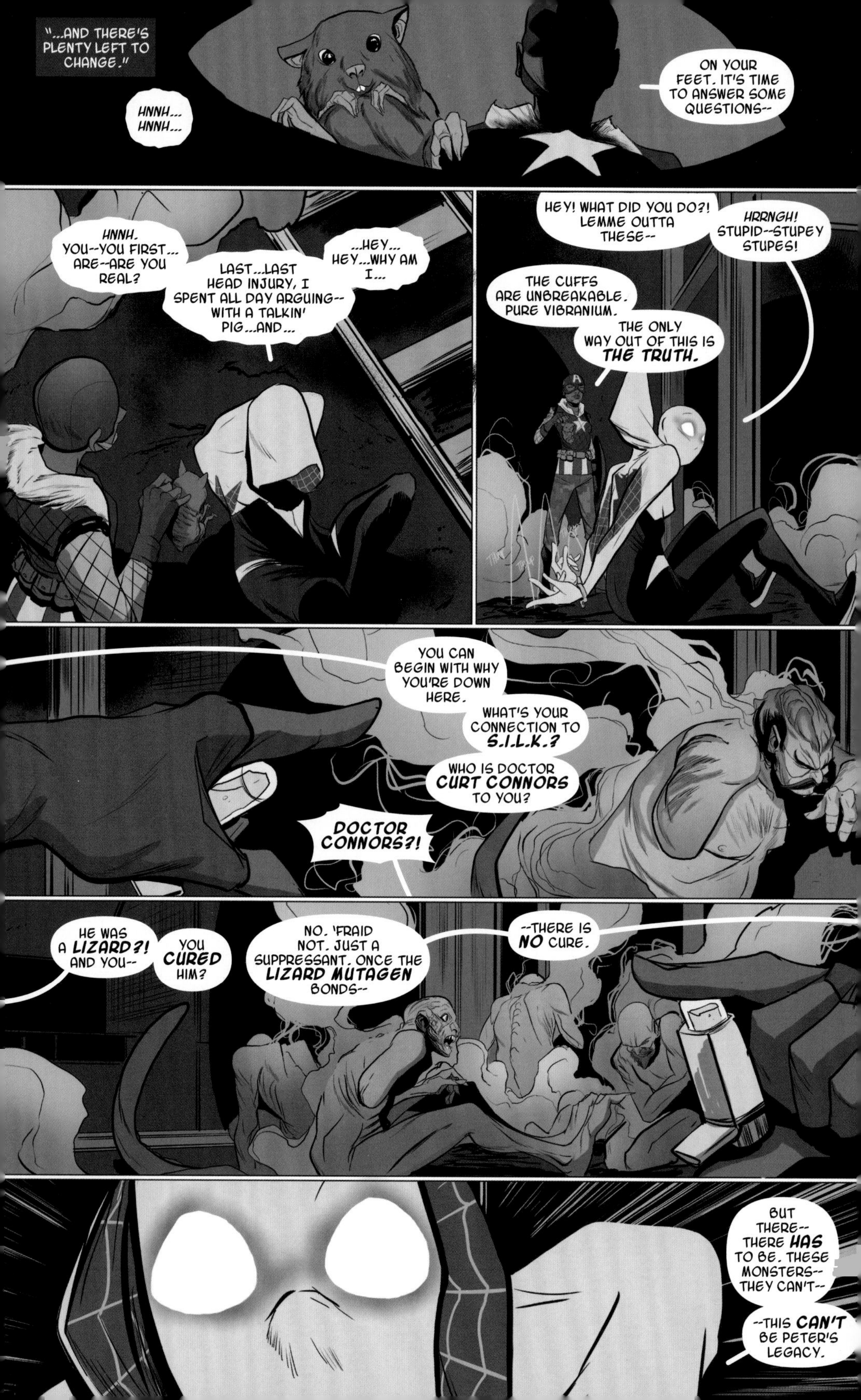
"...AND THERE'S PLENTY LEFT TO CHANGE."
HNNH... HNNH...
ON YOUR FEET. IT'S TIME TO ANSWER SOME QUESTIONS--
HNNH. YOU--YOU FIRST... ARE--ARE YOU REAL?
LAST...LAST HEAD INJURY, I SPENT ALL DAY ARGUING--WITH A TALKIN' PIG...AND...
...HEY... HEY...WHY AM I...
HEY! WHAT DID YOU DO?! LEMME OUTTA THESE--
HRRNGH! STUPID--STUPEY STUPES!
THE CUFFS ARE UNBREAKABLE. PURE VIBRANIUM.
THE ONLY WAY OUT OF THIS IS THE TRUTH.
YOU CAN BEGIN WITH WHY YOU'RE DOWN HERE.
WHAT'S YOUR CONNECTION TO S.I.L.K.?
WHO IS DOCTOR CURT CONNORS TO YOU?
DOCTOR CONNORS?!
HE WAS A LIZARD?! AND YOU--
YOU CURED HIM?
NO. 'FRAID NOT. JUST A SUPPRESSANT. ONCE THE LIZARD MUTAGEN BONDS--
--THERE IS NO CURE.
BUT THERE--THERE HAS TO BE. THESE MONSTERS--THEY CAN'T--
--THIS CAN'T BE PETER'S LEGACY.

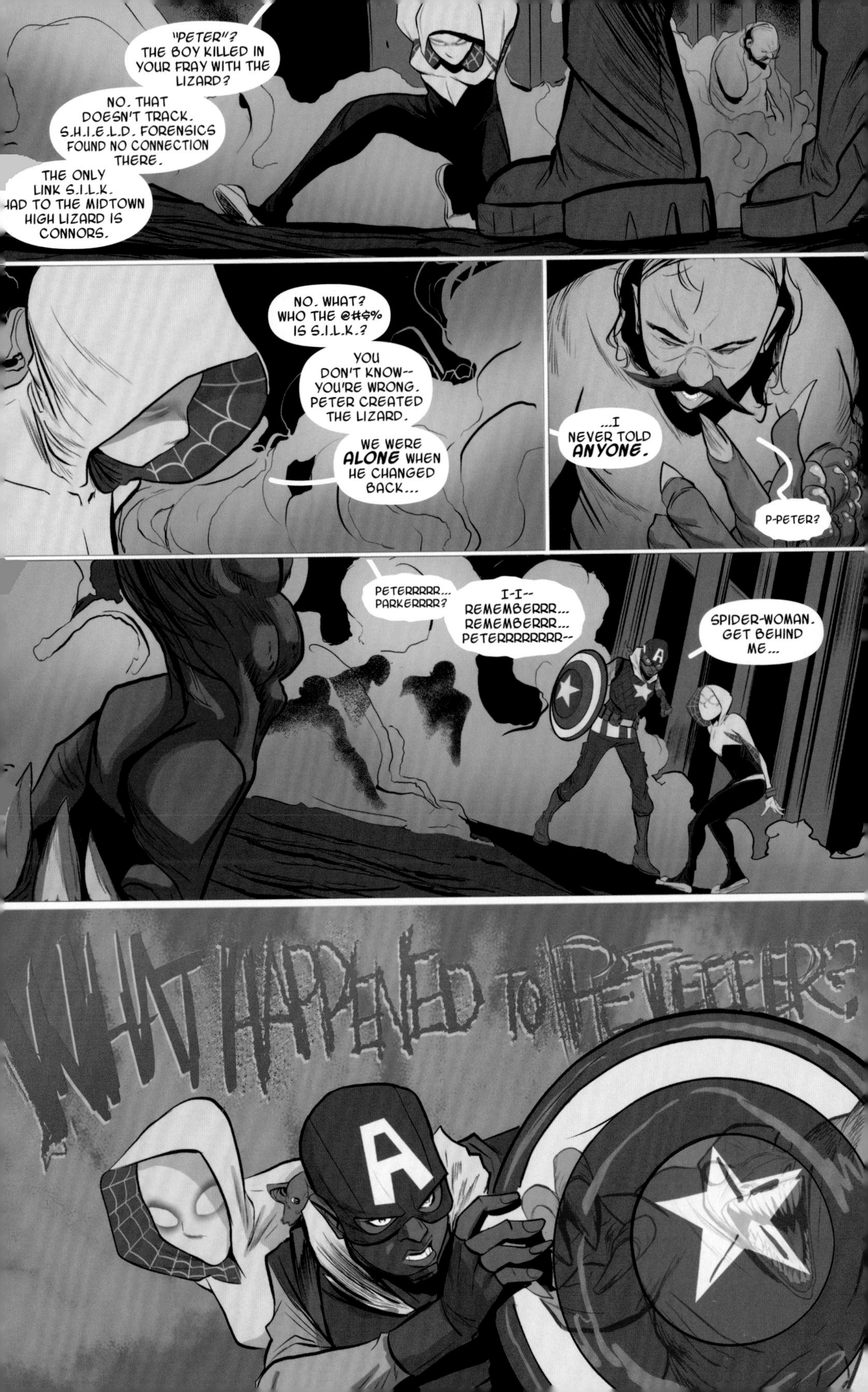
"PETER"? THE BOY KILLED IN YOUR FRAY WITH THE LIZARD?
NO. THAT DOESN'T TRACK. S.H.I.E.L.D. FORENSICS FOUND NO CONNECTION THERE.
THE ONLY LINK S.I.L.K. HAD TO THE MIDTOWN HIGH LIZARD IS CONNORS.
NO. WHAT? WHO THE @#$% IS S.I.L.K.?
YOU DON'T KNOW--YOU'RE WRONG. PETER CREATED THE LIZARD.
WE WERE **ALONE** WHEN HE CHANGED BACK...
...I NEVER TOLD **ANYONE.**
P-PETER?
PETERRRRR... PARKERRRR?
I-I-- REMEMBERRR... REMEMBERRR... PETERRRRRRRRR--
SPIDER-WOMAN. GET BEHIND ME...
WHAT HAPPENED TO PETEEEER?

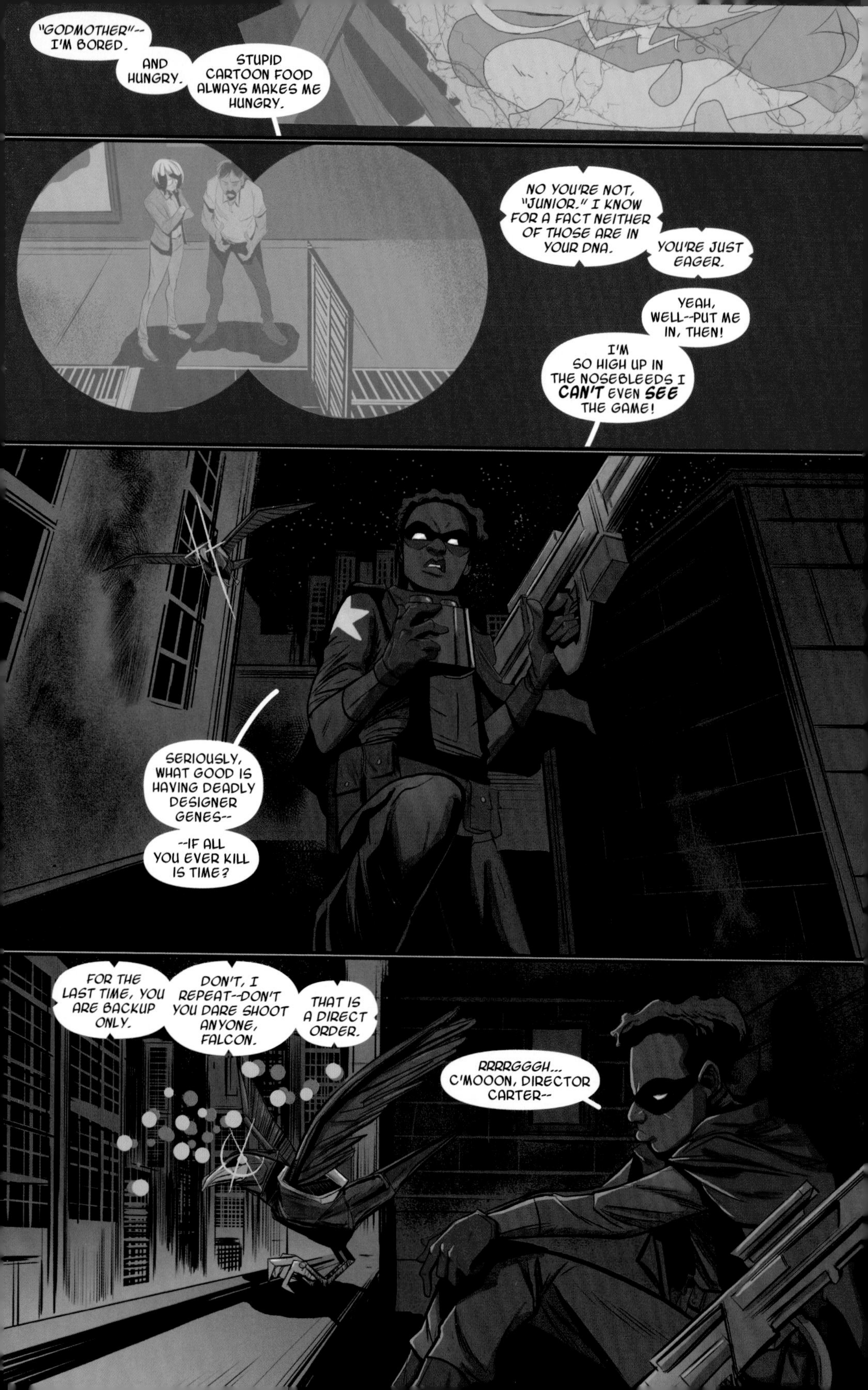
"GODMOTHER"-- I'M BORED.
AND HUNGRY.
STUPID CARTOON FOOD ALWAYS MAKES ME HUNGRY.
NO YOU'RE NOT, "JUNIOR." I KNOW FOR A FACT NEITHER OF THOSE ARE IN YOUR DNA.
YOU'RE JUST EAGER.
YEAH, WELL--PUT ME IN, THEN!
I'M SO HIGH UP IN THE NOSEBLEEDS I **CAN'T** EVEN **SEE** THE GAME!
SERIOUSLY, WHAT GOOD IS HAVING DEADLY DESIGNER GENES--
--IF ALL YOU EVER KILL IS TIME?
FOR THE LAST TIME, YOU ARE BACKUP ONLY.
DON'T, I REPEAT--DON'T YOU DARE SHOOT ANYONE, FALCON.
THAT IS A DIRECT ORDER.
RRRRGGGH... C'MOOON, DIRECTOR CARTER--

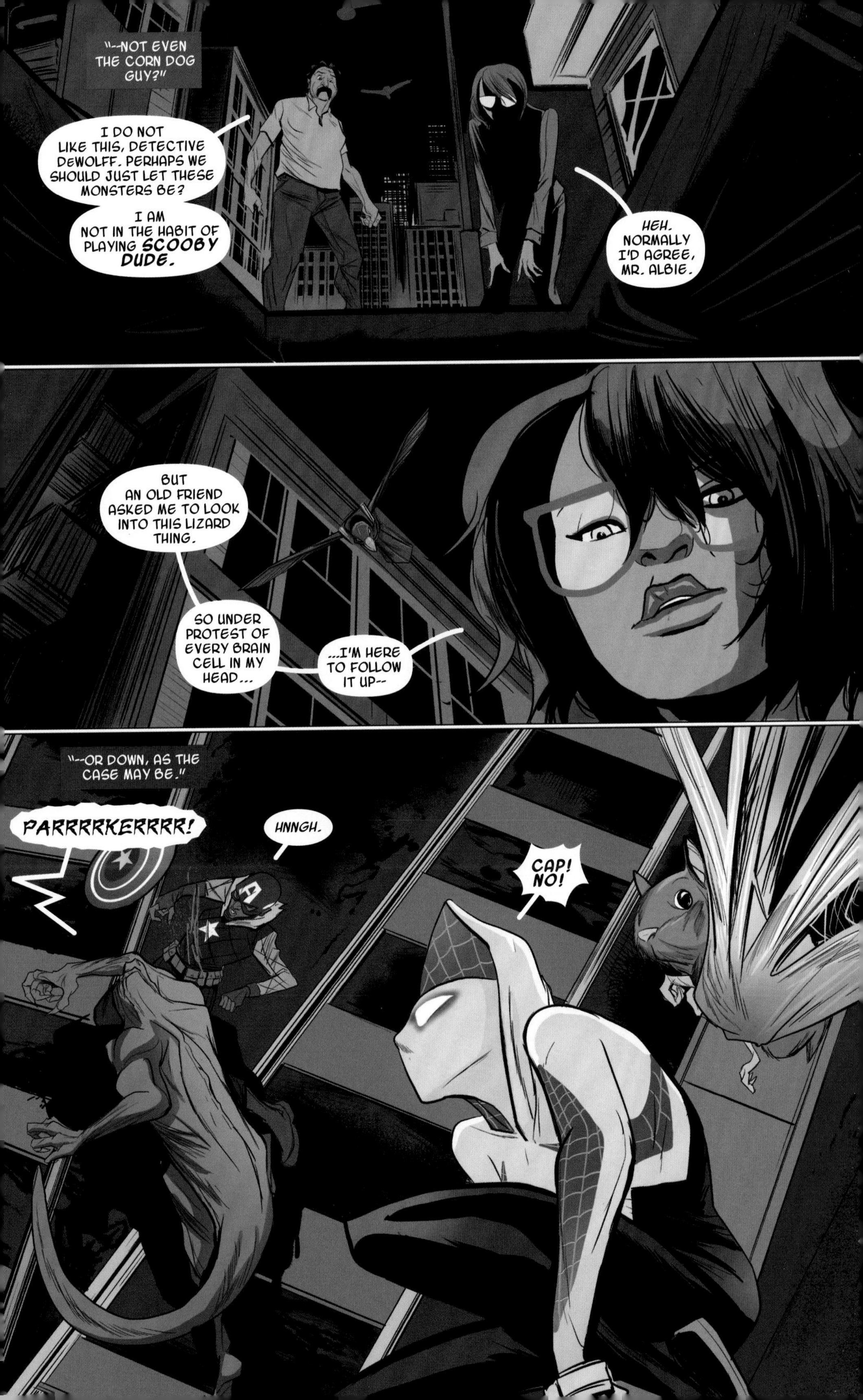
"--NOT EVEN THE CORN DOG GUY?"
I DO NOT LIKE THIS, DETECTIVE DeWOLFF. PERHAPS WE SHOULD JUST LET THESE MONSTERS BE?
I AM NOT IN THE HABIT OF PLAYING SCOOBY DUDE.
HEH. NORMALLY I'D AGREE, MR. ALBIE.
BUT AN OLD FRIEND ASKED ME TO LOOK INTO THIS LIZARD THING.
SO UNDER PROTEST OF EVERY BRAIN CELL IN MY HEAD...
...I'M HERE TO FOLLOW IT UP--
"--OR DOWN, AS THE CASE MAY BE."
PARRRRKERRRR!
HNNGH.
CAP! NO!

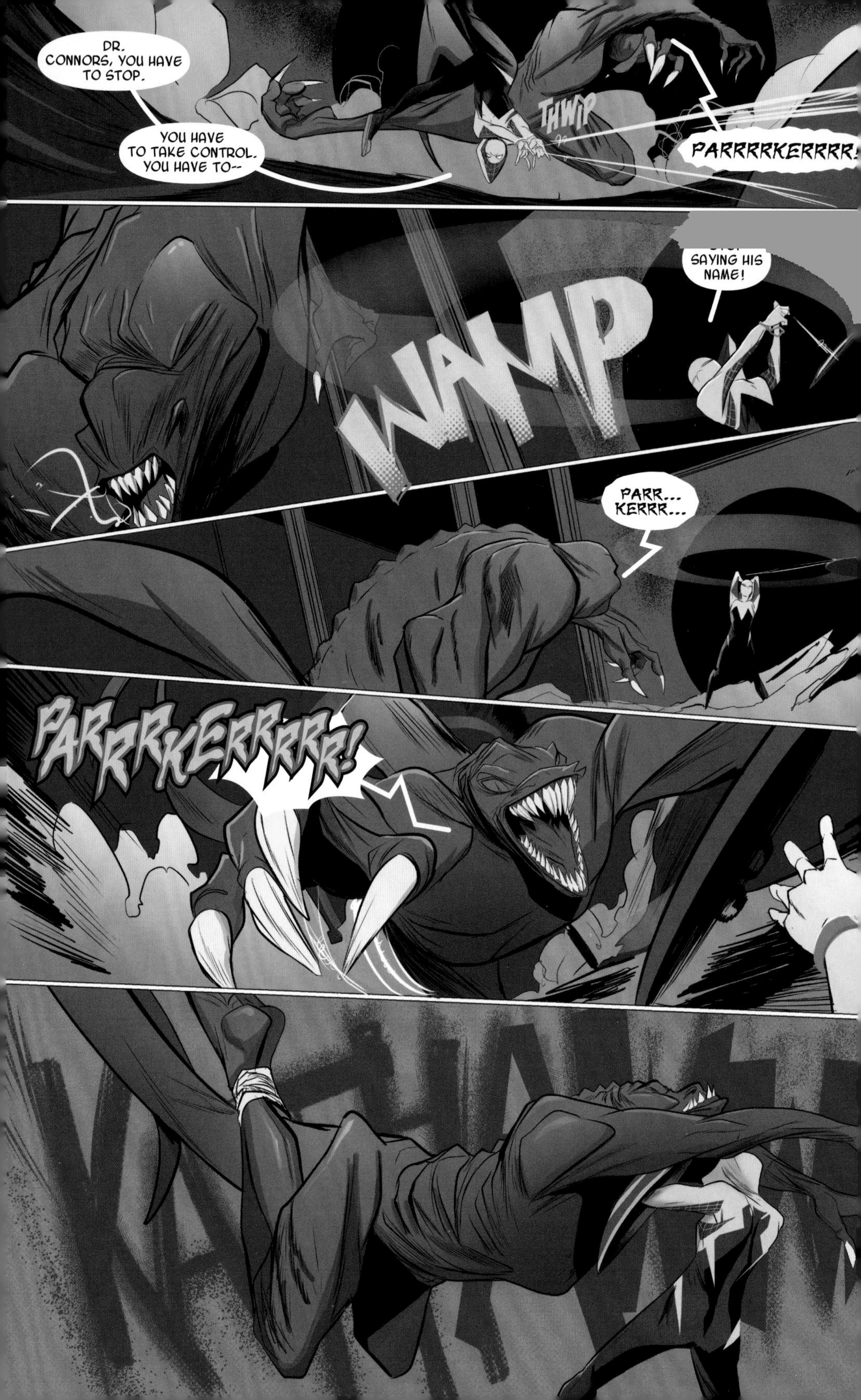
DR. CONNORS, YOU HAVE TO STOP.
YOU HAVE TO TAKE CONTROL. YOU HAVE TO--
THWIP
PARRRRKERRRR!
WAMP
SAYING HIS NAME!
PARR... KERRR...
PARRKERRRRR!

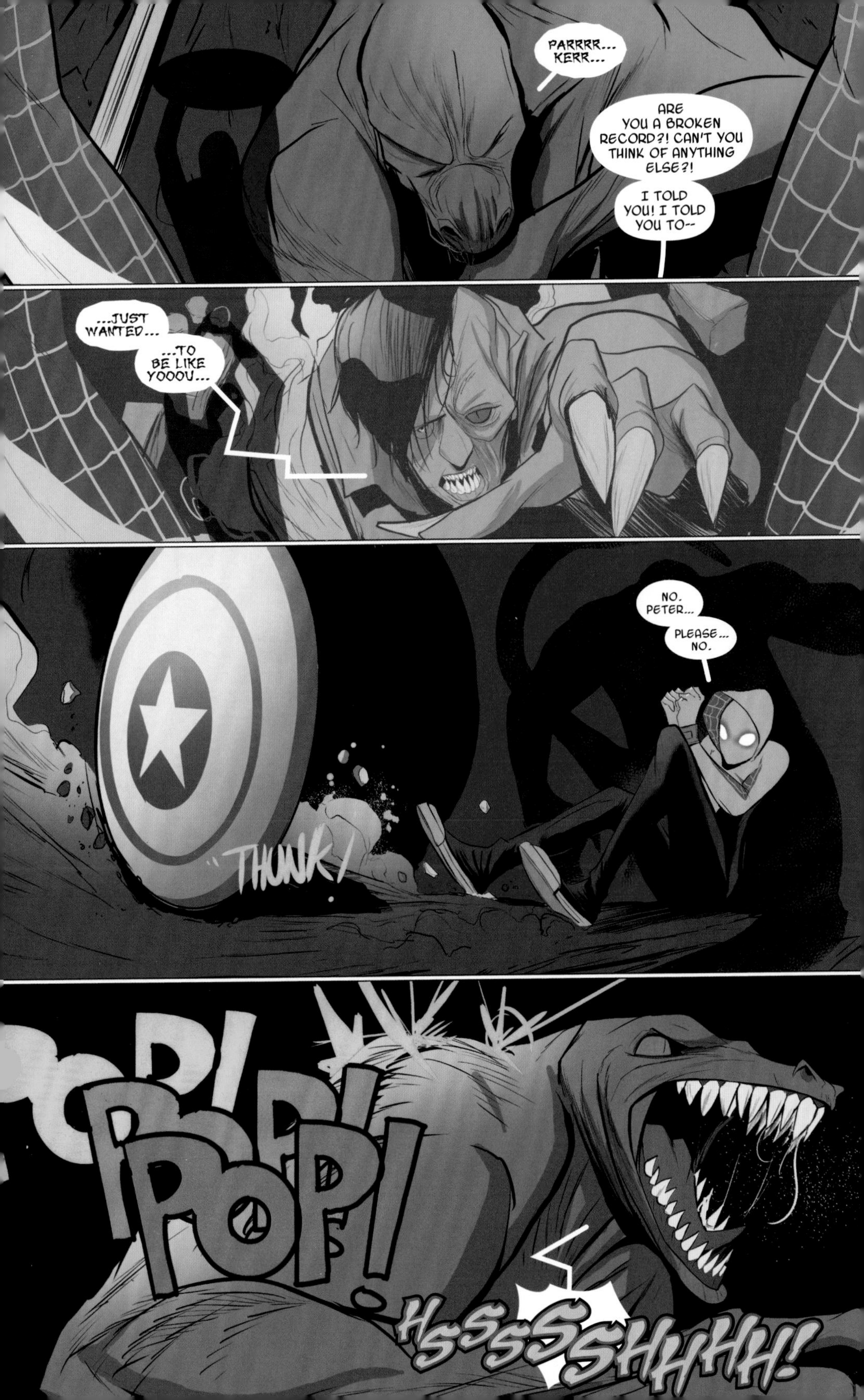
PARRRR... KERR...
ARE YOU A BROKEN RECORD?! CAN'T YOU THINK OF ANYTHING ELSE?!
I TOLD YOU! I TOLD YOU TO--
...JUST WANTED...
...TO BE LIKE YOOOU...
NO. PETER...
PLEASE... NO.
THUNK!
POP! POP!
HSSSSSHHHH!

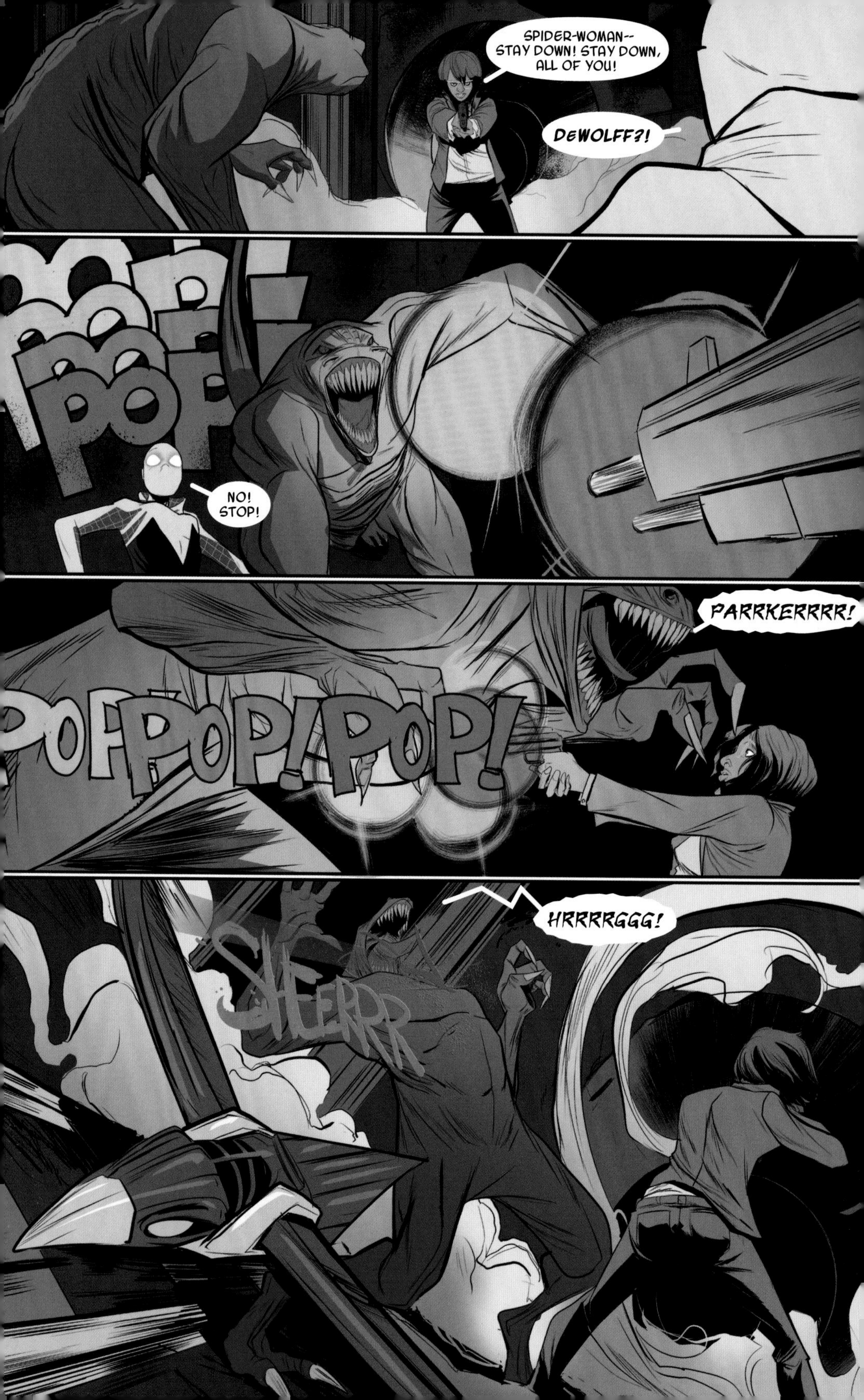

SPIDER-WOMAN-- STAY DOWN! STAY DOWN, ALL OF YOU!
DeWOLFF?!
POP! POP! POP!
NO! STOP!
PARRKERRRR!
POP! POP! POP! POP!
HRRRRGGG!
SHERRR

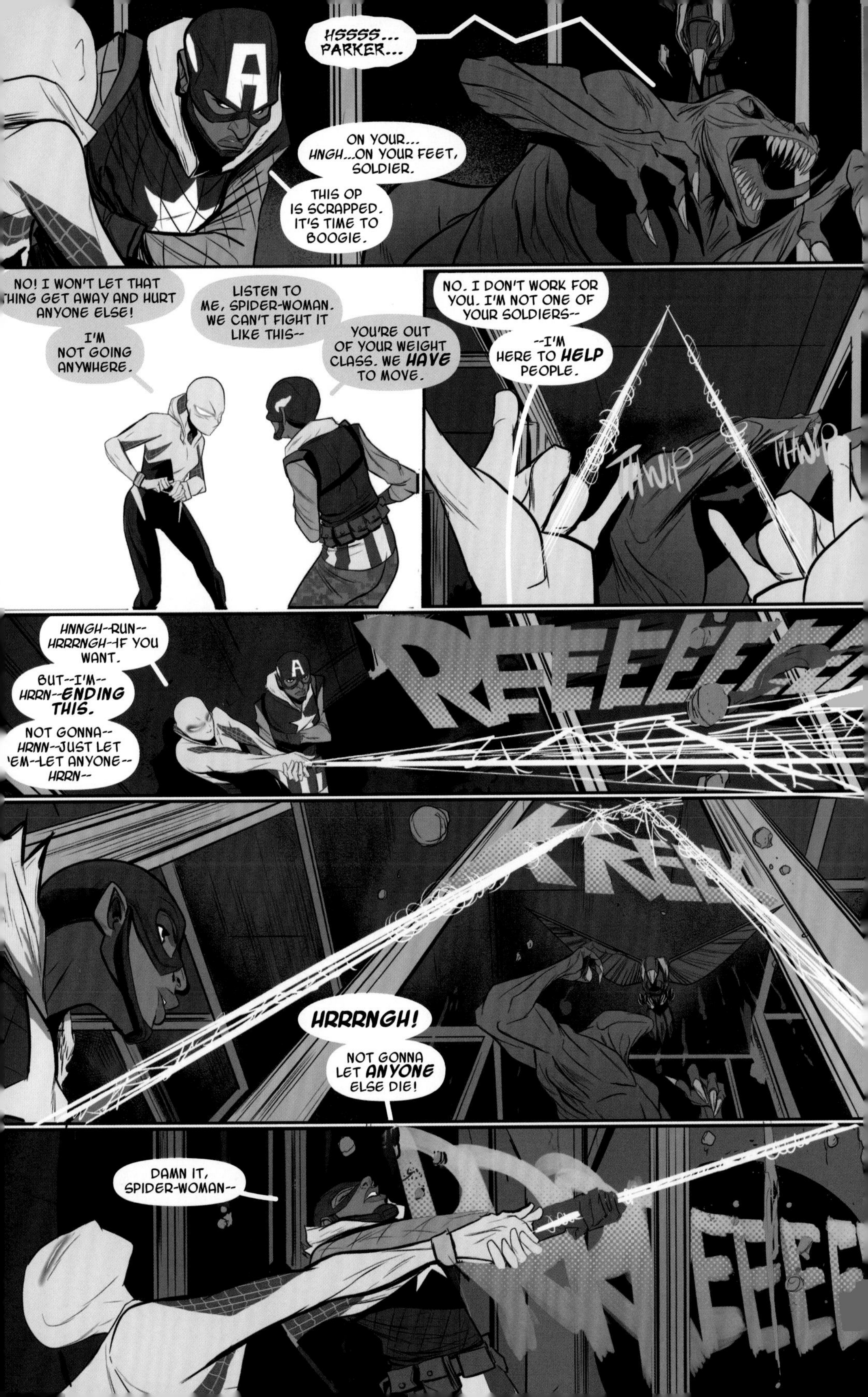
HSSSS... PARKER...
ON YOUR... HNGH...ON YOUR FEET, SOLDIER.
THIS OP IS SCRAPPED. IT'S TIME TO BOOGIE.
NO! I WON'T LET THAT THING GET AWAY AND HURT ANYONE ELSE!
I'M NOT GOING ANYWHERE.
LISTEN TO ME, SPIDER-WOMAN. WE CAN'T FIGHT IT LIKE THIS--
YOU'RE OUT OF YOUR WEIGHT CLASS. WE HAVE TO MOVE.
NO. I DON'T WORK FOR YOU. I'M NOT ONE OF YOUR SOLDIERS--
--I'M HERE TO HELP PEOPLE.
THWIP
THWIP
HNNGH--RUN-- HRRRNGH--IF YOU WANT.
BUT--I'M-- HRRN--ENDING THIS.
NOT GONNA-- HRNN--JUST LET 'EM--LET ANYONE-- HRRN--
REEEEEE
HRRRNGH!
NOT GONNA LET ANYONE ELSE DIE!
DAMN IT, SPIDER-WOMAN--

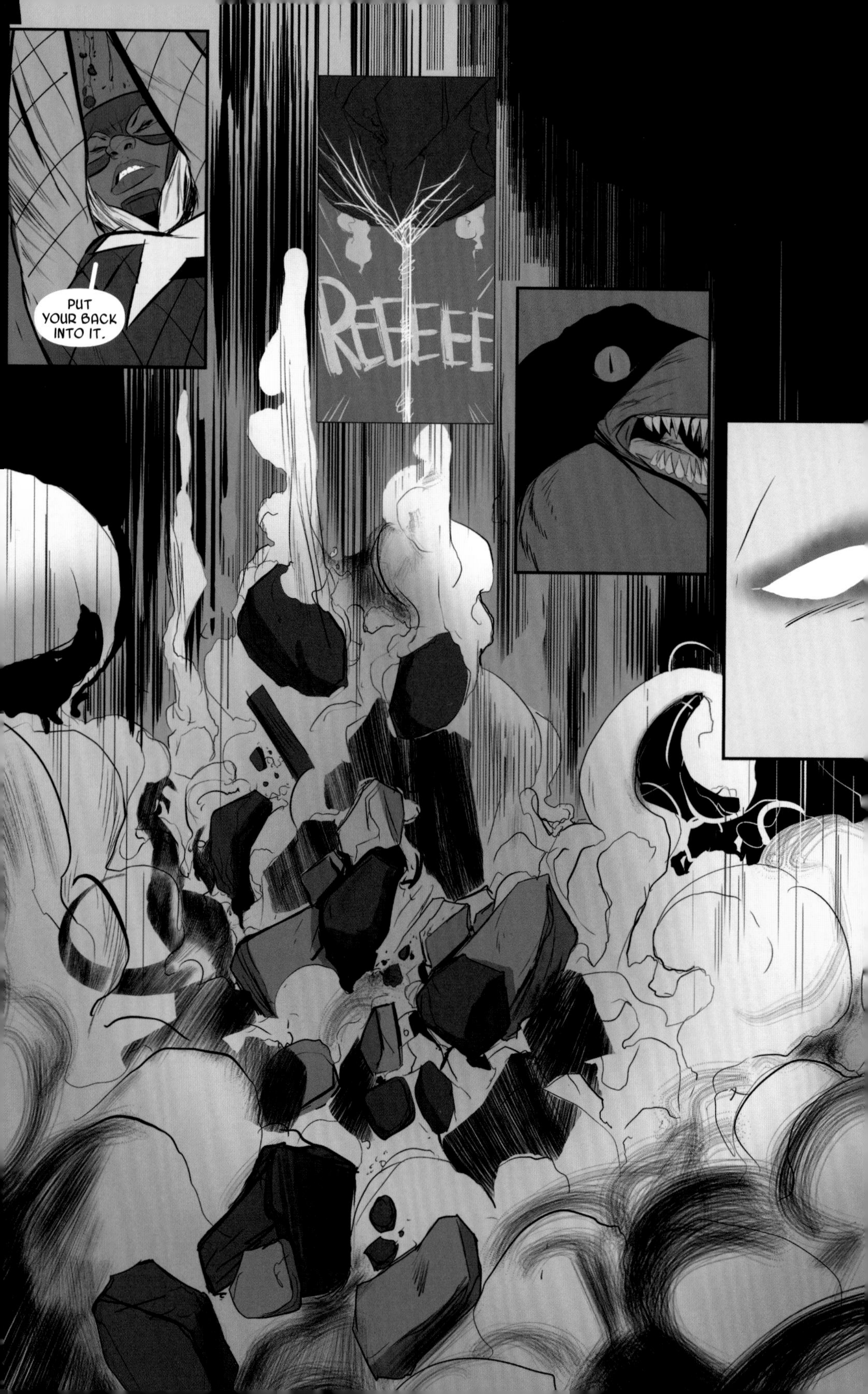
PUT YOUR BACK INTO IT.
REEEEE

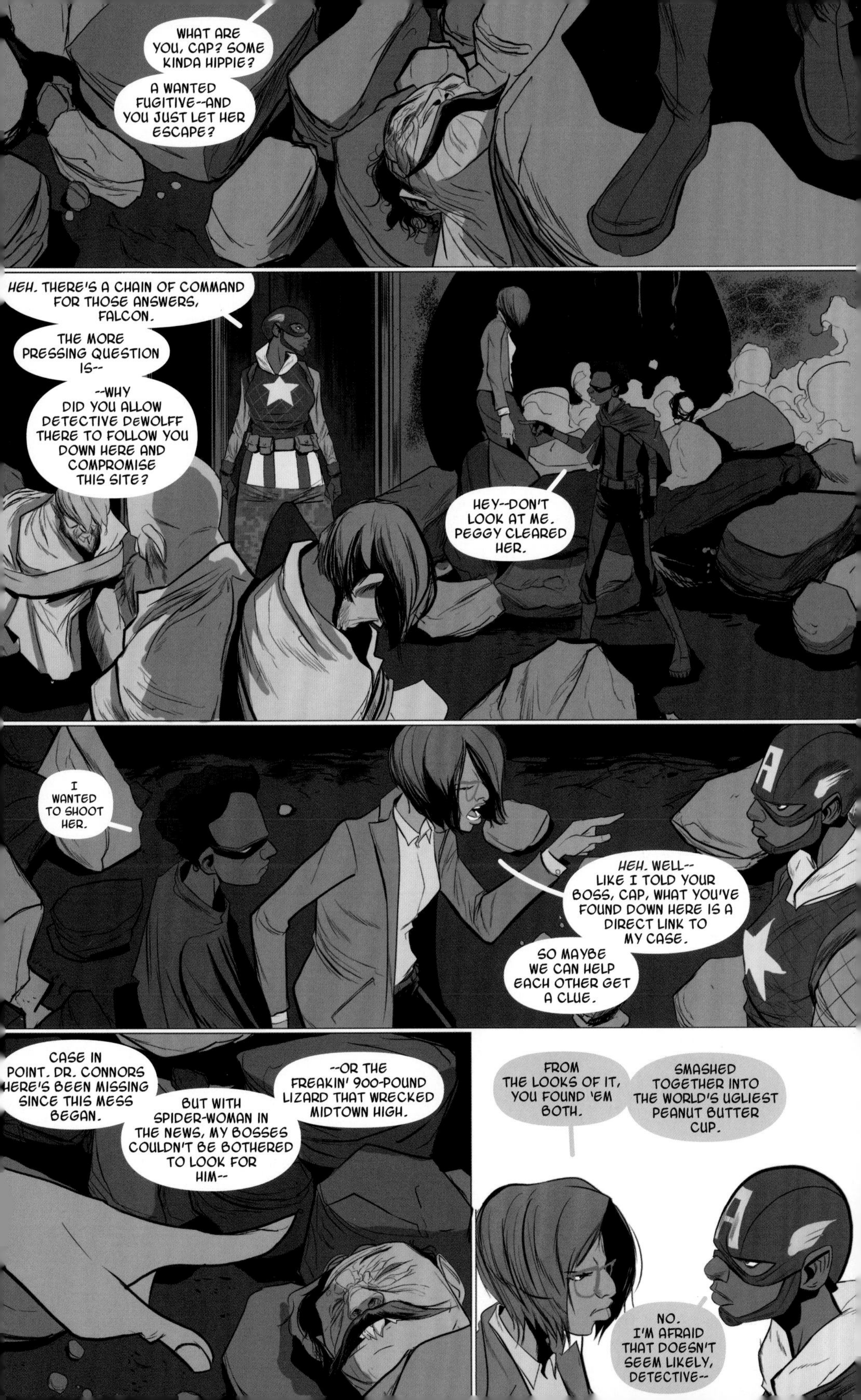
WHAT ARE YOU, CAP? SOME KINDA HIPPIE?
A WANTED FUGITIVE--AND YOU JUST LET HER ESCAPE?
HEH. THERE'S A CHAIN OF COMMAND FOR THOSE ANSWERS, FALCON.
THE MORE PRESSING QUESTION IS--
--WHY DID YOU ALLOW DETECTIVE DeWOLFF THERE TO FOLLOW YOU DOWN HERE AND COMPROMISE THIS SITE?
HEY--DON'T LOOK AT ME. PEGGY CLEARED HER.
I WANTED TO SHOOT HER.
HEH. WELL-- LIKE I TOLD YOUR BOSS, CAP, WHAT YOU'VE FOUND DOWN HERE IS A DIRECT LINK TO MY CASE.
SO MAYBE WE CAN HELP EACH OTHER GET A CLUE.
CASE IN POINT. DR. CONNORS HERE'S BEEN MISSING SINCE THIS MESS BEGAN.
BUT WITH SPIDER-WOMAN IN THE NEWS, MY BOSSES COULDN'T BE BOTHERED TO LOOK FOR HIM--
--OR THE FREAKIN' 900-POUND LIZARD THAT WRECKED MIDTOWN HIGH.
FROM THE LOOKS OF IT, YOU FOUND 'EM BOTH.
SMASHED TOGETHER INTO THE WORLD'S UGLIEST PEANUT BUTTER CUP.
NO. I'M AFRAID THAT DOESN'T SEEM LIKELY, DETECTIVE--

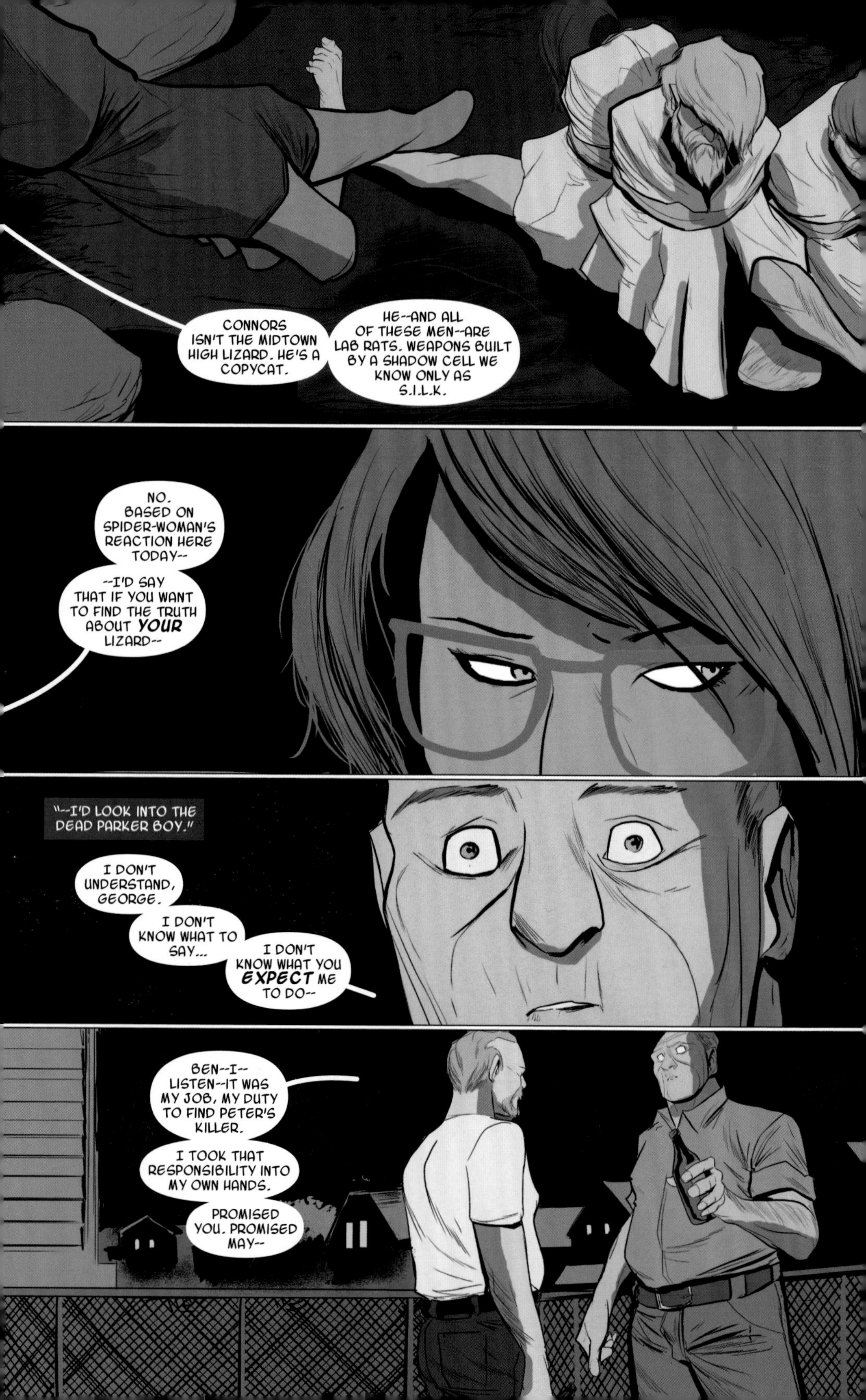
CONNORS ISN'T THE MIDTOWN HIGH LIZARD. HE'S A COPYCAT.
HE--AND ALL OF THESE MEN--ARE LAB RATS. WEAPONS BUILT BY A SHADOW CELL WE KNOW ONLY AS S.I.L.K.
NO. BASED ON SPIDER-WOMAN'S REACTION HERE TODAY--
--I'D SAY THAT IF YOU WANT TO FIND THE TRUTH ABOUT YOUR LIZARD--
"--I'D LOOK INTO THE DEAD PARKER BOY."
I DON'T UNDERSTAND, GEORGE.
I DON'T KNOW WHAT TO SAY...
I DON'T KNOW WHAT YOU EXPECT ME TO DO--
BEN--I-- LISTEN--IT WAS MY JOB, MY DUTY TO FIND PETER'S KILLER.
I TOOK THAT RESPONSIBILITY INTO MY OWN HANDS.
PROMISED YOU. PROMISED MAY--

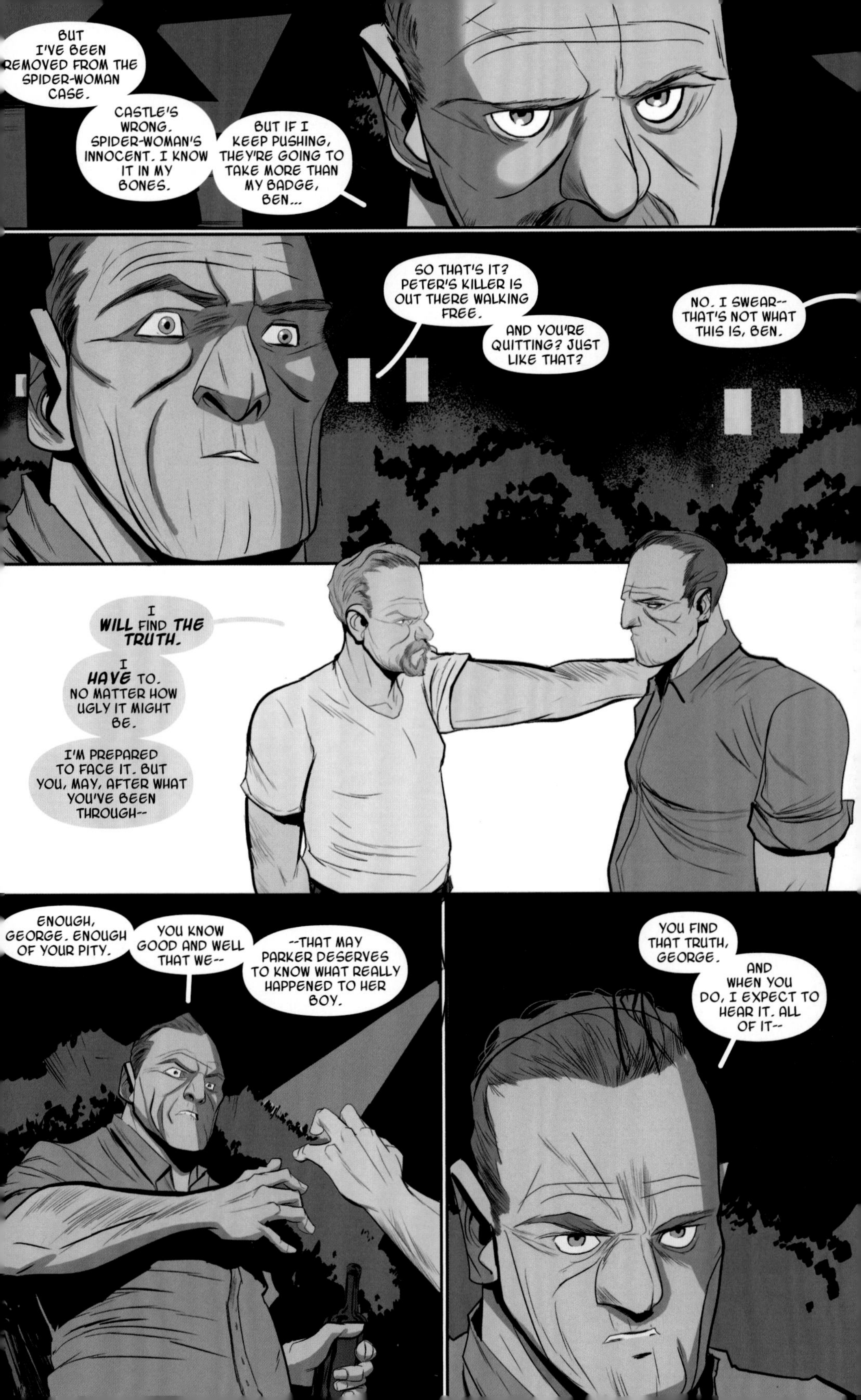
BUT I'VE BEEN REMOVED FROM THE SPIDER-WOMAN CASE.
CASTLE'S WRONG. SPIDER-WOMAN'S INNOCENT. I KNOW IT IN MY BONES.
BUT IF I KEEP PUSHING, THEY'RE GOING TO TAKE MORE THAN MY BADGE, BEN...
SO THAT'S IT? PETER'S KILLER IS OUT THERE WALKING FREE.
AND YOU'RE QUITTING? JUST LIKE THAT?
NO. I SWEAR-- THAT'S NOT WHAT THIS IS, BEN.
I WILL FIND THE TRUTH.
I HAVE TO. NO MATTER HOW UGLY IT MIGHT BE.
I'M PREPARED TO FACE IT. BUT YOU, MAY, AFTER WHAT YOU'VE BEEN THROUGH--
ENOUGH, GEORGE. ENOUGH OF YOUR PITY.
YOU KNOW GOOD AND WELL THAT WE--
--THAT MAY PARKER DESERVES TO KNOW WHAT REALLY HAPPENED TO HER BOY.
YOU FIND THAT TRUTH, GEORGE.
AND WHEN YOU DO, I EXPECT TO HEAR IT. ALL OF IT--

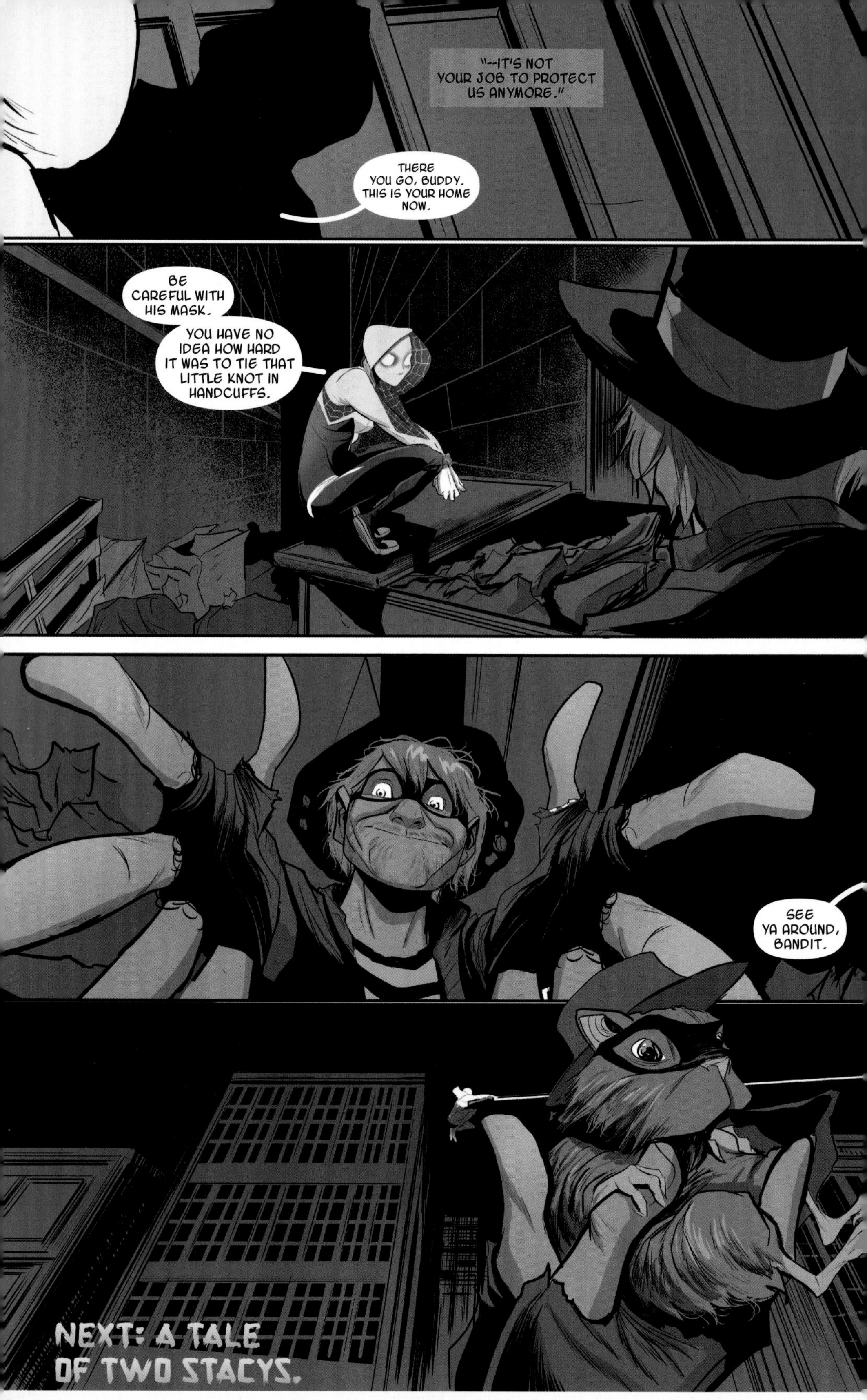
"--IT'S NOT YOUR JOB TO PROTECT US ANYMORE."
THERE YOU GO, BUDDY. THIS IS YOUR HOME NOW.
BE CAREFUL WITH HIS MASK.
YOU HAVE NO IDEA HOW HARD IT WAS TO TIE THAT LITTLE KNOT IN HANDCUFFS.
SEE YA AROUND, BANDIT.
NEXT: A TALE OF TWO STACYS.

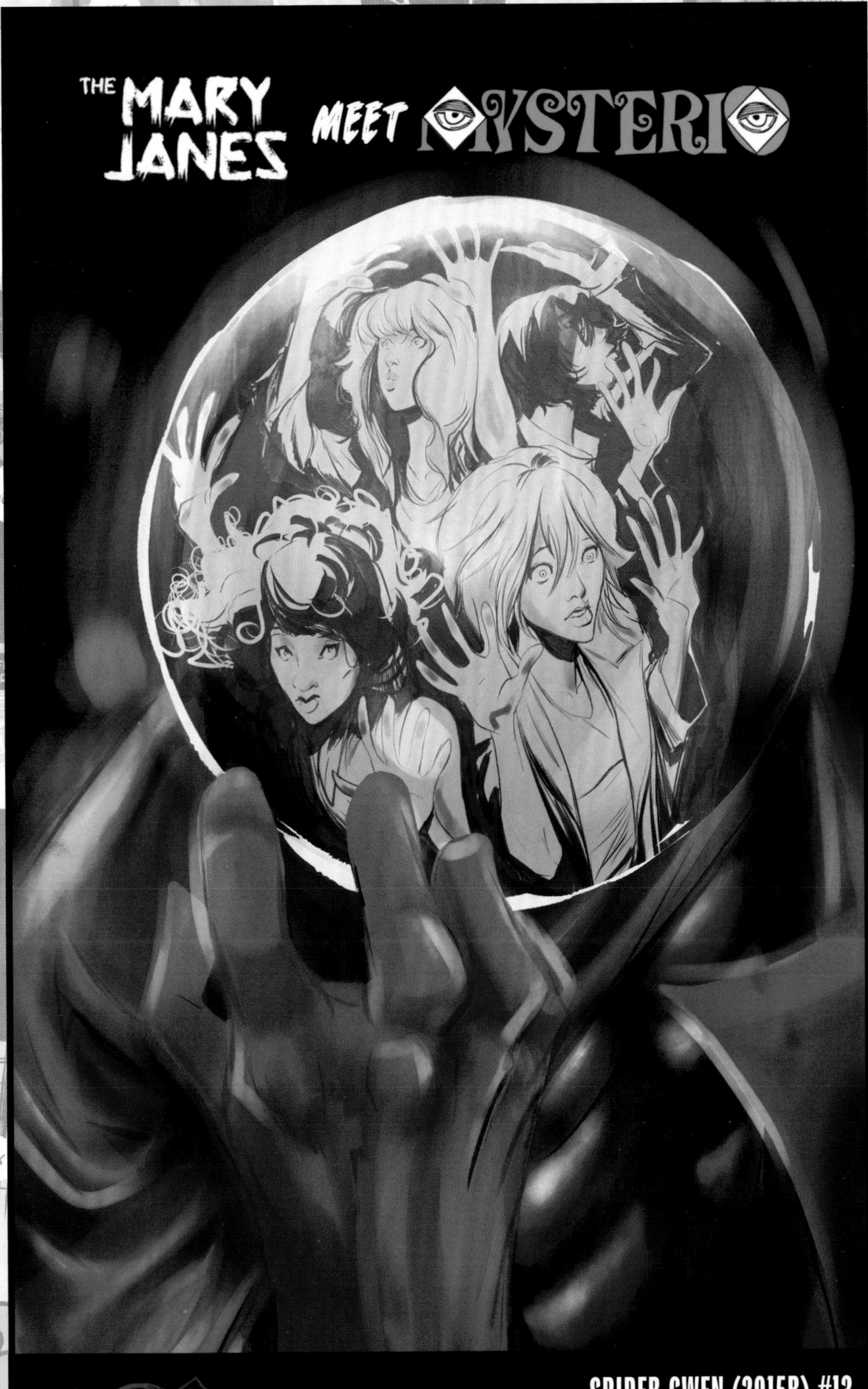
THE MARY JANES MEET MYSTERIO

SPIDER-GWEN (2015B) #13

THE MARY JANES ARE IN FOR A TRICK WHEN THEY VISIT MYSTERIO'S HAUNTED HOUSE!

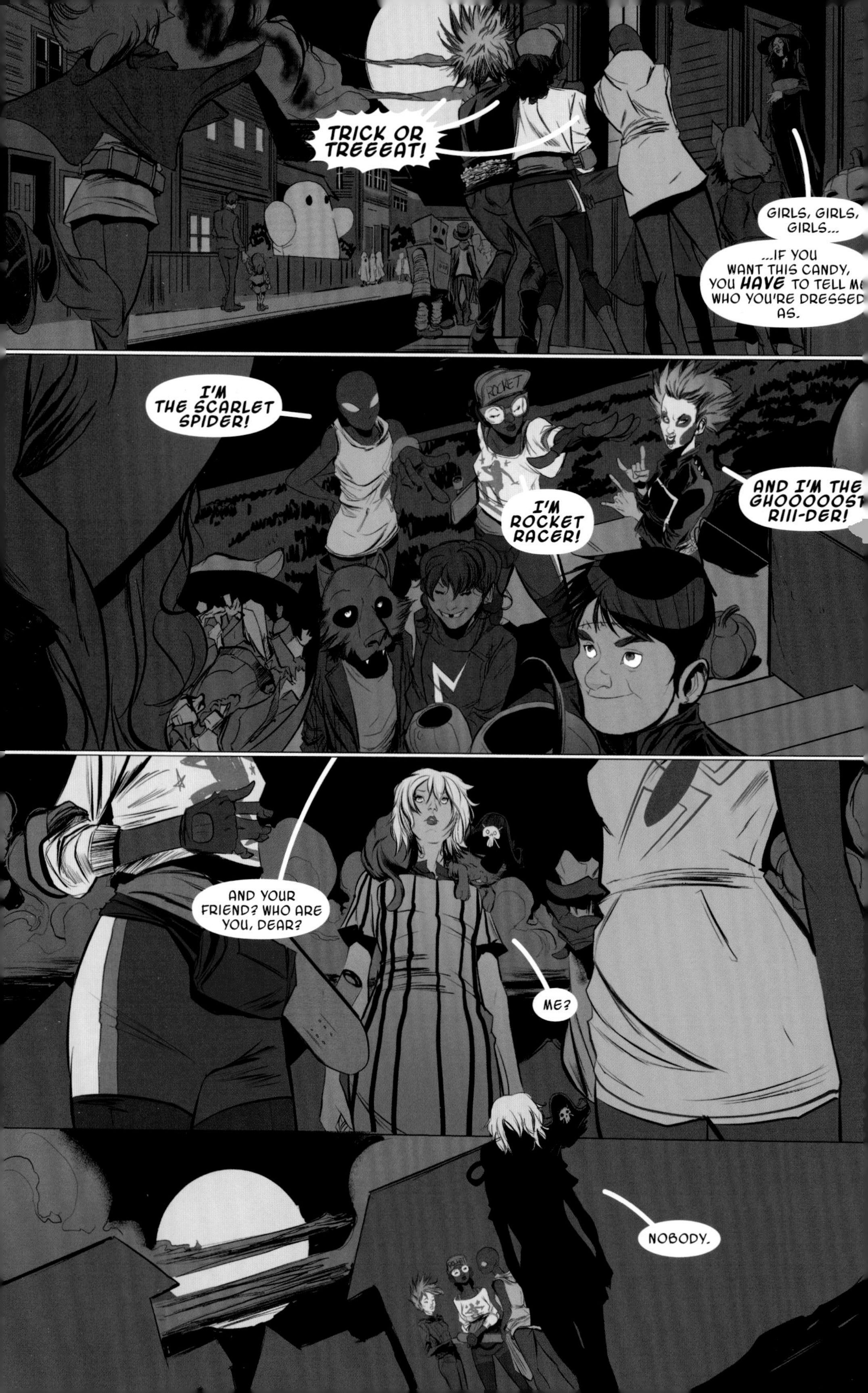
TRICK OR TREEEAT!
GIRLS, GIRLS, GIRLS...
...IF YOU WANT THIS CANDY, YOU HAVE TO TELL ME WHO YOU'RE DRESSED AS.
I'M THE SCARLET SPIDER!
ROCKET
I'M ROCKET RACER!
AND I'M THE GHOOOOOST RIII-DER!
AND YOUR FRIEND? WHO ARE YOU, DEAR?
ME?
NOBODY.

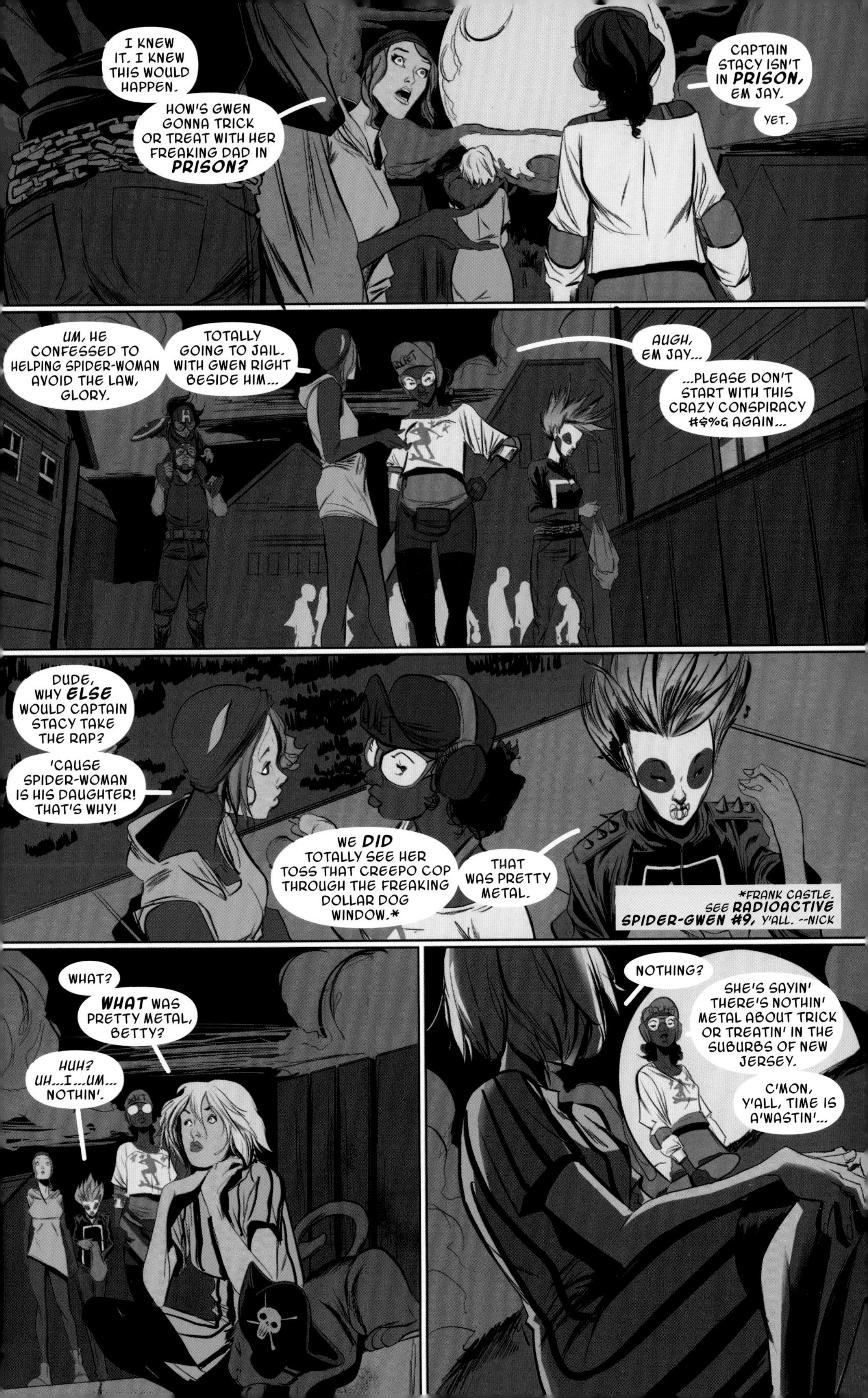
I KNEW IT. I KNEW THIS WOULD HAPPEN.
HOW'S GWEN GONNA TRICK OR TREAT WITH HER FREAKING DAD IN PRISON?
CAPTAIN STACY ISN'T IN PRISON, EM JAY.
YET.
UM, HE CONFESSED TO HELPING SPIDER-WOMAN AVOID THE LAW, GLORY.
TOTALLY GOING TO JAIL. WITH GWEN RIGHT BESIDE HIM...
AUGH, EM JAY...
...PLEASE DON'T START WITH THIS CRAZY CONSPIRACY #$%G AGAIN...
DUDE, WHY ELSE WOULD CAPTAIN STACY TAKE THE RAP?
'CAUSE SPIDER-WOMAN IS HIS DAUGHTER! THAT'S WHY!
WE DID TOTALLY SEE HER TOSS THAT CREEPO COP THROUGH THE FREAKING DOLLAR DOG WINDOW.*
THAT WAS PRETTY METAL.
*FRANK CASTLE. SEE RADIOACTIVE SPIDER-GWEN #9, Y'ALL. --NICK
WHAT? WHAT WAS PRETTY METAL, BETTY?
HUH? UH...I...UM... NOTHIN'.
NOTHING?
SHE'S SAYIN' THERE'S NOTHIN' METAL ABOUT TRICK OR TREATIN' IN THE SUBURBS OF NEW JERSEY.
C'MON, Y'ALL, TIME IS A'WASTIN'...

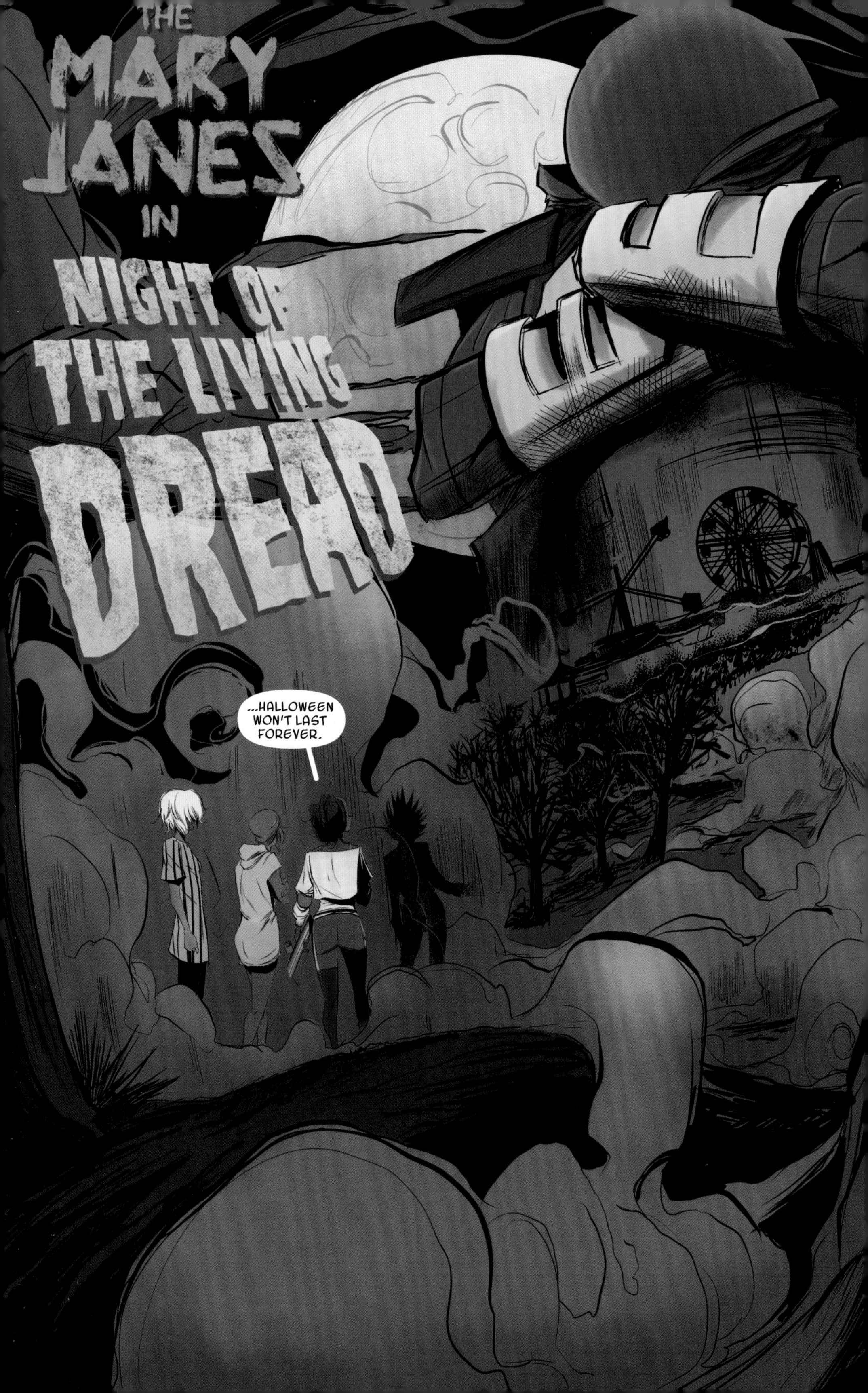
THE MARY JANES IN
NIGHT OF THE LIVING DREAD
...HALLOWEEN WON'T LAST FOREVER.

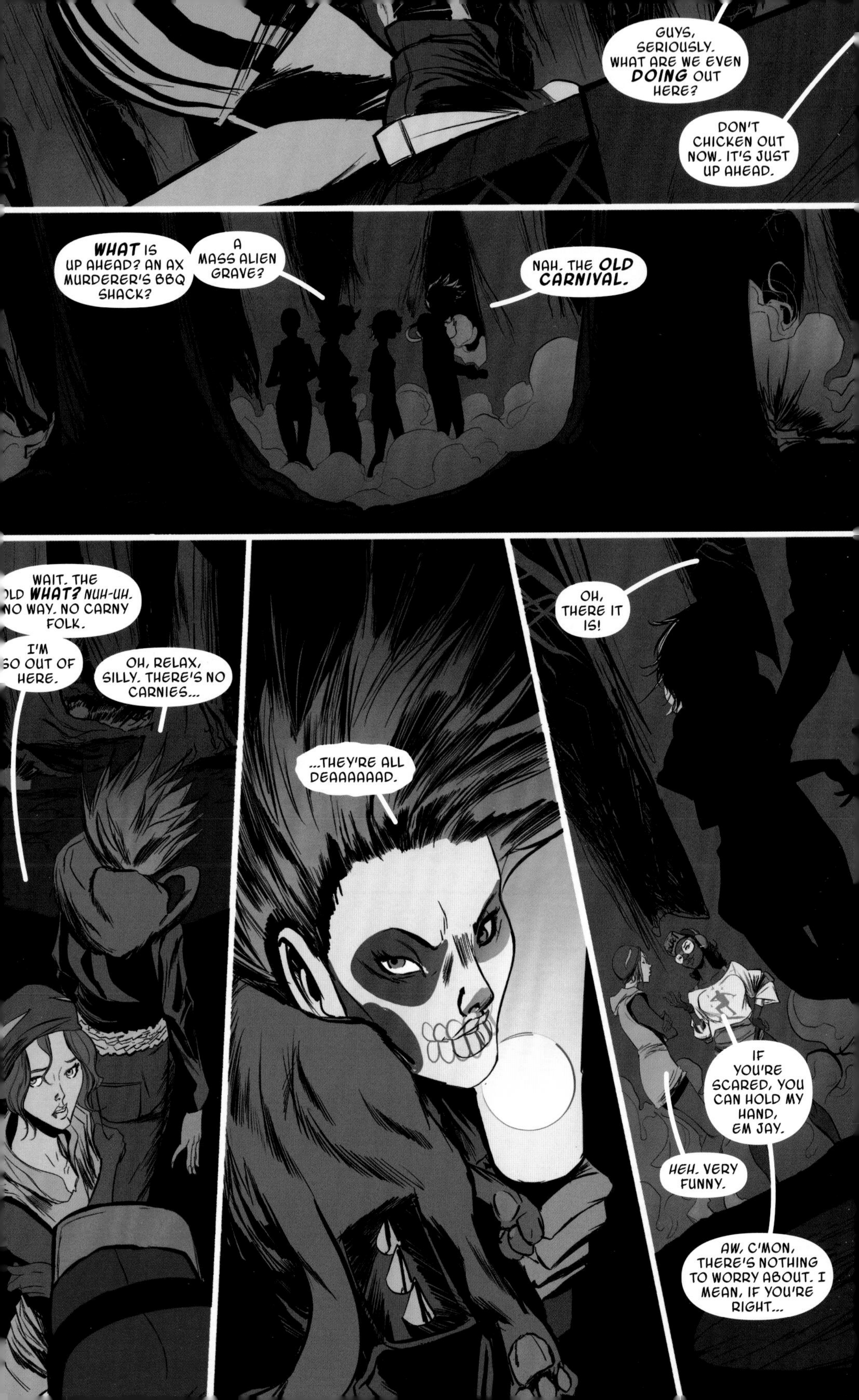
GUYS, SERIOUSLY. WHAT ARE WE EVEN DOING OUT HERE?
DON'T CHICKEN OUT NOW. IT'S JUST UP AHEAD.
WHAT IS UP AHEAD? AN AX MURDERER'S BBQ SHACK?
A MASS ALIEN GRAVE?
NAH. THE OLD CARNIVAL.
WAIT. THE LD WHAT? NUH-UH. NO WAY. NO CARNY FOLK.
I'M SO OUT OF HERE.
OH, RELAX, SILLY. THERE'S NO CARNIES...
...THEY'RE ALL DEAAAAAAD.
OH, THERE IT IS!
IF YOU'RE SCARED, YOU CAN HOLD MY HAND, EM JAY.
HEH. VERY FUNNY.
AW, C'MON, THERE'S NOTHING TO WORRY ABOUT. I MEAN, IF YOU'RE RIGHT...

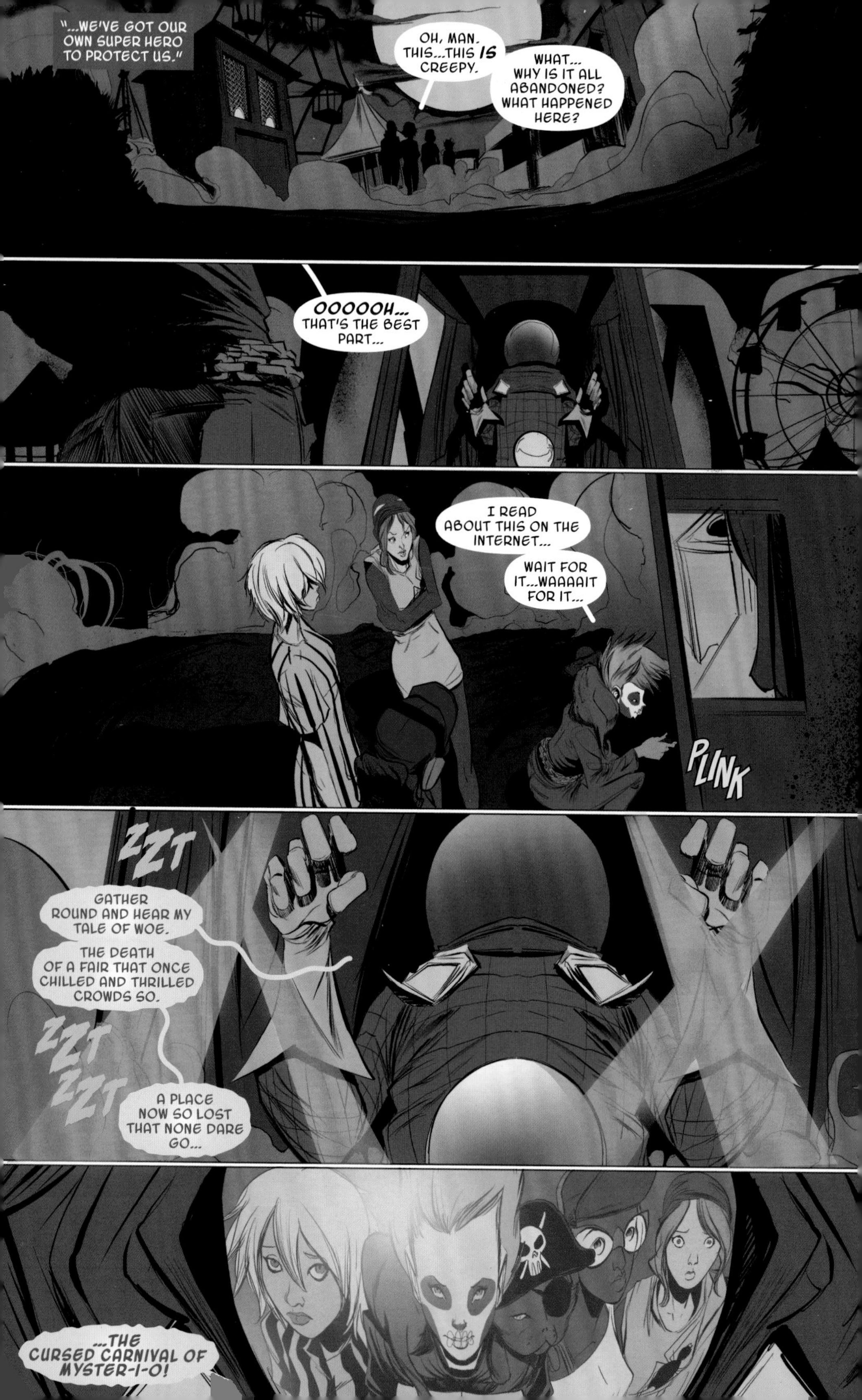

"...WE'VE GOT OUR OWN SUPER HERO TO PROTECT US."
OH, MAN. THIS...THIS IS CREEPY.
WHAT... WHY IS IT ALL ABANDONED? WHAT HAPPENED HERE?
OOOOOH... THAT'S THE BEST PART...
I READ ABOUT THIS ON THE INTERNET...
WAIT FOR IT...WAAAAIT FOR IT...
PLINK
ZZT
GATHER ROUND AND HEAR MY TALE OF WOE.
THE DEATH OF A FAIR THAT ONCE CHILLED AND THRILLED CROWDS SO.
ZZT
ZZT
A PLACE NOW SO LOST THAT NONE DARE GO...
...THE CURSED CARNIVAL OF MYSTER-I-O!

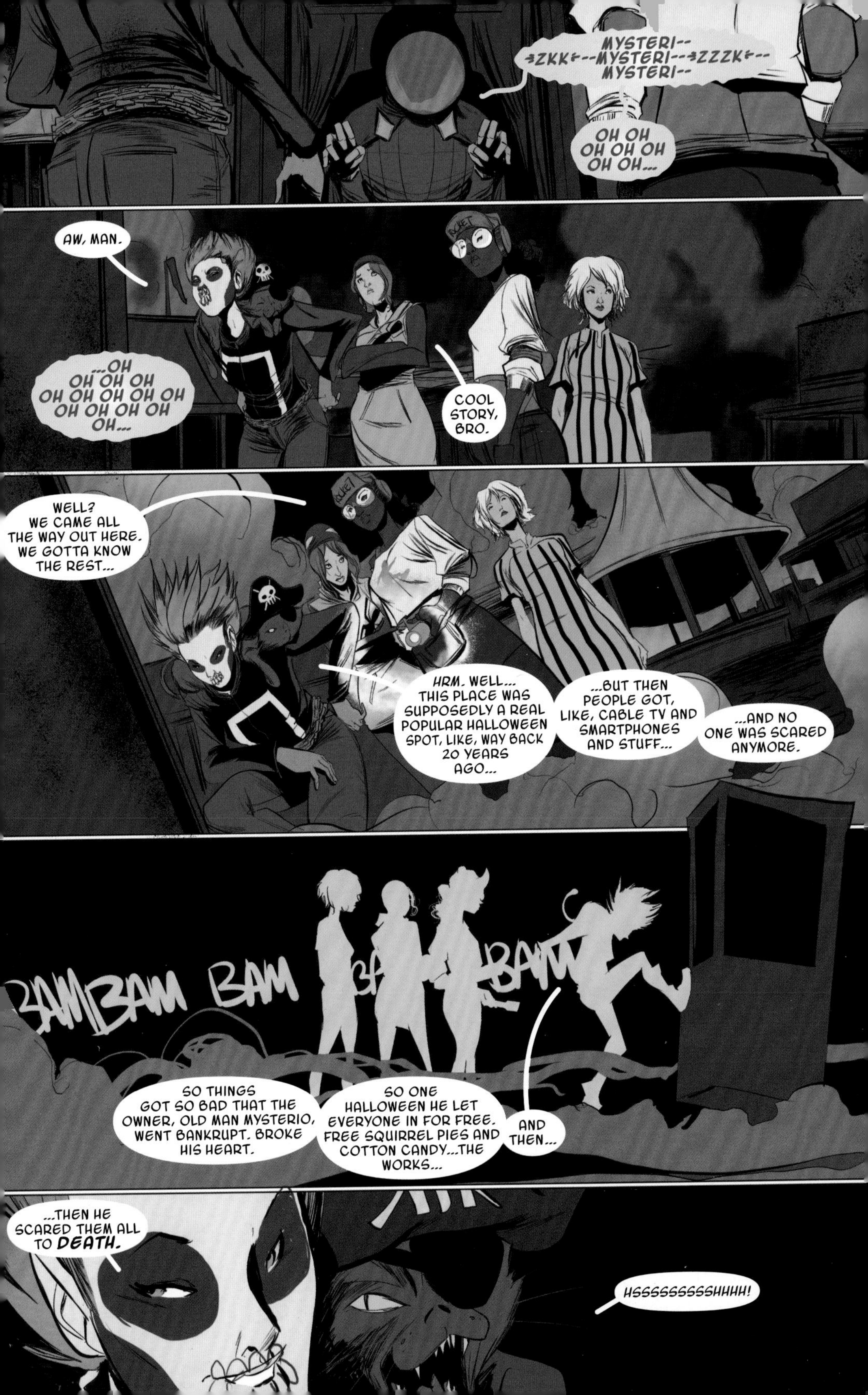
MYSTERI-- ZKK--MYSTERI--ZZZK-- MYSTERI--
OH OH OH OH OH OH OH...
AW, MAN.
...OH OH OH OH OH OH OH OH OH OH OH OH OH OH...
COOL STORY, BRO.
WELL? WE CAME ALL THE WAY OUT HERE. WE GOTTA KNOW THE REST...
HRM. WELL... THIS PLACE WAS SUPPOSEDLY A REAL POPULAR HALLOWEEN SPOT, LIKE, WAY BACK 20 YEARS AGO...
...BUT THEN PEOPLE GOT, LIKE, CABLE TV AND SMARTPHONES AND STUFF...
...AND NO ONE WAS SCARED ANYMORE.
BAMBAM BAM
SO THINGS GOT SO BAD THAT THE OWNER, OLD MAN MYSTERIO, WENT BANKRUPT. BROKE HIS HEART.
SO ONE HALLOWEEN HE LET EVERYONE IN FOR FREE. FREE SQUIRREL PIES AND COTTON CANDY...THE WORKS...
AND THEN...
...THEN HE SCARED THEM ALL TO **DEATH.**
HSSSSSSSSSHHHH!

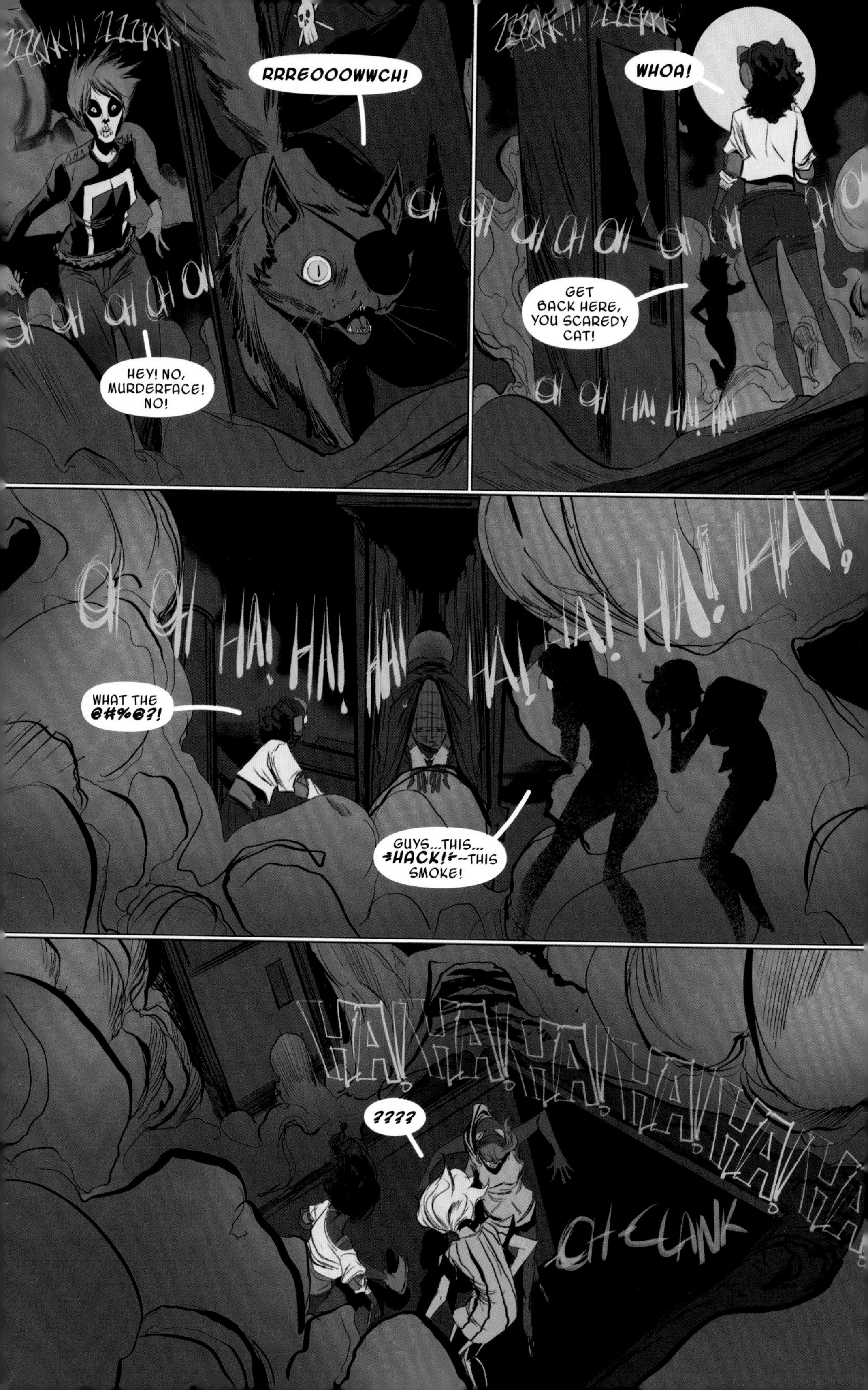
ZZZZAK!!! ZZZZCLAK!
RRREOOOWWCH!
HEY! NO, MURDERFACE! NO!
ZZZAK!!! ZZZCLAK!
WHOA!
GET BACK HERE, YOU SCAREDY CAT!
HA! HA! HA!
HA! HA! HA! HA! HA! HA!
WHAT THE @#%@?!
GUYS...THIS... *HACK!*--THIS SMOKE!
HA! HA! HA! HA! HA! HA! HA! HA!
????
CH-CLANK

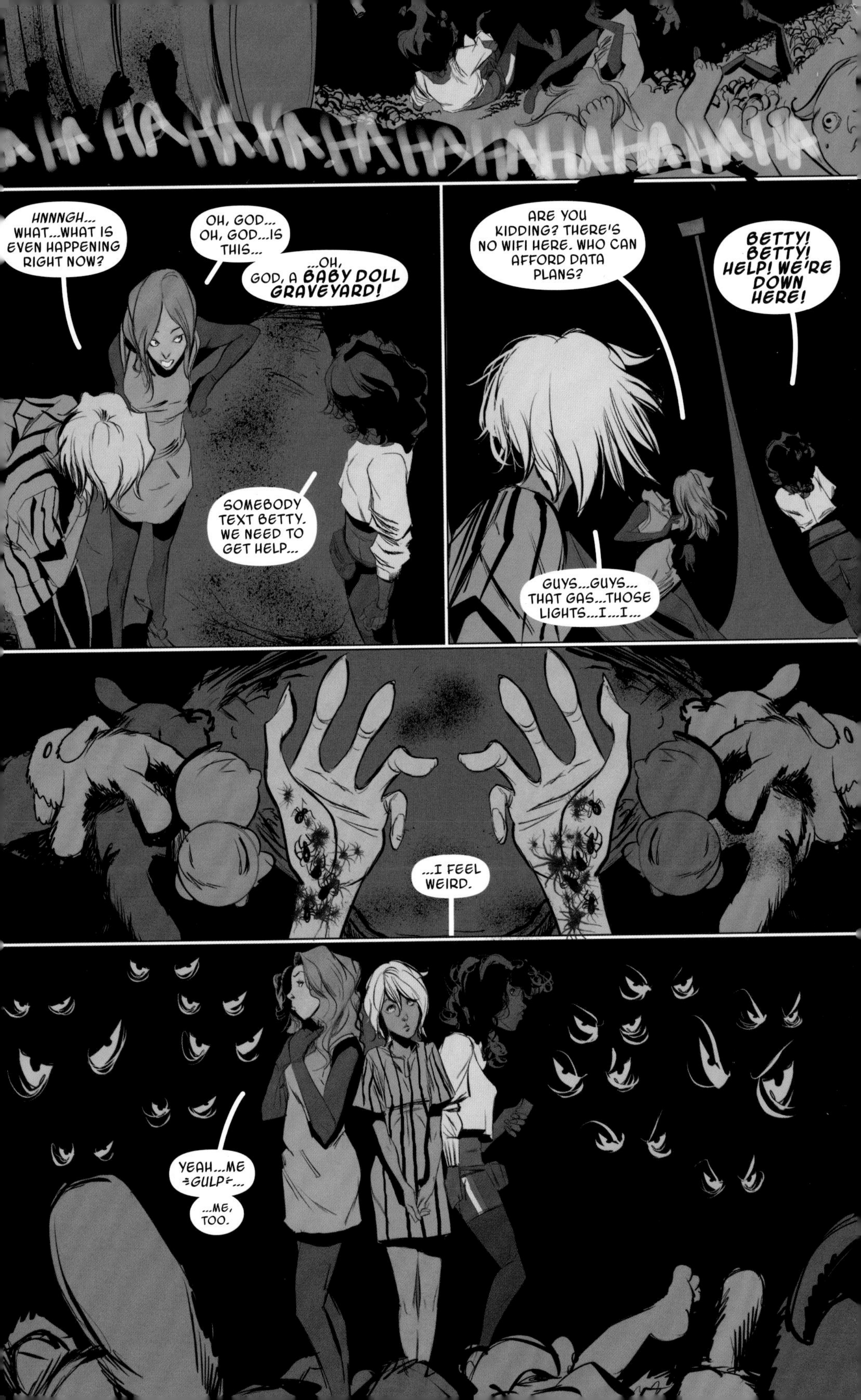
HAHAHAHAHAHAHAHAHAHAHAHA
HNNNGH... WHAT...WHAT IS EVEN HAPPENING RIGHT NOW?
OH, GOD... OH, GOD...IS THIS...
...OH, GOD, A BABY DOLL GRAVEYARD!
SOMEBODY TEXT BETTY. WE NEED TO GET HELP...
ARE YOU KIDDING? THERE'S NO WIFI HERE. WHO CAN AFFORD DATA PLANS?
BETTY! BETTY! HELP! WE'RE DOWN HERE!
GUYS...GUYS... THAT GAS...THOSE LIGHTS...I...I...
...I FEEL WEIRD.
YEAH...ME =GULP=...
...ME, TOO.

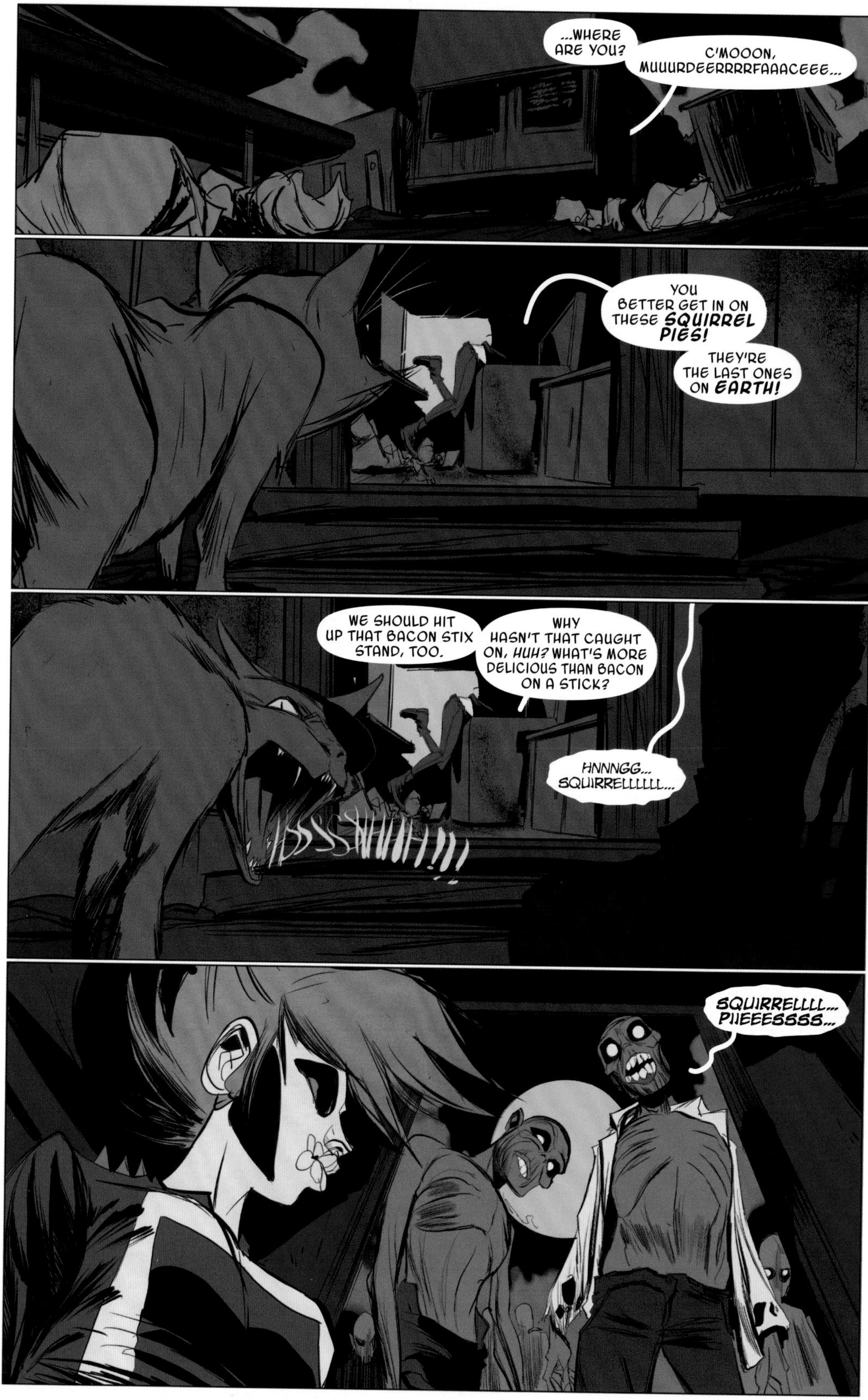
...WHERE ARE YOU?
C'MOOON, MUUURDEERRRRFAAACEEE...
YOU BETTER GET IN ON THESE SQUIRREL PIES!
THEY'RE THE LAST ONES ON EARTH!
WE SHOULD HIT UP THAT BACON STIX STAND, TOO.
WHY HASN'T THAT CAUGHT ON, HUH? WHAT'S MORE DELICIOUS THAN BACON ON A STICK?
HNNNGG... SQUIRRELLLLLLL...
HSSSSHHH!!!
SQUIRRELLLL... PIIEEESSSS...

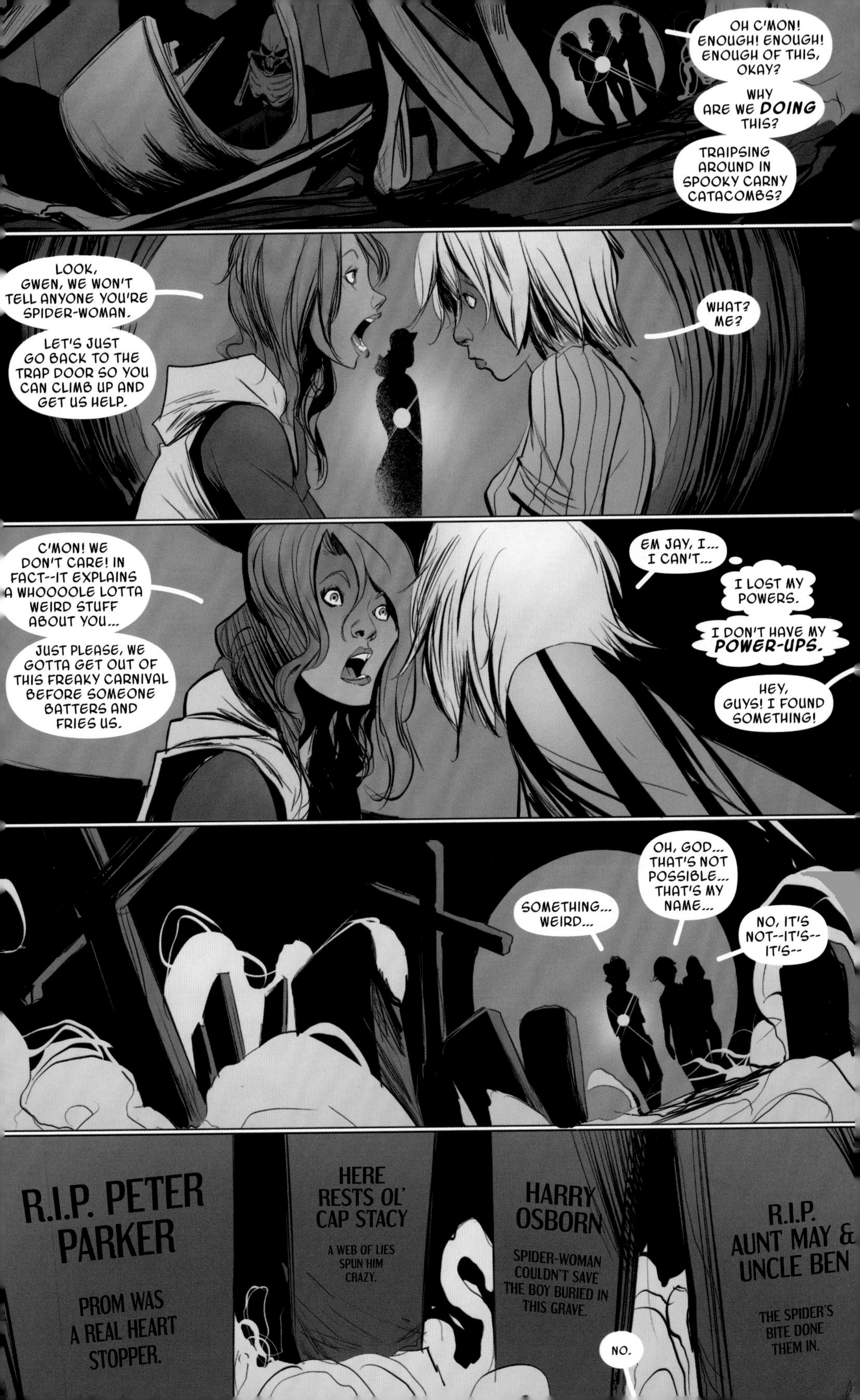
OH C'MON! ENOUGH! ENOUGH! ENOUGH OF THIS, OKAY?
WHY ARE WE DOING THIS?
TRAIPSING AROUND IN SPOOKY CARNY CATACOMBS?
LOOK, GWEN, WE WON'T TELL ANYONE YOU'RE SPIDER-WOMAN.
LET'S JUST GO BACK TO THE TRAP DOOR SO YOU CAN CLIMB UP AND GET US HELP.
WHAT? ME?
C'MON! WE DON'T CARE! IN FACT--IT EXPLAINS A WHOOOOLE LOTTA WEIRD STUFF ABOUT YOU...
JUST PLEASE, WE GOTTA GET OUT OF THIS FREAKY CARNIVAL BEFORE SOMEONE BATTERS AND FRIES US.
EM JAY, I... I CAN'T...
I LOST MY POWERS.
I DON'T HAVE MY POWER-UPS.
HEY, GUYS! I FOUND SOMETHING!
SOMETHING... WEIRD...
OH, GOD... THAT'S NOT POSSIBLE... THAT'S MY NAME...
NO, IT'S NOT--IT'S-- IT'S--
R.I.P. PETER PARKER
PROM WAS A REAL HEART STOPPER.
HERE RESTS OL' CAP STACY
A WEB OF LIES SPUN HIM CRAZY.
HARRY OSBORN
SPIDER-WOMAN COULDN'T SAVE THE BOY BURIED IN THIS GRAVE.
R.I.P. AUNT MAY & UNCLE BEN
THE SPIDER'S BITE DONE THEM IN.
NO.

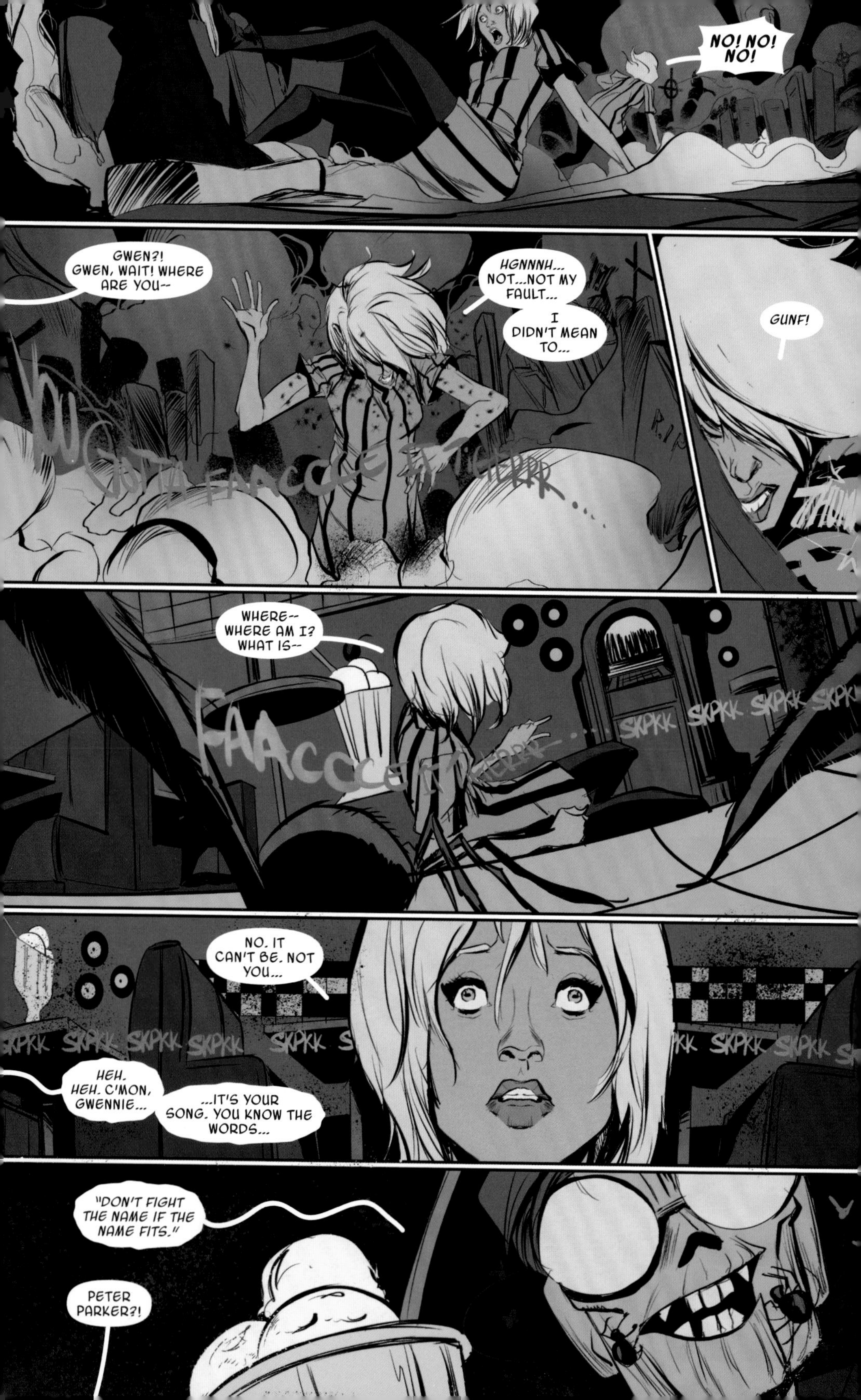
NO! NO! NO!
GWEN?! GWEN, WAIT! WHERE ARE YOU--
HGNNNH... NOT...NOT MY FAULT...
I DIDN'T MEAN TO...
GUNF!
WHERE-- WHERE AM I? WHAT IS--
SKPKK SKPKK SKPKK
NO. IT CAN'T BE. NOT YOU...
SKPKK SKPKK SKPKK SKPKK SKPKK
HEH. HEH. C'MON, GWENNIE...
...IT'S YOUR SONG. YOU KNOW THE WORDS...
"DON'T FIGHT THE NAME IF THE NAME FITS."
PETER PARKER?!

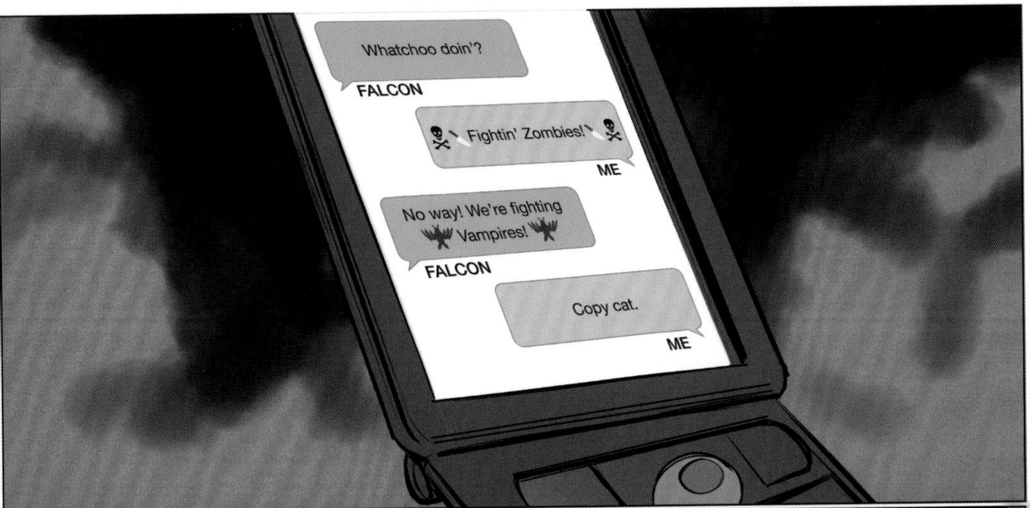

Whatchoo doin'?
FALCON
Fightin' Zombies!
ME
No way! We're fighting Vampires!
FALCON
Copy cat.
ME

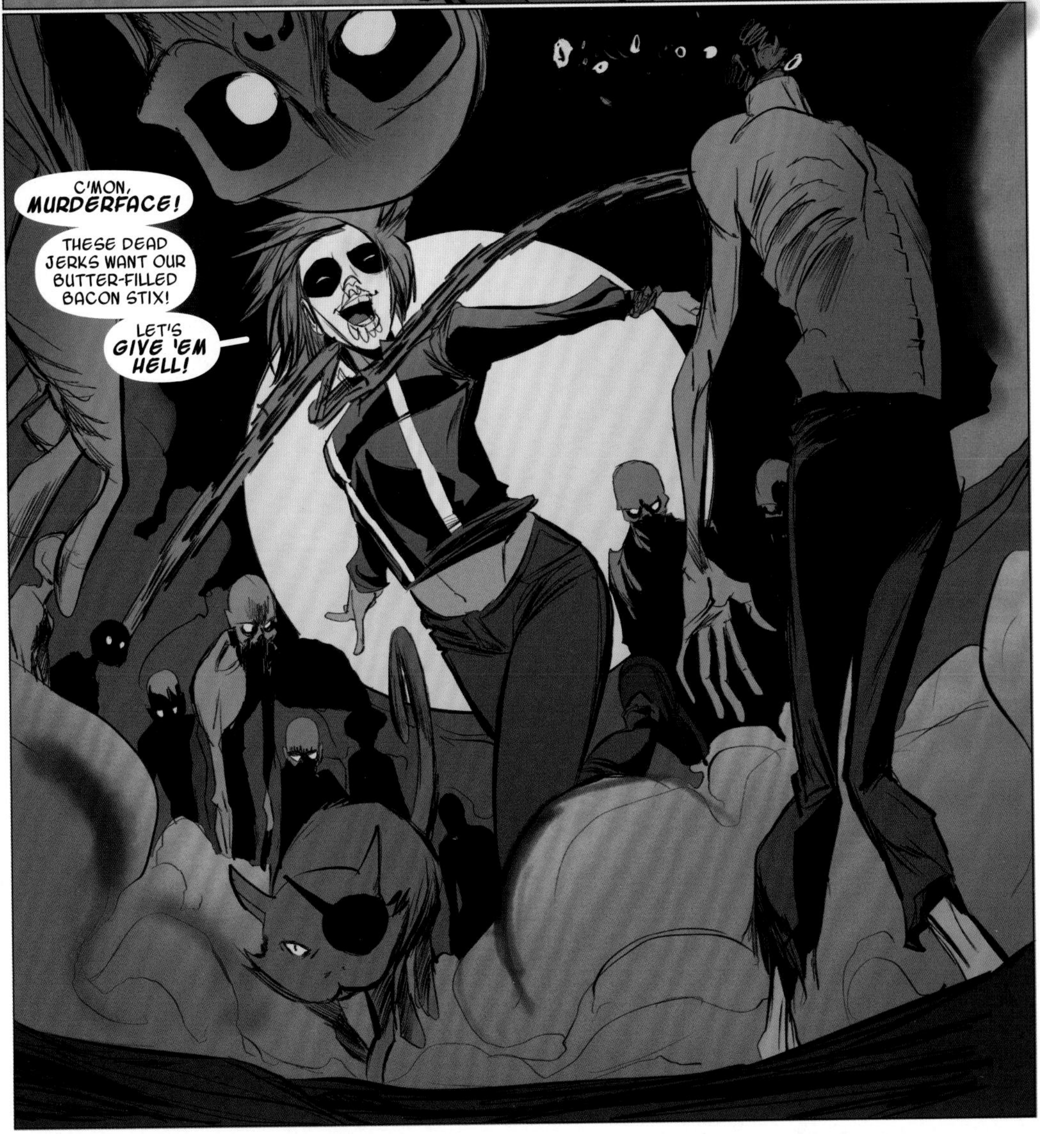

C'MON, MURDERFACE!
THESE DEAD JERKS WANT OUR BUTTER-FILLED BACON STIX!
LET'S GIVE 'EM HELL!

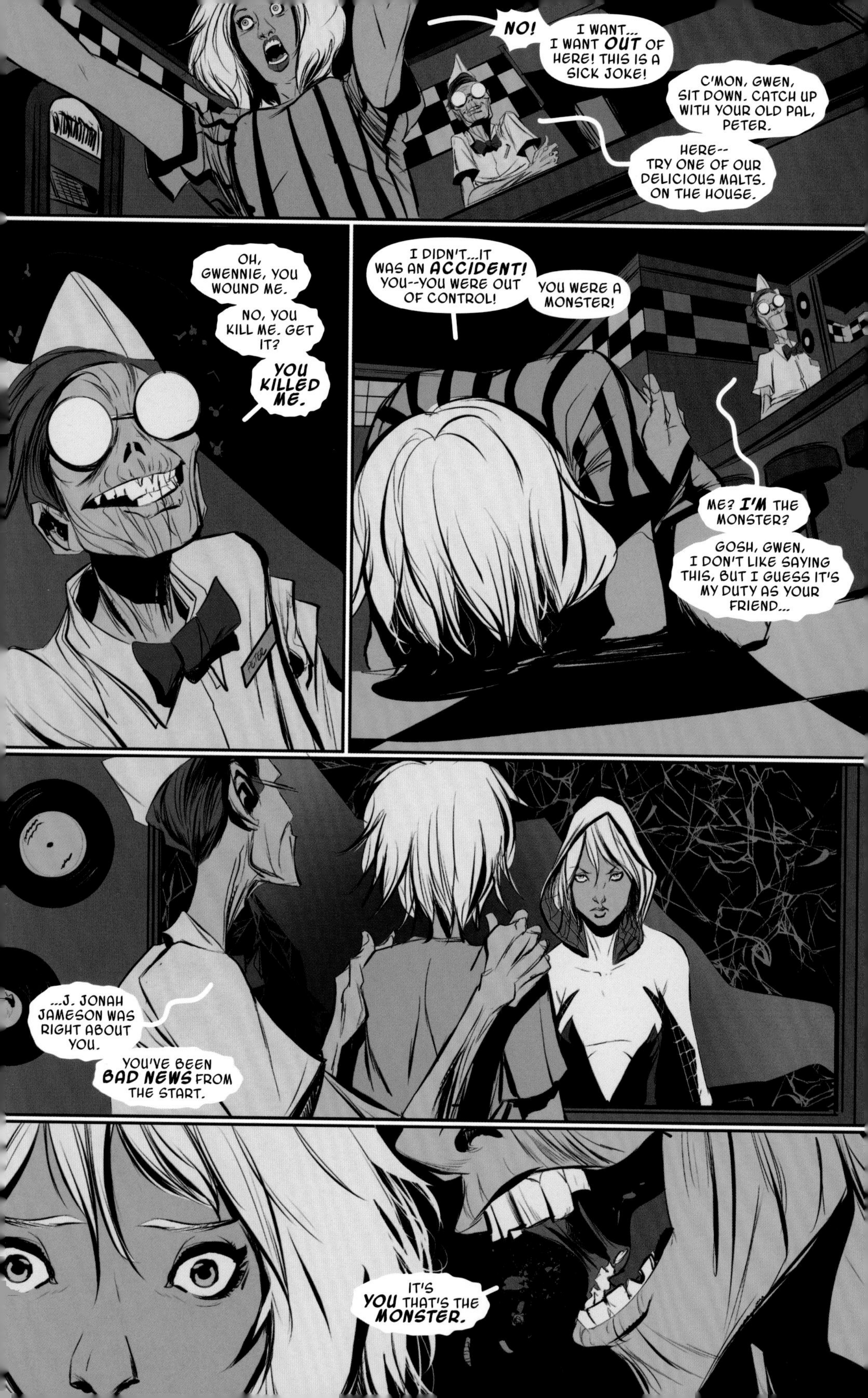
NO!
I WANT... I WANT OUT OF HERE! THIS IS A SICK JOKE!
C'MON, GWEN, SIT DOWN. CATCH UP WITH YOUR OLD PAL, PETER.
HERE-- TRY ONE OF OUR DELICIOUS MALTS. ON THE HOUSE.
OH, GWENNIE, YOU WOUND ME.
NO, YOU KILL ME. GET IT?
YOU KILLED ME.
PETER
I DIDN'T...IT WAS AN ACCIDENT! YOU--YOU WERE OUT OF CONTROL!
YOU WERE A MONSTER!
ME? I'M THE MONSTER?
GOSH, GWEN, I DON'T LIKE SAYING THIS, BUT I GUESS IT'S MY DUTY AS YOUR FRIEND...
...J. JONAH JAMESON WAS RIGHT ABOUT YOU.
YOU'VE BEEN BAD NEWS FROM THE START.
IT'S YOU THAT'S THE MONSTER.

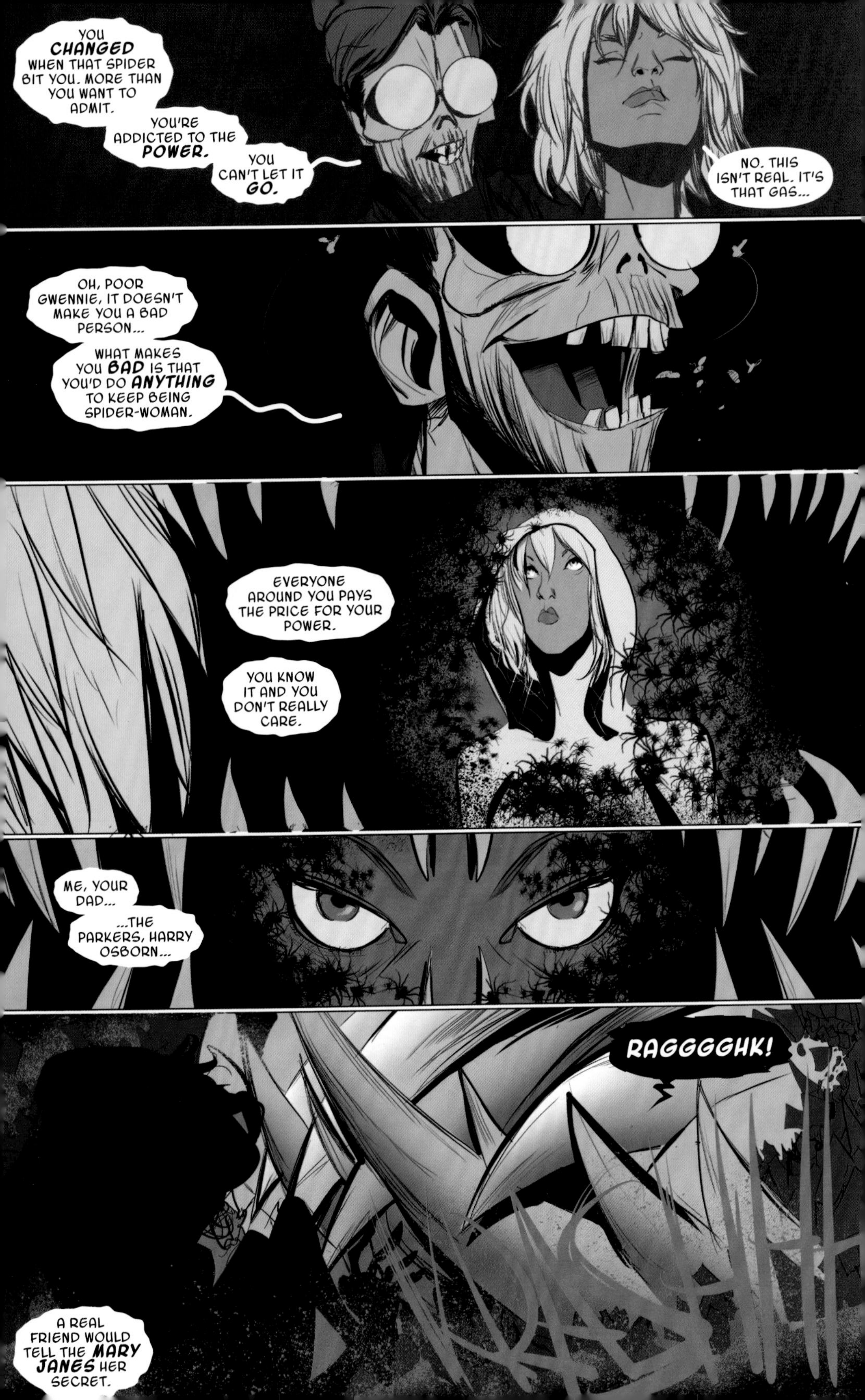
YOU **CHANGED** WHEN THAT SPIDER BIT YOU. MORE THAN YOU WANT TO ADMIT.
YOU'RE ADDICTED TO THE **POWER.**
YOU CAN'T LET IT **GO.**
NO. THIS ISN'T REAL. IT'S THAT GAS...
OH, POOR GWENNIE, IT DOESN'T MAKE YOU A BAD PERSON...
WHAT MAKES YOU **BAD** IS THAT YOU'D DO **ANYTHING** TO KEEP BEING SPIDER-WOMAN.
EVERYONE AROUND YOU PAYS THE PRICE FOR YOUR POWER.
YOU KNOW IT AND YOU DON'T REALLY CARE.
ME, YOUR DAD...
...THE PARKERS, HARRY OSBORN...
RAGGGGHK!
A REAL FRIEND WOULD TELL THE **MARY JANES** HER SECRET.

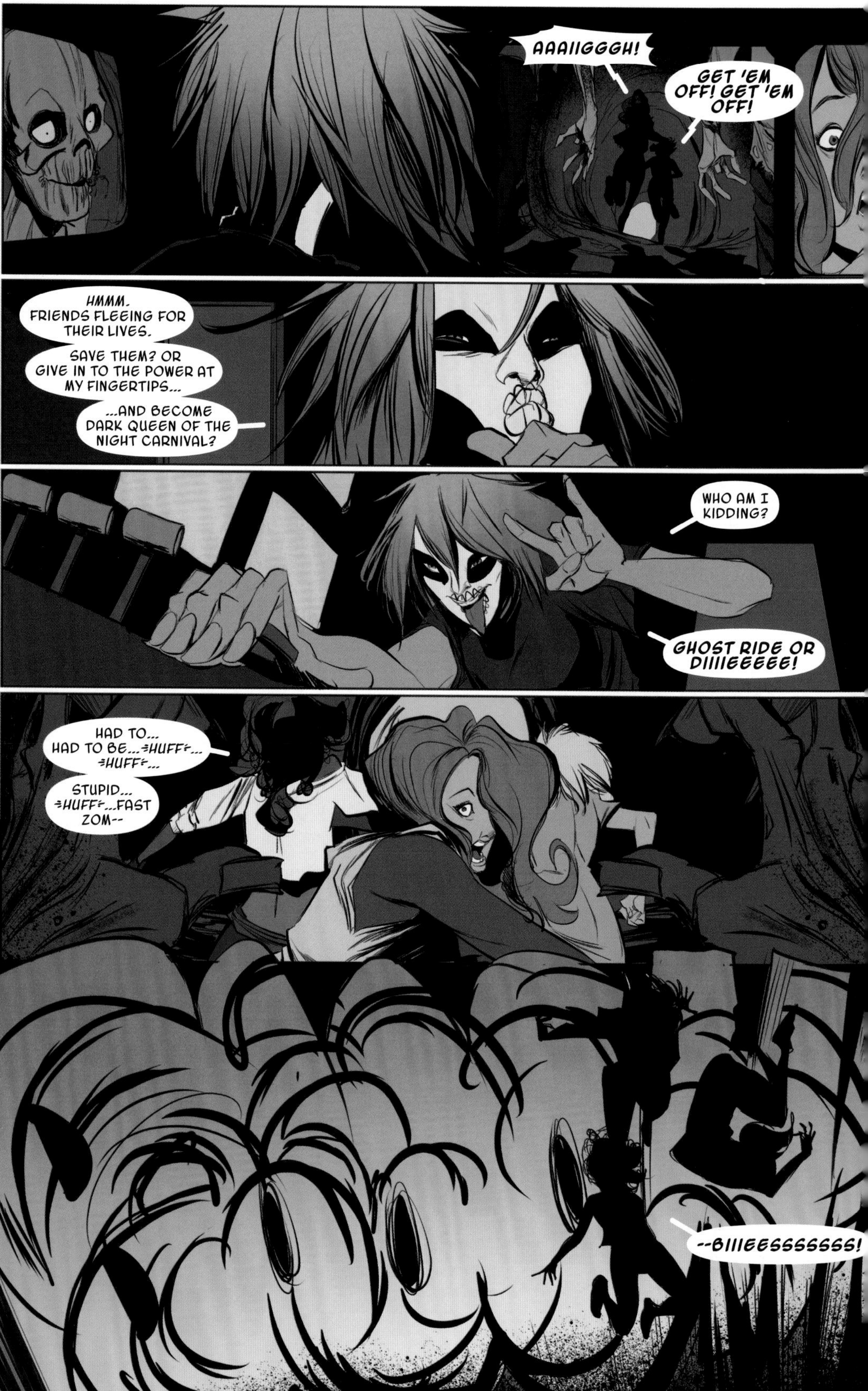
AAAIIGGGH!
GET 'EM OFF! GET 'EM OFF!
HMMM. FRIENDS FLEEING FOR THEIR LIVES.
SAVE THEM? OR GIVE IN TO THE POWER AT MY FINGERTIPS...
...AND BECOME DARK QUEEN OF THE NIGHT CARNIVAL?
WHO AM I KIDDING?
GHOST RIDE OR DIIIIEEEEEE!
HAD TO... HAD TO BE... =HUFF=... =HUFF=...
STUPID... =HUFF=...FAST ZOM--
--BIIIEESSSSSSSS!

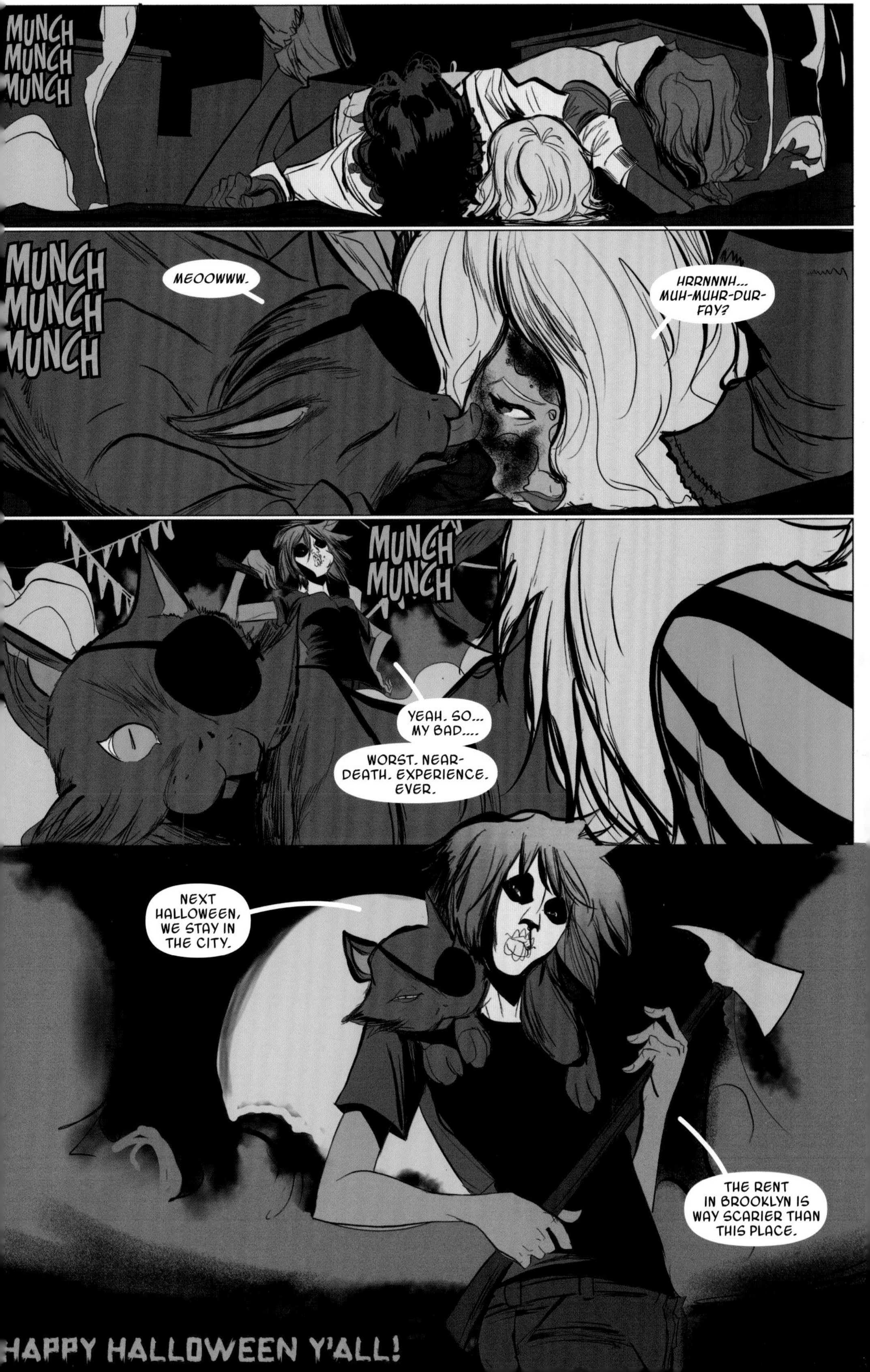
MUNCH MUNCH MUNCH
MUNCH MUNCH MUNCH
MEOOWWW.
HRRNNNH... MUH-MUHR-DUR-FAY?
MUNCH MUNCH
YEAH. SO... MY BAD....
WORST. NEAR-DEATH. EXPERIENCE. EVER.
NEXT HALLOWEEN, WE STAY IN THE CITY.
THE RENT IN BROOKLYN IS WAY SCARIER THAN THIS PLACE.
HAPPY HALLOWEEN Y'ALL!

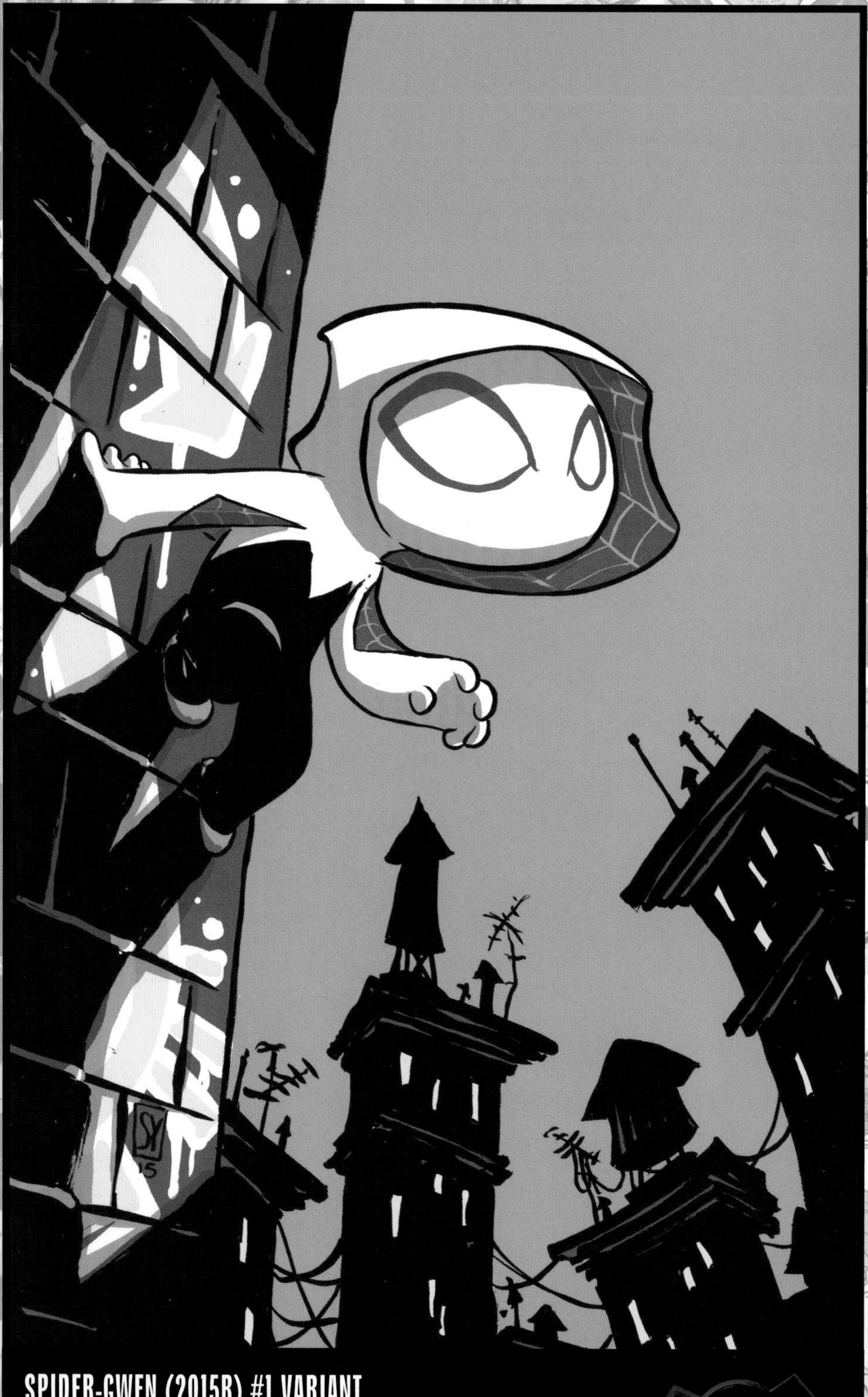

SPIDER-GWEN (2015B) #1 VARIANT

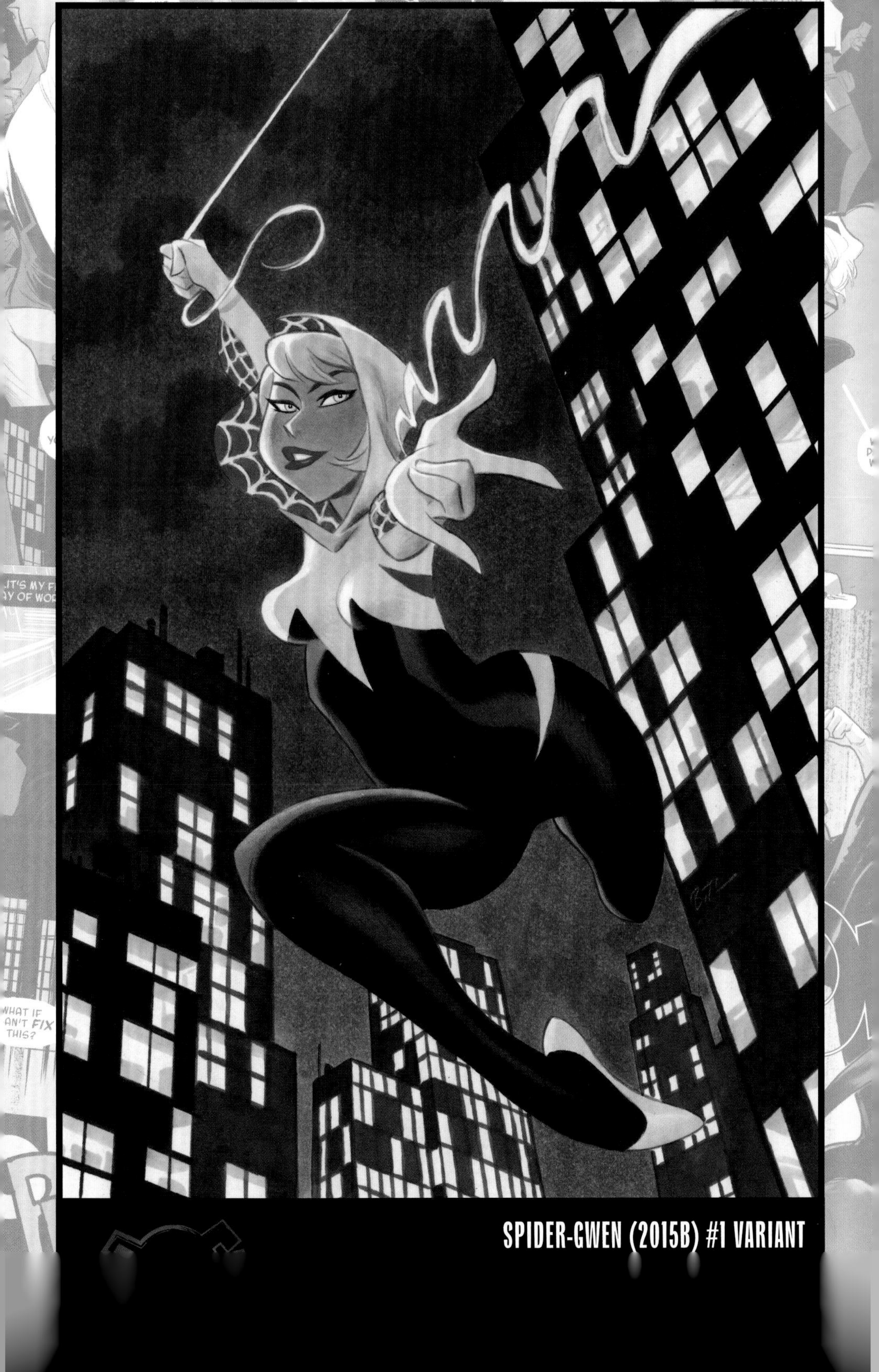

SPIDER-GWEN (2015B) #1 VARIANT

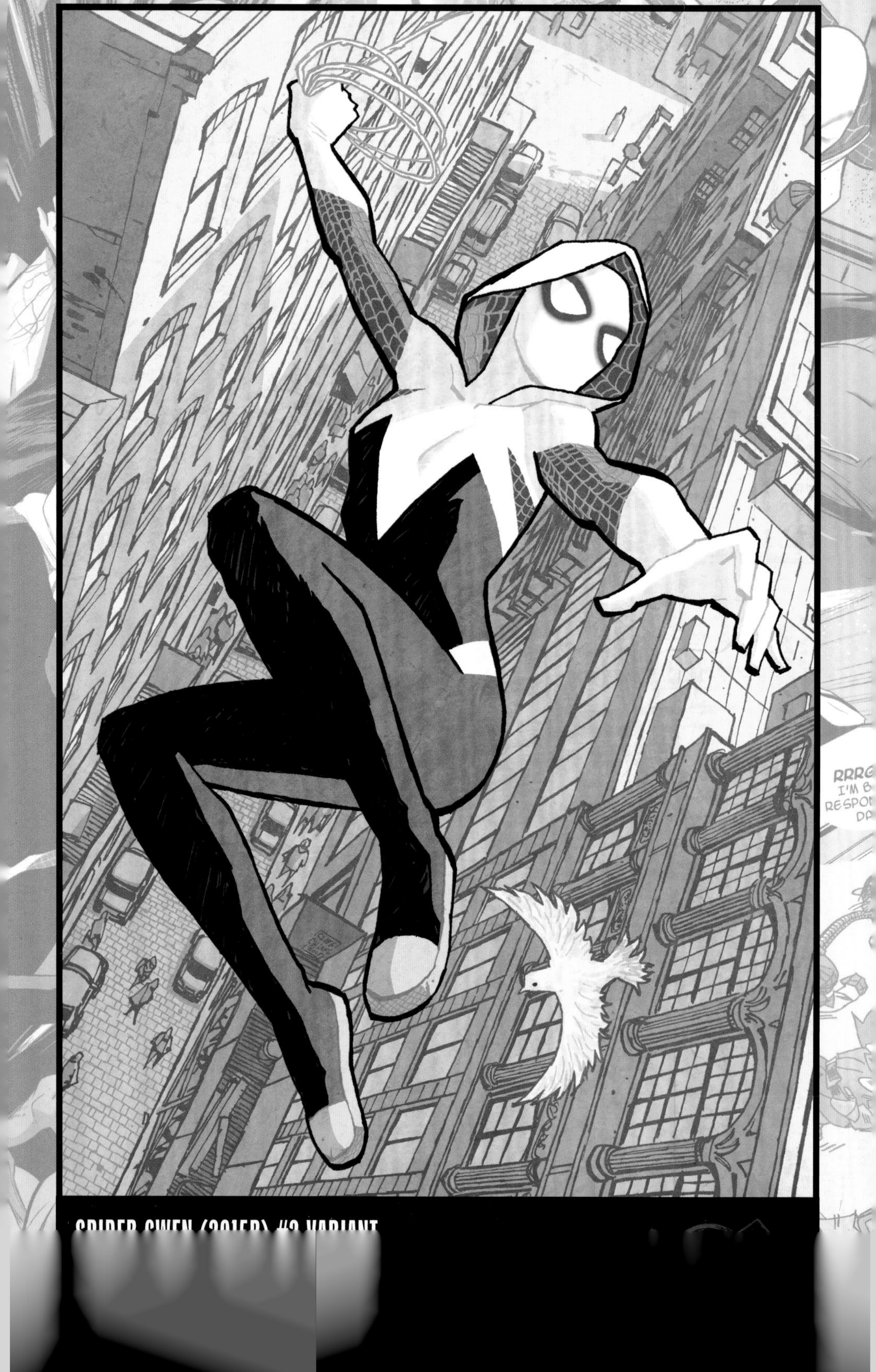

SPIDER-GWEN (2015B) #2 VARIANT